The Dream Team: Back row — Gary Waslewski, Jose Santiago, Gary Bell, Dave Morehead, Jerry Stephenson, Jim Lonborg, Darrell Brandon, Russ Gibson, Sparky Lyle, John Wyatt, Bill Landis, Lee Stange, Dan Osinski. All others standing — Keith Rosenfeld (batboy), Billy Rohr, Joe Foy, Mike Andrews, Ken Harrelson, Elston Howard, Mike Ryan, George Thomas, Dalton Jones, Norm Siebern, Jose Tartabull, Jimmy Jackson (batboy), Jerry Adair; Buddy LeRoux (trainer), Vince Orlando (equipment manager); Don Fitzpatrick (equipment manager). Sitting — Tony Conigliaro, Carl Yastrzemski, Rico Petrocelli, Sal Maglie (coach), Bobby Doerr (coach), Dick Williams (manager), Eddie Popowski (coach), Al Lakeman (coach), Reggie Smith, George Scott, Tom Dowd (traveling secretary). (Photo courtesy Boston Red Sox)

The Impossible Dream Remembered

The

Also by Ken Coleman

So You Want to Be a Sportscaster

Also by Dan Valenti:

Red Sox: A Reckoning
From Florida to Fenway
Cities Journey
December Sunlight

Also by Ken Coleman with
   Dan Valenti:

Diary of a Sportscaster

Impossible Dream Remembered

The 1967 Red Sox
by Ken Coleman and Dan Valenti

THE STEPHEN GREENE PRESS, Lexington, Massachusetts

Copyright © Ken Coleman and Dan Valenti, 1987
Foreword copyright © Jim Lonborg, 1987

First published in 1987 by The Stephen Greene Press,
Inc.
Published simultaneously in Canada by Penguin Books
Canada Limited
Distributed by Viking Penguin Inc., 40 West 23rd Street,
New York, NY 10010.
Photographs reproduced by permission of the Boston
Red Sox, Bobby Doerr, Russ Gibson, Billy Rohr, and
Dan Valenti.
Excerpts from his diary are reprinted by permission of
Bobby Doerr.

Red Sox logo reproduced by permission of
the Boston Red Sox.

Endpaper baseball cards used with permission from Topps
Chewing Gum, Inc.

Library of Congress Cataloging-in Publication Data
Coleman, Ken.
  The impossible dream remembered.

  Includes index.
  1. Boston Red Sox (Baseball team) — History.
I. Valenti, Dan.   II. Title.
GV875.B62C644   1987   796.357'64'0974461
86-25768
ISBN 0-8289-0556-8

Printed in the United States of America by The Alpine
Press, Inc.
designed by Robin Brooks
set in Baskerville and Avant Garde Gothic Book by
WordTech Corporation
produced by Unicorn Production Services, Inc.

Dedications

Sportswriters have a difficult job: they have to be objective about their work and report what they see. The beat writers can heap praise one day and criticism the next. Human nature being what it is, ballplayers like the praise, but not the criticism; that can make it tough for a writer.

Many of these men, who were my friends and traveling companions, are no longer with us. I dedicate this book to them. In alphabetical order they are: George Bankert of the *Quincy Patriot Ledger*; Roger Birtwell of the *Boston Globe*; Fred Ciampa and Larry Claflin of the *Boston Record American*; Ray Fitzgerald of the *Globe*; Bill Liston of the *Record American*; Hugh McGovern of the *Worcester Telegram*; Henry McKenna of the *Record American*; and Lin Raymond of the *Patriot Ledger*.

I also dedicate the book to Thomas Austin Yawkey, who made the baseball dream, as well as the dreams of thousands of people, possible through his support of the Jimmy Fund of the Dana Farber Cancer Institute. My final dedication is to Mr. Yawkey's widow, Jean, who cares about the Red Sox and the Jimmy Fund more than anyone I know.

— Ken Coleman

To the memory of Edith Stein and Simone Weil, and to my family.
— Dan Valenti

Foreword

In 1967 I enjoyed the finest year of my career. As I look back, I still feel a satisfying sense of accomplishment for what we did as a team; but the thing that most strongly remains with me from 1967 is the familiarity I feel with so many people. Total strangers who were fans in '67 will see me today, and it's as if we have instant communication. We've shared a wonderful baseball experience, and it breaks down what normally would be a lot of initial contact tension.

I run into people on the street or at parties — people I don't know — and they'll say things like, "You won't believe this, but in a scrapbook at home I've got a piece of your sweatshirt that I was able to tear from you down on the field on that final day."

Twenty years after the fact, my feelings about what happened in 1967 haven't diminished. In fact, if anything, they've become more romanticized. That year has become a very romantic part of my life.

What Ken Coleman and Dan Valenti have done in this book has made me realize this last point more clearly than ever. Reliving the particular moments of each day makes 1967 come alive again — alive with a sense of perspective that is both uplifting and upbeat.

I don't think any of us on that team fully realized what effect 1967 would have on our lives and on the lives of millions of baseball fans. It wasn't until the summers of years to come that the real feeling of that season became apparent to me personally. It first started to hit me in the winter immediately following the season. I could walk around Boston and walk into places and not feel like a stranger. It just became a warmer and warmer feeling as the years went along. And that contributed greatly to my decision to make New England my permanent home.

This book recaptures the excitement and the life of 1967 in a way that makes it happen all over again.

— *Jim Lonborg*
Scituate, Massachusetts

Acknowledgments

When two people collaborate on a book, the question remains as to who did what. So it is with this book.

I was on the scene in 1967, and most of the memories are mine. Much of the book's material came from interviews I had with the people involved. Also, Bobby Doerr sent me his personal diary that he kept of the season, and I'm grateful to this very special person for his help.

But my main acknowledgment is to Dan Valenti, the talented young man who worked with me to create this book. Dan is an extremely gifted writer whose command of the written word is nothing less than artistry. And the most succinct way I know of putting our collaboration into perspective is to say that I supplied the paint, and Dan painted the pictures. His dedication, literary skills, and hard work were just as important to this book as my having been there in 1967.

There were many invaluable resources for our research, especially the Boston newspapers, the *Sporting News*, the library at the National Baseball Hall of Fame in Cooperstown, New York, and the research staffs of the Boston Public Library and the Berkshire Athenaeum in Pittsfield, Massachusetts.

Dan and I would also like to thank the Boston Red Sox, particularly Chief Executive Officer Haywood Sullivan, PR Director Dick Bresciani, and his assistant, Josh Spofford; members of the 1967 team, who cooperated in so many ways, both large and small; Tom Begner and Rickie Harvey at The Stephen Greene Press; Thomas S. Hart Literary Enterprises of Boston; Stuart Savage of The Sox Exchange, Montpelier, Vermont; Jim Lonborg, for writing the foreword; the microfilm department of Williams College Library; Junebug Clark Photography of Farmington Hills, Michigan; Literations of Pittsfield; and all the many other people, organizations, and businesses — too numerous to mention — who helped out along the way.

— Ken Coleman
Cohasset, Massachusetts

As soon as I came into public view I began to weave, my head down, mumbling to myself. It is not easy to mumble to yourself if you don't feel moved to mumble. I didn't know what to mumble and finally began to mumble the starting lineup for the impossible-dream Red Sox team of '67. "Rico Petrocelli," I mumbled, "Carl Yastrzemski . . . Jerry Adair."

I sat on the front steps of the town library and took a swig from my bottle, blocking the bottle neck with my tongue so I didn't have to swallow any. What I was going to do didn't get easier if I did it drunk. A couple of high school girls in leg warmers and headbands skirted me widely and went into the library.

"Dalton Jones," I mumbled. I took another make-pretend swig.

A good-looking middle-aged woman in a lavender sweat suit and white Nikes with a lavender swoosh parked a brown Mercedes sedan in front of the library and got out with five or six books in her arms. She looked forcefully in the other direction as she edged past me.

"George Scott," I mumbled, and as she went by I reached up and pinched her on the backside. She twitched her backside away from me and went into the library. I sipped some more muscatel and let a little slide out and along the corner of my mouth and down my chin. I could hear a small commotion at the library door behind me.

"Mike Andrews . . . Reggie Smith . . . " I blew my nose with my naked hand and wiped it across my shirt. "Hawk Harrelson . . . Tony C." I raised my voice. "José goddamned Tartabull," I snarled. Up at the town hall a black and white Mill River Police car turned out of the parking lot in front and cruised slowly down toward the library.

I stood and smashed the muscatel bottle against the steps.

"Joe Foy," I said with cold fury in my voice.

— Robert Parker
A Catskill Eagle

Contents

1

Prelude to a Miracle

There is in all of us a yearning to go back. We are creatures of the past and are continually shaped in the present by what has happened before. At all different levels and in many different ways, human life involves a need to return; it's a vital, necessary process for it defines who we are now. When the past is a haunting one, we must come to terms with it. When it's a joyous one, we want to relive its memories; and our past becomes a way in which we can stay young in spirit. In short, we all want — and need — to go home again.

As I said, the desire to return involves many levels: it can be a complex thing, like childhood, when your mother got you out of bed in the morning and fed you at night. It can be simple, like listening to your favorite record over and over again or seeing a favorite film yet once more. It can involve something as disarming as our sense of play. And if you grew up in New England and got interested in baseball, your sense of the past usually revolved around the Boston Red Sox. For Red Sox fans, *the* year of the past that will forever be alive in the present is 1967, when what couldn't happen did. Wherever I go, on speaking engagements, public appearances, or just running into fans at the ball park, people invariably ask me what it was like in 1967, when a 100−1 shot cashed in on the American League pennant. And I should know because I was there for every single game, from the first inning of the grapefruit league opener in March at Winter Haven to the last out of the World Series.

That's what this book is about: the 1967 Boston Red Sox, Destiny's Darlings, the Cardiac Kids, the Impossible Dream.

The best place to begin this story of the past is even further in the past, at my start in baseball and how I came to be behind the mike for that incredible year.

I grew up a Red Sox fan in Quincy, just a few miles south of Fenway Park. I'd sit out in the sun-drenched bleachers at emerald-like Fenway Park and root as any other Sox fan. I never dreamt that years later I would be associated with the team in such an intimate way. I actually got interested in broadcasting as a result of a childhood accident suffered when I was in the eighth grade. I was a good baseball player, not good enough to go into professional ball, but accomplished on my own peer-group level. One day I was accidentally shot in the left eye with a BB gun, and I lost my vision in that eye. I continued playing ball in high school, legion, CYO, and the Quincy Park League; but the injury ended any aspirations I had of trying to make it as a baseball player. I knew only that I loved the game and that if it were possible, I'd try to be connected to it in some way.

When World War II broke out, I served in the army in India. Oddly enough that's where I got my first chance to break into radio . . . but I didn't take the opportunity. The idea of speaking to a lot of people in a place called Chabua, India, near Burma, frightened me; and I talked myself out of it. Feeling that I'd let myself down by not taking the job, I came back to the States and enrolled at Curry College, then located on Commonwealth Avenue in Boston. I went there for a year, and the experience restored my confidence. Mostly I learned to cope with the inherent shyness that had previously stood in my way.

My first radio job came in 1947 at WSYB in Rutland, Vermont. I got the position by doing a guest spot on Art King's show at WEEI in Boston. The show basically was a "job center of the air" for returning veterans. At WSYB I broadcast games of the Rutland Royals baseball team, which at the time included Johnny Antonelli. The manager was Ebba St. Claire, who went on to become a major league catcher with the old Boston Braves. Robin Roberts also pitched in the league, with Montpelier, Vermont. So it was a good league, and I got my feet wet as a broadcaster. I put in a year there, then went to work for WJDA in my hometown, Quincy. I was a sports announcer and program director from 1948 to 1951. It'd be more accurate to say that I was the station's all-around guy, its utility player. I did a bit of everything, from football games to newscasting to disc jockeying. My next stop was at WNEB in Worcester, where I got a job broadcasting Boston University football. Harry Agannis was the Terrier quarterback.

Those years of paying dues led to my first big break in 1952, when I landed the job as radio voice of the Cleveland Browns. Cleveland was looking for an aspiring broadcaster, someone who was good and who wasn't known in the Cleveland market. It came down to Lindsey Nelson and me — and luck was with me. Two years later my radio work for the Browns expanded to television, where I also became the voice of the Cleveland Indians. As my fortunes rose and I became known, I also landed work as early and late sportscaster for WJW-TV, WEWS-TV, and WKYW-TV. For more than a decade, I worked in Cleveland and settled into a very established, secure position. It looked as if I would never want to leave.

So had my career gone up to 1965 . . . a succession of stops that led me closer and closer — and finally into — major league baseball broadcasting but farther and farther — so it seemed — from Boston.

It wasn't to stay that way, however. One day during the winter of 1965, I was sitting in the Wig-Wam, the pressroom at Cleveland's Municipal Stadium. I was lunching with Gabe Paul and Herb Score. While we were eating, someone came in with word that Curt Gowdy had left his long stint as the voice of the Red Sox to go to work for NBC. As a result, of course, there was an opening in Boston.

I quickly got in touch with Red Sox general manager Dick O'Connell to let him know I was interested in the job. A couple of weeks had gone by when I got a call from O'Connell, asking me to come to Boston for an interview with him and Harold Clancy, then head of the *Herald Traveler* newspaper and WHDH, flagship station of the Red Sox radio/TV network. I told my wife, Ellen, that if all things were equal financially (we had five children), I would take the job in Boston. After all I had grown up in Quincy; and I knew that if I didn't take the job, I would wonder for the rest of my life what would have happened. I wasn't going to let myself down again as I had done so many years earlier in India.

Well, the offer was made. The money was actually better than it was for me in Cleveland; and that took all doubts away, doubts centered mainly on my comfortable, secure position in the Cleveland market. So I took the job. Although I was replacing a very fine broadcaster in Curt Gowdy, I made up my mind not to let that affect me. I wasn't going to try to be the new Curt Gowdy. I was going to be the very best that Ken Coleman could be.

There was only one potential ticklish matter in my coming to Boston. I knew that Ned Martin wanted the job as the number-one man. He'd been covering the team since 1961. I was a little worried about how Ned would take to me. If I had known Ned then the way I know him now, I wouldn't have been concerned. Once I got the job, I wrote Ned a letter and explained that I definitely was a guy that didn't have people working *for* me. My partners on the air worked *with* me, just as I worked with them. From that time Ned and I developed an excellent relationship on the air and off, a relationship that remains true to this day. He's one of my closest friends, and I think he's one of the best broadcasters working anywhere today. So I had made it to Boston . . . all of eight miles from my boyhood home in Quincy.

Though I didn't know it then, 1966 was exactly the right year for me to come to Boston, because the futility of the Red Sox perfectly set up the real impossibility of the Impossible Dream.

The first year I came to Fenway as a broadcaster was with Cleveland in 1954. The Sox were entering the middle stages of a decline that bottomed out in 1966 and were coming off a year when they went 62–100, for a .383 percentage, forty games out of first. They drew just 652,201 for 1965, or just over 8,000 a game. They had finished below .500 for seven straight years (making it eight in '66). It was a team that no one seemed to take seriously — not the media, not their opponents, not the fans. Or maybe it'd be more accurate to say that the fans had taken them too seriously for too long and finally responded to years of heartbreak by staying away. They were angry, an anger mixed with apathy and sorrow. In a sense they were jilted lovers. By 1966 Red Sox fans had forgotten how to have fun, how to laugh, how to rejoice in their team, almost how to enjoy the game itself.

Let's look at this a little closer, because by doing so, we'll have a better point from which to review what happened in 1967. The Red Sox fans didn't lose their joy overnight. The erosion took about twenty years and went back to Enos Slaughter's "mad dash," which scored the Cardinals' winning run in the seventh game of the '46 World Series, a series that the powerful Sox were favored to win by 20–7 odds. It was as if Slaughter never stopped running, and the energy drain continued through the playoff loss to Cleveland in 1948; the consecutive losses to the Yankees at Yankee Stadium to lose the 1949 pennant; the shattering of Ted Williams's elbow on July 11, 1950, in the All-Star Game, an injury that probably cost them the pennant; and the inevitable, inexorable advance of mediocrity through the rest of the fifties and early sixties.

If one had to pick a single moment as the official end of Fenway's festivities, you'd have to go with September 28, 1960, bottom of the eighth inning, with the Sox trailing Baltimore 4 – 2. This was Ted Williams's last at bat ever.

The day was overcast, the steely gray skies looming over the little ball park like a shroud. The wind was blowing in on the raw, cold afternoon. Williams, who knew Fenway as well as anyone, declared before the game that nothing would be hit out that day. By the sixth inning, the lights had to be turned on (John Updike likened them to headlights in a funeral procession).

People began to applaud as soon as Williams hit the on-deck circle. They continued as he stepped into the batter's box, where he was given a three-minute standing ovation during which play was halted. Baltimore's Jack Fisher, in relief of Steve Barber, fooled around nervously with the resin bag during the ovation. There were two things he didn't want to do: walk Williams or give him a hit.

Ted took the twenty-one-year-old's first pitch low for a ball, then swung and missed at a fast ball. With the count 1 – 1, Fisher tried again to blow the ball by the forty-two-year-old Williams . . . youth having a go at old age. The ball came in, and Williams swung with his classic form; the swing seemed to invoke his long baseball career in one fantastic, transfigured action. The ball cut through the damp air on a line, the last thunderbolt of an ancient god. Oriole outfielder Jackie Brandt went back to the bullpen wall in right center, leaped, but was unable to reach the ball, which landed in the bullpen. As the crowd screamed in disbelief, Williams calmly circled the bases in his familiar head-down Cadillac jog. He had *willed* a home run.

But another action, less dramatic, demonstrated what this really meant for Boston baseball. In the top of the ninth, Manager Mike Higgins sent Williams out to left one last time. Right behind The Kid, he sent caddy Carroll Hardy. The exchange neatly summed up the changing fortunes of the Red Sox — here was the greatest hitter of all time being spelled by a lifetime .225 hitter. A new era had dawned on Fenway.

During the Sox' six-year journey to oblivion from 1961 to 1966, there were certainly some good performances, which included the play of third baseman Frank Malzone, outfielder Carl Yastrzemski, and pitchers Bill Monbouquette, Earl Wilson, and Dick Radatz, but the overall movement was downward, relentlessly downhill. Some moments were truly forlorn:

May 10, 1961 — Seventeen Red Sox batters strike out in a game against the Los Angeles Angels.

June 20, 1964 — The Orioles score six runs in the first inning before the Sox can record the first out.

September 12, 1965 — A loss to the Minnesota Twins puts the Red Sox seasonal record against the Twins at 1–17.

September 28, 1965 — Attendance at Fenway for a game against the Angels is 461.

May 1, 1966 — The Sox hit into six double plays.

In a perverse sense, being a Red Sox fan during this period was easier than ever before because there was never any pressure, any excitement. There were no "must" games or "big" series. Instead of focusing on the season, which was always lost before it began, Boston fans simply lived from game to game. Losing was expected. And so the flood waters rose at Fenway, but help was on the way.

Though Ted Williams himself predicted greatness for the young man from Long Island ("Son, don't ever let them change your swing"), the headlines were slow in coming for Carl Yastrzemski. Yaz hit .266 with eleven homers, a performance overshadowed, in fact, by two other rookies on the club in 1961. One was Yaz's roommate, Chuck Schilling, who set an American League record for fielding at second base, turned the double play beautifully, and had more hits than either Roger Maris (sixty-one home runs) or Mickey Mantle (fifty-four home runs). From June 8 through July 17, Schilling played forty games in which he accepted 213 chances — 99 putouts, 114 assists — without an error. The other rookie who outshone Yaz was pitcher Don Schwall, who went 15 – 7 to win League Rookie of the Year honors.

Schilling and Schwall seemed too good to be true, and they were. The following year Schilling broke his wrist and three years later was riding the bench with an average below .200. Schwall hurt his arm the next year (9 – 15, 4.95) and, on November 21, 1962, was sent to Pittsburgh along with Jim Pagliaroni for slugger Dick Stuart and pitcher Jack Lamabe.

Yaz, however, got better each year. In 1962 he hit .296 with ninety-four RBIs. In 1963 he hit .321 for the batting title. He also established himself as the league's premier defensive left fielder.

His improvement seemingly went for naught, when, by 1966, the Sox finished ninth, one-half game ahead of the Yankees. The fact that the Red Sox finally finished ahead of the dreaded Bronx Bombers salvaged the season for some. In fact, very quietly, Boston played some of the best baseball in the league during the season's second half. Maybe something was afoot after all as they headed into 1967.

There's one story, though, that seems to sum up how it was around the ball park in 1966. It involved a live commercial I had to do between innings during State of Maine Day at Fenway. I was told about the commercial the day before. The sponsors said that, in the spot, I would have to hold a live lobster in my left hand. To keep it tranquil, they told me I had to simply rub its tummy just before we went on the air. I thought it was a joke. Well we went on the air, and I started into the commercial; but when I picked up the unrubbed creature, it started bucking, twisting, and snapping. Somehow I made it through with no loss of blood, but that's about all you could say — I got through it just as the team got through another poor showing.

As '66 progressed, however, you could see some of the seeds of '67 being sown. The Red Sox had one of baseball's best records from late July. Jim Lonborg was starting to mature as a pitcher, as was George Scott as a first baseman. The team picked up a fine pitcher in Jose Santiago; and on the farm, some real talent became evident. So, going into 1967, there was a feeling that the club would be better. Of course no one had even the slightest idea that the team would come *close* to the pennant, let alone win it.

To sum it all up, throughout the team's decline preceding the rise in 1967, Red Sox fans faced quite a problem: how could they be happy again? It wasn't a question of hope, necessarily, but its negative counterpart — resignation. Their cheers were always momentary cheers tinged with the gloom of tomorrow's expected loss. It was as if each win during these dry years was like something that didn't belong, like a sentence taken completely out of context so that it made no sense.

How to be happy again — a problem for a metaphysician, a psychiatrist, a priest maybe, but a baseball fan? It was a problem with no answer, really, except the totally improbable one generated by a remarkable collection of young men who for a storied, timeless summer gave us magic. Their play restored self-respect to Fenway and its fans, and the year turned everything around. And there was no reason to expect it. It couldn't happen. It was

Dick Williams: iron-fisted, caustic, head-strong, brash, authoritarian . . . and a winner. (Photo courtesy Boston Red Sox)

impossible. It was unthinkable. It was absurd. Ridiculous. Laughable. It was 1967.

The positive feeling going into 1967 intensified when the Sox named Dick Williams manager. To that time the Red Sox had the reputation of being baseball's country club. The public perceived and the press portrayed them as the Gold Sox, the Millionaires. From a PR standpoint, it was a real thorn in management's side. Williams's appointment did much to combat the problem.

From the very beginning, Williams made it clear to everyone that he was going to run a very tight ship. Dick was iron fisted, caustic, headstrong, brash, authoritarian. He said that as manager he wasn't going to try, as so many had before, to make his players happy. He was going to run the club *his* way, take it or leave it. He said he was interested in just one thing — winning — and he would do whatever he had to do to accomplish that, spare no one. Some thought it was a blustery wind before a big storm; others thought it was a much needed blast of fresh air. One thing was certain: the Sox were not to be the same in 1967.

Nineteen sixty-seven. It had been just four years since America lost its innocence on November 22, 1963, in Dallas, Texas. The Vietnam War was intensifying and was about to split the country in two. America's cities were plagued by racial tensions, and its youth, in growing numbers, were turning on and dropping out on drugs.

Against all this, baseball seemed insignificant, an irrelevancy worth no more than an afterthought or asterisk, some adult's beer-cooled distraction from a long day's work, some child's fantasy land of perfectly blocked box scores and players in snowy white uniforms. All of this made what happened in '67 all the more amazing, something so unlikely that it seemed to take on a significance — a life — of its own. For this was a happening that couldn't happen, or so the experts said when the chilling odds came out of the dry heat of Las Vegas in March. The Boston Red Sox, the "country club," were unceremoniously installed as 100 − 1 underdogs for the American League pennant.

To even call them underdogs was misleading because the word implies some slim, but plausible chance. Here there was none, at least according to the smart money. There were even snickers when Manager Dick Williams had the audacity to announce that the Sox would win more than they would lose.

After the last out of the last inning of the year's last regular-season game, however, the Red Sox had a pennant in its pocket, the sun of a championship in its heart. A twenty-one-year desert sojourn in search of the pennant had ended. All of New England, most of the country, and some of the world walked on the velvety-rich dirt of baseball's promised land . . . out of the land of sorrows and into a gemlike Fenway, green now not so much from paint as from the resurrected body of Boston baseball. It was like the moment in the *Wizard of Oz* when the screen changes from dreary black and white to Technicolor.

For the briefest of moments, everything seemed right. The war in Vietnam seemed to stop; the hippies and the establishment embraced; flowers grew out of riot clubs; and in our cities, blacks and whites raised a toast together to this miracle. Some might say the moment never happened; yet we know it probably did. It was a moment that turned a whole year into part of an eternal present, one we shall always carry with us: the memory of the Impossible Dream.

Let's now look, day by day, at how the dream unfolded.

February and March

Spring training began with high hopes under the high skies and steady sun of Winter Haven, Florida. Fans, players, the media . . . all were anxious to find out how Dick Williams would translate his no-nonsense ideas on running a ball club into action on the playing field. Even though Williams had two years as a Triple-A manager under his belt and even though many of the current Red Sox played *with* him in Boston or played *for* him at Toronto, the past seemed somewhat irrelevant. This was, after all, the Boston Red Sox. The reputed "country club," the Gold Sox. Discussions of Williams's approach boiled down to one question: would it work?

It worked.

He ran more of a boot camp than a spring training, especially when compared to his predecessors. He insisted that every player be on time, put in a hard day's work, not complain, and be there the next day for more. He wasn't interested in discussion or debate with his players. There was one chief in camp, and it was Williams. Dick and his coaches installed a precise schedule for workouts: every player knew where he had to be and what he had to be doing at all times. When nothing formal was scheduled, a player was expected to run or participate in volleyball games.

The rookie manager imposed a tight curfew, announced he would take no sore arms north with him, and said he wouldn't be afraid to send anyone down for not hustling. In effect he threw his fiery personality smack in the middle of the ball club and dared anyone to tell him what he could or couldn't do. Many grumbled, and a few made the mistake of doing it publicly; but no one actually challenged Williams. And so a funny thing happened on the way to the ball park — this unconnected bunch of young men developed into a spirited team whose fighting character reflected that of their manager.

SATURDAY, FEBRUARY 25

The Red Sox officially opened camp today. Dick Williams greeted twenty-four pitchers and four catchers. The rest of the team will report Tuesday night. Williams, coming off two successful seasons as manager of the Sox' Triple-A entry in the International League at Toronto, gave a brief talk regarding rules and regulations of camp. Most of the talk afterward came in reaction to his announcement that pitchers would be expected to play volleyball when not down for scheduled activity.

   Pitching coach Sal Maglie was not in camp. He was given personal time off because of his wife's death last week.

SUNDAY, FEBRUARY 26

Dick Williams made a quiet but potentially far-reaching move today by naming third-base coach Eddie Popowski as his second in command. Pop, who has coached and managed in the Red Sox' farm system for decades, is in his first season with the parent Sox. "If I'm sick or get thrown out, he'll be in charge," Williams said.

   The move takes on its significance when you consider Popowski's role as father figure to many of this team's young players, including George Scott and Rico Petrocelli. Many observers feel that Popowski's role as confessor will neatly complement Williams's role as captain of a very tight ship.

MONDAY, FEBRUARY 27

Most of the rest of the club checked into Winter Haven today, but an incident involving two borderline pitchers showed that Williams meant it when he said he'd take no guff . . . from anyone. Pitchers Dennis Bennett and Bob Sadowski showed up twenty-five minutes late. The roommates, both trying to bounce back from arm troubles, told Williams that the motel switchboard failed to wake

The Sox opened camp with one of baseball's best outfields: Carl Yastrzemski, Reggie Smith, and Tony Conigliaro. (Photo courtesy Boston Red Sox)

them on time. The rookie manager then rushed into his office, called the motel, and left emphatic orders that all players should be awakened each morning at 7 A.M. — three hours before practice. Williams then called Bennett and Sadowski in and, in a voice level that could be heard throughout the clubhouse, bawled them out and promised, "This will not happen again!"

Bennett underwent surgery on his pitching shoulder (left) last April. He was 3–3 in 1966 for Boston. Sadowski, sent down to Toronto last year because of arm problems, is still listed on the Toronto roster. Today's incident won't help his chances.

After workouts Williams met with the media and wouldn't discuss the Bennett/Sadowski incident; but he did say that he planned to let Tony Horton battle George Scott for the first base job. It seems that one of the ways the manager plans to light a fire under Scott is to plant these little uncertainties in his mind to get him to think more. Williams has lamented a couple of times about how difficult it is to "get through" to Scott.

TUESDAY, FEBRUARY 28

It was a quiet day today. Dalton Jones was hit below the knee in batting practice by Pete Magrini and is expected to miss two days.

WEDNESDAY, MARCH 1

General Manager Dick O'Connell put to rest trade rumors that have been circling Carl Yastrzemski like sharks since 1966 ended. O'Connell revealed for the first time that he and Yaz talked two weeks ago, and the club advised the star outfielder that he would not be traded. O'Connell did add a footnote, however, saying that if a team came up with an offer for Carl that was just too fat to turn down, the Sox would have to listen.

THURSDAY, MARCH 2

Joe Foy was 6 pounds over the 205-pound weight limit that the club set for him, and this had Dick Williams mad. Still the 211 pounds were less than what Foy weighed at any time during 1966, trainer Buddy LeRoux said.

The Sox are hoping Foy can avoid the slow starts that have plagued him throughout his professional career. Last year, for example, the 1965 International League MVP hit just .223 for the first three months of his rookie season and didn't hit his first home run until June. He came alive in the second half, though, and ended with respectable stats of fifteen home runs and a .262 batting average. Williams said he's convinced that Foy's perennial slow starts were due to his weight problem.

On the field Rico Petrocelli narrowly missed serious injury today in batting practice. Rico was at shortstop when Tony Conigliaro hit a savage line drive right at Rico's head. Rico wasn't looking, but somebody yelled. He skipped just in time, and the ball hit him on the backside. If he hadn't moved, the ball probably would have hit him in the face.

Dave Morehead pitched batting practice and looked strong. He said that he felt no pain in his recovering right arm.

FRIDAY, MARCH 3

The workouts continued today with veteran observers having remarked that the drills were the most organized they'd seen in a Red Sox camp in years.

You knew that this camp would be different when Dick Williams put on the gear and umpired intrasquad games in Winter Haven. (Photo courtesy Boston Red Sox)

SATURDAY, MARCH 4

The Red Sox suffered their first serious injury of the spring when second baseman George Smith tore up his right knee while practicing rundown plays between second and third. He was carried off the field, and the initial prognosis was that he'd be out at least eight weeks. Smith's injury points out a potential problem for Boston — its infield depth.

The other pure second baseman in camp, rookie Mike Andrews, has been hampered by a sore back. Speculation is that the Sox will call up someone from the minor league roster to fill in for the rest of camp. Most likely bet is Al Lehrer, who played infield (mostly shortstop) for Manager Williams last year at Toronto.

Dom DiMaggio was in camp today, and the ex-Red Sox center field great gave Reggie Smith some pointers on outfield play: "I told him that he took an extra step before he made his throw, which was bad. I told him how to field ground balls in front of him and not to the side. I told him to go fast to a ball and not glide to it. And I told him about wind currents and Fenway Park . . . . Reggie will be a better center fielder this year than he was a season ago [at Toronto]. Five years from now? He should be great."

SUNDAY, MARCH 5

Today George Smith flew to Boston for treatment on his leg.

MONDAY, MARCH 6

Dick Williams donned gear to ump the first intrasquad game today at Chain o' Lakes Park. Reggie Smith, Jose Tartabull, and George Thomas each cracked home runs. Rookie Billy Farmer was pulverized by Sox hitters. "That last inning took about a century," he remarked.

Reggie was almost badly hurt in a freak accident during batting practice. After swinging at and missing a ball, the bat flew out of his hands, struck a pole in the batting cage, and ricocheted back into his right shoulder. Smith went down in a heap, and at first it looked like the injury might be serious; but after quick treatment,

Spring Training: A Time to Dream

If life begins on opening day, as Thomas Boswell asserts, then its conception begins in spring training, when teams come together with their winter-borne aspirations. The February/March sun at first seems incongruous, especially in the initial days of camp. It is in these early days that the beat, or mood, of the camp begins to take shape. Almost without exception the character of a spring camp proceeds from hope.

Always in spring a ball club must dream. It must because spring is the only time it can do so with impunity. Spring training is that period of baseball between its image and its reality. All teams are undefeated, all are tied for first place, and there is no evidence whatsoever to dispute anyone's claim to upcoming greatness. Spring training is the timeless time that intervenes between the first dream of a pennant and the first pitch on opening day, when all bets are off, everything is for keeps, and no prisoners are taken. Once the season begins, reality takes over and most decidedly puts baseball back in time ... not the time of a clock, but the time imposed by a relentless 162-game schedule. With each at bat, with each inning, each win or loss of

the swelling went down and Buddy LeRoux gave Reggie the okay to play.

As expected the Red Sox called up Al Lehrer as the infield replacement for the injured George Smith. Meanwhile, Smith was in a hospital bed at Sancta Maria Hospital in Cambridge. The twenty-nine-year-old second sacker was to undergo an operation Wednesday morning to repair cartilage damage to his right knee.

"It was a tough break," Smith said. "I went into camp with all the confidence in the world. Then this happens. It was a tough break all around.

"We were practicing chasing men on rundown plays. I turned suddenly. Maybe I was on my heel, I don't know. Nobody was near me. But when I twisted, something snapped in my knee and it locked, as simple as that."

TUESDAY, MARCH 7

Expect the unexpected from Dick Williams. Better yet expect nothing at all, because if you do, you're likely to be wrong. During drills and a brief simulated game, the rookie manager shifted all-star first baseman George Scott to the outfield before a mid-morning downpour ended the workout. Later Williams said he would not hesitate to use Scott in the outfield "if needed" during the regular season.

the regular season, a case is being built — an argument being made — for or against one's spring dreaming.

Once the season begins, a team's foundation of hope comes under scrutiny. And as certain as three strikes is an out, some teams begin to lose hope. For some, dreams become walking nightmares — think of the 1965 Red Sox, who lost 100 games. For others hope is pushed beyond the point of return and enters the perfect despair of tragedy — the '48, '49, and '78 Sox come readily to mind. But occasionally a team finds its dreaming, its hoping justified. For them the season is fun and carries them beyond what they even dared pray for . . . and they win a pennant — like the Impossible Dream Red Sox.

But this is all for the regular season. Spring admits no losers, no .210 hitters, no earned run averages above four, no errors, no mistakes. All columns on all stat sheets bear the well-rounded form of zeroes. Baseball's perfect symmetry.

And what is this spring? Spring training is repetition . . . endless batting, running, and fielding drills, repeated cliches ("we're just one or two players away"). It's six weeks in a motel room, six weeks of running out of places to eat. This repetition breeds a feeling of security in baseball people. It's as if the fact that a team goes through its rituals — the drills, the exercises — will somehow ensure a measure of success for the regular season. How can a manager imagine his team doing poorly when he sees

Before the rains came, the team worked on Texas League pop-ups. Third base coach Eddie Popowski is a true master at hitting balls in the no-man's land just beyond the infielders and just in front of the outfielders. He had a lot of players huffing and puffing.

WEDNESDAY, MARCH 8

Ted Williams, in from the Florida Keys to offer batting advice, held court today with about ten pitchers. Ted had his audience enraptured as he spun tales about how certain batters reacted in certain situations and how sluggers like Jimmie Foxx used to approach hitting. The other Williams in camp — Dick — wasn't too thrilled and twice had to send pitching coach Sal Maglie over to break up the confab. The problem was that Ted's tales were keeping the pitchers from doing their running.

In the intrasquad game, Eddie Popowski's team defeated Bobby Doerr's 6 – 3. The Sox made a number of fundamental mistakes and glaring errors, and the manager was screaming how the team would be working extra hard on fundamentals from now on.

THURSDAY, MARCH 9

There was another simulated game today, and an interesting play developed that illustrated how seriously Dick Williams took train-

his pitchers covering first base correctly, his outfielders making perfect cutoff throws, his catchers making textbook throws in infield practice?

Spring training is the one time when all teams can truly participate equally in baseball. Even when the grapefruit and cactus games start, the results are meaningless. The action is baseball; the talk, baseball. Both are surprisingly pure, or one might say, simple. For this is a subtle game, and spring training is its most uncomplicated moment. To the fans exhibition results mean little. It is enough that baseball is being played (this is still winter, remember). If the home team wins an exhibition game, so much the better; but such a win is a bonus, added value. Rico Petrocelli, for example, makes a two-out error at

shortstop in a game against the Reds. Sure enough the runner eventually scores. But the fans at Chain o' Lakes laugh it off. They're in Florida, out of the steel gray shroud of New England's dying winter. How can an exhibition error bother them?

Of course the same error committed at Fenway Park will likely bring discontent from the fans and leads to a truism about Red Sox fans (and baseball fans in general): they are impatient over the quarter mile, but long suffering over the marathon; critical during the inning, understanding over the game; doubtful for the game, sympathetic for the season. Simply put, they forgive in the long run, but not always for the specific moment. And this makes spring training evermore special. Because the season is

Ted Williams, working with Yaz in spring training, taught him how to pull the ball. (Photo courtesy Dan Valenti)

so brief and because, when camp breaks, all the results are wiped out, everyone loves to forgive down here. The sun is warm, the sky is cloudless, the smell of oranges gives the air a kind of sweet aroma. Baseball fans love to forgive because they *can* forgive. We have, in short, baseball's equivalent to that wonderful state called peace of mind.

But for the players, or certain players, not all is so peaceful. You're reminded with regularity that there are guys fighting for jobs and working hard for an uncertain future. When a rookie pitcher takes the mound for his first appearance of the spring or a thirty-seven-year-old veteran finally gets an at bat late in the game as a pinch hitter, don't speak to him of spring's myth or magic. Talk to him, maybe, of sleepless nights, food that won't stay down, the fear of being cut. Talk to him of the possibility of being sent down. Talk of the bus rides, the inadequate meal money, the dimly lit parks with empty seats — if he somehow doesn't make the team.

Four kinds of players emerge in a spring training camp: the sure starters and stars (Carl Yastrzemski, Tony Conigliaro); those who are sure of making the team (Dalton Jones, Darrell Brandon); those who know in their hearts that they don't have a chance, at least not this year (Dick Baney, Bill Farmer); and those who are on the dividing line between success and failure, the "maybe-they-will/maybe-they-won't" group (Hank Fischer, Galen Cisco). By far this last group has it the toughest. This bunch consists of

ing. While umping, he called a balk on rookie pitcher Cecil Robinson and waved in a runner home from third base. "They'd call that on him in a real game, wouldn't they?" Williams asked.

FRIDAY, MARCH 10

The team traveled to Sarasota today for the grapefruit league opener. Before a sellout crowd (many of them Red Sox fans left over from when the Sox trained here between 1946 and 1958), Chicago won easily 8–3. Tony Conigliaro homered for Boston. Dennis Bennett, the starter and loser, gave up four runs in three shaky innings. Pete Magrini, pegged by some as the club's long reliever, was hit hard.

Williams once more proved he was not afraid to experiment. In today's game he videotaped batters and pitchers for later study.

SATURDAY, MARCH 11

Williams speculated on the team he'd take north with him and cautioned that what he said was subject to change at any time. He said he wanted three catchers, six outfielders, seven infielders, and "only healthy pitchers." He vowed that no pitcher with a sore arm would make the team. When asked about the starting rota-

rookies with fast-dying chances and veterans who may no longer have a fit. For them every pitch, every inning, every at bat looms large. For them it's always the bottom of the ninth of the seventh game of the World Series. Every action is critical.

Then there are the coaches, slow-moving men with time-wizened faces. They have seen it all before. Everything. For them spring is renewal, the chance to share the world of young men once again. Their eyes are as deep as wells when they look at young players. They see themselves, and aren't they right? Doesn't a good coach, by imparting his knowledge of baseball, offer nothing less than a part of himself, a part that can later find new expression through the career of a young man? That's why good coach-

ing is selfless. It gives of itself so that the self may live through the play of another. When one gives of the self, he doesn't lose part of himself, but gains a larger, less *selfish* identity. Wasn't Sal Maglie also on the mound when Billy Rohr almost no-hit the Yankees in the season's third game?

When a player fails to make it in baseball, as most minor leaguers will, the loss is momentary. For each failure there are ten, twenty, or more kids waiting for a chance to fill the uniform. In such a game, individual failure matters little. The empty spot on the roster will be filled tomorrow, or next year, until time and the forces of destiny produce a Tris Speaker, a Mel Parnell, a Jim Lonborg, a Carl Yastrzemski. And coaches know this. They know it without necessarily

Dick Williams meets with the press in Winter Haven. The Boss promised a winning year and delivered. That's Haywood Sullivan sitting on the counter at left, next to the cabinet. (Photo courtesy Boston Red Sox)

knowing they know. They have seen it all. And they will talk in baseballisms, sayings that are not so much platitudes as proverbs, some incarnating Wisdom itself: "It's not over 'til it's over." "You can't steal first base." "Blessed are they who hope, for they may see a pennant."

Eventually the time comes when the team packs up and heads to the chilly North. What have we learned down here? What have we unlearned? What have we gained? What have we lost? These are questions that have as many different answers as there are players on teams. Russ Gibson's conclusions will be totally different from George Scott's.

Overrated or underrated players, overpriced or underpriced players, and all those in between mat-

ter not in the long run. They play their careers — two months or twenty-two years — and exit. They leave us with memories, and we come to a great realization about baseball: they weren't driving the baseballs all those years; the baseballs were driving them.

The 1967 team got in their charter and flew north to Boston. Were they heading for the cold? To another losing season? No. They were heading to a land now ready for baseball's return. They flew to the pennant.

tion, he listed Jim Lonborg, Jose Santiago, Darrell Brandon, Hank Fischer, and Lee Stange.

SUNDAY, MARCH 12

Skinny, twenty-one-year-old rookie Billy Rohr turned in an impressive performance as the Red Sox beat the Kansas City A's 8 – 3 at Winter Haven. Rohr faced just nine batters over the last three innings and he struck out two. He used his changeup with great results. "Mace Brown showed me how to throw a changeup in the instructional league," Rohr said. "Give Mace the credit. It's an easy pitch [to learn] for some guys, but I had to work at it."

Jerry Stephenson, pitching well in three innings, gave up one run on a wind-blown homer by Joe Rudi. In the field rookie Al Lehrer made two outstanding plays at short.

Dick Williams, reacting to Reggie Smith's head-first slides into second and third yesterday against the A's, said he was impressed. "It may be some time since you saw a Boston player slide that way to get to a base, but there will be a lot more of them doing it for me."

MONDAY, MARCH 13

Mike Andrews collected five straight hits as the Red Sox dropped a 5 – 3 decision to the New York Mets before 1,034 people at Chain o' Lakes. Mike had been just 1 for 6 in previous action and complained about a "lazy bat." Bobby Doerr has been working with Andrews at the plate; and for today at least, it seems to have paid off.

Dennis Bennett, in his second outing, looked good. He held the Mets scoreless on one hit in three innings. Reggie Smith chipped in with a 420-foot home run off Jim Ray in the eighth inning with Andrews aboard.

Before the game Ted Williams and Mets coach Yogi Berra talked about the old days of the Red Sox–Yankee rivalry. The chat was cut short by Mets hitters, who crowded Ted for some hitting tips.

After the game Dick Williams announced his first cuts. Infielder Ken Poulsen and pitchers Cecil Robinson, Bill Farmer, Rob Snow, and Dick Baney (all rookies) were shipped to Ocala for reassignment in the minor leagues.

TUESDAY, MARCH 14

The Red Sox looked like their hapless predecessors of recent years in today's game at Winter Haven. They mixed poor base running with the blowing of a four-run lead as they lost to the White Sox 5 – 4.

Boston went up 4 – 0 on home runs by Tony Conigliaro and Rico Petrocelli. They lost the game in the ninth, but it was base running that had Dick Williams breathing fire. "We took away at least one run by running the bases poorly," Williams said. "You never get thrown out at third with one out. If you have to slide, you shouldn't be trying."

He was referring to a play in the first, when Jose Tartabull was thrown out at third base to end the inning. With pitcher Jose Santiago on second base to start the play, Tartabull tried to go from first to third on a single. He was cut down before Santiago could cross home with the run.

Tony Horton also made a base-running boo-boo when he was thrown out by Chicago center fielder Ken Berry after rounding second base and straying too far. Horton was caught dead in his tracks, and Williams was seething. "Those mistakes are not going to be tolerated when the season starts. If they continue we'll start hitting the wallet."

One bright spot was Conigliaro's hitting. Tony went 3 for 3, with two doubles to go along with his round tripper.

Eddie Popowski: The Buffer Man. (Photo courtesy Boston Red Sox)

WEDNESDAY, MARCH 15

This time it was Jerry Stephenson's turn to feel the heat of the manager. The Red Sox got a lead against Whitey Ford and the Yankees in the top of the first at Fort Lauderdale, but the Yanks came back against Stephenson in the bottom of the inning. He walked the first three batters he faced, gave up two singles, and walked another . . . all before getting the first out. "Jerry said his arm stiffened waiting for the top of the first to end. If that's the case, what's going to happen when he goes north and has to sit in the cold for a while. He won't be able to move his arm," Williams remarked.

The Red Sox were without Carl Yastrzemski, who stayed behind in Winter Haven to have a bad tooth x-rayed.

Someone asked Williams if George Scott was any better at laying off low balls, something that gave Scott fits in the second half of 1966. "Yes," the manager answered. "He's improved slightly. At least now he waits until they come up to his shins."

With a Little Help from the Coaches

One aspect of the 1967 Red Sox often overlooked is the contribution of the coaching staff. From his hiring Williams made it clear that he would rely heavily on his coaches for the day-to-day administration of his overall managerial duties. Besides the charter given to them by Williams, the coaches also took on particular importance because of the very personality of the manager. His no-nonsense, iron-willed, even acerbic approach to managing — which would tolerate no wasted effort and which heavily emphasized fundamentals — created the need for a buffer zone between him and his players. This was recognized, consciously or otherwise, when the coaches were selected. Williams's selections constituted a masterful display of team psychology that would have made Freud proud. The buffers were to take some of the edge off of Williams's dictates, especially among the younger and more sensitive players. The two men who contributed the most to this effort were third base coach Eddie Popowski and first base coach (and hitting instructor) Bobby Doerr.

Popowski assumed the role of chief buffer. Pop came to the parent club after thirty years in the organization as player, scout, and manager. He managed most of the homegrown Red Sox in the minors, for example, George Scott and Reggie Smith just two years earlier in Double-A at Pittsfield. Pop did an outstanding job with the players and served as a pressure valve, a sounding board, and equal parts father confessor, psychiatrist, guidance counselor, and guru. He was especially helpful to Scott, Smith, and Rico Petrocelli. He knew these guys, knew how to get them off the floor when they were in the dumps — especially Scott, who would have been lost without Eddie.

Pop could also ride players when they needed it — for example, he got on Tony Horton for not practicing his fielding around first base — but he could

---

This kind of needling appears to be getting to Scott, who isn't the bubbling, carefree man he was in spring training last year. Eddie Popowski, however, is doing a good job in getting George to stay cool.

THURSDAY, MARCH 16

Scott must be hoping third baseman Joe Foy stays healthy this year. George returned to first base today after spelling the injured Foy at third. Foy was back in position after missing four games with a stiff shoulder. Scott celebrated by blasting a home run, two doubles, and a single as the Red Sox edged the Mets in truly bizarre fashion by scoring ten runs in the ninth to win 23 – 18.

"I want to play first base," George told the press after the game. "I don't want to play nowhere else. I'll knock in 120 runs if I play first base this year." He was upset over Dick Williams's penchant

do so without Williams's cutting edge. His guidance and temperament counterbalanced the manager's perfectly and provided a balanced chemistry that served the Sox so well that year.

It's no doubt that Pop was highly responsible for the success of many players: Scott's .303 average and fielding; Smith's winning the Sox' rookie-of-the-year award; Petrocelli's being named the American League starting shortstop in the All-Star Game.

The other major contribution to the buffer role was made by Doerr. The Red Sox all-time great second baseman used his soft-spoken manner, incisive baseball smarts, and stable presence to great effect. He was very well liked by the players, knew all those who came up through the farm system (having worked for ten years as special scout), and helped out a great deal with his hitting instructions.

Rounding out the coaching staff were Sal Maglie as pitching coach and Al Lakeman as bullpen coach.

for moving him around defensively. Scott insisted that it affected his hitting.

Foy, in his comeback, got himself five hits, after which Williams emphatically announced that "Scott's going back to first, and Foy is staying at third."

The game was exhibition baseball at its best (or worst, depending on how you look at it). "It was the wildest game I've ever seen," said Mets manager Wes Westrum after the three-hour, forty-five-minute contest. *Exhibition* was indeed the correct word for this DeMillelike spectacle that saw forty hits and seventeen walks. It may have given birth to a new Mets joke as well: "How'd the Mets do today?" "They scored eighteen runs." "Yeah but did they win?"

Gary Waslewski, Dave Morehead, and Jim Lonborg were shelled. Morehead, who needed the work, got in about two weeks' worth, pitching the fourth and fifth and giving up ten runs. Darrell Brandon pitched a scoreless ninth to get the win.

Off the field Yaz had his aching tooth pulled.

FRIDAY, MARCH 17

The bringin' in of the green brought the Red Sox no luck today as they lost 7 – 5 to the Reds at Winter Haven. Cincy rookie first baseman Lee Maye had a double, triple, and home run. Reds' rookie Gary Nolan, eighteen, got the win. Nolan, an Irish lad, gave up just one hit in the last three innings, a pinch single by George Thomas. Pete Magrini took the loss. Hank Fischer pitched well in his first outing of the spring for Boston.

SATURDAY, MARCH 18

Tony Conigliaro, haunted by injuries his previous three years with the Red Sox, will fly to Boston today for x-rays and an extensive examination of his left shoulder. Tony, hit by a John Wyatt fast ball in batting practice, went down in a heap and was hurting bad. A preliminary exam showed that Tony suffered a slight crack of the shoulder. The injury doesn't appear serious, but the team is taking no chances and is setting up a complete exam in Boston.

This marks the fifth time Tony has had a bone broken by a pitched ball in the last five years. At the time of the injury, Tony was off to his best spring ever with a .588 mark.

In today's game at Lakeland, Dennis Bennett went five hitless innings as the Sox shaded the Tigers 3 – 2. Carl Yastrzemski homered off Denny McLain.

SUNDAY, MARCH 19

What strange magic is this? Voodoo? Sunspots? Double steal . . . hit and run with a runner on second . . . hit and run with men on first and second . . . the winning run squeezed home? Can this be the Red Sox? It was today. Boston looked more like the 1959 Go-Go White Sox as they beat Detroit 7 – 6.

With the bases loaded, Bob Tillman squeezed home Russ Gibson and left long-time Sox observers trying to remember when that had happened last. Scott, Thomas, and Gibson had three hits apiece. Williams was pleased with the way the club ran but also grumbled about the four errors.

Off the field there was good news as well. Tony Conigliaro was released from a Boston hospital and reported to camp for continued treatment by Buddy LeRoux, who correctly diagnosed the injury as a fracture of the scapula.

Later the Sox shipped out pitchers Dave Morehead, Bob Sadowski, Pete Magrini, and catcher Gerry Moses. They have a lot invested in Morehead, who, despite being just twenty-three years old, has been pitching with the Red Sox since 1963. Just eighteen months ago, he threw a no-hitter versus Cleveland at Fenway. When his arm is sound, Dave has one of the league's best curve balls.

Williams was frank in explaining the cuts and said that he could no longer experiment with fringe players and couldn't take chances on pitchers who needed warm weather.

MONDAY, MARCH 20

Jim Lonborg won his third game of the spring in as many decisions and appears to be the odds-on favorite to be the opening day pitcher. Jim seems on the verge of becoming the staff ace. Today he went the first five innings giving up no runs and three hits in the team's 5 – 3 win over the Pirates. In analyzing his performance, Jim said he was now convinced that "my fast ball is my best pitch. I can come back with my slider and not get hurt. That's exactly what I was doing today, and that's the way I'm going to pitch at Fenway Park."

Tony Horton came alive at the plate with three hits, including a home run. The team batting average is a lusty .317. The Red Sox pulled off five double plays. The win was their third in a row.

TUESDAY, MARCH 21

Philadelphia clobbered the Red Sox 10 – 5 today, but that took a backseat to the George Scott–Dick Williams defensive tête-à-tête. Williams played Scott in right field and put Tony Horton on first. Scott felt Williams was playing favorites with Horton since Tony played first for two years under Williams at Toronto. When Scott saw his name on the lineup card with "rf" after it, he shook his head and started mumbling to himself. He then went to Eddie Popowski and told Pop, "this is going to ruin my hitting."

Popowski replied, "How can playing right field ruin your hitting? The man [Williams] is trying to let you get some swings."

"Big deal," Scott shot back. "I can get my swings in the cage."

When told of Scott's reaction, Williams said, "I hear Scott doesn't like right field. Well if he doesn't want to play, that's okay with me."

Retrospective: Carl Yastrzemski Looks Back

KC: Was the off-season between 1966 and 1967 the first time you went to Gene Berde, physical therapist at the Colonial [resort in Wakefield]?

CY: Yes it was. I really didn't have the opportunity to work out before, because I would spend the wintertime finishing up work on my degree at Merrimack College. But during that off-season before '67, Gene worked with me all winter; and it really paid off. I had a good spring training. I noticed right away that I had more power. The ball was going another thirty or forty feet. That's when I decided to become a pull hitter; and at that time, we really didn't have that many home run hitters on the Red Sox. I felt I could help the ball club more by being a power hitter than by just hitting for average, so I made the transition in hitting style. It bothered me mentally for about the first month of the season. That's when Bobby Doerr sat down with me. We talked. We tried to figure it out. That's when we came up with the idea about raising the hands up high.

KC: You're referring to the morning of May 14, when you and Bobby went out to the park early before a doubleheader with the Tigers at Fenway. You and Bobby decided to make the adjustment in your swing, with the hands held high. What happened that day?

Later, the two crossed paths on the field before the game. "I'm not a right fielder," Scott told Williams. "You are today," the manager replied.

Horton may not be Williams's favorite as Scott claims, but he is getting a full shot at the first base job. Williams and Bobby Doerr like Horton's bat. The manager explained that Horton could only play first, while Scott was more versatile; so to get them both in the lineup, Scott had to play a different position. Incidentally Horton is the only player to have appeared in every exhibition game.

In the contest at Clearwater, Bob Tillman and George Thomas hit home runs in the loss. Brandon (five runs, eight hits in five innings) and Fischer (five runs, six hits in two innings) were pasted.

WEDNESDAY, MARCH 22

A newspaper report surfaced today that said the Red Sox were on the verge of a major trade involving George Scott and Jose Santiago. It was also reported that both players, along with Garry Roggenburk, were placed on waivers to see if any other club would put in a claim. After any claims the players would be withdrawn, and trade talks would begin with the interested club

CY: As I said 1967 was a year of transition for me as a hitter. Up to that time, I was a gap hitter to left center and right center and hit for average. I was almost like a Wade Boggs, except I pulled the ball a little more. Early in the '67 season, after I had made the transition to being a power hitter, a lot of my balls were dying in the outfield. They didn't have the take-off that they should have had. They were hopping to the fence, where they should have been in the bullpen. Being six feet tall and 180 pounds, I decided to raise my hands real high to get more lift on the ball. That was the only way I could generate extra lift. When we went to the park that morning, Bobby and I talked about it [see Bobby Doerr's diary entry on May 14]. We stayed out there about an hour and a half working on it. After I made the adjust-ment of the hands, I was hitting balls in the bleachers in batting practice. I said to Bobby, "I'm going to stay with it. I don't know if I can get to the ball in the game, because in batting practice, they're only throwing the ball eighty miles per hour, and in the game it's going to be ninety miles per hour. But I'm going to try it." In that doubleheader I hit two home runs against the Tigers. I was confident and stayed with that stance the rest of the year.

KC: Carl, there was a situation in Chicago when you wanted to do some extra hitting, but Eddie Stanky thwarted your efforts. Do you remember that?

CY: Yes. In 1967 I was really killing the White Sox. That's when Stanky came up with that statement "All-Star from the neck down." One day I stayed at the park after a game because I wanted to hit. Eddie

---

or clubs. That's one theory for why Williams would put a player of Scott's caliber on waivers. The other is that it's the manager's way of spurring on the young slugger to do better.

The waiver list can be meaningless, even absurd. Last year, for example, Manager Billy Herman put the *entire team* on waivers. At the time Herman thought he'd be back as Red Sox skipper and wanted to see what teams were interested in what players as a prelude to trade talks.

When asked if he were looking to make a move, Williams said, "Well I keep my eye on the waiver list every day."

In the game at Winter Haven, Santiago, Bill Landis, and Jerry Stephenson all looked strong as the Sox downed the Yankees 5 – 2. The good performances by Landis and Stephenson complicated Williams's decision on his future cuts. Landis's outing, coupled with Billy Rohr's fine pitching, gives veteran lefty Dennis Bennett something to think about. Bennett has been streaky so far, and Williams has repeatedly stressed that he wants consistency.

Carl Yastrzemski and Rico Petrocelli hit home runs. In his postgame remarks, Williams went out of his way to praise Yaz: "He's been playing tremendous for us all spring."

In addition to his home run, Yaz had a double and made a glittering one-handed grab on Bill Robinson's long fly with the bases loaded in the second.

had Ken Berry take some extra hitting before me. He had Berry hitting and hitting and hitting and hitting and hitting, so I just waited and waited and waited. Finally, when Berry got through, I thought we would finally get the field. So what does Stanky do? He goes in the clubhouse and comes back out and says, "You can't have the field," and he brings a dog out. And he's walking his dog all over the field! And we waited some more. We waited about an hour and a half. Finally Eddie realized we weren't going to leave, so he said, "Okay, you can have the field now."

Of course, he was a character. He was the first base coach for the '67 All-Star Game in Anaheim. I think I was on base four or five times in a row, and every time I came down to him, he put his arms around me and talked to me like I was his long-lost son. So I couldn't figure the guy out.

That '67 White Sox team had great pitching, but no offense. I was pretty good friends with Gary Peters [one of Chicago's aces that year]. One time Gary hit me in the shoulder, then came up and hit me in the neck. After being hit the second time, I was going to go out and fight Peters. Now Gary's six feet four inches and weighs 220. Bobby Doerr was going to fight him he was so mad. But Peters told me after the game, "We're ordered to do it. Anytime we are ahead in the game, the pitchers are ordered to try to hit you and get you out of the game."

KC: You joined the Red Sox in 1961. You had the tough job of replacing Ted Williams; and from 1961 to 1966, the team did not fare well. Was the fact that

The heart of the Red Sox batting order poses at Winter Haven: from left, Carl Yastrzemski, George Scott, and Tony Conigliaro. (Photo courtesy Boston Red Sox)

the team was in the race in '67 a real factor in the kind of year you had?

CY: Those first years with the Red Sox were very depressing. We'd get 700,000 fans a year. If you got 8,000 fans for a Friday-night game, you were lucky. And a lot of them were very boisterous in voicing their negative opinions [laughs], and you could understand that. In '67 we had some new kids. We were five or six games out early in the season, hung tough, then had that road trip in July when we won ten in a row. We made a move, and something changed. When we went to play a ball club, instead of expecting to lose a series, we expected to walk in and say, "Hey, why can't we beat these guys three out of four instead of them beating us three out of four?" And all of a sudden, it started happening.

Everyone participated in the effort, and we went through some tough times together. Probably the toughest was when Tony Conigliaro got hit. We suffered a tremendous blow in losing Tony, who was just coming into his own not only as a hitter, but as a defensive outfielder. With Reggie Smith in center and myself in left, it was a tremendous defensive outfield. We all could run, catch, and throw; then we lose Tony. When he got hit, I remember my reaction driving home that night. I said, "That's it. We don't have a chance at the pennant."

Then all of a sudden, Jose Tartabull comes in; and he plays like Superman for the last six weeks of the

---

THURSDAY, MARCH 23

George Scott's days as an outfielder probably ended for good today after the slugger knocked himself unconscious running into the right field wall at Winter Haven in a 7 – 4 win over the Dodgers. With two on in the top of the sixth, John Kennedy lined a long drive to right center. Scott at first broke the wrong way, then running full tilt, crashed against the fence. He was revived on the field by Buddy LeRoux. X-rays showed no broken bones, but a bruised wrist. Scott was hospitalized overnight at Winter Haven Memorial Hospital as a precaution.

"When he hit the wall, it made a noise like a gong," said center fielder Jose Tartabull, who had a closeup view. "If it were me, my jaw would have been torn right off."

"He went into it face first," said reliever Don McMahon, who was in the bullpen just fifteen yards away. "We were yelling 'The wall, the wall' — but he just kept on going."

Scott hit the wall so hard that he tore away skin about the size of a half-dollar from his chin. After the collision he staggered, then collapsed.

"He was out cold for a minute," said LeRoux. "Look at Zora Folley against [Cassius] Clay. He got knocked out but was back up in ten or twelve seconds."

"He moved the wall from 330 feet to 332," Mike Andrews quipped.

season. Jerry Adair — coming through in the clutch. And it got to the point where they couldn't pitch around me. People like Adair and Dalton Jones were always on base. They had to pitch to me because so many times I came up with guys on first and third, first and second. I just got into one of those grooves. I didn't even know I won the Triple Crown until the next day I read it in the papers after the last game of the season. My only thought was "Pennant, pennant. We got to win one for Mr. Yawkey." That's the way the whole ball club felt. It kept driving and pushing. Nothing was going to turn us back. We had the desire. Everybody pulled together. Somebody would make a good play — I'm not talking about a big hit, but about a defensive play — and the bench and clubhouse would react as if he had just hit a home run in the bottom of the ninth with two outs to win a ball game.

KC: What would you say about your relationship with Dick Williams?

CY: Everybody thought I had a problem with Dick Williams. I never had a personal problem with him. I was the only guy on the ball club with no curfew. I was the only guy who had a single room. Dick never bothered me. I had problems with the way he treated other ballplayers. I thought he should have reprimanded them in private. I thought he should have taken a ballplayer into his office and shut the door. I didn't like it when he went to the press with that stuff, like saying "talking to George Scott is like talking

---

"The ball tailed off, and I was going at top speed," said a groggy Scott later. "I knew I was on the cinder path, but I didn't realize I was so close to the fence."

Dick Williams all but put an end to Scott's outfield play saying, "I want George's bat in the lineup, but I don't want him running into fences. Scotty's outfield activities will be curtailed."

GOOD FRIDAY, MARCH 24

Williams gave the team the day off for Good Friday. George Scott, who suffered a concussion in his collision with the right field wall yesterday, was released from the hospital. He had orders to limit his activity to sitting on the motel veranda. LeRoux said Scott should be able to return to full-time duty Monday or Tuesday.

SATURDAY, MARCH 25

The Twins beat the Red Sox at Winter Haven today 8-3. Brandon and Stange were roughed up. Only Bennett pitched well.

EASTER SUNDAY, MARCH 26

The Sox laid an egg on Easter by losing 7-1 to Minnesota. After the game Williams said Reggie Smith would be moved from

to a block of cement." I think that kind of thing is embarrassing and degrading to a ballplayer. I think it hurt a ballplayer's performance.

But Dick probably had to do what he did. We had some young ballplayers who came up with him from Toronto, and he knew them. He was hard. Without any doubt he was the right guy at the right time in '67. I think the club needed his style. You can't take it away from him: he won the pennant. How he did it, with his methods, you have to give Dick 100 percent credit.

KC: On the last two days of the season, you had all your relatives in, and you stayed at the Colonial. Would you tell us what that time was like?

CY: I had about thirty relatives in, so there was no room at the home for me to sleep; so I went over to the Colonial for both nights. On Saturday night I went to dinner, then went to bed early, about ten o'clock. I stayed in bed, but I couldn't fall asleep. Finally, about two in the morning, I got up, went out, and walked . . . and kept walking. I think I walked to Route 128, ten to fifteen miles. By the time I got back, it was dawn. I had breakfast. When I got to the ball park, it was about 9 A.M. I felt very relaxed. I lay down on the clubhouse floor and took a nap for about three hours. I got up about noon and felt super.

But those two nights I didn't sleep a wink. It was from the adrenalin flowing so hard. Here was a chance. Here was an opportunity. You remember a couple of days before, we were really out of it. If the other teams had won some games on Thursday or Friday, we had no chance. But all of a sudden, we

---

center to second to replace Mike Andrews. Williams was livid over the fielding of Andrews, who had been keeping quiet about the extent of his back problems. It caught up with Mike — and the team — today. "Andrews has a bad back and can't bend. If he can't bend, he can't play," the manager said. He added that Andrews should have caught two balls that went for hits. "We can't wait any longer," Williams said. "It's a shame we had to wait this long to find out [about how bad Andrew's back really was]."

It was revealed that Andrews injured his back lifting weights in the off-season. His replacement played second base (a little, not much) in the minors. Reggie said he felt he could do the job. "I don't care where I play, as long as I play," Smith said.

The loss dropped the team's preseason mark to 9 – 9.

MONDAY, MARCH 27

With opening day just two weeks away, there is some concern over the number of injured players. The list of walking wounded has forced Williams to postpone a four-player cut that was expected today. The ailing include Tony Conigliaro (cracked left shoulder), George Scott (bruised wrist), Mike Andrews (pulled back muscles), Gary Waslewski (sore arm), George Smith (torn cartilage in his right knee), Dan Osinski (pulled rib cage muscle), and Jose Tartabull (pinched nerve in his leg).

learned they got beat. Now we had new life. I can remember when we got beat by Cleveland on Wednesday, everybody was talking about packing up and going home. All of a sudden, on Saturday morning, we were back in the pennant race. We had a chance. We had to beat Minnesota twice, and that's what we did.

KC: That season really turned the Boston franchise around.

CY: I think 1967 not only turned on the fans, but I think it turned the whole Red Sox organization around. I think we became winners instead of losers. We expected to go out and win, instead of lose. The thinking changed. We became winners. The attitude in the clubhouse was unbelievable! When you look back and compare our talent — who we had on the field the last six weeks of the season — with the other contenders, you wonder how we won. We should have finished ten games out of first place that year. That's why they call it the Impossible Dream, I guess.

Just as Williams thought it couldn't get worse, it did. In the game today, pitcher Jose Santiago, pitching in the 6−1 loss to Atlanta, developed a blood blister. But later in the day, the skipper got some good news: Tony C. was given permission to resume workouts.

TUESDAY, MARCH 28

Williams and the coaches started weeding out the roster by axing two pitchers. Garry Roggenburk and Dave Vineyard were sent to Deland for reassignment to Toronto of the international league.

Vineyard's story is a tragic one that few will ever really hear about since it doesn't look like he will make the majors. Three years ago Dave looked like one of the brightest prospects on the Baltimore staff, but an industrial accident damaged his left leg; and he was never the same again. The Red Sox had him in camp as a nonroster invitee. It looks now like his career is over.

Williams said he would cut two more players next week. The manager also unofficially picked George Scott over Tony Horton for the first base job — to the surprise of no one. Horton's hitting only .217. "Tony's pressing so badly he's all fouled up," Williams said. He added that "as soon as Scott is ready to play, he will go immediately to first base."

Scott resumed light workouts this week.

The game against the White Sox was rained out.

WEDNESDAY, MARCH 29

Carl Yastrzemski continues to show that his rigorous off-season conditioning program is paying off. He tagged two home runs off lefty Al Jackson. The blasts led the Sox to a 10 – 9 win over the St. Louis Cardinals. The homers off Jackson were doubly significant in light of Carl's anemic .198 average versus southpaws last year. Yaz also made the game-ending catch by spearing Jim Williams's fly to deep left. The Boston outfielder has played great defensive ball all spring.

Carl Yastrzemski's rigorous off-season training program led to a fast start in camp, then to what is probably the greatest all-around year a player has ever had. (Photo courtesy Boston Red Sox)

Yaz credits Ted Williams and Gene Berde for his great spring: "Ted told me to close the hip [point the right hip more toward the plate rather than opening it and pointing it toward first], and I went right to work on it. I can't see as much of the ball, but I'm not helping the pitcher either. This way I can wait and I have more leverage. I know I'm hitting better."

Gene Berde? He's the physiotherapist at the Colonial Country Club who put Yaz through his paces in the off-season. "He put me on a schedule of ninety minutes a day, six days a week. I was skipping rope for ten minutes straight, and then I was sprinting until I thought my lungs would burst. He gave me every exercise, except lifting weights, that anybody ever heard of; and he made me do them. Soon I was feeling better than I ever have in my life."

In his speculations on the opening day lineup, Williams jokingly answered, "Possibly George Thomas," for each position. He then said it would probably be Scott, Smith, Petrocelli, and Foy in the infield; Yaz, Tartabull/Thomas platoon, Conigliaro in the outfield; and a three-man platoon behind the plate (Mike Ryan, Russ Gibson, and Bob Tillman).

THURSDAY, MARCH 30

The team got a scare when Baltimore lefty Steve Barber hit Carl Yastrzemski on the hands with a fast ball in the sixth inning of today's 1 – 0 triumph over the Birds. Yaz was hit when one of Barber's pitches got away. Carl put up his hands to protect his face, and his right hand got clipped. Yaz left the game; x-rays fortunately showed no break, just a bruise. Ironically Dick Williams was talking earlier about his hopes that the rash of injuries was over, especially after George Scott and Tony Conigliaro returned to the lineup today for the first time since their injuries.

In the game Lee Stange worked five shutout innings and retired the last thirteen batters he faced. Hank Fischer may have won a spot on the roster by throwing shutout ball for the last four frames.

FRIDAY, MARCH 31

The Red Sox and Yankees made baseball history today by playing the first major league game ever in the Virgin Islands. The Yanks won 3 – 1 behind the pitching of Mel Stottlemyre. Jim Lonborg tuned up by going seven innings and giving up just four hits. The game drew a capacity crowd of 4,100 in St. Croix.

3

April

After the toughest and most productive spring training camp in years, the team broke camp and flew north to put it all on the line for real.

The Red Sox took the home opener 5 – 4 from Chicago in the Fenway freezer, then the next day lost 8 – 5 in the ninth. In ways both symbolic and spiritual, though, the *true* opening day did not happen until the third game of the season and Billy Rohr's near no-hitter against the Yankees in New York. No one knew at the time of Rohr's gem about anything like an Impossible Dream or an impending pennant and World Series, but there was a suspicion after this game in New York — an undefinable and unfocused suspicion — that something odd was going on. This was a game whose import went outside of itself by setting in motion the idea that anything was possible.

For the rest of April, the Red Sox played well overall and ended at 8 – 6, one game out of first place. The six losses included two 1 – 0 defeats and an eighteen-inning, 7 – 6 heartbreaker at Yankee Stadium. Any one of these three losses could have gone the other way.

Also during April Dick Williams continued to exert his influence over the team and established most decidedly that he was the only chief . . . all the rest were Indians. He was out to mold a club made in his own image, one that bore the stamp of his feisty personality.

SATURDAY, APRIL 1

In the second game on the Virgin Islands, the Sox turned the tables on the Yankees and clubbed them silly 13 – 4. The offensive fireworks helped islanders celebrate the fiftieth anniversary of the U.S. purchase of the islands.

SUNDAY, APRIL 2

The muscle show continued today with an 8 – 2 drubbing of the New York Mets at St. Petersburg. The win ran the Red Sox grapefruit record to 12 – 10 (including nine of the last fourteen). George Scott knocked in three runs with a home run and double.

MONDAY, APRIL 3

There was no game today, and Williams held a day-long workout on fundamentals. The team worked on cutoff plays, pick-offs, and rundowns. There was some trade talk, with Don Demeter's name popping up. Demeter appears to be out of the running for the center field spot, with Smith at second and Tartabull and Thomas being named in the platoon. Rumors were fueled when Dick O'Connell visited the A's camp in Bradenton.

   Players got a laugh reading Jimmy the Greek's odds on the '67 season. Greek had the Orioles 2 – 1 favorites to repeat, with the Sox listed as 100 – 1 long shots.

TUESDAY, APRIL 4

More fire erupted from the volcanic Williams today during a 3 – 1 loss to the Pirates. The game was scoreless going into the bottom of the eighth, with Darrell Brandon pitching seven shutout innings. Dennis Bennett came on in the eighth and with two out, two on, gave up a triple to rookie George Spriggs off the left field wall. During the play Bennett just stood on the mound. Williams shouted out some heated words from the dugout, Bennett glared back in, then Williams sprinted out to the mound. "I went to the mound to speak to him because he did not back up third base. I bawled him out . . . I also told him it was a lousy pitch," Williams said. "My little boy could have handled that pitch." He concluded by saying that he would tolerate no bellyaching on the team.

Managing to Get By

One of the misconceptions about the '67 Red Sox was that it was a "loose" team, that is, relaxed, fun-loving, young, and happy-go-lucky; but it wasn't. Dick Williams held the reins tightly, too tightly to permit that kind of attitude. Simply put Dick was an extremely tough manager who pulled no punches. Many of the players feared him.

Williams was a shrewd manipulator of the team's psyche. He manipulated it by his regular correcting of players in public through the press. Most managers, like Billy Herman, who preceded Williams, and Eddie Kasko, who followed, deal with a player's

---

WEDNESDAY, APRIL 5

A horrendous ninth inning by the Red Sox handed the lowly Washington Senators the game today 5−1. The ninth began with the score knotted at 1−1, but two wild pitches by Gary Waslewski, a dropped line drive by Tony Conigliaro, and a booted grounder by Mike Andrews at second led to four Nat runs.

Carl Yastrzemski strained his back and was listed by Buddy LeRoux as day to day. Back woes may also have sidelined Mike Andrews, but for a longer time. Andrews was in obvious pain and couldn't bend over properly when he made his ninth-inning error.

THURSDAY, APRIL 6

The team got below the twenty-eight-player limit today by sending rookie infielder Al Lehrer and pitchers Gary Waslewski and Jerry Stephenson to Toronto. Haywood Sullivan said Stephenson told him he wanted to be traded "if that's all the Red Sox think of me." Sullivan calmly dismissed the request because Jerry was "hot under the collar" and didn't mean it.

In today's game the Sox beat Detroit at Lakeland 4−1. Billy Rohr nailed down a spot on the roster by pitching six innings and giving up just one run. Galen Cisco also pitched well and may have secured his spot. Offensively Tony Conigliaro and

problems in private, in the manager's office, behind closed doors and shut lips. It's baseball's equivalent of a confessional: what goes on stays a private matter between the two parties. Williams could operate like that, but just as often wouldn't. He'd talk about a problem player with the writers and would blast, say, George Scott for not listening to instructions or Dennis Bennett when Bennett griped in the spring about being in the bullpen. Seeing something in print gives it a life of its own, a kind of instant validity. Williams believed that players would get his message more quickly and lastingly that way.

If you read only the papers, you got the impression that all kinds of nasty things were going on; but it wasn't as bad as it seemed. It was simply one of the ways that Williams maintained total control over his team.

A number of players literally feared Williams, which is not at all uncommon in baseball or in other professional sports. Fear can sometimes be a motivating factor, as Paul Brown and Vince Lombardi proved in football. Years later players look back at their service under such men, and they sometimes change the word *fear* to *respect*.

But I think it would go too far to attribute the team's success entirely or even primarily to Williams's iron fist. Somehow or other in 1967, the chemistry to do what was deemed impossible was there. It worked;

George Thomas had two RBIs each. Carl Yastrzemski sat out the game with a bad back.

Williams also announced his pitchers for the season's first three games: Jim Lonborg and Darrell Brandon to pitch the first two at Fenway versus Chicago, with Rohr to open up against the Yankees in New York.

FRIDAY, APRIL 7

On the off-day, Williams held a seven-inning intrasquad game between the regulars and the reserves. The regulars won 8–3, with George Scott crashing a mammoth home run. The manager raised a few eyebrows when he predicted the Red Sox would win more than they would lose in the regular season.

SATURDAY, APRIL 8

As camp eases down and the intensity eases up on the last two days, work goes on at a feverish pace at Boston's Fenway Park, where the grounds crew is trying to get the field in shape for the April 11 opener. Some 90,000 square feet of Maryland turf costing $11,000 is being laid in four-foot sections over the entire field. It's been a cold, wet spring in Boston; and to blow moisture off the ground, Fenway Park superintendent Dan Marcott has hired helicopters to rev up their blades over the field.

it was successful. After 1967 it wasn't. Williams's approach certainly was a major factor; but then it took Carl Yastrzemski's Triple Crown (something that hasn't been done in baseball since) and Jim Lonborg's Cy Young year to win the pennant by a game.

The manager's job is to get the best performance out of the people made available to him. I think for that year, for that ball club, Dick Williams did just that. He pushed the right button the right number of times. Norm Siebern might have been hitting under .200 on August 19, but Williams sent him up against the Angels with the bases loaded. Siebern cooly hit a three-run triple that keyed an 11−10 win.

Williams also knew how to use his coaching staff by expertly weaving the calming influences of Eddie Popowski and Bobby Doerr into the strings that pulled on the ball club. There is no question that Williams was then, and remains today, an excellent manager. He's proven that with his record and his longevity. I think, however, that players play better for so-called player managers such as Al Lopez and Ralph Houk. Ballplayers need to be loose, because of the day-in, day-out grind of the game. The more relaxed a player is, the better he is apt to play. By relaxed I don't mean a player thinking, "Now I can take it easy," but that he can simply feel as comfortable

---

In the next-to-last grapefruit game, the Sox ripped the Tigers at Winter Haven 6−2. The win assures them of a winning record for the camp. They are now at 14−12 with one game left. It marks the first winning camp in years.

SUNDAY, APRIL 9

In the last game, the Tigers beat the Sox 4−3 in ten innings. George Scott had four hits. Now that he has been given the first base job, Scott's mood has lightened somewhat. George smiled when asked about the problems this spring caused when Williams moved him around in the field. Right after the game, the team flew to Boston.

MONDAY, APRIL 10

Fenway Park was too wet for workouts so the team went across the Charles River to Cambridge and used the Harvard batting cage. The weatherman predicted cool but sunny for tomorrow's opener. An exhausted grounds crew battled the rain all day today as they tried to get the field into a semblance of playing shape.

Reggie Smith will be the fourth different player to open at second base in the last four years. George Smith opened last year, Felix Mantilla in 1965, and Chuck Schilling in 1964.

as possible within his own personality so that he can perform at his peak. Generally this attitude is something a manager can influence. Sometimes, as with the '67 Sox, the coaches play a big part. Sometimes the players do it themselves.

TUESDAY, APRIL 11

Temperatures in the high thirties, plus forty-mile-per-hour winds produced near-arctic conditions and forced the first postponement of a home opener since 1953. Despite the heroic work of the grounds crew, the field was spongy and unplayable. The team did manage to get in a brief workout after the game was called. The players then spent most of the day moving personal belongings, which arrived last night from Florida.

WEDNESDAY, APRIL 12

Governor John Volpe threw out the first ball; and four minutes later, at precisely 1:34 P.M., home plate umpire Hank Soar called, "Play ball," and 1967 arrived.

It was bitter cold, and Volpe ducked out too soon to see the Sox get off with a 5 – 4 win over Chicago before 8,234 hardy souls.

Rico Petrocelli led the way with a home run and four RBIs. Jim Lonborg opened and got the win with relief help from John Wyatt and Don McMahon. Rico's homer was hard to believe given the fierce crosswind prevailing at the time. It didn't seem possible that any ball could be hit out.

True to the new spirit of the club, the Sox — *Red* Sox, that is — had three stolen bases before the season was six innings old. They hustled the winning run in the sixth. Jose Tartabull beat out an infield hit, stole second, and scored when shortstop Ron

Hansen threw away a grounder by Carl Yastrzemski for a two-base error. The Red Sox got the last two outs in spectacular fashion, with Tony Conigliaro running down Hansen's liner in right and George Scott robbing Jerry Adair blind on a ball that seemed destined for right field.

THURSDAY, APRIL 13

It was another December-in-April–like day at Fenway, and the Red Sox responded to the cold weather by playing Santa Claus, literally handing over an 8 – 5 victory. Boston made five errors and gave up five unearned runs in the top of the ninth.

In the ninth, the Red Sox handled the ball like trained seals: Joe Foy bobbled two and Tony Conigliaro one as the White Sox pushed across one run and loaded the bases. Ron Hansen's double gave Chicago a 6 – 5 lead. Jerry Adair's two-run single wrapped up the scoring.

Hank Fischer was MVP for Boston — Most Victimized Pitcher. He came on in relief of starter Darrell Brandon, didn't allow a runner past second in his first three innings, and in the ninth pitched well enough to retire four batters. Yet he ended up with the loss.

The defeat snapped Boston's nine-game Fenway Park winning streak over Chicago, dating back to April 27, 1966.

"The Rohr of the Crowd"
Friday, April 14, 1967

Young Billy Rohr, part Cherokee Indian, stood tall on the mound today at fabled Yankee Stadium almost doing what all the ghosts of baseball's greats and near-greats failed to do. With the song of destiny quietly humming its haunting notes in the young man's head, the rookie found his rhythm quickly and came within one pitch of doing what had never been done before: pitching a no-hitter in his first major league appearance. When it was over, the baseball world stood admiring and dumbfounded. There was no point in attempting a heady analysis of Rohr's feat or in proposing logical explanations . . . there was just a blind and almost delirious acceptance.

After coming within one strike of history, Rohr settled for a one-hit, 3–0 shutout of the Yankees. The skinny, twenty-one-year-old lefty gave up five walks but no hits as he faced New York catcher Elston Howard with two outs in the ninth before 14,375 — including Jackie Kennedy and her son, John. Howard worked the count to 3 and 2 before stroking a line single to right. Tony Conigliaro had no chance to make a play. The New York crowd was still booing Howard's hit when Rohr retired Charley Smith for the final out.

Rohr threw 122 pitches, besting Yankee great Whitey Ford, who was making his four hundred thirty-second major league start. Ford pitched well, but the Sox got all they needed on Reggie Smith's leadoff home run in the first and Joe Foy's two-run shot in the eighth.

The drama crescendoed throughout the game, with the tension picking up noticeably after the sixth inning, as everyone became fully aware of what was going on. The usual carefree, staccato banter of the typical baseball crowd gave way to a building buzz. Shouts became murmurs. Almost instinctively people seemed to lower their voices as they would in a church or somewhere else holy. It was only in the ninth that they felt free to really cheer in support of the young Rohr.

Billy looked nervous on the mound at the beginning, which is understandable because it was his first appearance ever; but he quickly settled down and retired the first ten men to face him. He breezed through to the sixth, when he had to survive a scare. The scare came when Bill Robinson ripped a hard grounder up the middle. Rohr couldn't get his glove down in time, but the ball struck him on the left shin and ricocheted directly to third baseman Foy, who threw to Scott for the out. Dick Williams and trainer Buddy LeRoux came rushing out as Rohr limped around the mound. He walked it off, though, and five minutes later said he was okay. The crowd gave him a hand, and the game resumed.

After the Sox went down in the top of the ninth, all of the people in the stands stood up as Rohr emerged from the dugout. Rohr, looking determined, almost grim, made no acknowl-

RED SOX					YANKEES				
Name	ab	r	h	rbi	Name	ab	r	h	rbi
R. Smith, 2b . .	5	1	1	1	Clarke, 2b. . . .	3	0	0	0
Foy, 3b.	3	1	1	2	Robinson, rf. .	3	0	0	0
Yastrzemski, lf	4	0	2	0	Tresh, lf.	3	0	0	0
Conigliaro, rf.	4	0	1	0	Pepitone, cf. .	3	0	0	0
Scott, 1b.	4	0	0	0	Howard, c. . .	4	0	1	0
Thomas, cf. . .	4	0	0	0	C. Smith, 3b. .	4	0	0	0
Petrocelli, ss. .	3	0	1	0	Barker, 1b. . . .	2	0	0	0
Gibson, c. . . .	3	1	2	0	Kennedy, ss. .	2	0	0	0
Rohr, p.	2	0	0	0	Mantle, ph. . .	1	0	0	0
					Amaro, ss. . . .	0	0	0	0
					Ford, p.	2	0	0	0
					Clinton, ph. . .	1	0	0	0
					Tillotson, p. . .	0	0	0	0
TOTALS	33	3	8	3	TOTALS	28	0	1	0

	1	2	3	4	5	6	7	8	9
Boston	1	0	0	0	0	0	0	2	0	0
N. Y.	0	0	0	0	0	0	0	0	0	0

	IP	H	R	ER	BB	SO
Boston						
Rohr.	9	1	0	0	5	2
N. Y.						
Ford.	8	7	3	3	1	5
Tillotson.	1	0	0	0	2	1

edgment. Before making his first pitch, he looked around at his defense as if he were establishing a magical bond with each of his teammates, a connection that, in some wordless way, would help preserve the no-hit treasure.

First up for the Yankees in the ninth was Tom Tresh, who in one swing of the bat seemed to put an end to this real-life fantasy. His drive to left over the head of Carl Yastrzemski left a rising trail of blue vapor. Everyone knew the ball couldn't be caught — everyone except Yaz. At the crack of the bat, Yaz broke back, being guided by some uncanny inner radar. Running as hard as a man fleeing an aroused nest of bees, Yaz dove in full stride and reached out with the glove hand in full extension, almost like Michelangelo's Adam stretching out for the hand of God. At the apex of his dive, Yaz speared the ball, and for one moment of time that would never register on any clock, stood frozen in the air. He landed, did a full tumble, and triumphantly rose, holding the ball high in the air as if he were Liberty keeping the burning flame aloft. It was truly a *spectacular* catch, made all the more improbable coming when it did. The New York crowd went wild.

Joe Pepitone followed with a routine fly to right, which Tony Conigliaro handled easily. Of course anything would have looked routine coming on the heels of Yaz's grab. The stage was set for Howard. Ellie assumed his wide stance in the right batter's box and pumped the bat out to Rohr, measuring him up. Rohr worked Howard tough, running the count full. On the fateful pitch, Rohr threw a curve, which hung a fraction, enough for Howard to make solid contact for the base hit. It was over; and with the ending theatrics, a sense of the miraculous hung over this young Red Sox team.

Jackie and son, John, went to the dugout to congratulate Rohr, who was besieged by fans, fellow players, the media, everyone.

From Boston, Mayor John Collins sent this telegram: "You gave Boston an unforgettable day. Red Sox fans everywhere salute you and congratulate you on a fine pitching performance. May today's victory be the first of hundreds in your major league career."

In the clubhouse Rohr talked calmly with the press, a calm not unlike that which descends after the initial shock from a surprising event wears off; the calm someone has when they are emotionally drained: "It would have been nice to have a no-hitter, but it's awfully nice to be 1 – 0 in the big leagues. After Yaz made that catch — the greatest I ever saw — I felt I owed it to him to pitch a no-hitter. Howard hit a flat curve. It would have been a strike.

"We hadn't thrown him a curve before, but we decided to try it in the ninth. He swung in the dirt after the first curve I threw. When he hit the ball, I knew it was in there [for a hit]. The first I thought about a no-hitter was about the fifth or sixth inning. Nobody on the bench talked about it, and neither did the Yankee bench. Sure I'm a little disappointed, but he [Howard] gets paid more to hit than I do to pitch, so I guess he should get one."

Howard said he was just doing his job and added, "It was the first time I ever got a base hit and got booed in New York."

The line of the day, though, went to Russ Gibson before the game even started. For some reason the team took a bus from Boston to New York rather than fly, as they normally would do. Gibson grumbled in mock disgust: "I've been riding buses for ten years in the minors. I finally get to the big leagues, and on my first road trip, what happens? We take the bus."

After the game Dick Williams said he almost took Rohr out after Billy was drilled in the left shin: "I was afraid he might hurt his arm by favoring the sore leg. I told Gibson to let me know if Rohr was favoring the leg. An inning later Gibson told me the kid had better stuff than he had before he got hurt."

The night before his near-historic first start, Rohr spent a sleepless night. On Thursday Billy got permission to change roommates from Bob Tillman to Jim Lonborg. He said he wanted Lonborg to help him go over the Yankee hitters. "When we got to New York," Lonborg recalled, "I took him to Dawson's Pub for a big steak. Then we went to the Biltmore to go to bed. He couldn't sleep . . . he was tossing and turning all night."

When Rohr went on the field before the game, Dennis Bennett remarked: "If he gets by the first inning he'll be okay. But he's a nervous wreck right now."

Billy Rohr, cap flying, lets go a pitch in his startling near-no-hitter on April 14 at Yankee Stadium. (Photo courtesy Boston Red Sox)

Radio versus TV

In 1967 I did play-by-play on both radio and TV as head of the three-man crew that included Ned Martin and Mel Parnell. It was more enjoyable doing both, rather than one or the other; and I think in that situation, a broadcaster has a tendency to do a little better job because of being less likely to fall into a rut. Doing radio and TV keeps you a bit sharper, I think.

In '67 we broadcast all the games on radio and fifty-six games on TV. When we were doing a TV game, I would broadcast the first three innings on TV, the middle three on radio, and the last three on TV. Ned Martin would do just the opposite, 3 – 3 – 3 on radio–TV–radio. Mel would do nine innings of

---

Williams came out of the dugout in the ninth before Howard stepped in: "Watch that first pitch," Williams said. "This man's a dangerous batter on the first pitch."

Rohr started Howard off with a fast ball, and Ellie swung and missed. A fast ball outside made it 1 – 1. The rookie came right back with another heater, which Howard took for called strike two. Rohr then missed with two curves and ran the count to 3 – 2 before the hit.

This wasn't Rohr's first experience in no-hit land. "I saw a no-hitter once by Sandy Koufax against the Giants in the Coliseum. Imagine, I was almost in a league with Koufax today, my idol, that guy. But there was Howard on first base. I looked over at him. I wasn't mad, just disappointed."

Howard reiterated the fact that he was just doing his job and that he wasn't a villain: "I got three kids to feed, so I go up there to hit the ball . . . and I'm not a bit sorry because my job is to do that. When I got to first base and I looked at him, I knew he was hurt. But that's my job, man."

SATURDAY, APRIL 15

How could you possibly follow what Billy Rohr did yesterday? Well you couldn't, but Mel Stottlemyre gave it next best by

color on TV. Ned had a postgame television show; I did pregame TV and radio shows. Al Walker was our engineer on radio and, in effect, our producer.

One thing for which a broadcaster must always be on the alert when switching from radio to TV is to remember to "put on the brakes." By that I mean you have to cut your descriptions to the bone. I think one of the problems with televised baseball today, particularly on the network level, is that TV broadcasters talk too much. Radio and TV are two completely different mediums and should be treated as such. I have no idea why it is ever necessary to put three people in a booth to do TV play-by-play. The average, intelligent fan doesn't need, and doesn't

want, three people yakking at him or her to explain what's going on.

Almost all the broadcasters I know say they prefer doing baseball on radio. Baseball is a radio game, where your listeners can visualize what's happening on the field through your word pictures. And the radio audience very often is a bigger one than TV. For example, on a weekend, a radio audience is on the move, in cars, at the beach, around a picnic table, out of doors. They're not sitting in a living room when it's sunny and pleasant outside. Radio audiences are, I think, much more attentive than their TV counterparts. Because they bring their imaginations into play when listening to a radio description, they

---

outdueling Dennis Bennett in a 1−0 loss at the Stadium. The Red Sox not only didn't score a run, they didn't even dent third base. It was strictly hands off Stottlemyre, who allowed but four hits.

Bennett, who complained openly this spring about being used as a reliever, looked strong, with a good fast ball and a sharp curve. He went all the way and gave up five hits. His only mistake came on Horace Clarke's two-out single in the fifth, which produced the game's only run.

"I suppose I'll be cut to pieces for losing the ball game," Bennett remarked facetiously. "A man has to pitch a one-hitter around here to be greeted by the press," he laughed in a reference to the media attention given to Rohr.

Yaz robbed Tresh again, this time with two men on.

SUNDAY, APRIL 16

Today's game began in the cold and ended in the dark as the Sox lost an eighteen-inning death march 7−6. Joe Pepitone's line single off Lee Stange with two outs in the bottom of the eighteenth ended the five-hour, five-minute marathon in which 571 pitches were thrown.

Boston blew leads of 3−0 and 5−3 before tying the game 6−6 in the ninth. They could have won it there. Tartabull reached on

American League Standings April 15, 1967			
Team	W–L	PCT.	GB
Baltimore	3–1	.750	–
Kansas City . . .	2–1	.667	½
Washington. . . .	2–1	.667	½
BOSTON	2–2	.500	1
New York.	2–2	.500	1
Detroit.	2–2	.500	1
California	2–2	.500	1
Chicago	1–2	.333	1½
Minnesota.	1–3	.250	2
Cleveland	0–2	.000	2

tend to be more involved, more mentally active and alert.

For a broadcaster radio is simply more fun to do, because you have much more of a chance to exercise your creativity. You are, after all, creating — on the spot — images for the listeners' minds. On television, however, if you're broadcasting correctly, your words should never dominate, or even equal, the picture. What you say should be supplementary to what your viewers see. Your job is simply to put captions on those pictures.

I'm sometimes amazed at a strange reverse logic when it comes to this point, though. This happened to me when I was in Cleveland, when I was doing the Indians' television. People told me that sometimes they'd turn the TV sound down and listen to the radio description to accompany the TV picture. And now that I do radio, I've had letters from people telling me they do the same thing. They listen to me with the TV sound turned down. Boston Celtic fans do this frequently, pairing up Johnny Most's unabashed words with the TV picture. But oddly enough if a TV announcer would try to do what a radio announcer does, people would say, "What is that idiot doing?" You don't do this on TV play-by-play: "Morehead goes to the resin bag, now tugs at the bill of his cap. He looks in for the sign from Ryan, comes to the belt. He pauses, now pitches. It's a fast ball outside and low for a ball. Now he steps off the rubber." The viewer would say, "What's he telling me all this for?"

---

an error, Foy flied out, but Yaz singled and Tony C. doubled for a run. However, Charley Smith robbed Scott on a wicked smash between short and third, and the Yanks escaped.

The line score told the story of the Sox's futility in cashing in their runners:

$$Boston - 6 - 20 - 2$$
$$New\ York - 7 - 15 - 3$$

No less than thirteen times did the Red Sox have the chance to knock in the winning run from second or third. The breakdown was as follows:

Ninth inning: Scott lined out, Reggie Smith flied out.
Tenth inning: Thomas fouled out; Tartabull fanned.
Eleventh inning: Smith robbed of a hit by Len Barker.
Twelfth inning: Foy struck out.
Thirteenth inning: Scott fanned; Smith robbed of a home run by Steve Whitaker.
Fifteenth inning: Scott struck out.
Sixteenth inning: Demeter struck out; Tartabull popped out.
Seventeenth inning: Conigliaro and Scott fanned.

Failure to hold leads, plus this exasperating failure in the clutch, had Williams steaming in the clubhouse after the game: his comments were mostly unprintable.

MONDAY, APRIL 17

There was no game scheduled today, but things were popping otherwise as the Dick Williams–George Scott Show — erupting and simmering in alternating waves since early spring — surfaced again. Williams announced Scott would be benched in favor of Tony Horton for tomorrow's one-game "series" in Chicago. "I'll have Horton at first base. Scott has been awful hitting, and his fielding hasn't been so fabulous that Horton will hurt us out there," Williams said.

The manager made the switch after stewing over Scott's 1-for-8 performance yesterday in which he stranded seven runners in scoring position. They talk about a game of inches: an inch or two either way on Scott's smash, with runners on second and third in the ninth, would have prevented all this. But Charley Smith robbed George and took the game away from the Red Sox.

"The last three times up, he struck out with men on base. Trying to talk to him is like talking to cement," Williams lamented of Scott. He also pointed out that Scott had a .185 average with no extra-base hits or RBIs. Scott and Horton would not comment on the move.

Despite an early arrival in Chicago following yesterday's five-hour game, Williams ordered seventeen members of the team out of bed for an early morning workout at Comiskey Park. Even though Yastrzemski was one of the ten players excused from the workout (along with Tony Conigliaro, who had five hits yesterday), he went to the park anyway.

TUESDAY, APRIL 18

The team dropped to 2–4 as they lost to the White Sox 5–2 at Comiskey. Bruce Howard checked Boston on three hits until the ninth, when he lost his shutout on singles by Conigliaro, Smith, Horton, and Petrocelli's infield out.

There was more ragged play. Joe Foy made a costly error in the sixth, after which Williams yanked him in favor of Dalton

Retrospective: Dick Williams Looks Back

On managing his way:
"When I came to Boston in 1967, I had a one-year contract. Norma and I took a three-year lease on an apartment, and we purchased our furniture on a three-year-period payment. So if I was going to go down, I was going to go down *my* way. I made up my mind to run that club the way I wanted and the way it should have been run."

On the volleyball games for pitchers in spring training:
"They had fun doing it. Now if somebody had gotten hurt and landed on a shoulder, I would have been horse meat. And because pitchers were playing volleyball, they weren't cluttering up my outfield with guys standing around wondering who was next to be sent out. They were having fun; they formed teams. And my outfielders had room to practice running after balls off the bat. And it was good conditioning for the pitchers."

On George Scott:
"Scotty tried to pull a lot, and he'd take his eyes off the ball. With his power he didn't have to pull. He could hit the ball to the opposite field nine miles, and that's what we tried to impress on him. Dick O'Connell even went out and bought one of the first videotape machines, one that we could hook up on a long extension cord and have it right by the batting cage. We took shots of George chasing

---

Jones. Tony Conigliaro missed a cutoff on one of his throws, Reggie Smith (playing second) failed to cover first on a bunt in the sixth, and Petrocelli bobbled a grounder that was generously ruled a hit, also in the sixth.

Williams's postgame comments focused on Foy, who went 0 for 2, dropping his average to .083.

WEDNESDAY, APRIL 19

Falling snow, cold temperatures, and wet grounds forced a cancellation of today's Patriot's Day doubleheader.

Williams said that he'd bring down heavy fines against Joe Foy and George Scott if they didn't shed their excess weight. According to Williams Foy has gone from 202 to 212 pounds since spring training ended. Scott weighs 221 pounds. Williams said he was shocked when he learned that just two years ago at Pittsfield Scott weighed 198 (a year in which he won the Eastern League Triple Crown).

The manager said that Foy would stay on the bench with Jones remaining at third. And he didn't stop the juggling act there. He said that Reggie Smith would go back to center field, the Tartabull/Thomas platoon would be scrapped, and Mike

bad balls and pulling out. We told Scotty what he was doing, but he said he wasn't chasing balls. Once I remember taking him outside of the cage and showing him tapes of him in the cage fishing for balls. You know what he said? He said, 'That's not me!'

"George was a lot of fun, though. Everybody loved him. He was a great talent. But we kept after him to stop pulling everything. Dick O'Connell gave him twenty dollars for every hit he got to the right of the shortstop. If he got a hit that he pulled, it cost George ten dollars, cash on the barrelhead. He made some pretty good money. He started going up the middle more and hitting to right center, and he was a better ballplayer."

On Billy Rohr's one-hitter at Yankee Stadium:
"I think of that all the time because if I had just stayed in the damn dugout, maybe he'd have thrown a no-hitter. I went out and talked to him with two outs in the ninth. When I got back in the dugout, Elston Howard got the base hit over Mike Andrews's head. I felt bad about that. There weren't any words of wisdom I laid on him, but I just felt I had to go out there to talk to him."

Andrews would take over at second. Horton would stay at first in place of Scott.

The team worked out at the Harvard batting cage.

THURSDAY, APRIL 20

Today was a scheduled day off, and no workouts were held. The Yankees come into town beginning tomorrow night. Billy Rohr gets his second start.

FRIDAY, APRIL 21

For the second time in a week, Billy Rohr beat the Yankees with a strong, complete game. This one was a few miles below his first win in terms of dramatics, but the end result was just the same: a victory, this an eight-hit, 6–1 triumph before a good night crowd of 25,603.

The Red Sox put the game away with three runs in the fifth off nemesis Mel Stottlemyre. With the game scoreless in the bottom of the fifth, Dalton Jones rapped a two-out single. Carl Yastrzemski, George Thomas, and Tony Horton followed with consecutive doubles. They added three more in the seventh off

Steve Hamilton on Reggie Smith's double, Jones's home run, Horton's single, and a double by Rico Petrocelli.

Rohr lost his shutout in the eighth as his personal tormentor, Elston Howard, singled home Bill Robinson.

Rohr's been taking some good-natured kidding about his instant celebrity status. Last Sunday night he took a bow on the Ed Sullivan Show and picked up a quick $500. The club also rewarded him with a new contract, boosting him from $8,500 to $9,000 a year.

SATURDAY, APRIL 22

The Red Sox made it two in a row over the Yankees by winning 5 – 4 on an unearned run in the sixth. With the game tied at 4, New York reliever Dooley Womack hit George Thomas with a 3 – 2 pitch. Russ Gibson singled to center but was thrown out trying to stretch it into a double, Thomas taking third. With one out the Yankees brought the infield in. Mike Andrews then grounded to John Kennedy at short, but Kennedy bobbled the ball, Thomas holding third. George Scott then followed with a sacrifice fly.

The victory went to Jose Santiago, who pitched just two-thirds of an inning in relief of Jim Lonborg. Don McMahon preserved the win with three scoreless frames.

The hitting star for Boston? Carl Yastrzemski, who went 3 for 3 including a home run, his first of the year.

Reggie Smith sat dejected in the locker room after the game. He's had but six hits in his last thirty-seven times up. Dick Williams tapped him on the shoulder and said: "Get your head up. We won."

SUNDAY, APRIL 23

Elston Howard — who else? — belted a two-run double in the five-run fifth inning and led the Yankees over Boston 7 – 5.

The Sox simply blew this one. Led by Carl Yastrzemski's second home run of the season (two in two days), they jumped out to a 5 –1 lead. But starter Darrell Brandon set up the Yankees with three walks and a wild pitch in the fatal fifth. Williams was teed off over the walks.

Despite their win today, the Yankees aren't the Bombers of old. Howard's double in the fifth was their first extra-base hit in seven games. That span involved 287 at bats.

Williams was thrown out of the game in the fifth after heckling home plate ump Red Flaherty over a ball-strike call. It was the first ejection in Williams's brief career as a big league manager. Eddie Popowski took over. Amazingly it was the first time since 1964 that a Red Sox manager was tossed from a game at Fenway.

Williams wasn't the only one to go, as Flaherty ran Yaz in the fifth as well when Carl vehemently disputed a called second strike. This was just the second time in his career that Carl got the boot, the first coming on June 21, 1964, at Baltimore.

MONDAY, APRIL 24

Dalton Jones whacked three singles and Mike Andrews contributed a bizarre three-run dribbler as the Red Sox defeated the Senators in Washington before just 2,235 in thirty-degree weather.

The strangest play in this game came in the eighth, with Andrews up with two outs and the bases loaded. Mike worked the count to 3 – 2. With the runners breaking, Andrews sent a ground ball to first baseman Ken Harrelson. Harrelson came in but booted the ball (and the game). The ball rolled into foul territory on the first base side, and all three runners scored to give Boston a 7 – 4 win. John Wyatt, in relief of starter Dennis Bennett, got the win over Dick Lines.

Dalton Jones's three hits give him an 8-for-19 run (.421) since replacing Foy at third. Regarding the benched George Scott, Williams hinted that he might be in the lineup soon.

When Joe Foy got in Dick Williams's early-season doghouse, Dalton Jones came off the bench with some hot hitting. (Photo courtesy Boston Red Sox)

TUESDAY, APRIL 25

Reggie Smith led off the game against Washington's Pete Richert with his second home run, and there was no

Jim Lonborg kicks and fires on his way to the Cy Young Award. (Photos courtesy Boston Red Sox)

looking back from there as the Red Sox pasted the Senators 9 – 3. He was joined in the homer parade by Mike Andrews, who hit the first of his major league career (a three-run blast in the third), and Tony Conigliaro, who got his first of the year (also in the third). It was Tony's first game after missing a few with a bad back.

George Scott, also back in the lineup, celebrated by going 2 for 4. Hank Fischer pitched a complete game and evened his record at 1 – 1.

Conigliaro said the first home run felt good, but that his back wasn't quite 100 percent. "I wonder if I'm twenty-two or forty-two," Tony asked.

Tony Horton, back on the bench for his lack of hitting and his horrors in the field, took practice in the outfield before the game. Eddie Popowski got all over him for it. "Hey, Horton," Pop yelled, "come in around first base and field some balls. How do you ever expect to learn to field that way?"

WEDNESDAY, APRIL 26

Rain washed out the series' finale in Washington. The team flew to Boston to open up a series with Kansas City. There were some trade rumors, with Tony Horton and Don Demeter being mentioned.

THURSDAY, APRIL 27

Another day off, this one a scheduled one. Jim Lonborg, who has gone just 11 2/3 innings in his first two starts, pitches tomorrow night against the Athletics.

FRIDAY, APRIL 28

Dominating Kansas City, Jim Lonborg turned in the strongest game by any Red Sox pitcher this year. Jim threw a shutout, gave up just six hits, and struck out thirteen. Lonborg managed at least one strikeout an inning through the sixth. He struck out the side in both the fourth and sixth. He didn't walk a batter in the 3 – 0 whitewash. Only one Kansas City runner reached third.

The Measure of Change

Changes? The entire payroll of the 1967 Red Sox team amounted to $825,000, or less than half of what one of today's highest priced players makes.

Changes. They sometimes sneak up on us, inching their way into our lives silently. And it's only hindsight that lets us accurately measure how far we have come. That's why it's impossible to look back to 1967, so many years ago, and not be struck by how much baseball has changed. We may credit (or blame, as the case may be) change in baseball on many things, and the topic would not exhaust its own separate book-length treatment. One factor often cited is the big money that's become so routine today. This "money theory" sees the injection of megabucks in the late seventies and early eighties as the moral equivalent of baseball selling its soul to the devil. Big money and long-term contracts, so the notion goes, smother a player with so much security

---

A little over 9,000 fans braved the cold at Fenway. How cold was it? "It was so cold, I wore four jackets in the dugout," reported Kansas City starter and loser, Jim "Catfish" Hunter.

The Red Sox picked up all the runs they needed in the fifth on hits by Mike Andrews and Reggie Smith. Smith also made a great throw from center field to nail the speedy Mike Hershberger at third.

SATURDAY, APRIL 29

Wild. Heart-stopping. Crazy. Pick one of these adjectives, and you'd have a good description of today's 11 – 10, fifteen-inning win over Kansas City.

The Red Sox trailed early, 5 – 2, but they erupted for six runs in the third, the last two on Reggie Smith's double. The A's pecked away, though, finally knotting the score in the seventh 9 – 9. It stayed that way until the top of the fifteenth, when Rick Monday hit his first major league home run off Don McMahon to put the A's in front 10 – 9. It looked like it was over.

But it wasn't over.

that his competitive edge dulls and his inner fires die out.

This may be true . . . in some cases. But it would be unfair for this theory to stand as a generalization. It all comes down to the individual player. When a truly professional ballplayer goes out on that field, what he makes has nothing to do with what he does when he's playing the game. If a player is a professional — not just technically, but morally — he's going to work just as hard every time he goes out there. If he doesn't do that, he doesn't deserve to be called a pro. On the whole when a player is between the foul lines, I don't think salary matters too much.

When you look at players like Pete Rose and Carl Yastrzemski, they would go out there and go hard no matter what they were getting or how many years they had running on their contracts.

In 1967 there certainly was more of a perception of baseball as a game . . . a game first, a business second. In that sense it was a more innocent time.

You didn't hear much about or from agents, about contracts, players' strikes. Players were less occupied by off-the-field interests. On the 1967 team, almost no player had an agent. Agents can play hardball with owners when it comes to money and contracts. Before agents players just met with the G.M. in a room, and usually they were overmatched.

The question is, then: was this more "innocent" brand of baseball also a better brand of baseball? From a purist's standpoint, the answer is yes. Teams played more fundamentally sound baseball. But in relative terms, I think baseball will always be baseball — a game that provides a few hours of simple enjoyment to millions each year.

Tony Conigliaro opened the bottom of the fifteenth with a single off relief ace Jack Aker. Petrocelli sacrificed him to second. Scott then singled, with Conigliaro stopping at third. Dick Williams sent up Dalton Jones to hit for Russ Gibson, and Jones worked a walk to load the bases. The crowd got more and more excited. The manager then went to the bench again, hitting Jose Tartabull for Mike Andrews. The speedy outfielder singled to center through the drawn-in infield to score Conigliaro and Scott. The entire Red Sox dugout sprinted out on the field to congratulate Tartabull, and the 9,724 at Fenway joined in with ringing cheers. All in all it was a truly great win, not just for the dramatics, but also because it lifted the Red Sox into a first-place tie. The last time they found themselves at the top after playing at least ten games was in 1963.

The clubhouse was riotous after the game. "How do you like our chances now?" shouted Carl Yastrzemski.

Tartabull said he went up guessing: "Everyone in baseball knows I'm a high-ball hitter. Jack Aker, too. When I was going up to the plate, I told myself that Aker would not pitch one high . . . so I started looking for a low ball to hit, and that's what I got." This caused Williams to quip that when he was playing, he was a low-ball hitter and a high-ball drinker.

For his part Kansas City manager Al Dark was complaining about what he called John Wyatt's vaseline ball. Wyatt went 5 2/3 innings of shutout relief. When asked about possibly loading the ball up, he just smiled and said nothing.

Don McMahon got the win.

SUNDAY, APRIL 30

It was Bat Day at Fenway, but not on the field, as the Red Sox lost a tough 1–0 game. Danny Cater's home run into the left field screen accounted for the A's — and the game's — only run.

End-of-the-month Stats: 4/30/67

American League Standings
April 30, 1967

Team	W–L	PCT.	GB
Detroit	10–6	.625	–
New York	9–6	.600	½
BOSTON	8–6	.571	1
Chicago	9–7	.563	1
Baltimore	8–8	.500	2
California	8–9	.471	2½
Cleveland	7–8	.467	2½
Washington	7–8	.467	2½
Kansas City	6–9	.400	3½
Minnesota	5–10	.333	4½

Team Batting

Name	AB	R	H	HR	RBI	AVG.
Osinski	2		1			.500
Demeter	2		1			.500
Jones	21	6	8	1	2	.381
Conigliaro	48	6	16	1	7	.333
Petrocelli	54	8	18	2	10	.333
Fischer	6		2		1	.333
Brandon	6		2			.333
Andrews	28	6	9	1	6	.321
Gibson	40	3	12		6	.300
Yastrzemski	61	6	18	2	9	.295
Scott	40	7	10		3	.250
Smith	59	10	13	2	6	.220
Tartabull	24	4	5		2	.208
Ryan	10		2		1	.200
Thomas	16	3	3		2	.187
Horton	22	2	4		3	.182
Lonborg	8		1			.125
Foy	40	4	4	1	2	.100
Rohr	6					.000
Tillman	5					.000
Bennett	3					.000
Wyatt	3					.000
McMahon	2					.000
Stange	1					.000

Team Pitching

Name	IP	H	BB	SO	W	L	ERA
Wyatt	13⅔	6	6	12	2	0	0.00
Osinski	7	4	2	2	0	0	0.00
Cisco	3	3	2	1	0	0	0.00
McMahon	8⅔	6	4	3	1	0	1.00
Fischer	15	14	4	9	1	1	1.80
Rohr	21	14	8	10	2	0	2.57
Bennett	14	9	6	6	0	1	3.21
Lonborg	25⅔	23	9	26	2	0	3.46
Brandon	24⅔	23	13	11	0	2	4.32
Santiago	2	3	1	2	1	1	4.50
Stange	4	7	2	2	0	1	18.00
Landis	⅓	1	3	1	0	0	54.00

Leaders

Batting
(minimum of 40 at-bats)

Name and Team	At-Bats Avg.
Kaline, Det.	.383
F. Robinson, Balt.	.351
Casanova, Wash.	.341
Cater, K.C.	.339
Petrocelli, Bos.	.333
Conigliaro, Bos.	.333
Clarke, N.Y.	.333
Berry, Chi.	.333
Freehan, Det.	.327
Reichardt, Cal.	.325

Home Runs

Name and Team	#
Blefary, Balt.	5
F. Robinson, Balt.	5
Mincher, Cal.	5
Kaline, Det.	5
Freehan, Det.	4

Runs Batted In

Name and Team	#
F. Robinson, Balt.	14
Freehan, Det.	14
Kaline, Det.	13
Blefary, Balt.	12
Mincher, Cal.	11

Pitching
(minimum of 2 decisions)

Player and Team	Record	Pct.
Lonborg, Bos.	2-0	1.000
Rohr, Bos.	2-0	1.000
Clark, Cal.	2-0	1.000
Horlen, Chi.	2-0	1.000
McDowell, Cle.	2-0	1.000

May

May rolled in with a win and went out the same way. In between, the team traveled through the Death Valley of a pitching and hitting slump, yet had enough belief in itself to ascend to a more lofty position in the hearts of Boston baseball fans than any of their predecessors had in years. It was a month in which the team wrestled with its identity. The struggle was tough; but like wrestling with an angel, it yielded some heady results, the most positive of which was the notion among the players that they *could* actually be as good as Dick Williams was saying they were.

Searching for the right combination, Williams shuffled players in and out of the lineup. Injuries and army duty for some forced him to do this. But he also made changes when players weren't producing. He benched Joe Foy, George Scott, Reggie Smith, and — for one game — even Carl Yastrzemski. "I don't care what a man's name is or if he's a rookie or a star. If he isn't hitting, he isn't playing," Williams dictated.

Through the first part of the month, the club looked like the team that the cynics said they'd be, dropping nine of eleven after winning on May 1. In one six-game stretch ending May 17, the pitching staff gave up fifty-six runs. In the last thirty-seven innings of that time, they allowed seventeen home runs.

Trade talk and possible roster moves became as frequent and as potentially damaging as rumors of war. But Jim Lonborg, winning on May 19, proved a stopper. The team went on to win

The Team Bus

In 1966, when Billy Herman was manager, the media sat in the back of the bus. On team buses, the manager almost always sits in the right front seat. Alongside him you usually find his top aide or the traveling secretary. That was the case with Billy and with Dick Williams; but when Dick came in, he made a big change in seating arrangements. He told the press to sit up front, where he sat.

I think the main reason for doing so was to get more control over press relations. When the media sits in back, away from the manager, there's more of a chance that players, particularly after a bad game, will say some negative things. The same goes for players in the doghouse: with the press far removed from the manager's earshot, players tend to gripe more. So I think Dick's seating plan was one of the more shrewd and astute ways he quietly but effectively established and maintained some control of the media.

nine of their last thirteen. Included in that span: Darrell Brandon's first win; the "gutsiest game" Dick Williams said he ever saw pitched; the disintegration of Billy Rohr; the emergence of Reggie Smith; and on May 30, the largest crowd at Fenway in five years. Slowly you could see the team starting to click, the seeds of their talent beginning to bloom into colorful flowers of surprising and unexpected hue.

By the end of the month, those flowers actually started to resemble a garden. Fenway was rocking as it hadn't since Ted Williams was a young man. No one could openly hope for Eden, but everyone seemed to sense that something — an intangible but good something — was stirring. Magic was afoot!

MONDAY, MAY 1

Controversial lefty Dennis Bennett starred today on the mound and at the plate as the Red Sox got off on the right foot to start their long western road swing. Bennett fired a clean six-hitter to shut out the California Angels 4 – 0. He also provided three-quarters of the offense with a three-run home run.

Bennett allowed just one extra-base hit, and only one Angel reached third; it was the pitcher's first shutout since coming to the Red Sox in the Dick Stuart trade after the 1964 season. The whitewash enabled Bennett to collect on a two-year-old bet with the Boston baseball writers. The shutout was the wager, champagne the stakes. The writers paid up with a case of the best bubbly.

TUESDAY, MAY 2

Angel righty Jim McGlothlin, who's been burning up the league this year with spectacular pitching, set down the first nineteen Boston batters, then hung on for a 3 – 2 victory. The twenty-three-year-old had the crowd thinking about a perfect game before he walked Mike Andrews with one out in the seventh. Yaz followed with a ground rule double, and Andrews scored on Tony Conigliaro's sacrifice fly. The perfect game, the no-hitter, and the shutout were gone in three batters (baseball *is* a funny game).

The Sox are now 9 – 7, one game out.

WEDNESDAY, MAY 3

Jim Lonborg is ready to apply for charter membership in the Hard Luck Club after tonight's crushing game against the Angels. Jim had a no-hitter through six and nursed a 1 – 0 lead going into the ninth, thanks to Andrews's home run to left in the fifth. But in the Angel ninth, Jim Fregosi, Jay Johnstone, and Rick Reichardt singled for a run. With two outs and a runner on third, Lonborg uncorked a wild pitch. Johnstone scored, and the Angels won 2 – 1.

After the game the clubhouse was somber. This was the latest of several tough, one-run losses the Sox suffered this year. In fact, of the team's eight losses, five were by a single tally. These are the kinds of defeats that have the power to dampen a club's spirits. It will be interesting to see how the Red Sox endure. The best way to deal with the loss is to forget it (easier said than done); just go out tomorrow and play the game for the new chance it is. This is how adversity becomes, not so much an ordeal loaded with pitfalls, but a test of character, which, when overcome, can have a strong and lasting positive effect on a team.

An incident before tonight's game illustrated how serious Williams and the coaches were in establishing a workmanlike atmosphere. Eddie Popowski was hitting grounders to the Red Sox' second infield. Suddenly Pop called the drill off and went back to the dugout to the players' amazement. "Three fumbles and three bad throws," Pop grumbled. "I don't think they're interested." Williams agreed — in language not entirely appropriate for a family gathering. The second infield got the message.

THURSDAY, MAY 4

With today's off-day, most of the team visited Disneyland before flying out to Minnesota to play the Twins. Going to the Twin Cities, the Sox just might think they are back in Disneyland . . . the Haunted Castle, to be specific. Over the last three years, they have a 3 – 27 record in the chamber of horrors known as the Minnesota ball park.

One other unrelated but interesting note. In going 9 – 8 so far, the Red Sox have scored six fewer runs than they did a year ago at the same point, but the pitching staff has given up thirty-five fewer.

Happy Jose

Jose Tartabull was one of those people you loved being around. You had a wonderful feeling being near Jose, because he was always happy, upbeat, and singing. He loved to sing songs in the clubhouse and accompany himself on a set of bongo drums.

FRIDAY, MAY 5

Boston made it three losses in a row as the Minnesota curse dropped them to .500. Ron Clark hit his first major league home run, and Zoilo Versalles — American League MVP just two years ago — had four hits for the Twins.

Jim "Mudcat" Grant, who went in at 0 – 3, picked up the win in the 5 – 2 game. The loss went to Billy Rohr. Reality may be catching up with the young lefty. He was manhandled by the Twins and didn't get beyond the second, giving up two runs and six hits. It was his second straight ineffective appearance.

Williams made some changes: George Scott was the new clean-up man, and Bob Tillman replaced Russ Gibson behind the plate. "We're looking for some more batting punch," Williams said.

Tony Conigliaro injured his back in the game, and he may miss the rest of the series.

SATURDAY, MAY 6

Dean Chance looked extra tough today as he pitched a five-hitter to lead the Twins to a 4 – 2 victory. The loss ran the Sox skid to four (five of their last six) and put their record at 3 – 29 in their last thirty-two games in Minnesota.

SUNDAY, MAY 7

Dr. Van Helsing arrived in time to drive a stake through the monster's heart. Translation? At last a victory in Minnesota.

Rico Petrocelli's two-run single in the seventh inning broke a 5 – 5 tie, and two more runs scored on Ron Clark's throwing error. The final score was 9 – 6, Boston. Dan Osinski got the win in relief, with a save to John Wyatt. Jim Perry took the loss.

It looked like more of the same voodoo as the Sox fell behind 5 – 1, but they came back. Don Demeter, who's been in Williams's doghouse all year, started his first game and got two hits. Tony Horton contributed a game-tying, two-run, pinch-hit double.

George Thomas started in left in place of Carl Yastrzemski, who was benched for lack of hitting. Thomas himself had to be replaced by Jose Tartabull after George injured his left hand diving for a fly ball. Jose responded with three hits. Yaz went in defensively for the ninth.

Momentum? Not in Baseball.

The early losing streak the Red Sox suffered brings to mind some ideas on what is an overemphasized part of baseball: momentum. Momentum is the most overrated and least important in baseball, of all major sports. At first glance the opposite seems true; for what is momentum but the building of one feeling on another, the transfer of usually positive energy from one event to the next in such a way that the exchange increases the charge? Having momentum first implies the presence of a continuum, a series of closely related successive events. A snowball rolling downhill and getting bigger or the chain reaction of atomic fission are some conceptual examples. By the same charge, an isolated event can never know momentum because there is nothing to build on, no succeeding event to transfer to. And what is baseball but a series of games? What better continuum could there be than a 162-game season? Or nine innings following one after the other like metal ducks popping up on the revolving wheel in a shooting gallery? And each inning, doesn't it break down into a series of pitches and

---

In explaining why he sat Yaz down, Williams said, "I don't care how much they're making. I'm trying to win ball games." His reference was to Yaz's salary of $58,000, one of the highest on the team. Yaz low-keyed the benching.

MONDAY, MAY 8

The team had an off-day today. The Sox, 10–10 and three games out, meet the A's tomorrow in Kansas City for two.

The team worked out, and Dick Williams commented on his frequent lineup changes: "I don't care what a man's name is or if he's a rookie or a star. If he isn't hitting, he isn't playing." Williams then announced the benching of a rookie — Reggie Smith — and a star — Tony Conigliaro. Demeter will play right, Tartabull center, Williams said.

TUESDAY, MAY 9

The first thing of note was that Williams changed his mind on Conigliaro and decided to keep him in right. The second thing of note is that the Sox were lucky to escape with a split against the lowly A's in the twin bill. Trailing 3–0 in the opener, they tied it in the top of the seventh on Conigliaro's three-run homer; but that went for naught when reliever Don McMahon got wilder than the combat zone at midnight and walked three straight to force home the winning run in the eighth.

plays? The last out of the game is squeezed only to give way to the first ball of tomorrow. Surely momentum seems inevitable.

In truth, though, each baseball game is a self-contained world. No *man* is an island, but baseball games are. The game before won't influence tonight's game; tonight's game exists as if there were no tomorrow. In his last game, Ted Williams homered in his final at bat, and the Sox beat Baltimore 5 – 4. The day before, the O's pasted Boston 17 – 3. Momentum?

In fact a discounting of momentum is one way in which we can judge a ballplayer's professionalism. The true pro can give his best in every circumstance.

If a player goes 0 for 5 and lets that affect him the next night by dogging it, by not playing hard, we might doubt his athletic integrity. Or what would we think of a team that couldn't come back from adversity, say, a tough loss or being down early in a game? A team like the '67 Red Sox, which came back so many times, tends to support this view of momentum.

One of the lessons Carl Yastrzemski said he learned from the pressure-packed games of the '67 stretch drive was that you had to play each game on its own terms . . . not let the highs get too high or the lows too low. You had to play on an even keel. It's an important step in an athlete's career to realize this, for

In the nightcap the A's led 2 – 0 going into the ninth. With ace reliever Jack Aker on the mound, it looked like certain defeat; Aker had already saved Game One. But Tony C. opened the ninth with a walk, Rico Petrocelli singled him to second, and both runners moved up on Mike Andrews's sacrifice bunt (apparently yesterday's bunting drills weren't for nothing). Bob Tillman, following with a base hit, scored Conigliaro. With one out Jose Tartabull walked to load the bases. Joe Foy also drew a walk to force in the tying run. Carl Yastrzemski put the game away with a bases-clearing double.

Jose Santiago went seven innings before being lifted for a pinch hitter. John Wyatt got the win.

In the first game, two pitchers battling to stay on the roster did well. Galen Cisco and Bill Landis pitched scoreless relief. The team must get down to the twenty-five-man limit by midnight tomorrow.

WEDNESDAY, MAY 10

The club, staggering like a boxer tagged with a crusher to the jaw, lost again to Kansas City 7 – 4. Again poor defense killed them in the late innings. Leading 4 – 3 in the seventh, the Sox let the A's tie it with an unearned run. Mike Andrews made the big error. In the eighth, Don McMahon gave the embedded dagger a final twist by walking four men in a row. Paul Lindblad bested Lee Stange in relief.

in doing so, he frees himself and his performance from the failures of the past. Such a ballplayer plays unconditionally, independent of how things are going for him personally. If he's slumping at the plate, he'll still play well in the field. A ballplayer playing this way is a mature ballplayer. This kind of maturity was an attribute of the entire '67 team. Despite the overall youth and inexperience, they played mature, level, yet intense baseball, especially in the big games. This maturity, this subconscious discounting of momentum, really was the secret of the club's remarkable comeback ability.

The '67 Red Sox did not rely on momentum and therefore could not be stopped by adversity. How else could a team lose a Tony Conigliaro in late August and not let that stop them? How could they, just two days later, sweep a doubleheader at Fenway against the California Angels and win game two after trailing 8 – 0?

If there's one danger in the notion of momentum, it's this: it can become an excuse for losing. Losers talk about not getting the breaks, about injuries; and they let one bad break affect their performance tomorrow . . . and tomorrow . . . and tomorrow.

Billy Rohr started and was once more shelled. He got knocked out in the third. In his last three starts, Rohr hasn't reached the fourth inning. In his last 7 2/3 innings, he's given up twelve runs and fifteen hits.

The Red Sox will try to rebound at home Friday as they begin an eleven-game home stand.

The team got down to the twenty-five-man limit by optioning catcher Russ Gibson, who has been suffering from a hand infection, to Pittsfield of the Eastern League. It was a phantom move. When Gibson's hand heals (about ten days), he'll be called up again. In the meantime Boston will try to work out a trade or decide to cut someone else. In effect the ghost move of Gibson to the Pittsfield roster buys the Sox about ten days.

Regarding a trade, what does the team want? "We'd like a utility infielder with the ability to play shortstop in case something happens to Rico. We'd also like another left-handed hitter," said Haywood Sullivan.

THURSDAY, MAY 11

There was an off-day today. It was revealed that Tony Conigliaro will be lost from May 19 to June 3 for two weeks of active duty with the army reserves at Camp Drum in upstate New York.

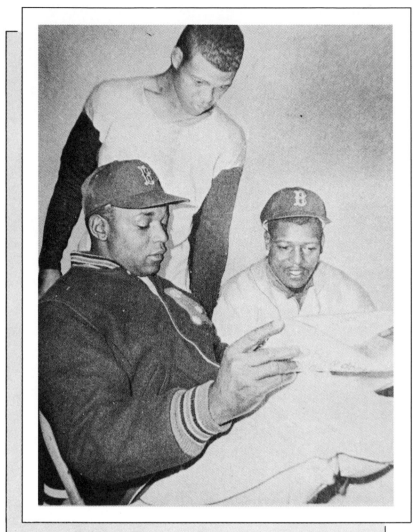

John Wyatt (seated left), Reggie Smith (standing), and Joe Foy read a newspaper account of Wyatt's beaning at the hands of his own catcher, Bob Tillman. It was one of the strangest plays of the year. (Photo courtesy Boston Red Sox)

FRIDAY, MAY 12

Are the fans ready to send out an S.O.S. — for Same Old Sox? Maybe. Just maybe, as the team continued its slide by handing the Tigers a 5 – 4 win at Fenway. The streaking Tigers scored three runs without a hit and added a fourth on a bizarre error. The third inning typified the team's woes as Darrell Brandon walked three and gave up a wild pitch to hand over two runs.

But the strangest run of all was Detroit's final run in the eighth. Al Kaline drew a walk off John Wyatt. On the second pitch, Al broke for second on an attempted steal. Catcher Bob Tillman unleashed a throw from behind the plate. The throw never made it to second; instead it skulled Wyatt. The ball bounded away, all the way to the batter's circle between home and first; and Kaline continued to third. After a few moments to clear out the cobwebs, Wyatt gave up the run on a sacrifice fly.

"I threw the heck out of it," Tillman said later. "I think it would have been right on target. It was probably the best throw I made all year. There was no chance for me to yell [to Wyatt]."

For Wyatt it was a little déjà vu. "For the second time in my life," he said, "there I was, stretched out on the Fenway mound." The first time came in 1963, when he was pitching for Kansas City and he took a smoking line drive flush in the mouth off the bat of Lu Clinton.

SATURDAY, MAY 13

The Red Sox found yet another way to achieve the depths, this one a 10 – 8 loss to Detroit. They lost on six runs in the ninth. The crowd got on Williams for allowing Wyatt to get bombed for all six runs in the ninth. Wyatt hadn't allowed an earned run in his previous nine appearances (18.1 innings).

Wyatt actually started out his day of work looking good and protecting a 5 – 4 lead for 1 2/3 innings. In the ninth, though, he hit the leadoff batter. That was followed by a double, a home run, an infield out, a double, a home run, a fly out, a hit batter, a double, and finally — mercifully — a fly ball for the third out. The Sox made it interesting by rallying for three in the bottom of the ninth.

In the clubhouse some of the pitchers were fuming at Williams for having left Wyatt in for the beating. Wyatt wasn't saying much: "I'm a pro," the reliever said, "and I got to eat, so I don't say nothing. That's all, man."

The last time a Sox pitcher was left in for as severe a beating was on July 22, 1962, when Mike Higgins left Galen Cisco in for thirteen runs and sixteen hits in less than five innings against the Senators.

SUNDAY, MAY 14

Third base coach Eddie Popowski did a fair impression of a windmill, or was it a traffic cop, as the Red Sox broke out of their slump today by sweeping the Tigers 8 – 5 and 13 – 9 before an appreciative gathering of 16,436 at Fenway. "I was out there a long time today, but it's something you don't mind doing when you're scoring. That's the kind of business I like," Pop said.

Pop made himself available to the press for postgame comments when Dick Williams wasn't talking. Williams was incommunicado, still bothered by the lambasting he took from the papers for leaving John Wyatt in for his beating yesterday. Pop's gesture relieved some of the pressure over Williams's not talking and generally defused what could have been an awkward situation. This illustrates again how important Pop is to the chemistry (and to the press relations) of this ball club.

In game one Jim Lonborg won with the help of Hank Fischer. Jose Santiago, with assists from Don McMahon and Galen Cisco, took the nightcap. Rico Petrocelli and Carl Yastrzemski had two homers on the day. Joe Foy and Santiago also homered. George Scott contributed a bases-loaded triple in the first game and three hits in game two. To kill a Tiger rally, he also started a spectacular 3 – 2 – 3 double play in the second inning of the second game.

The Adjustment

The following is excerpted from the May 14 entry in the 1967 diary of Hall of Famer Bobby Doerr.

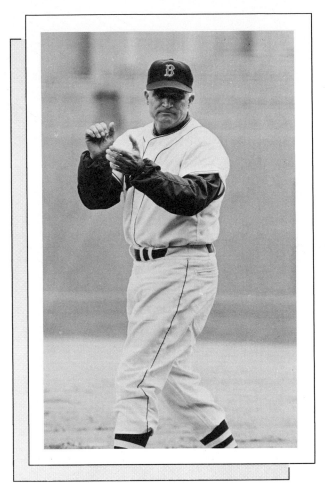

First base coach Bobby Doerr had a steadying influence on the club's younger players. Doerr's gentle but effective coaching style contributed greatly to the team's success. (Photo courtesy Bobby Doerr)

After last night's game, Yaz asked me if I would come out to the park with him this morning to throw him some batting practice. We went to the park about 9 A.M., before to-day's doubleheader against the Tigers.

Yaz has been in a little slump. He's tried many different things to get out of it. During the batting session this morning, I thought Carl's hands were a little low. We discussed it a bit, and Carl felt we were on to something. When he got back in, he held his hands higher, about to the level of his left ear. He started hitting the ball all over, with power. Yaz said he was sure he corrected the problem this way. After the adjustment, he started to hit almost everything real good. By raising his bat, he leveled his swing and the ball carried with a good back spin.

Up to now, with his hands dropped, he's been hitting with an uppercut, causing an overspin on the ball. A lot of potential home runs were sinking, and dying in the outfield. I think this will help Yaz a lot with his production. That seems to be what happened to-day. He hit a home run into the centerfield bleachers his first time up in game one, and also homered in the second game.

It should be noted that, up to the doubleheader against the Tigers, Carl had only two home runs on the season. After the adjustment suggested by Doerr, Carl went on to hit forty-two more.

The Tigers had a run in and the bases loaded with one out. Don Wert bounced to Scott, who had to reach high to bring the ball down. Scott looked to second to start a 3 – 6 – 3 double play, but he was in an awkward position from fielding the oddly hopping grounder. Instead he instinctively rifled a bullet to the plate, thus forcing Bill Freehan. Mike Ryan got the ball back to Scott to complete the play. "I've never made that play before in my life," Scott said later of the stunning defensive gem.

Also of note, the two teams combined for twenty-eight extra-base hits in the doubleheader and established a new American League record. The old one of twenty-seven was set in 1905 by the Red Sox and the Philadelphia A's. For the first ten games played at Fenway this season, there were thirteen home runs hit: five by the Sox, eight by opponents. Today there were twelve — six by each team.

The double win launched the Red Sox from eighth place to a third-place tie (at 13–14) with World Champion Baltimore.

And in New York today, Mickey Mantle hit his five-hundredth career home run. It came off the Oriole's Stu Miller.

MONDAY, MAY 15

Rain washed out tonight's game with Baltimore at Fenway.

The Red Sox, six games behind Chicago, face a real test against the Birds. Last year Baltimore took eight of nine games played between the teams at Fenway.

TUESDAY, MAY 16

The Orioles did it again at Fenway by beating up the Sox 8–5. John Wyatt took his second straight loss in relief.

Boston went into the eighth with a 5–4 lead on Carl Yastrzemski's home run in the seventh, but Wyatt gave up a two-out, three-run home run to Paul Blair to lose it. After having pitched scoreless ball for his first twenty innings of the year, Wyatt has given up ten runs in his last three innings. The Red Sox had three stolen bases, giving them twenty-one in twenty-eight games.

After the game Williams announced another lineup change. He said Don Demeter would go to right to replace Tony Conigliaro, who starts two weeks of active duty in the army reserves tomorrow.

WEDNESDAY, MAY 17

It could have been subtitled "The Jersey Street Massacre," or simply "Slaughterhouse." Instead it will be recorded as one loss, this 12–8 fiasco to the Orioles. Baltimore launched seven home runs (four in the seventh). The Sox added three of their

American League Standings May 15, 1967			
Team	W–L	PCT.	GB
Chicago	18–7	.720	–
Detroit.	17–9	.654	1½
Kansas City . . .	14–14	.500	5½
BOSTON	13–14	.481	6
New York.	12–13	.480	6
Cleveland	12–13	.480	6
Washington. . . .	12–15	.444	7
Minnesota.	11–15	.423	7½
Baltimore	11–15	.423	7½
California	13–18	.419	8

own, two by Yaz and one by Don Demeter. The ten combined home runs were just one shy of the major league record, but set the house record at Fenway. Yaz's two blasts give him five in four games, the best streak of his career.

The four home runs were part of the nine runs the Orioles thundered across in the seventh. Galen Cisco gave up five of them on two home runs and a double. He gave way to Bill Landis, who wasn't much better, yielding two homers and four runs. The crowd booed Williams when he came out to get Cisco.

When asked after the game if he was glad to see the Orioles leave town, Williams snapped: "It's not so much *them* leaving town. I think maybe some of our pitchers will have to leave town."

Red Sox pitchers, in dropping four of six on the home stand, gave up eighteen home runs . . . three a game on average. In those six games, the staff allowed fifty-six runs for a 9.33 ERA. In the last thirty-seven innings, the staff has allowed seventeen home runs.

THURSDAY, MAY 18

Today was a day off, and Williams let the club rest. He was on the move, however, traveling to Pawtucket, Rhode Island, to speak to the Rotary Club. The main topic was the shell-shocked Red Sox pitching staff.

FRIDAY, MAY 19

Jim Lonborg, who has emerged as the stopper, put to rest — for now, at least — complaints about the pitching with a route-going, twelve strikeout win over the Cleveland Indians at Fenway. Lonnie gave up just four hits in the 3 – 2 victory. The win leaves the Red Sox at 14 – 16.

The Tribe got their two runs in the first on Leon Wagner's wind-blown, two-run home run. The homer just made the nets in left field and made Lonborg furious. "I was mad," Jim said. "I've never been madder. Emmett Ashford [home plate ump] tried to joke around about it, but I just wasn't in the mood." So Jim took his anger out on the Indians by holding them scoreless the rest of the way.

The Sox needed last-inning dramatics to pull this game out. They trailed 2 – 1 going into the ninth, on a great pitching performance by the Indians' Gary Bell. But pinch hitter Jose Tartabull opened the Boston ninth with a single. Reggie Smith tripled Tartabull home with the tying run. Smith scored moments later on Tony Horton's pinch single off reliever Orlando Pena. "After I hit the ball into right field, I almost forgot to run. That's how excited I was," Horton said.

The Red Sox first run came in the seventh on a solo homer by Joe Foy.

SATURDAY, MAY 20

Today was the comeback that wasn't. Trailing the Indians 3 – 0, the Red Sox tied it up in the bottom of the seventh. The key hits were a two-run double by Dalton Jones and Rico Petrocelli's RBI single.

The score stayed 3 – 3 until the top of the tenth, when Chuck Hinton's two-run home run off Don McMahon proved the game winner. Hinton's blast was the twenty-first home run off Red Sox' pitching in the last eight games.

SUNDAY, MAY 21

From the pit to the mountaintop in one day.

There was new life at Fenway today as the Red Sox came back once more in a 4 – 3, 6 – 2 sweep of Cleveland.

George Scott's two-run home run into the right field bullpen capped a four-run eighth inning, when the Sox scored all their runs. The other two tallies came in on Carl Yastrzemski's savage triple by the 420 sign. The comeback marked the third straight time the Sox had come back from a deficit in the late innings to either tie or win.

The Sox clubhouse was joyous between games, while the Indians were in a fog. The Indian team may have been adversely affected by an incident in game one, when, with the bases loaded against John Wyatt, Manager Joe Adcock pulled Rocky Colavito for a pinch hitter. Rock heaved his bat and had words with his manager.

Back to Scott. The home run was his third of the season. Since getting back into the lineup after his early-season benching, he has raised his average to .298.

In the second game, Darrell Brandon won his first in five decisions by going the route in the 6 – 2 win. Again the club-

Getting Warm

In 1967 Jim Lonborg was the last Red Sox pitcher ever to warm up on the mound they had beside the first base dugout between the dugout and the screen area. It was fun for the fans to watch him work out there. In 1968 the warm-up mounds were removed; and from then on, all pitchers warmed up in the bullpen.

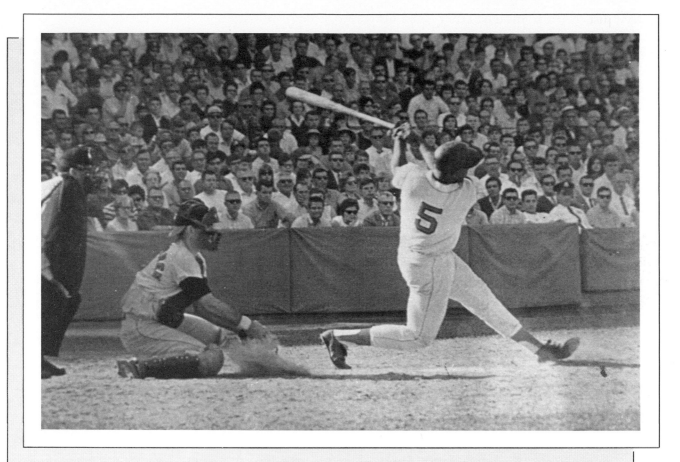

Never shy about his swing, George Scott lets go from the heels. The catcher is Orioles' Andy Etchebarren. (Photo courtesy Boston Red Sox)

house was a happy place. "The beers are on Brandon," shouted clubhouse man Don Fitzpatrick. "Beer, hell," retorted Brandon's roommate, Jose Santiago. "Make it champagne."

Perhaps the most important factor in Brandon's complete game was control. He didn't walk a batter. "I quit trying to be so careful," he said. "[Pitching coach Sal] Maglie's been all over me about that."

The win moves the team back to within one game of .500, at 16–17, .485, in fourth place, 5½ behind Chicago.

MONDAY, MAY 22

The team enjoyed another day off on the schedule. Dick Williams took the time to talk about George Scott: "He's found himself.

Scotty's just trying to hit the ball up the middle, not aiming for the left field fence. He doesn't have to pull the ball. He has proven he's so strong he can hit it out in any direction, in any park."

TUESDAY, MAY 23

The Red Sox climbed back to the .500 mark tonight (17−17, five games out) as they began a six-game road trip in Detroit. They beat the Tigers with classic form: good pitching combined with timely hitting.

After spotting the Tigers a first-inning run, lefty Dennis Bennett bore down the rest of the way to run his record to 2−1. John Wyatt nailed down the 5−2 victory for Bennett.

The Sox got homers from Rico Petrocelli, who hit his fifth blast in the second, and Yaz, who contributed a two-run shot in the eighth. Rico had three hits on the night.

The game wasn't without a miniconfrontation between Williams and Bennett. When the Tigers loaded the bases with two out in the fifth and Al Kaline up, Williams went out to the mound and appeared to be lecturing Bennett. When asked about it later, Bennett said Williams told him: "If I didn't get Kaline out, 'I'm coming after you.' " He got the Tiger slugger on a deep fly to center.

With Bennett's win and Lee Stange possibly starting Sunday, the new forgotten man on the staff is Hank Fischer. Fischer's troubles began a few weeks ago in a game in which Bob Humphreys hit Petrocelli with a pitch. Williams and Sal Maglie told Fischer to knock Humphreys down on his next at bat, but Hank didn't, which didn't set well.

WEDNESDAY, MAY 24

"The guttsiest game I've ever seen pitched in my life." That's how Williams described Jim Lonborg's clutch, 1−0, eleven-strikeout masterpiece against Detroit at Tiger Stadium. The win gave Boston sole possession of third place.

Third baseman Dalton Jones, starting for the first time in two weeks, led off the second inning against Denny McLain with a home run into the seats in right for the game's only run. Dalton always hit well in Tiger Stadium and was in the lineup in place of Foy for that reason.

Retrospective: George Scott Looks Back

On Dick Williams:
"I love Dick Williams. I love him because he had the ability to drive me, to get the maximum out of me. Now Dick Williams called me a lot of names that I don't think were justified, but I still love him because I think he was a great manager. He gave me a hard time as a way of motivating me, but he gave *everyone* a hard time, including Yaz. I think Dick made me a better ballplayer by our run-ins. I hope he didn't take my [criticisms] of him personally. But he made me a better ballplayer because he made me realize that baseball is a dog-eat-dog game, a game where people don't have a whole lot of passion for you. You've got to go out and do your job and move along. He taught me you've got to be a dog in this business. It helped me throughout my whole career. He made me a better person."

More on the manager:
"I remember in '67 we were in a short rainout game. We were leading, and Dick Williams told everyone to go to home plate and try to make an out. I told

Dick Williams in the dugout: 'Put someone else at first base, because it's hard enough when I *try* to get a base hit. I am not going to home plate to try to make an out. If you want to have that happening, you're going to have to put somebody else at first base, because I don't play baseball that way.' He didn't take me out."

And more:
"My relationship with Dick Williams in 1967 was off and on, up and down because Dick thought I didn't respect him as a manager; and I sometimes thought he didn't respect me as a player. But I honestly think it wasn't his thought to try to harm me or hurt me. It was his way of trying to get the maximum out of me. My thoughts were negative at the time, but later on I realized what he was doing."

On his infamous weight problem:
"It came to a head out in California. Dick made me weigh in. I got on the scales. He watched. I was two pounds overweight. He just said, 'You're not playing.'

After the Jones home run, it was all Lonborg. This was a night in which he didn't have his best stuff, and the Tigers had him on the ropes several times. But Jim came up with the big pitch every time he needed it. The shutout was his second of the season, with a record of 5–1.

Lonborg got out of a first-and-third, two-out jam in the second, a bases-loaded, one-out mess in the seventh, and also Houdinied his way out of a runner on third, one-out situation in the eighth.

He had help. Scott, in a brilliant play on Dick McAuliffe's slow roller in the seventh with the bases loaded, forced Norm Cash at the plate with a rifle throw.

THURSDAY, MAY 25

All good things must pass, as did the winning streak tonight. The Tigers clubbed them into submission, 9–3. The Bengals

were paced by Jim Northrup's grand slam in the sixth off Lee Stange, who didn't do much for his chances of getting back into the rotation. Dick McAuliffe added a home run.

Earl Wilson went the distance to win his sixth game. Starter Jose Santiago took the loss. Mike Ryan hit a home run for Boston in the third.

FRIDAY, MAY 26

The team dropped below .500 again by losing 4 – 3 to the Orioles at Memorial Stadium. They fell behind 4 – 0 on a three-run Oriole fourth (with Dave Johnson's bases-loaded single being the big hit), but they came back with three of their own in the fifth.

Singles by Joe Foy, Mike Ryan, Reggie Smith, and Mike Andrews — plus Carl Yastrzemski's infield out — pulled the Sox to within a run. With the tying run on third and one out, Oriole

That was it, and he walked away. I was two pounds overweight, and he put me on the bench! I went out that day and I ran with a sweatsuit on to get the two pounds off, and he still wouldn't let me play. I never will forget it. We lost each game in that series by one run. I'm almost sure if Dick Williams had to do it over again, he would do it different. After many years to think about it, I'm almost sure that he wouldn't take that gamble again. He took his best hitter on the club against California and put him on the bench. I wore California out that year. I could understand if I was five pounds overweight, but two pounds, man. That's running things a bit thin. I couldn't believe it. I couldn't believe it, man. I said to myself, 'What is this guy trying to do to me?' There was one time in that series where I was actually about six inches from going after Williams. I started to go after him. The devil kept telling me, 'Go and get him.' But my intelligence told me, 'No,' because you can't win. But my jaws were so damn tight it was a shame."

On winning the pennant:
"After the last out, I got to Jim Lonborg, and my stomach felt just like it was loaded with lead. For a min-ute there, I woke up. I was in dreamland, and I woke up. Gee, man. When I heard that California beat the Tigers, I can't even explain the feeling in that clubhouse. It was unbelievable. You really can't put it into words, that feeling. When that last pop-up went to Petrocelli, and he brought it down, my stomach felt like someone was holding me to the ground."

---

manager Hank Bauer brought in last year's World Series hero, Moe Drabowsky. Moe struck out two in a row to end the threat. That was the closest the Red Sox came the rest of the way.

This road trip has been a rough one for Scott. He has made only one hit in fifteen at bats, with eight strikeouts. After the game Williams announced that Scott would be out of the lineup for tomorrow's game: "Horton will be at first base."

Scott, having struck out four times tonight, prompted this remark from his personal guardian, Eddie Popowski: "He chirped for fifteen miles on the bus from the airport last night telling everybody how far he was going to hit the ball. Did you see any balls go over the fence? Neither did I. Jerking his head and trying to kill everything. If he thinks about getting thirty-five home runs, he'll hit two."

A matter of equal, maybe more, concern, however, is the pitching of Billy Rohr. The rookie had another poor outing and failed to last the fourth. He's now 2 – 2 and hasn't done anything since winning his first two games. It seems the more he falls behind hitters, the more he starts pressing, so that he abandons his natural motion and aims the ball.

The win tonight put Baltimore a game ahead of Boston in third place. Haywood Sullivan sat with O's general manager Harry Dalton, and trade speculation started again. The hottest rumor has the Sox giving up Lee Stange for outfielder Sam Bowens.

SATURDAY, MAY 27

It was as if Dick Williams (or somebody) went to sleep and dreamed of a baseball game. Only the dream turned into a nightmare; and instead of facing the Baltimore Orioles, the Sox found themselves lined up against Bela Lugosi's Transylvanian All-Stars under a full moon in the Balkans. Today's 10 – 0 loss was that bad.

The Red Sox infield was good for six errors: two by Tony Horton (starting in place of Scott) and one each by Mike Andrews, Dalton Jones, Joe Foy, and losing pitcher Darrell Brandon (1 – 5). Horton, in particular, looked bad. Besides his two errors, he tumbled over a tarpaulin trying for a ball and was slow on a bunt play. To make the shutout even worse, the Red Sox collected ten hits, but they stranded an equal number and blew numerous scoring chances.

Tom Phoebus went all the way and pitched his second straight shutout. Frank Robinson smacked his eleventh and twelfth home runs, giving him the American League lead. The O's scored three in the first and seven in the fourth. Garlic, anyone?

After his two early wins against the Yankees, Billy Rohr found the waters rough. (Photo courtesy Billy Rohr)

SUNDAY, MAY 28

The team pulled itself off the killing floor of yesterday's debacle to squeeze Baltimore 4 – 3. The Sox were led by Reggie Smith,

Uniformly Different

The uniforms of 1967 tell their own story. First they were made of flannel, not of today's double knits. There was no form-fitting opulence. The uniform shirts, with the fiery red "RED SOX" on the home whites and the block-letter blue "BOSTON" on the road grays, girdled the upper body, not in the tight caress of today's jerseys, but in what was more like a loose pat on the back. There was room for movement. Players seemed less muscular, with the strict outlines of their well-honed torsos hidden by the curtainlike folds of the shirts. These folds caught the shadows from the sun or the stadium lights in ways that — on today's uniforms — are unknown.

A player wearing a 1967 uniform seemed sculpted, because of this play of light . . . maybe less chic compared to the painted-on stylish dictates of today, but certainly more artistic, more heroic. It was as if each ripple in the uniform, the harsh play of light

---

who lashed out three hits and scored three runs. Jim Lonborg, with a save from John Wyatt, took the decision over Steve Barber.

This win was important because it proved to the club that it could come right back, shake off a truly horrendous day, and play good baseball.

MONDAY, MAY 29

The schedule maker gave the team the day off. Tomorrow the team plays the Angels for a doubleheader in Boston.

TUESDAY, MAY 30

Even the Old Towne's starting to talk. They came into Fenway hoping. They left believing.

The largest crowd at Fenway in five years, 32,012, witnessed in delight as their team trimmed the Angels twice in the Memorial Day doubleheader. The 5 – 4, 6 – 1 deuce was Boston's third straight doubleheader sweep at Fenway.

and dark, was chipped by a Michelangelo. That's how it looked in certain photos, anyhow. This chiseled look, lending in its roominess a subtle, unfixed form that seemed a neat counterpart to yesterday's less sophisticated circumstances, disappeared when the current spray-painted look became vogue.

The old uniforms flapped when a player went hard, and they seemed to accent motion. For baseball — a game composed mostly of stillness punctuated by five-second bursts of movement — the old style was perfect.

Next the socks. Nineteen sixty-seven was long before the stirrups disappeared in baseball. Today most players opt for fashion by pulling their socks up high enough to show only a narrow strip of sock. But the '67 socks were on full view: a red stirrup with the shallow white crescents of sanitary hose capped by alternating white and blue stripes . . . the sock "as it was" . . . the "suchness" of the sock. No stylized parading of the thin red strip of today.

Finally the shoes. We see in photos from 1967 the unvarying black of worn baseball spikes . . . spikes, not cleats. Real men wore spikes. No endorsement contracts, no racing stripes on the side, no space-age polyester materials. Just steel spikes and leather, sharpened steel gripping the real grass lawns of old ball yards. Think of the sound Carl Yastrzemski's spikes made as they tore up the outfield grass in a desperate race to make a miracle catch. Now think of the synthetic squeak made by the molded cleats making surface contact with a plastic rug. You can't prove anything by this, but you can hear in your memory some qualitative sound that speaks deeply of baseball past.

In the opener Tony Horton's pinch double broke open a 4–4 tie in the eighth and gave Dan Osinski his second win in as many decisions. Bill Kelso was tagged with the loss. In the top of the eighth, the Sox got a break. The Angels had Don Wallace on third with only one out. Buck Rodgers flied to Jose Tartabull in right with a ball so deep that one writer cracked that a Spanish-American War veteran could have scored with no trouble, not even a slide. But Wallace left third too early and had to retreat and retag, by which time it was too late to score. He died at third, setting the stage for Horton's heroics in the bottom of the inning. Horton, with six pinch hits in his last thirteen tries, has emerged as the team's best pinch hitter and one of the best in the league.

In the second game, Don Demeter's two-run double and Rico Petrocelli's single in the fourth gave the Red Sox all the runs they needed in the 6–1 win. An inning later two runs scored on Rico's squeeze bunt and a throwing error by Angel catcher Orlando McFarlane. The daring bunt had the crowd on its feet screaming. Dennis Bennett went all the way and pitched a strong five hitter to up his record to 3–1.

George Brunet took the loss.

The sweep had the whole town buzzing, and not since the days when Ted Williams was young has a Red Sox team turned on Boston baseball fans as this team has.

"It's been years since fans have seen the hit-and-run, and base stealing, and squeeze bunts. It keeps them interested and it keeps the other team off balance," said Bobby Doerr. He didn't have to convince any one of the 32,012.

WEDNESDAY, MAY 31

It was out with Angels and in with Twins in Fenway's revolving door. The Twins arrived for the two-game set confident that their dominance over the Sox would continue. But they were looking to the past, and this was a new Red Sox team. Boston proved it by putting on another show for the wild fans.

The Red Sox rode Carl Yastrzemski's ninth and tenth home runs to a 3 – 2 win. Yaz said later that he enjoyed playing in close games, especially with the Sox still in the race (22 – 20, 4 1/2 games behind the Tigers): "Every at bat means something now," Carl said. "We're playing tight ball games, and you've got to be bearing down all the time."

His leadoff homers in the fourth and seventh innings gave Boston a 2 – 0 lead; but true to the team's aggressive character, the winning run was scored on a suicide squeeze by Mike Ryan. The 12,335 went crazy.

"Before I left the dugout, Dick [Williams] told me to squeeze on the first pitch, no matter what . . . so we didn't even use a sign. He [Jim Perry, Twins' pitcher] threw a slider, and I was able to get the ball down," Ryan explained.

His bunt marked the second straight game in which the Sox squeezed a runner home from third. Beneficiary of tonight's running was Darrell Brandon, who was starting in place of Billy Rohr. Rohr was called for duty by his army reserve unit last night. Johnny Wyatt, getting the save, pitched a scoreless ninth. Wyatt said he was lucky because he didn't have anything on the ball: "If you ain't lucky in this game, you may as well pack your lunch pail and go home," Wyatt said.

"I've said it before the season that this team will win more games than it loses, and I still believe that," said a buoyant Williams after the game.

The team's 22 – 20 mark compares with a 16 – 26 record a year ago at this time.

American League Standings
May 31, 1967

Team	W–L	PCT.	GB
Detroit	26–15	.634	–
Chicago	25–15	.625	½
BOSTON	22–20	.524	4½
Cleveland	21–20	.512	5
Baltimore	20–20	.500	5½
Minnesota	20–22	.476	6½
Washington	19–23	.452	7½
New York	18–22	.450	7½
Kansas City	19–24	.442	8
California	18–27	.400	10

Leaders

Batting
(minimum of 80 at-bats)

Name and Team	At-Bats Avg.
Kaline, Det.	.347
Mincher, Cal.	.338
F. Robinson, Balt.	.333
Petrocelli, Bos.	.325
Carew, Minn.	.320
Northrup, Det.	.309
Conigliaro, Bos.	.304
Yastrzemski, Bos.	.299
Tovar, Minn.	.296
Berry, Chi.	.292

Home Runs

Name and Team	#
F. Robinson, Balt.	14
Mantle, N.Y.	11
Howard, Wash.	11
Yastrzemski, Bos.	10
Killebrew, Minn.	10

Runs Batted In

Name and Team	#
F. Robinson, Balt.	37
Kaline, Det.	35
Killebrew, Minn.	32
Yastrzemski, Bos.	31
Howard, Wash.	30

Pitching
(minimum of 4 decisions)

Player and Team	Record	Pct.
Horlen, Chi.	6-0	1.000
Sparma, Det.	4-0	1.000
Lonborg, Bos.	6-1	.857
McGlothlin, Cal.	4-1	.800
Chance, Minn.	8-2	.800

Team Batting

Name	AB	R	H	HR	RBI	AVG.
Santiago	7	1	3	1	3	.429
Petrocelli	154	23	50	6	24	.325
Horton	37	2	12		9	.324
Conigliaro	92	13	28	2	15	.304
Yastrzemski	154	30	46	10	31	.299
Ryan	64	10	19	1	8	.297
Andrews	124	16	36	2	11	.290
Demeter	42	7	12	1	4	.286
Jones	60	10	17	2	7	.283
Scott	144	18	39	3	19	.271
Fischer	8		2			.250
Osinski	4		1			.250
Gibson	56	4	14		6	.250
Brandon	18	1	4			.222
Tartabull	97	14	24		3	.247
Smith	146	22	31	2	13	.212
Thomas	20	3	4		3	.200
Foy	120	17	23	4	9	.192
Tillman	26	2	5		2	.192
Bennett	19	1	2	1	3	.105
Lonborg	25		2			.060
Rohr	10					.000
Wyatt	5					.000
Cisco	3					.000
Stange	2					.000
McMahon	2					.000

Team Pitching

Name	IP	H	BB	SO	W	L	ERA
Osinski	21	16	5	14	2	0	1.29
Fischer	23⅔	22	8	16	1	2	2.62
Cisco	16	11	5	5	0	1	2.81
Lonborg	70	57	22	71	6	1	3.09
Bennett	51⅔	45	16	18	3	1	3.12
Wyatt	27⅔	15	14	21	3	2	3.21
McMahon	16⅓	15	13	3	1	2	3.37
Brandon	65	55	28	42	2	5	4.03
Rohr	36⅓	35	17	13	2	2	4.25
Stange	17⅓	21	5	22	1	2	4.76
Santiago	30⅓	37	11	26	2	2	6.30
Landis	5	6	6	6	0	0	10.80

5 June

For the first two months of the season, the Red Sox went through what all young teams with new bosses do, they struggled to establish an identity, to achieve some confidence in who they were and what they could do. With its blend of new management, rookies, newcomers, and veterans, the team went through its growing pains. But in June the character of the club began to take definite shape.

June began with two key acquisitions: infielder Jerry Adair from the White Sox and starting pitcher Gary Bell from the Indians. Most observers felt that Adair and Bell would greatly help the team, though no one could have predicted how important Adair would become. The moves made it clear that the Red Sox' front office would not sit back — it believed as much as Dick Williams did that the Sox had a chance for the pennant, and they were going to go after it.

Two specific games went a long way in determining the temperament and the tempo of the club. On June 15, trailing 1 − 0 in the bottom of the eleventh inning against Chicago, they rallied for a two-out deuce to win 2 − 1. Tony Conigliaro's home run was the winner. On June 21 at Yankee Stadium, there was a bench-clearing brawl that made it official: these weren't the laid-back "country clubbers"; they were a bunch of fighters who would back down from nothing. In effect the game exemplified how they had taken on the aggressive qualities of their manager.

For his part Williams was proving himself a very effective manager. He could be tough and abrasive when he had to be, but he could also handle players with sensitivity when required — for example, he stuck by and encouraged Reggie Smith when the young center fielder got off to a slow start at the plate.

But most important of all in June, the Red Sox stayed reasonably close to first place. They did nothing to shake the growing confidence in Boston baseball circles that the team was for real.

THURSDAY, JUNE 1

The four-game winning streak came to an abrupt halt tonight at Fenway at the hands of Dean Chance. The talented Minnesota righty celebrated his twenty-sixth birthday with a four-hit, 4 – 0 shutout. Chance struck out ten.

The Sox reactivated outfielder George Thomas today. Thomas was out for almost a month recovering from a hand injury. To make room for Thomas, pitcher Hank Fischer was put on the disabled list with a sore arm.

FRIDAY, JUNE 2

Jim Lonborg upped his record to 7 – 1 with a brilliant three-hitter against the Indians at Fenway Park. Jim needed to be brilliant, as his mates pushed across just two runs in the 2 – 1 win. Lonnie had a no-hitter for 7 1/3 innings before Tribe catcher Duke Sims, hitting just .177 going into the game, belted a ground rule double to right.

Carl Yastrzemski continued his big hitting and won the game with a two-run home run in the bottom of the sixth over the right field fence. Besides winning the game, Yaz's homer ended a sixteen-inning scoreless streak for Boston.

SATURDAY, JUNE 3

Dennis Bennett, one of Dick Williams's early-season sparring partners, let his pitching do the talking today by going six strong innings against the Indians at Municipal Stadium. The Sox prevailed 6 – 2, with Bennett upping his record to 4 – 1. Gary Bell took the loss. Bennett gave up six hits but only one earned

The Bosox Club

We started regular meetings of the Bosox Club in 1967. We had the Wahoo Club in Cleveland when I was there. When I came to Boston in 1966, I sat down with Red Sox PR director Bill Crowley to try to set up a similar club in Boston. We had several meetings, and I remember a conference call we had with Gabe Paul and Al Rosen of the Cleveland front office. They shared with us ideas and procedures on running such a club.

The purpose of the Bosox Club is to promote baseball in New England on all levels, from Little League to the pros. We have about 500 members, largely from business; and it's turned into the most successful club of its kind in the country.

The thing I remember about '67, our first year, was the fact that Dick Williams attended and spoke at every single meeting we had. He couldn't have been more cooperative.

The Front Office

The front office is not one of the major features of this book, and it is not intended to be. I think most baseball fans focus their attention on what happens on the playing field and that they care only marginally for what happens in the front office. That's as it should be. They pay to see action.

But no team succeeds without an effective front office. In 1966 General Manager Dick O'Connell brought Haywood Sullivan back into the Red Sox organization from the Kansas City A's. Sullivan was a major factor in the acquisition of Lee Stange in 1966 and Jerry Adair, Gary Bell, Elston Howard, Norm Siebern, and Ken Harrelson in 1967. Crucial also to the team's success was owner Tom Yawkey. The three men — O'Connell, Sullivan, and Yawkey — worked in unison, and the issue was somewhat cloudy as to who did the most. And to their everlasting credit, no one claimed the glory for himself.

In spring training in 1985, Carl Yastrzemski and I talked about 1967 over a couple of beers; and Yaz pointed out that, on a personal level, Tom Yawkey made a major emotional contribution. A shy man who stayed out of the public eye, Yawkey in '67 was a constant visitor to the clubhouse, where he offered encouragement to the players, veterans and rookies alike. An owner who really knew the game, this quiet man's support blended into the intangible chemistry of the team.

---

run. Jose Santiago pitched the last three innings and was perfect; he gave up no hits or runs and struck out two.

The Red Sox put the game away early by scoring two in the second and three in the third.

The win leaves the Red Sox at 24 – 21, in third place, 3½ games out. But even more important than today's win was the news the team made off the field. Haywood Sullivan and Dick O'Connell made good on their trade promises by acquiring veteran infielder Jerry Adair from the White Sox in exchange for reliever Don McMahon and minor league pitcher Rob Snow. The deal was made to strengthen the bench and to provide insurance in the infield, especially at short. The versatile Adair can play third, short, and second and has been noted through the years for his steady play, especially in the field.

McMahon made himself expendable with some recent wild streaks, and he didn't figure in the Sox' pitching plans because of that. Snow was a throw-in.

In another roster move, the Red Sox made room for Tony Conigliaro by optioning reliever Galen Cisco to Pittsfield in the Eastern League.

SUNDAY, JUNE 4

The recent trend for low-scoring games continued today in Cleveland, as the Indians' Steve Hargan blanked the Red Sox

3–0. It was Hargan's fourth shutout for the season. Hargan got all the support he needed for his five-hitter from Leon Wagner, who hit his eighth home run to lead off the fourth. The Red Sox' bats were completely muffled, and they didn't come close to scoring.

Fifteen minutes after the game, the Red Sox announced their second trade in two days, this one somewhat of a blockbuster. The Sox acquired starting pitcher Gary Bell from the Indians in return for enigmatic first baseman Tony Horton and reserve outfielder Don Demeter. Both Dick Williams and Dick O'Connell said that Bell might be the missing link that could make the Red Sox contenders. "This is one of those years when it looks like the pennant is up for grabs," O'Connell said. "I think we can win it. We've bolstered our starting pitching with experience and ability."

When asked how he felt about getting Bell, Williams replied with one word: "Overjoyed." Williams said that Bell would go into the starting rotation immediately.

Horton is a kid with a world of potential. But he has yet to show he's mastered his biggest opponent: himself. He was unable to dislodge George Scott from first base this spring, his third shot at the Red Sox.

The acquisition of Gary Bell from Cleveland on June 4 was one of the key front office moves of the year. (Photo courtesy Boston Red Sox)

MONDAY, JUNE 5

On today's off-day, all the talk was about newcomers Adair and Bell. Dick Williams said he planned to start Adair at third immediately in place of Joe Foy. Foy's been slumping all year and is hitting just .204. Williams said that starting Adair at third might "build a fire under Foy."

TUESDAY, JUNE 6

The Red Sox were a little red faced tonight after two former mates helped the White Sox to a 5–3 victory at Comiskey Park. It didn't start out that way, as Boston got off to a 3–0 lead with two in the second on Mike Ryan's single and one in the third on Carl Yastrzemski's base hit; but Chicago battled back to tie it in the fifth.

After that, Don McMahon, obtained from the Red Sox for Jerry Adair just three days ago, and Wilbur Wood, who failed in his try to make the Red Sox a few years ago, shut the door. Boston starter Darrell Brandon went into the seventh giving way to Jose Santiago, who gave up a bases-loaded, two-run single for the deciding runs. Brandon took his sixth loss in eight decisions.

In other news the Red Sox were getting ready to open the checkbook for a bonus payment to sign seventeen-year-old Mike Garman. Boston selected the young man from Caldwell, Idaho, as their first pick in today's free agent draft.

After the game tonight, Tony Conigliaro had to fly home to attend a National Guard meeting in Lynn. He will miss tomorrow's twi-night doubleheader.

WEDNESDAY, JUNE 7

The White Sox went ahead quickly in tonight's first game; then, almost on cue, the skies opened up. After waiting for almost two hours for the skies to clear, umpire Bob Stewart called both games. One of the rained out games has been rescheduled to follow tomorrow night's scheduled single game.

THURSDAY, JUNE 8

Carl Yastrzemski smoked four hits in five tries, including his twelfth home run, to salvage a split of tonight's doubleheader with a 7 – 3 win in the nightcap. Boston dropped the opener 5 – 2. Yastrzemski's four hits gave him 11 for 22 on the six-game road trip and put him among the league leaders with a .322 average and thirty-six RBIs to go with his dozen home runs.

In Game One Joel Horlen won his seventh without a loss. Tommie Agee had three hits, with Jerry McNertney and Ken Berry belting home runs. Dennis Bennett, who went all the way, took the loss. Joe Foy hit his fifth home run of the year, and Yaz had two doubles and a single.

In the second game, Gary Bell made his Boston debut a winning one by throwing a complete game. The team backed up their new pitcher by banging out 15 hits. The Red Sox won it with a five-run second, featuring a two-run double by Foy and RBI singles by Russ Gibson, Bell, and Yastrzemski. Jerry Adair had three hits.

The Sox now stand at 25 – 24 in a fourth-place tie, 5½ behind Detroit.

Bell was affable in the clubhouse and showed a quick wit. At a recent luncheon, Bell was asked what kind of hitter Dick Williams was when the two faced each other as players. Bell looked at Williams, also seated at the head table, and said, "Without a doubt, the toughest hitter I ever faced."

FRIDAY, JUNE 9

It was Yaz and Foy again tonight as the Sox squeezed by Washington 8 – 7 at Fenway. Carl's thirteenth home run with a man on tied the game in the first. His fourteenth in the seventh snapped a 6 – 6 tie. Foy homered in the fifth and eighth, with Reggie Smith also hitting one out in the fifth. The five home runs put the crowd in a festive mood, a festivity with an edge on it because of the tight score.

Yaz (twenty for his last thirty-nine at bats) was brilliant in the field, too. He robbed Mike Epstein and Bob Saverine with glittering catches in left. John Wyatt preserved the win for Jose Santiago in the ninth.

Before the game Bob Tillman, who hasn't started a game since he beaned Wyatt with a throw on May 13, defended the play: "That [throw] plain wasn't my fault, but I was the fall guy in the papers. I don't mean this in criticism of Wyatt, but he was standing straight up when I threw the ball. I said it at the time, and I still say it, there was nothing wrong with the throw."

Some news of note came from Minnesota today as the Twins announced that they had fired Sam Mele as manager and replaced him with Cal Ermer.

SATURDAY, JUNE 10

Fenway was hot today, but the Red Sox were not as they did a swan dive before the big stick of Frank Howard. Howard's thirteenth and fourteenth home runs of the season gave the Senators a 7 – 3 win in the ninety-five-degree heat.

Three members of the '67 broadcasting lineup: from left, Ned Martin, Ken Coleman, and Mel Parnell. (Photo courtesy Boston Red Sox)

Camilo Pascual had his great curve doing the cha-cha off the end of a table; Pascual settled down nicely after giving up a two-run home run to Reggie Smith in the first and a solo shot to Rico Petrocelli in the third.

Meanwhile Tony Conigliaro, struggling through one of the worst slumps of his career (3 for 27, all singles), worked long after the game — in the heat — on extra batting practice. George Thomas volunteered to pitch to Tony, and Bobby Doerr shagged balls.

Some 15,634 saw today's game. This brought attendance to 320,670 — 79,264 ahead of last year.

SUNDAY, JUNE 11

The Red Sox split another doubleheader, this one against the

Partners

My three associates in the broadcasting booth in 1967 were Ned Martin, Mel Parnell, and Al Walker.

Ned was the veteran. Ned broke in with the Red Sox along with Carl Yastrzemski in 1961 following five years of broadcasting minor league ball in Charleston, West Virginia. From 1961 to 1966, Ned was part of some terrible Boston teams. That's why 1967 was a very special time in his life. He loves the game, and he responded beautifully to the excitement of the Impossible Dream. The team was winning, there were big crowds, lots of drama. I know it meant a lot to Ned.

In my opinion Ned is the consummate professional and one of the best broadcasters ever to have been associated with baseball. I have been blessed to work with Ned as a colleague and know him as a friend. He's intelligent, astute, well read, and wonderfully sensitive.

My other colleague in the booth that year was Mel Parnell. Mel handled color commentary on radio and TV and lent creative insight to our broadcasts. Mel was easy to work with and dependable. Also, the fact that he was — along with Babe Ruth — the premier left-handed pitcher in Red Sox history lent a unique perspective to our work in 1967.

The final member of the booth crew was Al Walker, our engineer. Al, who's now retired and living in Methuen, Massachusetts, started engineering Boston baseball in 1952 and continued until games switched from WHDH to WITS in the early seventies. During the course of those years, Al probably saw more Red Sox games than anyone else alive. Al was a quiet, intense guy and one of the most conscientious workers I've ever met. He'd come to the park at 2 P.M. to check all the equipment and make sure everything was okay and set up right for a night game. I remember Al drumming his fingers on his console. That was a habit of his. And before each game, he would say, "Go get 'em kids."

These three men gave us probably the strongest broadcasting team in all of baseball in 1967. Certainly that comes across on each relistening of "The Impossible Dream" record album we did following the '67 season. That record went on to become the greatest selling sports album in history and sold more than 100,000 copies.

Senators before 16,599 at Fenway.

In the opener they battled back from a 3–0 deficit to win 4–3. The Senators knocked out Darrell Brandon in the fifth, but Jose Santiago and John Wyatt shut them out the rest of the way and gave Boston a chance to pull it out. It was a chance they cashed.

The Red Sox got two in the sixth on Mike Andrews's single followed by doubles from George Scott and Joe Foy. Santiago's double and Jose Tartabull's single tied it in the seventh. Rico Petrocelli's base hit plated the game winner in the eighth.

In the second game, rookie Gary Waslewski from Meriden, Connecticut, made his major league debut; but he lasted only three innings in the starting role.

It looked like they might pull this one out, too, but finally went down 8–7. The loss went to Dan Osinski. Tony Conigliaro, whose extra batting practice paid off, hit a three-run home run.

MONDAY, JUNE 12

Gary Bell made it two in a row as a member of the Red Sox by winning his Fenway debut 3−1 over the Yankees before 18,932, who waited out an early evening thunderstorm. Bell pitched his second straight complete game (the staff's fifteenth, compared to eight a year ago) and gave up seven hits, fanned eight, and walked only one.

Russ Gibson hit his first major league home run with one on, one out in the second off Joe Verbanic to give Bell all the help he needed. The rookie took some ribbing over his blast, with Mike Andrews telling him the ball didn't really go out, but went through one of the holes in the scoreboard. Gibson also called an excellent game and handled Bell intelligently. George Scott went 2 for 3.

Gibson said he needed to work on his home run trot.

TUESDAY, JUNE 13

The Yankees got a split of the two-game series and beat Jim Lonborg 5−3. It was the second straight time Lonborg failed to win his eighth game. The Red Sox got out in front 2−0 on back-to-back home runs by Joe Foy and Tony Conigliaro in the second, but they couldn't hold on.

Dick Williams blasted Tony Conigliaro's base-running blunder, when he was thrown out at second trying to stretch a single into a double leading off the top of the seventh. The Sox were down three runs at the time.

WEDNESDAY, JUNE 14

The Red Sox seem to be developing a split personality when it comes to twin bills. The White Sox won today's opener at Fenway 8−7 on home runs by Tommie Agee, Dick Kenworthy, and Walt Williams. It was an agonizing loss. The Red Sox had the bases loaded with two outs in the ninth, but Wilbur Wood came on to fan George Scott to end it. Scott and Rico Petrocelli hit home runs.

In the nightcap Scott and Carl Yastrzemski hit home runs as Boston rebounded 6−1. Lee Stange won his first game. Eddie Stanky, who earlier called Carl Yastrzemski "an All-Star from the neck down," mildly surprised everyone by admitting that Yaz should be the starting left fielder next month for the American League.

"Tony C and the Team that Could" Thursday, June 15, 1967

Since the hiring of Dick Williams, since the winning grapefruit record, and especially since the season's start — in which the Red Sox' early play has given birth to a kind of good feeling not felt around Fenway for a long, long time — since all this there's been a movement under way, a faint but steadily growing ripple of the dramatic that periodically demands release. This impulse is felt only on winning teams and not on losing ones (remember, a cadaver has no pulse). This ripple, when expressed, is felt like the early volcanic activity that presages a genuine volcano, the treelike shaft of lava, sparks, and orange, pizza-looking glows. In short, before the true eruption come the warnings.

There have been several such warnings — the many come-from-behind wins and, most notably, Billy Rohr's one-hitter and the 12–11 win against the A's in fifteen at Fenway. But before tonight these games could have been dismissed by the cynical and near cynical as isolated events, unrelated happenings, flukes that spoke, not of the club's heart-stopping ability to win lost games, but only of the freak chances of the game of baseball. Until tonight, and the eruption.

For the Red Sox fan who wasn't at Fenway tonight and missed the game on radio, the wire service report of the 2–1, eleven-inning win over the White Sox would seem satisfying, but other than that nothing out of the ordinary. But for those who were there, for those who listened on the radio, even those who were blessed with the detailed account of a friend who was there or listened, it was a different matter.

Tonight's game revealed a truth that often goes unobserved in low-scoring contests, a truth moving beyond the kind of built-in

WHITE SOX					RED SOX				
Name	ab	r	h	rbi		ab	r	h	rbi
Williams, rf. .	5	1	2		Smith, cf.	5		1	
Buford, 3b. .	5				Andrews, 2b. .	5		1	
Agee, cf. . . .	5				Yastrzemski, lf	5		1	
Berry, lf.	4	2	1		Scott, 1b.	4		1	
McCraw, 1b. . .	4				Foy, 3b.	5	1	1	
Hansen, ss. . .	3	1			Conigliaro, rf. .	4	1	2	2
Stroud, pr. . . .					Petrocelli, ss. .	4		2	
Martin, c.					Gibson, c. . . .	4		1	
Causey, 2b. .	3	1			Waslewski, p. .	3			
Weiss, ss. . . .	1	1			Wyatt, p.	1			
McNertney, c.	3								
Ward, pr.									
Buzhardt, p. . .									
Howard, p. . . .	2	1							
Burgess, ph. .	1								
Wilhelm, p. . . .									
Kenworthy, 3b.	1								
TOTALS	37	1	8	1	**TOTALS**	40	2	10	2

Team	1	2	3	4	5	6	7	8	9	10	11
Chicago	0	0	0	0	0	0	0	0	0	0	1
Boston	0	0	0	0	0	0	0	0	0	2	2

Name	IP	H	R	ER	BB	SO
Minn.						
Howard	7	7			2	6
Wilhelm	2	1				4
Buzhardt (l)	1⅔	2	2	2		2
Boston						
Waslewski	9	6			2	5
Wyatt (w)	2	2	1	1		3

Support for Rico

Rico Petrocelli often opened up to me about his concerns. I remember once having a talk with Rico. He told me he was a worrier, especially since the birth of his twins. With a wife and three kids to support, Rico said he let things like job security get the best of him sometimes. But Rico said Eddie Popowski was a big help.

During the '67 season, Pop constantly reassured Rico by patting him on the back and telling him how good he was. Even Dick Williams made it a point every now and then to give Rico some words of encouragement.

Once, Rico, Dick, and I were sitting around and talking in the clubhouse. Dick said to Rico: "What you ought to do, for God's sake, is go out and find a house and buy it [at the time, Rico was renting a house, saying he couldn't go out and buy one because he had no sense of job security]. I don't say go out and get one like Yaz, but get a comfortable place for your family and your wife [Elsie]. It'll take a big worry off your mind. I'll tell you how much guts I have. I've only got a one-year contract, but I've got a two-year lease on my place and we bought all our furniture on time."

admiration that the term *pitcher's duel* engenders. The truth is this: where there is a lack of runs by both teams in the same game, there is also less distraction for fans.

Often the high-scoring, home run-laced slugfests are like quick hits from a popular drug: the high wears off just as quickly as it comes. Fans are diverted from the game itself by the Zorbalike dancing and celebration of, say, the long ball or a six-run inning. They are like all revelers, with senses partially lost through unrestraint. And this is not to say that such revelry hasn't a place in baseball, for it is dearly important. But it is a fact that during such outbursts, which every fan lives for, your attention is scattered.

A 0 – 0 game like tonight's (scoreless through ten) is a pleasure of a different kind. It is the pleasure built on suspense, of keeping one's self in check, of literally having your attention hang on every pitch. In such a game, every movement is consequential. There is no lost motion (or emotion). The pitcher, for instance, backs off the rubber in a crucial spot. The crowd follows his every move. In such a game, the crowd makes note of every incident and anticipates what next may happen. Will he throw over to first? Will he use the fast ball up and in or a curve low and away? Will the manager pinch-hit? Will he hit and run? All possibilities are examined. Minds start working. This cannot happen in the raucous undertow of a three-run homer, for example, that puts a game out of reach. A big home run stays with fans much longer than a string of zeroes. The ball will clear the fence, and the crowd won't stop cheering until long after the player is in the dugout. The next batter may ground out or single, and many may not even notice. But in the low-scoring game, all action is observed. Which leads to another difference: in low-scoring tilts, the cheers come for the defense and the pitcher.

The cheer for a run scored is different from that for a run prevented. The first is boisterous, outgoing; the second is more a letting go of held breath, a true release. Even the appreciation for a pitched ball holds its own unique quality in the pitcher's duel. During the late innings of a scoreless game, every pitch becomes a game in itself, a mini drama. When your team is on the field, your eyes are riveted on the pitcher and your defense. You follow the movement of the ball to the plate and care deeply about its *exact* location.

This long examination is necessary to begin a discussion about tonight's very special contest. For ten innings the Red Sox and the White Sox matched zeroes and formed a game with the classic dimensions and symmetry of a set of dueling pistols with precious gems inlaid in the ivory handles. The line score was a mirror reflection of circles, like so many perfect spheres casting identical images into a dead-still pond:

```
            123456789 10
Chicago   000000000  0
Boston    000000000  0
```

And then came the top of the eleventh, and a wind blowing over the surface of the water rippled it and virtually guaranteed an end to the hypnotic, identical reflections. Chicago scored a run.

Walt Williams led off against John Wyatt with a double into the left field corner. Don Buford followed. With the Red Sox expecting a bunt, the corners of the infield charged in. George Scott was in bunt zone when Buford tried to cross everyone. He swung away and sent a wicked liner down the first base line. What followed almost could not be believed, as Scott dove desperately for a ball just about behind him, somehow made a one-handed catch, and retired Buford, Williams taking third. No one else in baseball could have made the play Scott did. Wyatt bore down and got the dangerous Tommie Agee on strikes for the second out. But Ken Berry, on a twenty-game hitting streak, singled to right to plate Williams with the first run.

The "1" on the scoreboard in left changed from temporary yellow to permanent white when the inning ended; it looked ominous, like a loaded missile poised to rain hideous destruction over Fenway Park. The missile appeared ready to detonate into another 1 – 0 heartbreaker, especially when Chicago reliever John Buzhardt got Carl Yastrzemski on a pop-up and George Scott on a soft liner to start the bottom of the eleventh. Joe Foy was the last hope, and he came through with a ground single to left.

Tony Conigliaro walked slowly to the batter's box, and the crowd of 16,775 buzzed in nervous anticipation. Conigliaro set himself with the patience of a saint; he seemed to move in slow motion, like a slice of life slowed down for effect in a Stanley Kubrick movie.

What a spot for Tony, who'd been trying to regain his batting eye since coming off his two-week stint in the reserves. Had he left his bat at Camp Drum? Ironically, because of his slump, he

American League Standings June 15, 1967			
Team	W–L	PCT.	GB
Chicago	33–23	.589	–
Detroit........	32–25	.561	1½
BOSTON......	30–28	.517	4
Minnesota.....	30–28	.517	4
Baltimore	28–28	.500	5
Cleveland	28–30	.483	6
New York......	28–30	.483	6
Kansas City ...	29–31	.483	6
California	28–33	.459	7½
Washington....	25–35	.417	10

Tony Conigliaro's dramatic home run in the bottom of the tenth to beat Chicago on June 15 was one of the early milestones of the season. (Photo courtesy Boston Red Sox)

was batting in the sixth spot in the batting order. Buzhardt had a great curve ball working, and he started Tony with two benders that broke sharply and unmercifully. Tony swung and missed at each of them. Things seemed utterly hopeless. Buzhardt then played cat and mouse and teased Tony with two more curves, each of which just missed. The crowd groaned on each pitch. Buzhardt then came in with a fast ball that Tony took just inside to run the count to three and two. At 10:57 P.M. Buzhardt threw the game's last pitch, a curve ball that was like the punctuation mark ending a brilliant novel, say, the period that ends *Moby Dick.* Tony uncoiled his bat in what could only be described as a retaliatory strike and sent the ball fifteen feet up into the left field nets to give the Red Sox a 2 – 1 miracle win.

After a split second of shocked silence, the homer triggered a wild celebration, one long, abdominal cry of relief — the fans reacted as if the pennant had been won. Tony's teammates poured onto the field and surrounded the plate to greet the hero. They overwhelmed him.

"It was wonderful to see those guys waiting for me," Tony said.

Wyatt got the win in relief, but rookie Gary Waslewski deserved it. The kid went nine shutout innings and, to a standing ovation, left in the tenth after he pulled a back muscle and gave up back-to-back leadoff singles to Ron Hansen and Al Weis. It was at this point that Wyatt came in to get out of trouble.

He struck out the first man he faced, pinch hitter Pete Ward. White Sox manager Eddie Stanky went to his bench again, sending up pinch hitter Dick Kenworthy and Ed Stroud to run for Hansen at second. With a count of no balls and one strike on Kenworthy, Stroud tried to steal third and was cut down on a great throw by catcher Russ Gibson. This started an argument that got Stanky and Smokey Burgess thrown out of the game. The argument was not actually on the call at third, but with home plate umpire Larry Napp's ruling that Kenworthy had swung at the pitch (on which Stroud tried to steal) and made the count nothing and two. Stanky argued that Kenworthy checked his swing in time, but the argument was to no avail. Stanky left the field and threw his cap to the ground in disgust. When Wyatt struck Kenworthy out on a three-two pitch to end the inning, Stanky erupted again from the dugout and fired out a stream of invectives in Napp's direction.

There was an interesting development in the case of Stroud. About forty seconds after he was thrown out at third, he was traded to Washington. Chicago general manager Ed Short simply waited until Stroud was out of the game before announcing the deal, which will bring left-handed-hitting outfielder Jim King to the White Sox.

All in all it was a night not to be forgotten.

FRIDAY, JUNE 16

The Red Sox journeyed from the apex of elation to the depths of depression in the short space of one day as they dropped a pair to the lowly Senators in Washington tonight 1−0 and 4−3.

This was a Rod Serling kind of night: weird, bizarre, twisted. One half expected to see the man with the narrow lapels and skinny tie doing a voice-over something like this: "Witness, if you will, the Boston Red Sox, a young hustling team that just one night ago celebrated the sweet taste of extra-inning magic in a little drama called baseball. And witness now, if you will, these same Red Sox a day later but no wiser and in the dying seconds of a doubleheader loss that began in Washington but ended in the Twilight Zone."

Fade to black.

In game one Boston dropped another 1−0 zinger. Gary Bell pitched brilliantly and gave up just five hits. One of them was Ken McMullen's double leading off the bottom of the third. He went to third on an infield out and scored on a squeeze bunt by winning pitcher Bob Priddy. It was a soft, silent kind of run that leaves you thinking you're Napoleon, especially when it comes in a 1–0 game. To add to their frustration, the Red Sox banged out nine hits (three by Carl Yastrzemski, two by Tony Conigliaro), but they left nine runners on base. Seven times in the game the Sox had the leadoff man on to start an inning; three times they got the first two aboard. The worst of all came in the third, when Mike Andrews led off with a single and Yaz singled him to third with no outs. George Scott followed with a two-hopper down the third base line. McMullen speared the ball and threw home just ahead of Andrews. The next two hitters went out quietly. No runs.

Could it have been worse? Yeah. Priddy hadn't lasted four innings in any start this year.

In the nightcap the Red Sox, holding a 3–0 edge going into the bottom of the ninth appeared headed for a split. Darrell Brandon had given up just two hits through eight innings; but in the ninth, he folded faster than Myron Floren's accordian. Ed Stroud (remember him?) opened with a double. Singles by Fred Valentine and Frank Howard produced a run and chased Brandon. Dick Williams brought in Dennis Bennett, who got Mike Epstein to pop up. John Wyatt replaced Bennett to face McMullen, who singled to score Valentine. Dick Nen then drew a walk to load the bases. Wyatt got Ed Brinkman to bounce to Foy. Foy looked home, but had no play there. He then rushed a throw to first. The throw was low and to the home plate side of the bag and drew Scott off the base and allowed Hank Allen (running for Howard) to score the tying run. Paul Casanova then hit a high bouncer to Scott at first. George threw home, but was too late to get McMullen, who slid across with the winning run.

The Sox walked off the field dejected, dressed in silence, and didn't blink an eye to see Rod Serling behind the wheel of the bus ready to take them back to the hotel.

Well, not really . . . but almost.

SATURDAY, JUNE 17

The Lonborg Express rolled through Washington today letting no one off (no scramblers, no gamblers, no midnight ramblers) in a nine-inning, five-hit, 5–1 win over the Senators. Lonborg, now 8–2, walked two and struck out six. Jim's performance was the perfect antidote to the double dose of poison swallowed by the team last night in the nightmare losses.

Yaz and Tony C. gave Gentleman Jim all the help he needed. Tony led off the second inning with his sixth home run, this off Barry Moore. In the third, Reggie Smith and Mike Andrews singled with two outs. Yaz drove both home with a double.

For good measure Lonborg established control of the plate with chin music served up to several Washington batters. There was one hit batsman — Eddie Brinkman. Lonnie hit him in the helmet, which cracked open. Only 3,944 turned out for the game, but one of them was Supreme Court Justice Earl Warren.

SUNDAY, JUNE 18

The Red Sox slithered out of D.C. today smarting from their third loss in four games to the lowly Senators. The Sox dropped a ten-inning, 3 – 2 grinder.

Hank Allen, batting for the much ballyhooed rookie Mike Epstein, singled home Bob Saverine with two out in the tenth to pin the loss on Jose Santiago, who's now 4 – 3. The loss dropped Boston back to .500 again, 31 – 31 and 6 1/2 behind the White Sox.

The flight out of Washington to New York was a rough one. At one point the plane dropped fifteen hundred feet in an air pocket. Gary Bell eased the tension by saying: "I don't care if this thing goes down. I'm only three and six."

But for one member of the Red Sox, the trouble was just beginning when the team arrived in New York. Joe Foy got into town just in time to lead his parents from their burning house in the Bronx, just thirteen blocks from the House That Ruth Built. Foy stays with his parents when the team is in New York. He said he found the house on fire and his parents inside, confused by smoke. He rushed in, helped his folks to safety, and could only watch as the blaze leveled the three-story house. Joe lost all his clothes, trophies, and scrapbooks.

MONDAY, JUNE 19

Bill Landis was rained out of his first start of the year tonight in New York. The game has been rescheduled for Thursday. Dick Williams took the time off to juggle the lineup again and is hoping to find some combination that will score more runs.

Fear of Flying

The flight from Washington into New York on June 18 was as turbulent a flight as I've ever been on. The only other time I've been on a plane where it was even close to being as rough as this one was when I was with Cleveland and we got into some nasty weather. Bob Feller, who is a pilot, was on that plane with me. When I saw beads of sweat on *his* face, I thought, oh, God, if he's scared, I'm scared, because he knows what we're into.

As with any group of people, we had a few players who had a fear of flying. Yaz was one of those players who was bothered by planes. He'd get on board and immediately get into a card game or something else to get his mind off the flight. If we hit a little turbulence, his face would turn white. He had real difficulties with it; it took Yaz a couple of days to get over this flight.

As the plane bobbed up and down, we were all scared. Some of the players actually got sick. It was an extremely rough flight that we later learned was close to being in some real danger.

Bob Tillman, who hasn't started since hitting Wyatt in the head over a month ago, will catch and bat seventh. Reggie Smith, hitting just .187, will drop from leadoff to the number eight position. Mike Andrews, at .268, will go to the leadoff spot, with Joe Foy taking over the second slot.

TUESDAY, JUNE 20

Joe Foy, heroically blocking out the pain of the fire that destroyed his family's home, belted a grand slam home run to lead the Red Sox to an easy 7–1 victory over the helpless Yankees. Foy, who went into the game hitting just .240, cleared the bases after Mel Stottlemyre loaded them up on two walks and a hit. It was Foy's second major league grand slam. Since his earlier benching, he has raised his average from .192 and has hit five home runs with sixteen driven in.

Carl Yastrzemski followed Foy with a home run of his own (Carl's seventeenth), an upper deck job to right. Gary Bell won for the third time in four tries with the Red Sox. Bob Tillman celebrated his return from Siberian exile by going 2 for 4. After the game Dick Williams went to Tillman in the locker room and shook the catcher's hand. You don't think Tillman was out a long time? Before the game, when Williams taped the lineup card to the dugout wall, he had spelled Tillman's name with one "l."

"A Night at the Fights" Wednesday, June 21, 1967

It's a marvelous thing to see an identity form. It is at the same time miraculous *and* commonplace — miraculous because it testifies to the presence of impulses that are, strictly speaking, otherwise unknowable, that is, the creative forces that work each moment of each day throughout our lives. It's commonplace because the experience of identity is truly universal: if you survive childhood, you have first-hand knowledge.

As character takes shape, one has a wondrous sense that because growth is taking place, almost anything can result. The very nature of change precludes you from knowing for sure what the outcome will be. Now, you ask, what does all this have to do with the '67 Red Sox? Simply this: ball clubs also strive toward and achieve identities. Teams go through the same cycles of change as people do: they are born, they mature, they even die. To some extent it's the struggle that every club faces each year and that commences in spring training: what will it become? It was a question that loomed large for the '67 Red Sox, especially given their new manager with such a different approach from Red Sox bosses of the past.

We have already seen the pattern of the club emerging: its ability to come back from adversity, its tendency never to give up on itself, a dictate that Tony Conigliaro's eleventh-inning home run the other night at Fenway cast permanently in stone. It was not surprising, then, that just six days later Boston played another game that solidified even further its growing sense of self. This was tonight's game against the Yankees in New York, a game in which the Red Sox served notice on the rest of the American League that they would not be intimidated, would not back down from a fight, and would not be messed with, period. This was the game that proved it: the Sox had truly embraced their manager's philosophy.

The final score, Boston 8, New York 1, seemed to indicate little more than a one-sided, probably boring game. But the story of this game was not the game, really, but the wild brawl that developed, one the Red Sox walked away from with fists and heads held high. The fight unified this team and cloaked twenty-five separate individuals with one seamless fabric.

It all began in the second inning. Yankee pitcher Thad Tillotson was working against Joe Foy. Because of Foy's grand slam last night, Tillotson worked Foy extra tight. Finally he plucked Foy with a fast ball right on top of the batting helmet. Foy fired an icy stare at Tillotson on the mound, then trotted down to first. Nothing more happened except that the Sox scored a run to boost their lead to 5 − 0.

There was grumbling in the Red Sox dugout after Foy was hit; and in the bottom of the second, Jim Lonborg delivered Boston's response. But before we look at that, remember that throughout the early season, Jim shed his image as a nice guy on the mound, much to Dick Williams's delight. The once-gentle giant developed a blazing fast ball that—when it had to—could rise high and tight and force the hitter to eat dirt pudding. Chin music . . .

RED SOX					YANKEES				
Name	ab	r	h	rbi		ab	r	h	rbi
Andrews, 2b. .	3	3	1		Clarke, 2b. . .	3		1	
Foy, 3b.	2	2	1		Amaro, ss. . . .	5		1	
Jones, 3b. . . .	1				Mantle, 1b. . .	3		2	
Yastrzemski, lf	4	1	3	3	Hegan, 1b. . .	1			
Thomas, lf. . .	1		1		Pepitone, cf. .	1			
Conigliaro, rf.	4	1	3	4	Robinson, cf. .	4		1	
Tartabull, rf. . .	1				Whitaker, rf. . .	5			
Petrocelli, ss.	4				Tresh, lf.	5		1	
Adair, ss.	1				Gibbs, c.	2		1	
Scott, 1b. . . .	4	1	1	1	C. Smith, 3b. .	4			
Tillman, c. . . .	4				Tillotson, p. . .				
R. Smith, cf. .	4		2		Monbouquette, p				
Lonborg, p. . .	4		1		Howser, ph. . .				
					Kennedy, pr. . .			1	
					Reniff, p.				
					Tepedino, ph. .				
					Peterson, ph. .				
					Sands, ph. . . .			1	
					Womack, p				
TOTALS	37	8	13	8	TOTALS	34	1	7	−

Team	1	2	3	4	5	6	7	8	9	
Boston	4	1	1	2	0	0	0	0	0	8
NY	0	0	0	0	1	0	0	0	0	1

Name	IP	H	R	ER	BB	SO
Boston						
Lonborg (w).	9	7	1		6	7
NY						
Tillotson (l).	3⅓	7	8	8	3	3
Monbouquette.	1⅔	2				1
Reniff.	1					1
Peterson.	2	3				3
Womack.	1	1				

shave ball. . . . how are you fixed for blades? This was the Lonborg that Tillotson found himself up against in the bottom of the second.

Lonborg nailed the Yankee pitcher in the shoulder. The two pitchers exchanged words; then Foy, shouting at Tillotson, walked in toward the plate. Both benches emptied, and a wild melee ensued. It took twelve special policemen (including Rico Petrocelli's brother) to break it up. Before it was over, Petrocelli and Joe Pepitone were going at it like Martin and Lewis, and Reggie Smith had body-slammed Tillotson in the dirt between first and second. Amazingly no one was ejected. Pepitone, flattened by a punch, could not continue and left the game.

In the third, it happened all over again. Tillotson hit Lonborg with a pitch, and once more the benches emptied. But probably because everyone was all punched out, there were no punches, just some heated words and shoving. In the bottom of the inning, Lonborg went to work again, brushing back Charley Smith and beaning Dick Howser. At this point the umpires stopped the game and summoned both managers to the bench. They made it clear that the head hunting had to stop. After a long discussion in which Williams and Ralph Houk pleaded their cases, play resumed. Howser and Lonborg agreed that the pitch that hit the Yankee infielder was an accident. Maybe. But it did run Lonborg's hit batsmen total to ten on the year, tops in baseball.

The message had been served.

The game was lost to the extracurricular activity: the catcalls, beanballs, and fists were the main attraction, though the brawl itself was a draw. After five minutes of rolling, shoving, glaring, cursing, and punching, the teams went back to their dugouts with escorts from the umpires and the Yankee Stadium police. The leading individual contestants were Petrocelli and Pepitone.

Petrocelli and Pepitone — both born in Brooklyn — needled each other all the time. Each said they weren't fighting, just

Joe Foy won a game on June 20 against the Yankees with a grand slam. The next night he was skulled by a Thad Tillotson pitch, starting a Night at the Fights. (Photo courtesy Boston Red Sox)

kidding. "That's right," Rico said. "We were just kidding, and the next thing I know, everybody was fighting. The reason why I came over toward first was I thought a couple of guys were coming out of the Yankee dugout after Lonborg."

And Pepitone's version? "I was having this session with Rico. We were kidding. All of a sudden, somebody said something I didn't like. Maybe it was Rico. Pretty soon I was on the ground. I don't know who got me, but he was mussing up my hair, and I don't like that. All I know is I grabbed some dirt and half tossed it at Rico to joke, and the whole place was in a jam."

Reggie Smith's body slam on Tillotson also was a focal point: Reggie gave it the full Killer Kowalski treatment by picking Tillotson up, spinning him around, and throwing him to the ground. This brought the entire Yankee bullpen onto Smith. "[Elston] Howard grabbed my leg, and [Dooley] Womack my neck, and [Hal] Reniff was on my back," Smith said.

It was also about that time that Charlie Sands tackled Tony Conigliaro from behind. "It was definitely an illegal block and a fifteen-yard penalty," Tony quipped.

The only one who didn't get into the fight was Gary Waslewski, who was in the whirlpool bath and listening on radio. Someone remarked later to Gary that he could have stopped everything simply by getting out of the bath and walking out on the field.

Someone else asked Lonborg if he threw at Tillotson. Jim answered: "What do you think? I have to protect my players."

Then they asked him about the number of hit batsmen this season: "I want to be the best in my business," Lonborg answered. "I'm not going to let anything interfere. The batters took too many liberties with me my first two years. I didn't throw at anybody. But I can't let them dig in on me anymore."

The victory left Jim at 9 – 2, with a 3.03 ERA and a league-leading 105 strikeouts.

The game? Oh yeah, the game. The Sox got all they needed on Tony Conigliaro's three-run blast, George Scott's solo shot, and Carl Yastrzemski's three hits and three RBIs.

THURSDAY, JUNE 22

Bill "Raindance" Landis lost out to Mother Nature again as showers prevented his first major league start for the second

*Jim Lonborg, 1986.
(Photo courtesy
Dan Valenti)*

time in a row. People are starting to call Landis the "human rain delay."

"Oh well, I guess I should apply to some team in the desert for a job," Landis said.

FRIDAY, JUNE 23

Joe Foy's two-run triple and two-run single led a thirteen-hit Boston attack in an 8–4 win over the Indians at Fenway. Foy had four hits, which boosted him to .244, fifty points from where he was just two weeks ago. Chipping in were Tony Conigliaro, who drove in two with a single and a home run, and Carl Yastrzemski with a single and run-scoring double. Reggie Smith also had two hits. The crowd, eager to welcome the club home, was in the game all the way, all 30,223 of them. Lee Stange pitched a complete game to raise his record to 2–4.

The one sour note came in the seventh inning, when Rico Petrocelli was hit on the left wrist by George Culver. He crum-

Retrospective: Jim Lonborg Looks Back

On the volleyball games in spring training:

"They were great! They were held down in the left field corner at Chain o' Lakes Park in Winter Haven. The games made the camp light. Pitchers were always kind of bored, anyways, because if they weren't pitching, they had to shag in the outfield. You can shag only so much before you get tired of it. I think Dick [Williams] wanted to have the pitchers do something fun that would not only take away from the boredom, but would improve their other skills and their conditioning. Volleyball's a strenuous game."

The brawl at Yankee Stadium on June 21:

"Joe Foy had hit a grand slam the night before and had another home run his first time up the next night. So when he came up again, bingo, [Yankee pitcher Thad] Tillotson went after Joe and got him in the head. There was no doubt in my mind that I would be going after Tillotson. The thing that was so surprising to me was the fact that Tillotson even came to the plate later in the fourth or fifth inning,

or whenever it was. We were way ahead by then, so it was surprising that Ralph Houk would even let him bat. Tillotson knew he was going down. It was probably the only time in my career that I ever intentionally threw at anyone."

On his habit of going to the movies on game day:

"Going to afternoon movies became part of the routine for my game in general for night games in 1967. It was a relaxing way for me to spend the day. I'd have a pregame meal, go to the show, then just sit back, watch the movie, and completely relax. It was better than sitting in your room and watching TV or going to the park early and just hanging around. In the movies it was easy for me to sit down and let someone else entertain me."

On serving in the reserves:

"It didn't bother me to fly back from Atlanta for games. When you're that young, and you have so

bled to the ground in pain, and it seemed certain he had broken the wrist; but it turned out to be a severe bruise, bad enough to keep him out of the lineup for at least a week.

SATURDAY, JUNE 24

Leon "Daddy Wags" Wagner spoiled Family Day for 30,027 at Fenway this afternoon with a home run, and Indians' starter Steve Hargan made it stand in Cleveland's 3 – 2 win over the Red Sox.

SUNDAY, JUNE 25

A two-run homer by Carl Yastrzemski (his eighteenth) and solo shots by Bob Tillman (first) and Joe Foy (tenth) led the Red Sox to an 8 – 3 win over the Indians at an ovenlike Fenway Park. Gary Bell, with the help of Jose Santiago, picked up the victory

much energy, and you have that much confidence because of the way the season was going, it never really dawns on you that commuting by plane is a problem. In Atlanta, where I was stationed, I was able to work out with the Braves; and that was helpful."

On the season's final game — Sleeping Saturday night at Ken Harrelson's room at the Boston Sheraton:

"Being single in Boston is a wonderful thing. It really is a great town to be single in. There really is an awful lot of . . . you might say . . . action in town [laughs]. There was a lot going on at the apartment where I stayed, and I didn't think there would be much of a chance to get a good night's sleep. Plus, another superstition of mine was that I always felt comfortable pitching on the road, so I kind of pretended that I was just in another hotel room and that this was a road game. So I got the privacy and quiet that's necessary before a big game like that."

On why he chose reading The Fall of Japan *that night:*

"The guy who wrote it, Bill Craig, had written an article on me that summer for *The Saturday Evening Post*. Bill was a would-be pitcher from Medford. We hit it off really well, and we are still very close friends to this day. *The Fall of Japan* just happened to be his latest book. But I remember saying that I was reading *The Fall of Japan* and quickly fell asleep. Bill's editor later wrote him a note that said: "This doesn't look good!"

On the bunt:

"I had bunted successfully before during the season. It was one of those things Bobby Doerr used to talk about all the time, and he helped me work on my bunting. I saw Cesar Tovar back, and I was able to hide the bunt well. I didn't make an initial movement to show the bunt. I caught them off guard. When I stood on first, I remember thinking how much it might upset [Minnesota pitcher Dean] Chance that I had reached. I was the leadoff guy, and I know how much of a hole you're in as a pitcher when the leadoff man gets on. It had to be tough on him; he was trying to protect a 2 – 0 lead in the sixth in Fenway Park."

against his ex-mates. It was Bell's one-hundredth career win. Luis Tiant took the loss.

Tillman, benched for thirty-eight games earlier in the season for beaning Johnny Wyatt, played a big part in today's win. Besides the home run, the strapping catcher from Tennessee had two singles and a walk before giving way to pinch runner Jose Tartabull in the eighth. Tillman's offensive outburst raised his average fifty-four points to .244.

The three Cleveland games drew 83,779 and raised the season's total to 495,790 in twenty-nine home dates. With forty-seven home games remaining, the Sox should go over the one million mark, something they haven't done since Ted Williams retired in 1960.

Most of the talk off the field came regarding two roster moves the Red Sox made last night. They traded Dennis Bennett and sent Billy Rohr to Toronto. Bennett, who's had run-ins all season long with Dick Williams, was sent to the New York Mets for

On the final out:

"I think Scotty was the first guy I saw. We were jumping around like kids, hugging each other. As the moments unraveled, the fans were on the field. I can remember players just running by me. They were going straight to the dugout. And I was surrounded by a sea of people. Pretty soon the sea was moving. I looked around, and I didn't see anyone I recognized. They were all strangers. And I was going in the wrong direction! I wanted to be going toward the dugout, but we were moving towards right field, where Al Forrester used to bring the bullpen carts out. We weren't going where I wanted to go at all. It was scary. Some security guys finally got through and escorted me to the dugout.

"You can see the madness of the moment in some of the photos taken. Somebody from *Sports Illustrated* really captured a hell of a picture . . . there are two Boston policemen, and they've got me by the arms, and they're escorting me. My shirt is all ripped up, and my eyes have that urgent look as if pleading 'God! Get me back to the dugout!'

"One of the pictures taken that moment was of me in the middle of the crowd. I was examining the picture one evening during the winter of '67 with some friends. And then I noticed something. About eight or nine rows back, I see a familiar face. I said, 'That couldn't be.' But sure enough it turned out to be a guy named Jerry Torrance. He was a fraternity brother of mine from Stanford. He happened to be living in Cambridge at the time and was out at the ball park that day. He went on the field later. The photo shows me standing in the middle, and you can see Jerry some eight rows back trying to reach up to say 'Hi.' "

---

outfielder Al Yates. The Sox assigned Yates to Toronto. Bennett left with a record of 4–3 and a 3.91 ERA. He started just four games of the thirteen he's been in and pitched well on occasion; but he's been complaining openly about not being used exclusively in the rotation, and that hasn't set well with Williams.

Bennett was a flaky, fun-loving type, a man dubbed "Boston's last link with Dick Stuart." (The two were traded for each other following the 1964 season.) One night in spring 1965, when the Sox still trained in Scottsdale, Arizona, Bennett fired off what he called "a half a dozen rounds" from two pistols at the door of the team's motel. When asked why he did it, he replied: "I had these two pistols and it was Arizona, so why not?"

When he pitched his first complete game for Boston later that year, he threw a champagne party for the writers. This year the writers reciprocated when he pitched his first shutout in the American League in Anaheim against the Angels. The party was held at the Playboy Club.

"Number 23 [Dick Williams] wasn't too happy about the party," Bennett said. "He told the rest of the team not to come, but some of them did anyway."

Rohr departed quietly. After his two early complete-game wins over New York, he was completely ineffective, so his demotion comes as no surprise. He was 2 – 3 in nine games.

MONDAY, JUNE 26

Unfortunately for the Red Sox, there is no cure for the common cold. Tonight that may have cost them a ball game. With Carl Yastrzemski staying back in his hotel to nurse a heavy cold, the team dropped a 2 – 1 decision to the Minnesota Twins in Minnesota. They could have used Yaz's bat.

The lack of offense wasted a shining effort by Jim Lonborg, who pitched a complete game, gave up just six hits, and struck out ten, which, incidentally, increased his league-leading total to 115.

Tonight's loss dropped the Red Sox into a third-place tie with the Twins, six games out.

Yaz took his illness in stride: "I guess Lou Gehrig's record is going to be safe after all," he joked.

TUESDAY, JUNE 27

Dick Williams keeps rolling the dice and coming up with sevens. He puts the loaded gun to his head and hits the empty chamber. He turns his cards over and finds he has black jack.

He did it again tonight by starting rookie Gary Waslewski — who came in with no record in just twelve innings — against the league's top winner, Dean Chance, who was after his eleventh triumph. The two hooked up, with Waslewski the unlikely winner of the 3 – 2 game. More important, the victory gives the Red Sox sole possession of third place, a game up on the Twins and just one-half game behind second-place Detroit.

Waslewski went six innings and gave up just three hits. He struck out four before being lifted for a pinch hitter in the seventh. John Wyatt came on to preserve the win.

Like yesterday the Red Sox got the quick lead as Tony Conigliaro followed Joe Foy's first-inning single with a 381-foot home run into the Twins' bullpen in right center. It stayed 2 – 0

The Grind

Part of the hidden game of baseball for those who make their living off of it is what I call "the grind." The grind is a day game following a twi-night doubleheader. The grind is getaway day to embark on a two-week road trip. It's the road itself, a circuit of cities, airports, and hotels that are the counterfeit of home. The grind is bus rides in city traffic. It's packing and repacking your suitcase. It is the 162-game schedule following six weeks of spring training. For a broadcaster it's calling a 12 – 3 game with the home team losing.

until the Twins' second, when Tony Oliva launched a solo home run almost to the same spot as Conigliaro's.

Boston pushed across the game winner in the seventh. Jerry Adair singled. He moved up on Bob Tillman's single and scored on Reggie Smith's hit, the third straight two-out base hit. The Twins got their final run in the ninth as Wyatt gave up three hits, but he had enough working on his fast ball to strike out the side and hold onto the game.

Yaz, still groggy from his cold and flu, returned to action tonight.

WEDNESDAY, JUNE 28

Dave Boswell struck out twelve batters in the first five innings for the Twins, who beat the Red Sox 3 – 2. The win once again put Minnesota in a third-place tie with Boston.

Most of the lineup looked pathetic tonight, with Boston's first five men in the order going a combined 1 for 19. George Scott threw in two errors in the field.

Only Jerry Adair did well. Jerry, filling in for the injured Rico Petrocelli, had a single and a home run. He's been great in the clutch and solid in the field.

THURSDAY, JUNE 29

The Sox had the day off today and traveled to Kansas City. Gary Bell (4 – 1 with the Red Sox) is scheduled to open the three-game series tomorrow night.

Over the past two weeks, the Red Sox outslugged their opponents 64 – 38, yet their record in that time is only 8 – 7. The results show why: many of the wins have been lopsided, with all seven of the losses by one run. The team is 14 – 16 in the all-important one-run-game category.

Jerry Adair has done well filling in for Rico at short; but because he's starting, the bench is weakened. With Dalton Jones gone for two weeks of army training, the Red Sox have called up nineteen-year-old rookie Ken Poulsen from Winston-Salem, North Carolina, the club's A farm team. Poulsen's surprise promotion to the major leagues put a sudden halt to his wedding to Vicki Swaton of Winston-Salem. The couple was expected to say "I do" tomorrow, but with his joining the Red Sox, Poulsen temporarily has to say "I can't."

Jerry Adair came over from the White Sox on June 3, when the Red Sox were 22–21. With Jerry the team went 70–49. He hit .291, and it seemed every hit was a clutch one. (Photo courtesy Boston Red Sox)

Some twenty-five guests had been invited, the pastor engaged, and both sets of parents were ready to fly to Winston-Salem from California. Then Boston called.

"She was stunned," Poulsen said of his bride-to-be. "But she was happy I got the chance to be with the Red Sox." Miss Swaton looked at it philosophically: "We can always get married, but how often does a guy get sent up to the big leagues?"

Poulsen doesn't figure to be with the Red Sox long. The Sox told him he would be back at Winston-Salem when Jones rejoins the club.

The Tenth Player

Carl Yastrzemski and Jim Lonborg rightfully got the crush of headlines, attention, recognition, and awards. But if there had been a "Tenth Player Award" for the '67 Red Sox — one given for the most unexpectedly vital contribution — it would have to go to Jerry Adair. On a team that became known for its clutch performances, he was Mister Clutch, not in the overtly dramatic way of Yaz, but maybe with a quieter regularity.

The Red Sox picked him up on June 3 for pitchers Don McMahon and Rob Snow. On that day they were 22 – 21. They were 70 – 49 after that. In his eighty-nine games with Boston, Adair hit .291 and played all three infield positions. He's most remembered for his eighth-inning home run to beat the Angels 9 – 8 on August 20. The hit capped a comeback from an 8 – 0 deficit. But his contribution was just as large when he filled in at short from June 24 to July 25 after Rico Petrocelli got hurt. In that month Jerry didn't make an error, and the club went 19 – 9. He also exerted a steadying influence on the young infield of Andrews, Foy, and Scott.

Off the field he was a quiet guy and didn't have a lot to say to a lot of people. His personality seemed gruff at times. As a result he was tough to go on the air with for an interview. He liked to drink beer, one of his favorite spots being the Charles Cafe across from the Biltmore Hotel in New York. Usually he'd drink alone. If you went over to talk to him, he'd be pleasant enough, but never gregarious.

He did have some personal problems — including a very sick child who later died of cancer — and they certainly must have contributed to his quietness and reserve. A story comes to mind that seems to typify Adair. During the team's raucous pennant celebration in the Fenway clubhouse, everyone got involved with pouring and spraying champagne . . . everyone except Jerry, who sat on the trainer's table and quietly sipped his from a cup.

FRIDAY, JUNE 30

The Red Sox rode a three-run, tape-measure clout by Tony Conigliaro to a 5 – 3 win over the A's tonight in Kansas City. Tony's mammoth clout — measured at over 450 feet — made a winner of Gary Bell, who's now 5 – 1 since the Sox picked him up (or is "rescued" the word?) from Cleveland. Bell had help from John Wyatt, who snuffed a K.C. rally in the eighth, then pitched a scoreless ninth. George Scott also homered for Boston, who beat Jim Nash for the first time ever. Scott's home run, his tenth, tied the game at 1 – 1 in the fifth and set the stage for Tony's blast.

In the sixth, Joe Foy doubled and Carl Yastrzemski walked with two out. Tony then rocketed a ball over everything — over the 370-foot marker in left, over the 20-foot fence, and over the street behind the ball park. The ball came to rest 30 feet into a parking lot. The home run brought gasps from the crowd. It was Tony's tenth of the year and eighth in his last nineteen games.

Conigliaro's monster smash may well have been in celebration because earlier in the day Oriole manager Hank Bauer named him to the American League All-Star team in right. He joins Carl Yastrzemski and Rico Petrocelli on the All-Star roster.

American League Standings
June 30, 1967

Team	W–L	PCT.	GB
Chicago	42–28	.600	–
Detroit	38–33	.535	4½
BOSTON	37–34	.521	5½
Minnesota	36–34	.514	6
Cleveland	37–35	.514	6
California	38–38	.500	7
New York	33–38	.465	9½
Baltimore	33–38	.465	9½
Kansas City	34–41	.453	10½
Washington	32–41	.438	11½

End-of-the-month Stats: 6/30/67

Leaders

Batting
(minimum of 100 at-bats)

Name and Team	At-Bats Avg.
F. Robinson, Balt.	.337
Yastrzemski, Bos.	.331
Kaline, Det.	.328
Carew, Minn.	.315
Conigliaro, Bos.	.308
Blair, Balt.	.301
Mincher, Cal.	.298
Petrocelli, Bos.	.296
Hershberger, K.C.	.290
Northrup, Det.	.288

Home Runs

Name and Team	#
Killebrew, Minn	22
F. Robinson, Balt.	21
Yastrzemski, Bos.	18
Howard, Wash.	18
Kaline, Det.	15

Runs Batted In

Name and Team	#
F. Robinson, Balt.	59
Killebrew, Minn.	59
Yastrzemski, Bos.	53
Kaline, Det.	53
Blefary, Balt.	46

Pitching
(minimum of 9 decisions)

Player and Team	Record	Pct.
Horlen, Chi.	9-1	.900
Sparma, Det.	8-1	.873
Tiant, Cleve.	7-2	.777
McGlothlin, Cal.	7-2	.777
Lonborg, Bos	10-3	.754

Team Batting

Name	AB	R	H	HR	RBI	AVG.
Santiago	12	2	4	1	3	.333
Yastrzemski	253	47	84	18	53	.331
Conigliaro	195	32	60	11	43	.308
Petrocelli	223	29	66	8	32	.296
Scott	256	31	74	10	37	.289
Andrews	224	33	58	2	14	.259
Foy	230	41	57	10	24	.248
Tartabull	142	15	35		5	.246
Ryan	101	9	24	1	12	.238
Gibson	95	6	22	1	10	.232
Jones	78	10	18	2	7	.231
Tillman	54	4	12	1	4	.222
Adair	153	13	35	1	14	.229
Smith	235	29	48	4	22	.204
Thomas	32	6	6		3	.188
Osinski	6		1			.167
Waslewski	6		1			.167
Brandon	26		4			.154
Fischer	7		1		1	.143
Stange	15	2	2			.134
Bell	34	3	4		1	.118
Lonborg	45	1	5		3	.111
Wyatt	7					.000
Cisco	2					.000

Team Pitching

Name	IP	H	BB	SO	W	L	ERA
Waslewski	18	13	9	9	1	0	1.00
Osinski	31⅓	26	17	20	2	1	1.72
Cisco	19⅔	16	6	8	0	1	2.84
Lonborg	124	102	41	120	10	3	2.96
Wyatt	41⅔	27	18	34	4	3	3.06
Bell	107⅔	88	34	67	6	6	3.09
Stange	59⅔	62	12	41	2	5	3.77
Santiago	56⅓	54	18	46	4	3	4.18
Brandon	91⅓	79	36	59	2	7	4.24
Landis	7	7	6	8	0	0	9.00

July

With the team's identity in place and first place within sight, the Red Sox were ready to assert themselves as July rolled in. At first it didn't look like that would happen. A string of agonizing, one-run losses snake-bit the team. None was tougher to take than the July 5 game in Anaheim, when George Thomas's two-out, two-run home run gave them the lead in the top of the ninth only to have Don Mincher win it for the Angels with a home run of his own in the bottom of the inning. The Sox ended that road trip by losing their last five, but they wouldn't give up on themselves.

When the All-Star Game rolled around on July 11, Boston was 41–39, in fifth place, six games out. They placed four on the All-Star roster: Carl Yastrzemski, Jim Lonborg, Rico Petrocelli, and Tony Conigliaro.

After the midsummer classic in Anaheim, the Red Sox put it in high gear. Beginning on July 14, they went on to win ten in a row, capped by a doubleheader sweep of the Indians in Cleveland on the twenty-third. The town went wild, and some 15,000 fans were on hand to welcome the Red Sox at Logan International Airport on the evening of the twenty-third. It was a mob scene, bigger even than the crowd the Beatles drew at Logan the year before.

Williams didn't let up; for example, he pulled George Scott out of the lineup in one game for not hustling and called Darrell Brandon's pitching style "pussyfooting." Lee Stange got hot and threw several fine games, and Yaz continued his heavy hitting. They brought up Dave Morehead from Toronto and started him the next day. When the dust had settled on July 31, they were in second place, two games behind the White Sox.

No one could deny it now — the team had a pennant race on its hands.

SATURDAY, JULY 1

Oriole manager Hank Bauer named Jim Lonborg to the American League All-Star team, and Jim celebrated by winning his tenth of the year, 10 – 2, on a muggy night at Municipal Stadium in Kansas City. Lonborg got great support from fellow All-Star Tony Conigliaro, who hammered three hits, including his eleventh home run (and ninth in his last seventy-two at bats).

Tony, Mike Ryan, and George Scott each drove in a pair for the Red Sox, who — by virtue of their win and Detroit's 6 – 5 loss to Chicago — moved into a second place tie with the Tigers. The win upped their mark on the current road trip to 3 – 2.

Boston got all they would need early, with two in the second and one in the third. The third was a strange inning: the Red Sox got four straight hits, but only one run, thanks to some adventuresome base running. With one out, Carl Yastrzemski singled and went all the way to third on a wild pitch. Conigliaro singled him home. Tony then stole second and, running through Dick Williams's stop sign (Williams was coaching third in place of Eddie Popowski, who was attending his daughter's wedding in New Jersey), tried to score on Scott's single to center. Conigliaro was an easy out at the plate on Rick Monday's strong throw. Scott took second on the throw home. Jerry Adair followed with a single up the middle. Second baseman John Donaldson made a fine play by cutting the ball off before it made the outfield. When he realized he had no play at first, Donaldson alertly threw to third and picked off Scott, who had rounded the base too far. So Conigliaro and Scott had become galloping ghosts, and the Sox had just one run in the frame.

But it was enough for Lonborg, who went seven innings, gave up five hits, and struck out five. Jose Santiago pitched the last two innings. Lonborg now leads the American League not only in wins, but in strikeouts — 120 in 125 innings.

Tell Me No Stories

I'd like to talk a little about my counterparts in the media: the baseball writers. The job of writer and the job of broadcaster share their main purpose, which is to inform. They both seek to provide information, but along with that to inform with a style. In baseball writing, style is to use words to inform and — in a sense — entertain. Writers such as Ray Fitzgerald and Larry Claflin, who were such a part of 1967, come to mind.

Of current baseball writers, one of my favorites is Joe Falls, who writes for *The Detroit News* and is best known to baseball fans around the country through his columns in the *Sporting News*. Joe is a nostalgia buff and often writes about the past. I

After saving a game against his old mates, the A's, John Wyatt skipped off the mound like a kid. Wyatt was the stopper in '67, with ten wins and sixteen saves. (Photo courtesy Boston Red Sox)

once told him that one of the reasons I enjoyed his writing, his style, was because when I read his column, I get the feeling he's talking to me. He replied, "Ken, that's because my style is no style at all. I love to write, but I'm not what I'd consider a good writer, at least in a technical sense. I write best when it's like a personal letter."

Joe also made an interesting comment regarding the comparison between players today and players of the past, such as 1967. "Players today don't have any stories to tell, any baseball stories, for example, recalling a game played several years ago when the score was 2–2 in the ninth and a pitcher got a slider up for a home run."

Joe says that to get his stories today, he goes to the managers and coaches. The players simply don't have stories to tell. The game is a business first, and the ball park is a player's office. Joe points out that when the game is over, today's players go on to other matters. In the past, players used to hang around the park to talk baseball.

I think Joe is right. Yet maybe the stories are sometimes still there, but players don't share them with the media. And when they do, they wait until they themselves become coaches and managers. Maybe then they feel safer talking with the press or understand the new importance that the press assumes as these ex-players become management.

Williams blamed himself for his team's poor base running: "I messed it up. I stand farther down the line [nearer to the plate] than Pop. That's the way I operated at Toronto. Scott and Conigliaro hadn't played for me there, and they were confused. It was my fault. I was so far down toward the plate, I guess they were on their way home before they saw me."

Popowski is scheduled to rejoin the club next Friday in Detroit. "But when he hears how I'm coaching, I wouldn't be surprised if he grabbed a plane and flew to rejoin us tomorrow," Williams cracked.

SUNDAY, JULY 2

The Red Sox swept the A's and won today's squeaker 2–1 on Gary Waslewski's three-hit pitching and Joe Foy's timely hitting. Waslewski was brilliant in getting his second major league win against no defeats.

Kansas City opened the scoring in the first on a Rick Monday sacrifice fly; but Waslewski allowed only one hit the rest of the way up to the ninth, when Mike Hershberger led off with a single. Waslewski got an out, and Hershberger took second with the tying run. Dick Williams called on John Wyatt from the bullpen. Wyatt got the two men he faced to save the game. The pitcher, who rarely shows emotion when he pitches, skipped off the mound like a child.

The Sox first run came in the second on Mike Ryan's single. They got the winning run in the eighth when Joe Foy blasted a long home run that hit the scoreboard in center. He became only the sixth player in the history of Memorial Stadium to hit the scoreboard with a batted ball.

By winning, the Red Sox went five games over .500, the first time that happened since June 27, 1963.

Before the game, a telegram from Sayerville, New Jersey, arrived at the park for Dick Williams. It read: "DICK WILLIAMS: NICE GOING. A GOOD LAUGH. STAY WHERE YOU ARE. I WILL STAY IN DUGOUT. POP." Eddie Popowski sent Williams the needle for the manager's calamitous coaching job yesterday.

MONDAY, JULY 3

Lee Stange hadn't beaten the California Angels in more than two years, but that was then . . . this is now. And for now the righty held the Angels to three hits and a run in seven innings, as the Red Sox built up a big lead en route to a 9 – 3 laugher at Anaheim Stadium.

Mike Andrews, Reggie Smith, and Tony Conigliaro supplied the muscle by hitting home runs. Tony's was powered well past the 393-foot sign in center and gave him ten homers in his last twenty-one games, the best streak of his career.

Rookie Sparky Lyle made his big league debut on July 4. He turned in the staff's lowest ERA, 2.30. (Photo courtesy Boston Red Sox)

TUESDAY, JULY 4

There were no fireworks today for the Red Sox as they failed for the third time this year to extend a four-game winning streak. The Angels won 4 – 3.

Gary Bell had nothing; he walked five in 4 1/3 innings (in his first thirty-nine innings with Boston, Bell had walked just ten). Sparky Lyle made his major league debut by mopping up with a scoreless eighth and ninth.

On the health front, Rico Petrocelli is listed as day to day with his sore wrist. George Scott had to leave the game in the seventh inning with back spasms. Handyman George Thomas took over at first.

WEDNESDAY, JULY 5

This one was gut wrenching . . . slow torture . . . agony . . . as a great ninth-inning comeback crash-landed into the twisted wreckage of another heart-breaking one-run loss.

The Red Sox went into the ninth trailing 2 – 1, their only run coming in the fourth on Joe Foy's thirteenth home run. After that hit Angel starter George Brunet gave up only one hit.

It looked hopeless for the Red Sox when the first two men went quietly in the ninth, but Jerry Adair beat out an infield hit. Dick Williams sent in pitcher Bill Landis to run for Adair. This brought up George Thomas, hitting all of .171 . . . to grossly understate, an unlikely candidate for a hero's wreath. Thomas was playing only because regular first baseman George Scott was still out with his bad back.

With the count 1 – 0, Thomas lined his first homer of the year into the left field seats and gave Boston a 3 – 2 lead. But Jose Santiago couldn't hold the lead in the bottom of the ninth. Jim Fregosi opened with a single, and Don Mincher poled a home run over the right field fence for a 4 – 3 Angel win. The normally laid-back California crowd reacted as if their team had won the World Series. As the 16,952 in the stands whooped it up, the Red Sox trudged trancelike into a death-quiet locker room.

The last nine Red Sox losses have been by one run.

THURSDAY, JULY 6

On the day off, the Red Sox flew from the Coast to Detroit, where they will open up a four-game series tomorrow night. Gary Waslewski will pitch against Joe Sparma.

FRIDAY, JULY 7

Dick Williams and team may be looking for a new theme song. Unfortunately it won't be "Happy Days Are Here Again," but more like "They're Coming to Take Me Away."

The normally dignified confines of Tiger Stadium were more like the padded walls of an isolation cell as the Red Sox lost again by one run. Again it was a torturous loss, a loss that left you with dark circles under the eyes and muttering incoherently . . . 5 – 4 Tigers in eleven innings.

As during Wednesday's game in Anaheim, the Red Sox fought back from an apparently hopeless situation. For 8 2/3 innings Joe Sparma blinded them on two hits; but with two outs in the ninth and trailing 4 – 1, the Sox made like Lazarus and came up with three runs to tie.

With two outs Tony Conigliaro hit his thirteenth of the year with no one on, and the score became 4 – 2. George Scott and Rico Petrocelli then singled as Tiger fans got edgy. Tiger manager Mayo Smith pulled Sparma for Mike Marshall, who promptly gave up a run-scoring single to Reggie Smith. Dick Williams sent up Jerry Adair to pinch-hit for Bob Tillman, and Adair pulled a clutch game-tying double out of his hat.

The score stayed deadlocked until the Detroit eleventh. Jim Northrup led off against John Wyatt and beat out an infield hit. He then scored all the way from first on catcher Bill Freehan's double to left field, a double that Yaz just missed.

SATURDAY, JULY 8

Today's loss was different: it was by *two* runs. But it was still good (or bad) for Boston's fourth straight defeat as the team's futility continued in the 2 – 0 loss to Denny McLain. Once more the Red Sox left their bats at the hotel, and the dozing offense squandered fine pitching.

Lee Stange was the no-luck loser, as he gave up just one run in eight innings.

SUNDAY, JULY 9

The Red Sox were horrible in dropping their fifth straight 10 – 4 (longest losing streak of the year) in today's first game. With the Sox reeling going into game two, Jim Lonborg knew there was a lot riding on his broad shoulders. If ever the Red Sox needed a stopper, it was today.

"I felt more pressure before this game than most any other I pitched this year," Lonborg said. He came up with such an effort on a stifling, hot, muggy day that he literally left the mound babbling, completely spent and out of his head. "After we lost the first game, I could sense that the other guys were really counting on me. I'm supposed to be the stopper on the club, so I felt it was up to me to go out and end the losing streak."

And that he did, pitching seven brilliant, gutsy innings to lead the club to a 3 – 0 win over Detroit. Lonborg had to leave after seven because of the heat and humidity. He lost twelve pounds before Dick Williams took him out. "I completely blacked out on the mound in the sixth inning. I tried to bend down and took a deep breath, and the next thing I knew, I blacked out."

Lonborg returned to pitch a 1 – 2 – 3 seventh, but he couldn't remember doing it, that's how disoriented he had become. "I was out of it. It was so hot I couldn't concentrate, and everything was hazy. Actually I was incoherent."

Williams knew it was time to get Lonborg out when the pitcher came into the dugout after pitching the seventh. "He started babbling about some play that took place a few innings before, and I decided he was pitched out," Williams said. He brought in John Wyatt, who preserved the win and the shutout. It was Lonborg's eleventh win. The Sox runs came on Reggie Smith's two-run home run and a solo shot by Carl Yastrzemski. Yaz broke out of a slump by getting five hits in the twin bill.

Today's games were the last before the All-Star Game in Anaheim on Tuesday night. The Red Sox will be represented by Yaz, Lonborg, Rico Petrocelli, and Tony Conigliaro.

It's for You

The team comedian was George Thomas, assisted by Gary Bell and Joe Foy. One of Thomas's favorite gags was to carry a fake telephone hidden under his coat. Sometimes on a team bus he'd hand you the phone and say, "Hey, this is for you. It's Mr. Yawkey." He would even pull his phone gag on street corners with total strangers.

MONDAY, JULY 10

Many of the Red Sox headed to South Yarmouth for the annual clambake there. Jose Tartabull made the biggest error by dropping a lobster. Jose promptly retrieved it, held it high, and signaled a clean catch.

Lonborg, Yaz, Rico, and Tony took a plane for the West Coast. Dick Williams headed west, too, but went only as far as Pittsfield, where he was visiting friends.

The starting lineups for tomorrow night's game show a glittering array of names:

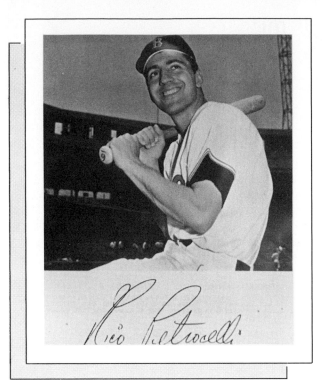

Rico Petrocelli led all American League short-stops in '67 with seventeen homers and sixty-six RBIs. His performance earned him starting honors in the All-Star Game. (Photo courtesy Boston Red Sox)

NATIONAL LEAGUE	AMERICAN LEAGUE
Lou Brock, lf	Brooks Robinson, 3b
Roberto Clemente, rf	Rod Carew, 2b
Hank Aaron, cf	Tony Oliva, cf
Orlando Cepeda, 1b	Harmon Killebrew, 1b
Richie Allen, 3b	Tony Conigliaro, rf
Joe Torre, c	Carl Yastrzemski, lf
Bill Mazeroski, 2b	Bill Freehan, c
Gene Alley, ss	Rico Petrocelli, ss
Juan Marichal, p	Dean Chance, p

TUESDAY, JULY 11

In the longest All-Star Game ever played, the National League prevailed 2–1 in fifteen innings on a home run by Tony Perez off Jim "Catfish" Hunter of the Kansas City A's.

It was a game of home runs, strikeouts, and zeroes. The pitchers on both teams recorded thirty Ks. The other two runs of the game came on solo homers: Richie Allen of the Phillies and Brooks Robinson of the Orioles.

Family Affair

Rico Petrocelli was the American League's starting shortstop in the 1967 All-Star Game. He also went on a few years later to set a league record for home runs by a shortstop. I think Rico was one of the greatest clutch hitters in Red Sox history. All of this was made possible by the very literal support of his family. When his family realized that Rico might have a chance to go somewhere in baseball, his parents and brothers decided that Rico would not have to work a regular job. He was allowed to concentrate on his game, which was quite a sacrifice for the hard-working family. The Petrocellis had the attitude of "let's give the kid a shot and see if he can make it." And he did.

Rico's strong family ties came out in another more specific way on June 21, 1967, when his brother, then working at Yankee Stadium as a policeman, came on the field to protect Rico after the wild brawl that erupted following the Jim Lonborg-Thad Tillotson beanball war.

For the Red Sox, Yaz was on base five times with three hits and two walks. Tony Conigliaro was 0 for 6, but he made the defensive play of the game with a fine running grab off Orlando Cepeda in the top of the tenth. Rico Petrocelli was 0 for 1 before being lifted because of his still-mending wrist. Jim Lonborg didn't play.

WEDNESDAY, JULY 12

The day after the All-Star Game was no day of rest for the Red Sox as Dick Williams called a 10:30 A.M. workout at Fenway. Williams, in a roaming discussion of the pitching staff, said Darrell Brandon's stuff was too good to nibble. He called Brandon's style "pussyfooting."

THURSDAY, JULY 13

In the "businessman's start" (12:55 P.M.), the Red Sox were all business and kicked off the second half with a 4 – 2 triumph over

Baltimore in the first game of the day-night doubleheader. In the nightcap, though, the business went under as the Sox were flailed 10−0. The Red Sox, however, could look at the bright side of this — they scored one earned run in the two games and came out of it with a split.

FRIDAY, JULY 14

You knew it would happen sooner or later, and it did tonight as the bats unlimbered from their long hibernation for an 11−5 pounding of Baltimore before 27,787 at Fenway.

Tony Conigliaro's propensity for mammoth home runs is well known, but tonight in the first inning he outdid himself against nineteen-year-old Oriole starter Mike Adamson. With Mike Andrews aboard, Tony lost a ball over everything in left: over the wall, the screen, Lansdowne Street behind the wall, the Massachusetts Turnpike behind Lansdowne Street. Many observers couldn't recall a ball hit harder or longer at Fenway.

Carl Yastrzemski hit his twentieth home run of the season in the sixth for one of his three hits. Jim Lonborg got the win.

Brooks Robinson made the play of the game on George Thomas with a sensational backhand stab of a ball headed down the line. Always clever with a line, Thomas deadpanned: "The report on Robinson is that he isn't a bad fielder."

SATURDAY, JULY 15

In the top of the first inning, in six seconds time, the Red Sox completely reversed the flow of the game and turned what appeared to be a long afternoon into the momentum that led to sweet victory.

Russ Gibson's alertness — before the game even began — may have been responsible for the win. After catching starter Gary Waslewski in the bullpen before the game, Gibson went to Dick Williams to report: "The guy's got nothing. Better get someone up and ready."

Williams took the advice and started warming Jose Santiago. Sure enough the game began and Waslewski came out throwing grapefruits and walked Luis Aparicio and Russ Snyder to start the game. When Waslewski went to 2 and 1 on Paul Blair, Williams made his move and brought in a ready Santiago. Jose ran the

American League Standings July 15, 1967			
Team	W–L	PCT.	GB
Chicago	49–35	.583	–
Minnesota	46–37	.559	2½
Detroit	45–38	.542	3½
California	46–42	.523	5
BOSTON	43–40	.518	5½
Cleveland	42–44	.488	8
Baltimore	40–45	.471	9½
Washington	39–47	.453	11
New York	38–46	.452	11
Kansas City . . .	36–50	.419	14

count to Blair to 3 and 2. On the payoff pitch, Oriole manager Hank Bauer started the runners; Blair whistled a liner to Joe Foy's left, slightly below the knees. Foy speared the ball with the glove hand, threw to Mike Andrews at second to double up Aparicio, and Mike relayed the ball to George Scott at first to nail Snyder. Triple play. It was like a last-second reprieve from the governor; just like that, the Sox were out of the inning. For the rest of the way, it was Santiago and Gary Bell (used for the first time in relief); and Boston was a 5 – 1 winner.

Russ Gibson's alertness in the bullpen gave Dick Williams a tip to win a game on July 15 against the Orioles. Gibson stuck out ten years of minor league ball before getting his shot in '67. (Photo courtesy Russ Gibson)

SUNDAY, JULY 16

The Red Sox moved into a third-place tie with Detroit by virtue of today's 9 – 5 win over the Tigers at boisterous Fenway. Tony Conigliaro belted his fifteenth home run of the year and Carl Yastrzemski his twenty-first (a career high).

Today started with a game — the annual Father-Son Game — being called because of rain and wet grounds. But the dads got their chance in the real thing. Conigliaro's blast capped a five-run second.

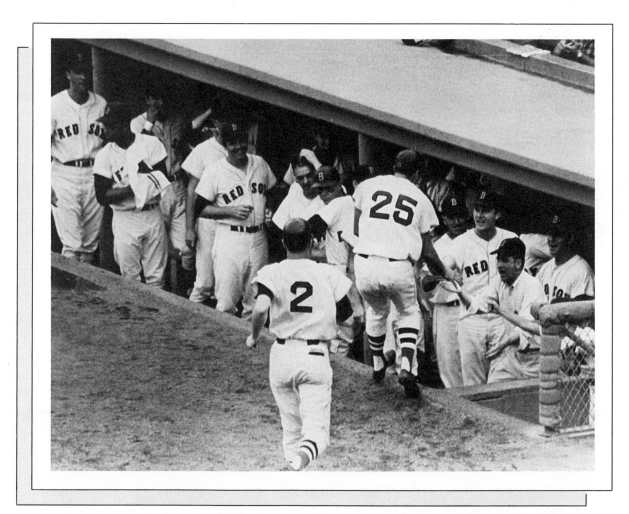

The bench greets Tony Conigliaro following his home run with Mike Andrews (2) aboard. (Photo courtesy Boston Red Sox)

The team made another move to bolster the bench by announcing the pickup of first baseman Norm Siebern from the San Francisco Giants in exchange for infielder George Smith. Smith hasn't played at all this year since tearing up his knee in spring training.

MONDAY, JULY 17

The Tigers and the Red Sox appear, for the moment at least, to be two teams heading in opposite directions: the Tigers south, the Red Sox north. With their 7 – 1 win, Boston took over sole possession of third place and handed Detroit its seventh straight loss.

Lee Stange, who looks better each time out, pitched a complete game and brought his record to 5 – 6. Stinger gave up just seven hits, walked no one, and struck out four. In seven of his nine innings, he threw nine pitches or less . . . that's what kind of control he had today.

The Sox are now making a habit of getting the early lead. Tonight it was three runs in the first; they never trailed after that. Denny McLain was handed his eleventh loss in twenty-one decisions. Yaz, continuing to roll, hit his twenty-second home run and a double and drove in three. Joe Foy, also red hot, had 3 for 4, an RBI, and three runs scored.

Someone asked Foy if he thought the Sox would finish in first division. "First division?" he sneered. "That's fifth place. Forget that. Why not go all the way?"

Just a few weeks ago, Foy's utterance would have drawn snickers and cynicism; but no one's laughing now. All are thinking: Can it be? Can it really be?

TUESDAY, JULY 18

The road made no difference to the revitalized Red Sox, who made it five in a row by thumping Baltimore at Memorial Stadium 6 – 2. Jim Lonborg got his thirteenth win (he leads the major leagues), the team went to seven games above .500, and the world seems, of late, a nicer place. The Sox now trail first-place Chicago by just 2 1/2 games.

Lonborg will leave July 29 to serve two weeks with the army in Atlanta. Jim said he's hoping he'll be able to fly back when it's his turn to pitch.

Talking Heads

The easiest man for me to interview on the '67 club was Rico Petrocelli. Rico was one of those people who would expand intelligently on his answers. One thought would lead to three others. In 1967 my dugout show was fifteen minutes long; that meant eleven minutes of actual content. Rico was the kind of guy I'd go to on a day when I didn't feel sharp (broadcasters have their off days, too). I knew Rico would carry the show. Mike Andrews and Jim Lonborg were like that, too. I think the hardest man to interview was Jerry Adair, who just wouldn't expand on anything he said. Nor was Yaz an easy subject, at least in '67. He was cooperative, certainly, but he tended to give short, quick replies, the kind that put pressure on the interviewer to keep things rolling. It was only later in his career that he became a truly excellent interviewee, mostly because he was doing it so often.

WEDNESDAY, JULY 19

It's all but official: a diagnosis of pennant fever for the Hub. Tonight the rocketing Red Sox made it six in a row, moved to within 1 1/2 games of first, and dumped Baltimore 6 – 4.

Trailing 1 – 0 after four, the Sox rode the big inning again and scored five times in the fifth. The big hit was Mike Andrews's three-run home run with two out.

THURSDAY, JULY 20

It took Mother Nature to cool off the Red Sox, as the heavens wept, washing out tonight's game with the Orioles. Unfortunately the rains came with Boston leading 2 – 0 in the third.

Before the game, Dick Williams and Eddie Popowski did some good-natured kidding. Their target? George Scott. Scott came in the dugout after having several of the Orioles practically on the ground with laughter in a discussion near the Orioles dugout.

WILLIAMS: Looks like it will be a fifty-dollar fine for fraternizing with the enemy.

SCOTT: Fraternizing? I was only talking to them.

POPOWSKI: What do you care with all your money? You're not like Joe Foy here, but I remember in Pittsfield when you were living on french fries.

SCOTT: What're you supposed to eat in the bushes, steak?

FRIDAY, JULY 21

Make it seven in a row, nine of ten, for the streaking Sox. This time it was Darrell Brandon's turn to shine, and he beat the Indians at Municipal Stadium with a route-going 6 – 2 win. It was just his second complete game of the year. The win put the Red Sox in sole possession of second place.

Newcomer Norm Siebern, playing for the first time, spelled Scott at first late in the game.

On a sad note, former Red Sox slugger and all-time great Jimmie Foxx died today of a heart seizure.

SATURDAY, JULY 22

They are page-one news. Radio stations give periodic updates of scores. They are the talk of New England; and today they set more

Vaseline? What Vaseline?

Once a reporter asked Dick Williams, for the record, about John Wyatt's "fork" ball, that is, about Wyatt's alleged doctored pitch. Wyatt was rumored around the league to "load 'em up." Williams wouldn't answer the question, but the reporter kept after him. The reporter asked Williams if Wyatt used Vaseline on the ball.

"Vaseline? What Vaseline," Williams replied with mock innocence.

"Well, you know, the stuff Wyatt is supposed to put on his pitches," the reporter answered.

"Vaseline? Never heard of it," Williams said with a straight face. "Vaseline? News to me!"

tongues to buzzing with their eighth consecutive win, this a brilliant 4 – 0 Lee Stange shutout of Cleveland. The win vaulted the team to within a half game of first-place Chicago, who lost to the last-place A's 9 – 3.

Stange, who has been the team's hottest pitcher, struck out four, walked just one, and didn't allow a runner past second. The game was really over on its second pitch, when leadoff man Mike Andrews deposited a ball into the left field seats. Yaz added his twenty-third home run in the eighth. Andrews finished with three hits, and smokin' Joe Foy had a pair.

"Ten in a Row" Sunday, July 23, 1967

It took sixteen years and two months to happen; for not since May 1957 had the Red Sox won ten in a row. But the only loss that Dick Williams suffered in ten days was his wife. That happened tonight at Logan Airport in Boston, where he was separated from wife Norma as 15,000 fans created bedlam by welcoming the team back from their wildly successful road trip, capped today by an 8 – 5, 5 – 1 sweep of Cleveland.

"They told us on the plane that there'd be fans at the airport," the manager said as he pushed his way through the delirious crowd to look for his wife. "But I never expected anything like this. It's really something."

A few moments later, Dick located his wife, who didn't know what to say. "I'm just in a daze," Norma said.

The frenzied crush caused one of the biggest traffic jams in the airport's — even the city's — history. Many travelers rushing to catch flights were simply out of luck. There was no way in . . . or out, for that matter. One airport official said the crowd was even bigger than the one that welcomed the Beatles a year ago.

Boston is now a changed city, as is all of New England: it is unified by a common entity (the Red Sox) and a common cause (a pennant). It's a city unraveling the threads of heartache, of missed opportunity, of bad luck, that have enshrouded it for so long. It's

RED SOX				INDIANS			
Name	ab	r	h rbi	**Name**	ab	r	h rbi
Andrews, 2b..	2	1		Maye, lf......	5		
Jones, 2b....	2			Davalillo, cf...	4		
Foy, 3b......	4	2	1 4	Colavito, rf...	3		
Yastrzemski, lf	3	1	1 1	Whitfield, 1b..	3	1	
Tartabull, lf...				Alvis, 3b.....	4	1	1
Conigliaro, rf.	4	2	3 2	Sims, c......	4		2 2
Thomas, rf...	1			Fuller, 2b....	4	1	2 2
Scott, 1b....	2			L. Brown, ss..	4		1 1
Siebern, 1b..	1			O'Donoghue, p			
Adair, ss.....	3	1	1	Demeter, ph..	1		
Petrocelli, ss.	1	1		Bailey, p.....			
Smith, cf....	4	1	3	Hinton, ph...	1		
Ryan, c......	2			Pena, p......			
Gibson, c	1			T. Horton, ph.	1		1
Lonborg, p...	4			R. Allen, p...			
				Wagner, p.....			
TOTALS	34	8	10 7	**TOTALS**	34	5	7 5

Team	1	2	3	4	5	6	7	8	9	
Boston.........	2	4	1	0	1	0	0	0	0	8
Cleveland.......	0	2	0	1	0	0	0	0	2	5

Name	IP	H	R	ER	BB	SO
Boston						
Lonborg (w).................	9	7	5	5	2	11
Cleveland						
O'Donoghue (l).............	2	4	6	6	6	1
Bailey......................	2	2	1	1	1	2
Pena.......................	3	3	1	1	1	3
Allen......................	2	1			1	2

a city freeing itself of twenty-one years of frustration, disgust, disappointment, anguish, and apathy. Its numbed emotions have come back, and the feeling that one has feeling, that one can have feeling, has in itself engendered a positive, buoyant, infectious optimism. It's as if all the stains encrusted on the edifice of Boston baseball by the misdeeds of the past have now been scrubbed away. The edifice has been sandblasted of all its ugliness, and underneath we have discovered a structure, a design so old and forgotten that its beauty is experienced as something new. It's almost as if each win in this ten-game streak — certainly the last five and especially today's two — has been like an encyclopedia's acetate overlays on the human body. Each one lifted off takes away more detail. Only in this case the body is the body of Boston baseball. Each win is one of the overlays; and when it is lifted, it dispels more frustration, exorcises one more demon, until, at the end, the figure exists in all its purity . . . all reborn, all new. In the end there are 15,000 human bodies collectively realizing the kind of joy that happens maybe three or four times in a lifetime.

Now to today's doubleheader.

Jim Lonborg started the afternoon on cue. He won his fifth in a row and fourteenth overall and struck out eleven. He left no doubt that he was okay after being hit with a line drive yesterday in batting practice. The game's big hit came in the second inning on Joe Foy's second grand slam of the year (his fifteenth home run overall) off John O'Donoghue. Foy's slam followed Tony Conigliaro's two-run shot in the first inning. That was a history-making blast for it was Tony's one-hundredth career home run. At twenty-two years, six months, and sixteen days, he became the youngest player in baseball history to reach the 100 mark. Carl Yastrzemski added his twenty-fourth home run of the year.

Jerry Adair doubled to start the second. Reggie Smith, hustling like a man trying to cool off a hot foot, beat out an infield hit. Mike Ryan and Lonborg went out, but Mike Andrews kept the inning alive by working a walk to load the bases. Foy wasted no time going to work and drilled a fast ball twenty rows into the left field seats. The players set up a wild reception committee for Foy at home; and an even more thunderous welcome followed in the dugout, which seemed to be floating two feet off the ground.

Lonborg, soaking wet on this hot day, pitched a tough nine innings and gave up seven hits and five runs. He tired in the ninth, where he gave up a pair of runs; but by that time the Red Sox had a big lead and it really didn't matter.

There were only about twenty minutes between games. After game one ended, Yaz and Andrews beat everybody to the clubhouse and greeted everyone as they came in. "Stay sharp," Yaz said to each player as they went by, and he shook hands with everyone. When Foy entered the locker room, he boomed: "Cool down, men . . . we're gonna win this thing. I just know we are."

The players had quick sandwiches and soft drinks. Some showered and changed uniforms; others sat around and talked about the second game. Yaz patrolled the clubhouse and yelled: "One more. One more. We gotta have it."

They had to have it, and they did have it. In the second game, it was Gary Bell's turn. Bell, ineffective in his last several starts, went in struggling; but he redeemed himself by throwing a complete game, 5 – 1 win. He allowed but five hits, struck out five, and — most important — walked no one.

The Indian fans treated Bell to a lusty round of boos in the first, boos that turned into vindictive cheering when Lee Maye doubled, went to third on a wild pitch, and scored on a sacrifice fly to give the Indians a 1 – 0 lead. It looked like the start of another long day for Bell, but Gary straightened himself out and had the last laugh in Cleveland by throwing shutout ball the rest of the way.

The Red Sox took the lead in the fourth on some sloppy play by the Tribe. Scott reached on a throwing error by third baseman Max Alvis. Adair singled to the left. Smith then singled to score Scott; and when Maye threw high to third from right field, Reggie motored into second. Cleveland starter Luis Tiant threw a ball in the dirt. Adair tried to score from third, but was thrown out at home. On the play Smith took third. Mike Ryan drew a walk, then promptly stole a run for his team. Mike, taking Indian catcher Joe Azcue completely by surprise, broke for second. Azcue threw weakly to second. Smith alertly broke for the plate and easily beat Chico Salmon's throw. The Indian fans now directed their boos at their own infield. The Red Sox dugout, meantime, was roaring with delight.

Boston added two more in the fifth on Tony Conigliaro's two-run home run. Tony ended the trip with 10 for 24, two doubles, two triples, two home runs, and six RBIs. The Sox added a single run to close out their scoring in the sixth.

How good are things going? The team hasn't made an error in sixty-seven innings. The pitching's been so good (six complete games in the last seven) that relief ace John Wyatt hasn't been to

RED SOX					INDIANS				
Name	ab	r	h	rbi		ab	r	h	rbi
Andrews, 2b. .	5				Maye, lf.	4	1	2	
Foy, 3b.	4				Fuller, 2b. . .	2		1	
Yastrzemski, lf	4	1	3		Colavito, lf. . .	4		1	
Conigliaro, rf	4	1	1	2	Azcue, c.	4			
Scott, 1b. . . .	3	1	1		Alvis, 3b.	4		1	
Adair, ss. . . .	3		1		Horton, 1b. . .	4			
Smith, cf. . . .	4	2	2	1	Hinton, cf. . . .	3			
Ryan, c. . . .	3		2	1	Salmon, ss. . .	3			
Bell, p.	4				Tiant, p.	1			
					Davilillo, ph. .	1			
					Culver, p. . . .				
					Whitfield, ph. .	1		1	1
					Allen, p.				
TOTALS	34	5	10	4	TOTALS	31	1	5	1

Team	1	2	3	4	5	6	7	8	9	
Boston	0	0	0	2	2	1	0	0	0	5
Cleveland	1	0	0	0	0	0	0	0	0	1

Name	IP	H	R	ER	BB	SO
Boston						
Bell (w).	9	5	1	1		5
Cleveland						
Tiant (l).	6	8	5	3	3	5
Culver.	2	1				
Allen.	1	1				

Welcome Back

On the plane ride from Cleveland to Boston, an announcement was made that something out of the ordinary was happening at Logan with the fans. The cryptic announcement made us curious. When we landed, the mystery was cleared up. We saw the thousands and thousands of people and couldn't believe it. Players were shaking their heads; some looked out of the windows with open mouths.

The plane was ordered to pull up to a very remote section of the airport. When it stopped we were hustled into a waiting bus. That's when the fans came rushing out. They started shaking the bus, and it became scary. I was more concerned with the safety of the fans, being on the runway and all.

Their reception for us was a beautiful, wonderful thing. It was a real high. None of us had ever seen anything like it. We were dumbfounded. I think that was the critical turning point in the emotions of the team. We knew then and there — once and for all, beyond all doubt — that the fans believed in us.

the mound in ten days. In the winning streak, Boston has outscored its opponents 67 – 26. Seven different regulars have knocked in the winning run in the ten games, and the starting pitchers have won all ten.

The locker room after game two was even more energized, but Williams tried to keep a level head. Happy, yes . . . out of control, no: "When I was with Kansas City, we won eleven straight ball games; and the manager, Harry Craft, had a mild breakdown, and we went from there to lose thirteen games. So I'm careful. I don't expect we will lose thirteen games. We will win more than we lose. But that's as far as I want to go at the minute."

Now back to Logan Airport. The mob that greeted the team made movement anywhere just about impossible. The team bus had to wait in its tracks. There were just too many people to risk moving at all. The state police had to summon aid from neighboring barracks to contain the crowd. The original airport plans for the team had to be changed. The crowd was so big that hundreds of fans spilled over onto the runway, where a jet was taxiing for takeoff. Airport officials had the team get off at the Butler Aviation Terminal, then bussed them to the United gate to meet fans.

"How can we lose with people like this behind us?" Conigliaro yelled above the din.

Policemen had to form a flying wedge so the players could move into a nearby waiting area, where families and friends waited for them. The police were shoved, pounded, clawed as the fans desperately tried to get a close-up look at their heroes. One airport official said: "You have heard of crowds being overestimated. Well this is one crowd that has been underestimated. I can't recall a crowd this large at the airport."

Later the Red Sox made a policy decision that would stick for the rest of the season. For the safety of their fans, they would make no more public announcements about the team's travel plans, that is, departures and arrivals.

Now the Red Sox prepare to meet the Angels on Tuesday, when the Sox will open up what promises to be the biggest, most popular, most exciting home stand in years.

MONDAY, JULY 24

Players used the day off to regain their sense of reality after yesterday's circus at Logan. All during the day, fans lined up on Jersey Street to wait sometimes for hours for the privilege of getting tickets for the home stand.

TUESDAY, JULY 25

It was like an auction as the Red Sox resumed play tonight, with the auctioneer barking out to the curious crowd: "I have ten in a row. I have ten. Will anyone give me eleven? Do I hear eleven?"

The Red Sox and their fans wanted to bid eleven. The Sox got ten hits and trailed by just two runs after six. But it wasn't to be, as the California Angels (on a roll themselves with thirty-three wins in their last forty-five games) popped Boston's balloon (for now, anyway) with a 6 – 4 triumph.

A rumor that the game had sold out early resulted in thousands of tickets going unsold.

WEDNESDAY, JULY 26

There was no ticket snafu tonight, and 32,403 filled Fenway on Family Night. The Red Sox came off without a hitch, too (well, just about), and parlayed a wild seventh inning into a gratifying 9 – 6 win over the Angels. This win gave Bill Landis his first major league victory.

Through seven, the Red Sox looked like sleepwalkers, as California built a 4 – 1 lead off Darrell Brandon. Through six innings Angel lefty George Brunet gave up one hit, an infield job to Joe Foy in the fourth; but in the seventh, the Sox rolled a lucky seven.

Tony Conigliaro started things with a ringing double off the wall in left. George Scott, going the other way, leaned into a Brunet fast ball and lined it to the bullpen wall in right for a triple, scoring Conigliaro. Angel manager Bill Rigney replaced Brunet with his top reliever, Minnie Rojas. Rojas got Rico Petrocelli to fly to left, but the ball was deep enough for Scott to tag and score. Then the Red Sox got lucky. Reggie Smith reached on a bad-hop single over the glove of first baseman Don Mincher. Norm Siebern, hitting for Bob Tillman, hit what looked like an inning-ending double play ball to slick-fielding second baseman Bobby Knoop; but Knoop dropped the ball, and everyone was safe. With the fans rocking venerable Fenway, Dalton Jones,

"1967 was a tremendous year. It seems like yesterday. I loved it and wish I could relive it. . . . George Thomas and I helped keep the team loose. And Sparky Lyle, he was a maniac! That was before he became 'known' as a character. Thomas was just one of those guys who kept everyone loose. George couldn't hit, so he had to do *something* to help out!"

batting for Landis, flied deep to right to move Smith to third. Up came Mike Andrews.

"I saw [Angel third baseman Woody] Held playing deep, so I thought about the bunt. When I went to the plate, I tipped off Reggie. The slider came. I bunted it to third" for a base hit that tied the score at 4 – 4.

Foy then beat out an extremely close play on a grounder, and the bases were loaded. Many thought he was out . . . but not first base umpire Bill Haller. Yaz cashed in by roping a Rojas slider against the wall in left center. This cleared the bases and gave the Red Sox a 7 – 4 lead.

The Angel dugout rode Haller for his call on Foy, and they tossed helmets onto the field. Haller then chased Jack Hamilton, Johnny Werhas, and Rigney from the Angel bench. Rigney left shouting to Haller: "Are you doing this for the home fans?"

California added runs in the eighth and ninth, but the Sox pushed across two more in the bottom of the eighth on leadoff back-to-back home runs by Conigliaro and Scott.

THURSDAY, JULY 27

Fantastic. That's all you can say about this team and this afternoon's rousing win, their greatest comeback of the season. The first eight innings of the game were like the appetizer to a great meal, a preliminary meant to do little more than whet the palate for the more exotic and exquisitely tasty fare to follow. Boston went ahead 2 – 0 on homers by Yastrzemski (his twenty-fifth) and Scott (his twelfth) in the first and second innings, respectively. But Angel righty All-Star Jim McGlothlin waltzed through the rest of the game up to the eighth. He held a 5 – 2 lead going into the bottom of the ninth.

The game's last two innings were everything.

As Boston came up in the ninth, pitching coach Sal Maglie looked around at the 34,193 (biggest crowd since April 15, 1958) and said to Dick Williams: "Hell, no one's going home. We might as well win it." And that's what they eventually did.

Mike Andrews led off the ninth with a single to left. Joy Foy took one pitch for a ball, then lined a drive into the left field screen for his sixteenth home run to bring the Sox to within one.

"The main thing I was thinking," Foy said, "was to stay out of the double play. I hit it pretty good, but I didn't think it was hard

Tony Conigliaro ties the game in the ninth with his home run against the Angels. The Sox went on to win, 6 – 5 in ten. (Photo courtesy Boston Red Sox)

enough. I was running hard coming around first when I looked up and I didn't see anyone playing the ball. Then I heard the crowd yelling. So I slowed down."

Yelling? It was more like sweetly amplified histrionics, for there was still only one out, and it would be fair to say that the fans *expected* the Sox to get more.

After Foy's home run, Rigney pulled McGlothlin for left-hander Clyde Wright, who got Yaz on a fly ball to center. Rigney then took Wright out for righty Bill Kelso to face Tony Conigliaro.

On the first pitch, Tony answered the crowd's prayers by blasting the ball into the screen to tie the game. In the stands bedlam ensued. It would probably be the literal truth to say that there had never been more noise coming out of the Fenway stands.

In the top of the tenth of the 5 – 5 game, Williams brought in Sparky Lyle. With one out Mincher singled. Bill "Moose" Skowron, batting for Jimmie Hall, laced a liner to left center. Yastrzemski, running at top speed, speared the ball one-handed to rob Skowron blind for the second out.

"I was playing him shallow," said Yaz, "figuring if he got under the ball, it would be off the fence. My first glance at the ball, I thought 'No.' My second glance, I thought 'Yes.' "

But the drama of the inning wasn't over. Bubba Morton reached on Foy's second error of the game, and Bob Rodgers followed with a single to left. Yaz charged the ball like an infielder as Mincher roared around third. Yaz cannoned a throw that was so perfect it was almost scary. The ball went all the way in the air to Russ Gibson, directly on the plate. Mincher was out by fifteen feet.

In the bottom of the tenth, with Fenway a wall of noise, Reggie Smith led off by slashing a 3 – 2 pitch from Kelso into the right field corner. The tricky angles of the corner victimized Morton, and the ball got by him.

"I tried to open up coming around second," Smith said. "I had visions of an inside-the-park home run when I saw the ball caroming around."

But third base coach Eddie Popowski, with Solomon-like wisdom, held Smith. Gibson flied to short left for the first out. Jerry Adair, hitting for Lyle, then bounced one to third; but it took a tricky hop and skidded by Paul Schaal to score Smith with the winning run.

After an appropriately spontaneous celebration on the field, the Sox poured into the locker room. "We cannot be beat," Conigliaro thundered. Yaz stood in the doorway and greeted each player as he clapped his hands enthusiastically and screamed unintelligibly. When he finally sat down, Carl stirred a mixture of ice cream and soda in a paper cup ("a strawberry/vanilla/chocolate shake laced with two root beers").

Across the way in the Angel locker room, a somber Bill Rigney sat contemplating his hard luck over the last two games. He summed up his feelings this way: "The Red Sox broke my streak last night. But they broke my heart today."

FRIDAY, JULY 28

Almost as a way of relieving the mounting frenzy of the fans, the baseball fates decreed tonight's game to be far different from yesterday afternoon's waking dream. End result? Jim Lonborg was shelled off the mound (3 1/3 innings pitched, six hits, seven runs) in a 9 – 2 thumping at the hands of the Minnesota Twins. This was Lonborg's last start before beginning his two weeks of army duty in Atlanta.

SATURDAY, JULY 29

What's the news these days? Is it this young team's confidence? Its cockiness? Its ability to come from behind? Is it the Fenway crowds (35,469 today)? Maybe none of it is news anymore, the way these things have become almost commonplace. Well Boston combined all of this once again today in the first game of the doubleheader with the Twins and rallied for a 6 – 3 victory. In the nightcap it was all different; and the team, looking like it missed a collective wake-up call, got bombed 10 – 3.

The excited game one crowd saw a dandy, which boiled down to the effectiveness of Boston's bench and the right arm of Carl Yastrzemski. It was another of those "typical" Red Sox games. They appeared headed for defeat, but pulled it out with a big rally. They trailed 3 – 2 going into the bottom of the eighth, when Dick Williams went to his bench.

Norm Siebern and Dalton Jones each came through with pinch hits. With two men out and George Scott on first, Siebern singled hard to right center off Al Worthington. Jerry Adair singled to right to tie the game. With the Fenway throng going bananas, Jones, hitting for John Wyatt, bounced a single off of Cesar Tovar's glove at second for the lead run. Foy then plated two more with a double to left center.

Yaz's arm saved some serious damage. In the fourth, Carl threw out a runner at third to kill a rally. In the seventh, he threw out the quick Ted Uhlaender trying to score from third on Jim Kaat's fly ball.

SUNDAY, JULY 30

The Twins made like Wallenda, walking a tight rope, slipping, only to hold on by five fingers. One by one the fingers slipped off

Superstitious

I think people get superstitious in a pennant race. I had a little superstition that I shared with Mrs. Tom Yawkey as the race went down to the wire. Mrs. Yawkey scored each home game. About two-thirds of the way through the season, before the start of each game, she would wave down to me in the broadcasting booth from her box; and I would wave back. It was our ritual to keep the good vibes going.

until they were hanging by one. The last finger started slipping, too; but just as it was about to lose its grip, it held, and the team staggered away with a 7 – 5 win.

It was the Red Sox' fourth loss in the first seven games of the home stand, but they almost turned another pumpkin into a royal coach. The game proved true an old Boston saw, the one about a lead never being safe in Fenway.

Boston trailed 7 – 1 going into the ninth. Darrell Brandon, who gave up four runs in 3 2/3 innings, looked deader than a cracked, twenty-year-old garden hose. Harmon Killebrew and Rod Carew hit home runs thirty-two and seven, respectively, to give the Twins their comfortable pad.

Then in the ninth, the Red Sox did it again. Incredibly it all happened with two outs and Tony Conigliaro (single) on first. Reggie Smith singled, and Russ Gibson doubled; these hits were followed by three straight singles by Dalton Jones, Mike Andrews, and Joe Foy. This left runners at first and third with the score at 7 – 5 Twins. With Carl Yastrzemski due up, Twins manager Cal Ermer brought in lefty Jim Roland.

Yaz worked the count his way to 3 – 1 and got the green light, and Roland came in with a high slider. Yaz got under it just a bit, and with his hard swing, sent a towering pop-up between the mound and home plate, just to the first base side. Third baseman Rich Reese came in calling for the ball, but both catcher Jerry Zimmerman and Roland were yelling for Cesar Tovar to take it. As it developed, no one could hear anything above the roar of 24,459 partisan Sox fans. The six-foot, three-inch Reese and the five-foot, nine-inch Tovar collided. Reese made the catch; but on the collision, the ball squirted loose and Reese fell backward. As he did he reached for the ball again, somehow one-handed it in his glove, and tumbled to the ground with the out. The entire park groaned.

In a move made to bolster the starting pitching, which lately has had its troubles, the team sent Gary Waslewski to Toronto and recalled veteran Dave Morehead. At Toronto this year, Dave was 11 – 5 in seventeen starts and gave up just 115 hits in 122 innings. He struck out 109 and had an ERA of 3.21. Morehead has a great curve ball and a live fast ball. He first joined the Red Sox in 1963 and was their rookie pitcher of the year with a 3.81 ERA. Just two years ago, he pitched a no-hitter against the Indians at Fenway. He's young enough to come back . . . at least that's what the Red Sox are hoping.

Jim Lonborg, pulling army duty in Atlanta, worked out with the Braves today. Jim is expected to fly back for his next start.

The Sox also put in a claim on Twins pitcher Jim "Mudcat" Grant, whose name showed up on the waiver wire. "We are interested," said Haywood Sullivan.

MONDAY, JULY 31

Little Big Man Lee Stange provided instant respite for the Sox pitching woes today by throwing a 4–0, three-hit gem against the Twins. Stange was perfect for 6 2/3 innings, before Harmon Killebrew singled in the seventh to a chorus of Fenway boos. Before Stange's shutout today, the Red Sox used twenty-eight pitchers in the last seven games.

Yaz gave Stange all the support he needed by hitting his twenty-sixth home run, a three-run job, in the third. The Sox added a final run in the fourth on a bases-loaded walk to Mike Ryan.

Lee "Stinger" Stange whitewashed the Twins on July 31. His 2.77 ERA led all Sox starters. (Photo courtesy Boston Red Sox)

*End-of-the-month
Stats: 7/31/67*

American League Standings
July 31, 1967

Team	W–L	PCT.	GB
Chicago	58–42	.580	–
BOSTON	56–44	.560	2
Detroit	53–45	.541	4
Minnesota	53–47	.530	5
California	55–49	.529	5
Washington	51–53	.490	9
Baltimore	45–54	.455	12½
Cleveland	46–56	.451	13
New York	44–56	.440	14
Kansas City . . .	44–59	.427	15½

Team Batting

Name	AB	R	H	HR	RBI	AVG.
Yastrzemski	357	63	115	26	75	.322
Conigliaro	294	53	89	19	61	.303
Scott	350	49	101	13	51	.289
Petrocelli	272	32	73	9	39	.267
Andrews	324	55	83	5	24	.266
Smith	342	43	86	6	33	.251
Lyle	4		1			.250
Osinski	8		2			.250
Foy	352	57	87	17	45	.247
Tartabull	151	16	37		5	.245
Jones	87	11	21	2	9	.241
Ryan	160	15	37	1	18	.231
Adair	219	20	50	1	21	.228
Santiago	18	2	4	1	3	.222
Gibson	114	6	24	1	12	.211
Tillman	64	4	12	1	4	.188
Brandon	33	3	6			.188
Thomas	49	7	9	1	5	.184
Siebern	64	8	10		4	.156
Fischer	7		1		1	.143
Lonborg	59	3	7		5	.119
Bell	46	4	5		1	.109
Stange	31	2	2		1	.065
Wyatt	9					.000
Landis	1	1				.000

Team Pitching

Name	IP	H	BB	SO	W	L	ERA
Lyle	16	13	4	20	1	0	1.68
Wyatt	55	36	25	47	5	4	2.45
Osinski	47	47	9	27	2	1	2.54
Stange	113⅓	97	18	61	7	6	2.78
Lonborg	167	133	49	152	14	4	3.34
Bell	141⅓	123	46	87	7	9	3.62
Brandon	118⅓	111	45	75	4	8	4.33
Santiago	77⅔	83	23	60	6	4	4.40
Landis	17	16	7	12	1	0	6.35

Leaders

Batting
(minimum of 225 at-bats)

Name and Team	At-Bats Avg.
F. Robinson, Balt.	.331
Kaline, Det.	.325
Yastrzemski, Bos.	.322
Carew, Minn.	.303
Conigliaro, Bos.	.299
Blair, Balt.	.289
Scott, Bos.	.289
Horton, Det.	.287
Fregosi, Cal.	.282
Tovar, Minn.	.280

Home Runs

Name and Team	#
Killebrew, Minn	32
Howard, Wash.	28
Yastrzemski, Bos.	26
F. Robinson, Balt.	21
Conigliaro, Bos.	19

Runs Batted In

Name and Team	#
Yastrzemski, Bos.	75
Killebrew, Minn.	75
Howard, Wash.	67
Conigliaro, Bos.	61
F. Robinson, Balt.	59

Pitching
(minimum of 10 decisions)

Player and Team	Record	Pct.
McGlothlin, Cal.	9-2	.818
Horlin, Chi.	13-3	.813
Lonborg, Bos.	14-4	.778
Sparma, Det.	10-4	.714
Merritt, Minn.	7-3	.700

August

Hot August was an alpine kind of month: it was thirty-one days of the highest peaks and the deepest crevices. If it could be read out on a screen, the lifeline of this month would jag its way up and down in an irregular jerking that gave witness to the strong pulse of this team.

The greatest high came on August 20, when the Red Sox swept the Angels at Fenway Park to win the second game 9 – 8 after trailing 8 – 0. Another glorious experience was finally getting into first place. The low point by far was two nights earlier, on the eighteenth, when Tony Conigliaro was almost killed after being hit in the face by a pitch from Jack Hamilton. Some said such a young team couldn't weather the loss of such an important player in so close a pennant race. But once more the Red Sox refused to bow their heads. They bounced back by filling in with Jose Tartabull, George Thomas, and — for six days — Jim Landis. When he had to, Dick Williams even put Joe Foy in right during a game.

The club also continued to make moves off the field as it went after and got free agent Ken Harrelson, obtained savvy veteran catcher Elston Howard from the Yankees, and brought up Dave Morehead from Toronto. And Dick Williams continued to be Dick Williams. For example, he benched George Scott for a key series with the Angels in Anaheim because Scott was overweight. When people questioned the wisdom of benching Scott, Williams fired back: "I'm not going to change [my ways] now just because we're in a race."

Near the end of the month, the first *BIG* series of the season arrived: five games in Chicago with the teams tied for first. The Sox passed the test by winning three of five, including the game that ended with Jose Tartabull's unlikely throw from right to nip Ken Berry at the plate.

August simply was one of the most exciting, drama-packed months in Boston baseball history.

TUESDAY, AUGUST 1

With the last-place Kansas City A's in town, 26,750 of Fenway's faithful came expecting a Red Sox sweep, but they had to content themselves with a split. In fact they walked away feeling lucky that the team managed to salvage the second game.

In the opener the A's Chuck Dobson fired a five-hitter to best Dave Morehead, who was making his 1967 debut for Boston. Morehead looked shaky and nervous.

Between games someone asked Dick Williams what he thought of Morehead's effort: "Not much," the manager shot back. Actually, Williams was more hot about Morehead going home to Toronto from Columbus before reporting to Boston. The team had told him to come direct from Columbus. "Maybe he's not used to our operation. Maybe he thinks it's the way it used to be."

In the nightcap Mike Ryan belted a three-run pinch-hit home run in the seventh to break up a 4 – 3 game, and the Red Sox went on to win 8 – 3.

Private first class Jim Lonborg flew in from Atlanta just in time to get his fifteenth win. Lonborg struggled for 5 1/3 innings and gave up eight hits and all three Kansas City runs. He gave way to Sparky Lyle in the sixth; the rookie was overpowering, striking out four.

WEDNESDAY, AUGUST 2

After the game, Carl Yastrzemski sat numbly on a stool in front of his locker. He flipped a half-filled (to Yaz, it was half empty) beer cup into a nearby trashcan. "This stuff doesn't taste any good after losing one like that. And that was a tough one."

Tough it was, because the Red Sox not only lost to the lowly A's 8 – 6, but in the process also lost a chance to gain on the White Sox, who lost to the Indians 5 – 1.

Mike Andrews hit his sixth home run (and first at home) in the second. John Wyatt took the loss.

THURSDAY, AUGUST 3

At Yankee Stadium the phone rang in manager Ralph Houk's office. Houk answered, then called for Elston Howard. "Elston. Mr. Yawkey of the Red Sox wants to talk to you." Fifteen minutes later, Howard was a member of the Red Sox. "I've never enjoyed a telephone call more in my life. Mr. Yawkey said to me 'Elston, we want you in Boston.' "

When the news broke in the Boston clubhouse, the players reacted unanimously in favor: "Howard is the best catcher I've ever seen for calling a ball game," said Carl Yastrzemski. "He's the best handler of pitchers and the best at setting up hitters."

Consensus is that Howard's experience will help the young team down the stretch. The thirty-eight-year-old catcher will join the team in Minnesota tomorrow.

In the game tonight at Fenway, Bill Landis started, and it didn't rain. Landis had been rained out of his three previous starts. But the A's rained on him for three runs in the first inning; and for a while, this game looked like another pitching failure, another loss. But Dick Williams played a hunch and brought back Dave Morehead for a second chance, just two days after his failure as a starter. As have so many of Williams's gambles, this one paid off; and Dave threw five innings of shutout relief. By the time Morehead left, Boston had a 4 – 3 lead, which Sparky Lyle and John Wyatt protected for an eventual 5 – 3 victory. For Wyatt the save was sweet revenge for yesterday's cuffing at the hands of his former team. "I thought I'd never get over losing to them cats the night before," Wyatt said. "But you can forget things easily when the next day comes and things get brighter."

Yaz made a big defensive play in the sixth. With the A's leading 3 – 2, Mike Hershberger doubled to right. Dick Green then singled to left. The ball slowed up in the outfield grass, and it looked like the speedy Hershberger would be home with the run; but Yaz

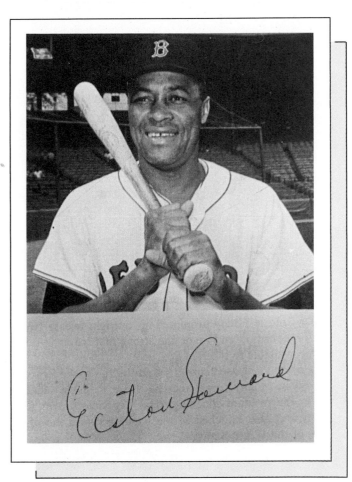

Elston Howard's influence on the pitchers during the stretch run probably meant the pennant. (Photo courtesy Boston Red Sox)

A death threat to Mike Andrews brought in the FBI. (Photo courtesy Boston Red Sox)

gave it one of his patented infield charges and threw a perfect strike to Mike Ryan for the out. It was his fourth assist in the last five games.

The Red Sox went ahead in the sixth on Mike Andrews's two-run single. Andrews ended the scoring in the eighth with a solo homer.

In the top of the ninth, Haywood Sullivan called Howard in New York. "We've been working on the deal for two or three days . . . I'm sure the guy can help us," said Sullivan.

The move left the Red Sox with four catchers: Howard, Ryan, Russ Gibson, and Bob Tillman. To make room for Howard, they sent outfielder Jose Tartabull to Pittsfield; but Jose is not expected to stay long in the Berkshires. The Sox are trying to unload Tillman; and when they do, Tartabull most likely will rejoin the club.

Death Threat

One of the very little known events of the '67 season was the death threat to Mike Andrews. One day Dick O'Connell came into the clubhouse with representatives from the FBI and told Mike that death-threat letters had been sent by someone in Chicago to the starting second basemen of the three contenders: Mike, Rod Carew of Minnesota, and Dick McAuliffe of Detroit. Apparently the letters were from someone who had a lot of money bet on the White Sox to take the American League pennant.

The club and the FBI talked it over with Mike. They made the decision, with Mike's agreement, that the threat would best go unreported and that no one else on the team, other than Dick Williams, would be told about it.

I'm sure it weighed on Mike's mind, and he did confide in his close friend Russ Gibson, who was the only other player on the team to know of the problem. The FBI gave Mike protection for a few days because they couldn't afford not to take the threat seriously.

Fortunately, of course, the threat wasn't acted upon. Mike went on to have a fine season for Boston that year and continued a successful career. Mike, a native Californian, has come to make his home in New England; and he's been a wonderful man for the New England community, primarily through his work with the Jimmy Fund of the Dana Farber Cancer Institute, of which he is chairman.

Sullivan also confirmed that the deal for Mudcat Grant was dead.

FRIDAY, AUGUST 4

The Red Sox began their road trip in Minnesota, where they ran into lefty Jim Merritt, who did a credible impression of a buzz saw. Merritt got into trouble only once in his 3 – 0 gem, in the eighth. It was trouble of a curious sort, when a bug flew into his mouth, almost choking him. "I was opening my mouth to breathe," Merritt said. "I saw him and then — whoosh! — he was in there . . . My eyes [watered] and I gagged a couple of times. Then I finally got him down."

The Sox went down a whole lot easier on five hits (two by Yaz).

Elston Howard reported to the club before the game. He was given number 18. Players came over to him and introduced themselves, going out of their way to make Ellie feel at home.

SATURDAY, AUGUST 5

From the start things went the wrong way for the Red Sox in Minnesota today. In the Twins' first, Tony Conigliaro lost a ball in the sun for a double and a run. After Rico Petrocelli tied the score in the second with his tenth home run, the Twins answered in the third on a solo shot by Zoilo Versalles. And that was the extent of the scoring, as the Twins rode the strong pitching of Dave Boswell for the 2−1 win.

SUNDAY, AUGUST 6

> Where has all the offense gone,
>> Long time passing?
> Where has all the offense gone,
>> Long time ago?

Words to a sad folk song that the folks in New England would rather not hear; but for the third straight game, they got a full sixteen bars as the Red Sox' bats turned up nothing — literally nothing — as Dean Chance threw a rain-shortened, five-inning, perfect game. It left the Sox with a grand total of one run scored here in the three-game set.

"Gentlemen, it was a cheapie," Chance said later of the perfect game, but added that he'd take it any way he could get it. The closest the Red Sox got to a hit was Elston Howard's hard line drive in the third. It sliced away from Bob Allison, but he made a nice running grab.

The Red Sox have now lost thirty-one of their last thirty-six games here, going back to 1964. The only break they got all day was from the Orioles, who beat the White Sox twice.

MONDAY, AUGUST 7

The team traveled to Kansas City for a doubleheader tomorrow (did they pack their bats?). Dave Morehead (1−1) and Gary Bell (7−9) will pitch against Catfish Hunter (9−11) and Blue Moon Odom (3−4).

TUESDAY, AUGUST 8

After losing tonight's first game 5 – 3 to the thorny A's, Dick Williams took no chances in the nightcap. He played it as if it were a World Series game: he used nineteen players, including seven pitchers and four pinch hitters, in an equatorially hot, muggy Kansas City night.

In game one, the A's built a 5 – 0 lead off Dave Morehead, who was ineffective as a starter, although he struck out six in 4 1/3 innings. The Red Sox mounted a comeback of sorts with the long ball. Rico Petrocelli's solo shot in the eighth made it 5 – 1, and Tony Conigliaro's two-run job brought it to 5 – 3. But Jack Aker came on to get Rico for the final out with a man on.

They fell behind early in game two as well, and the evening had the makings of a total disaster — the A's, after all, are tied with the Yankees for the American League basement. Williams wanted to avoid a double loss at all costs. In fact he shook up the lineup in the nightcap. Reggie Smith was benched, Carl Yastrzemski was moved to center, and Norm Siebern took over left. In the infield slumping Joe Foy sat down at third in favor of Jerry Adair.

The new lineup was no good for Gary Bell, who gave up three runs; after six, the Sox trailed 4 – 1. But three in the seventh tied it, and three in the ninth pulled it out . . . all this while Dan Osinski, Hank Fischer, and John Wyatt held the A's scoreless in relief.

In the seventh, with Blue Moon Odom on cruise control with a four-hitter and the first two men out, Reggie Smith drew a walk. Jerry Adair singled (his third hit of the game). Manager Al Dark brought in lefty Tony Pierce to face Yaz, but Carl singled up the middle on a 3 – 1 pitch to score Smith. Conigliaro's double off Aker tied it up. The winning rally in the ninth came off ex-Yankee Bill Stafford. Again there were two out. Yaz doubled off the left field wall. Conigliaro and Foy were walked intentionally to get to Siebern; but Norm fouled up the strategy by lining the first pitch into left for two runs. When Jim Gosger threw the ball into the dugout, the third run was home. The A's got a run in the bottom of the ninth to make it 7 – 5 and loaded the bases, but Darrell Brandon came on to get pinch hitter Ted Kubiak to bounce back to the box.

Haywood Sullivan announced that catcher Bob Tillman had been sold to the Yankees for the $20,000 waiver fee. Tillman's spot on the roster was taken by Fischer, who was reactivated from the disabled list. Sullivan also said that if no deal could be worked out for a pitcher, the team would recall Jerry Stephenson from Toronto.

WEDNESDAY, AUGUST 9

After the long twi-night doubleheader last night, the team got to bed about 3 A.M. Despite that Williams called a special workout at 10 A.M. for Reggie Smith, George Scott, Joe Foy, Elston Howard, and Dalton Jones. All the coaches were ordered to be there, and they threw batting practice. Howard remarked (complained would not be the word) how he thought Williams was giving him the silent treatment; Ellie's had a sore finger, which has hampered his performance.

In the game the Red Sox beat Kansas City 5 – 1 behind Jim Lonborg, who again flew in from Atlanta on an overnight pass. The win was number sixteen for Jim, tops in the majors. The win brought the Sox to 1 1/2 games of the first place White Sox, who lost to Detroit.

Both in the field and at bat, Boston looked sharp tonight. For the second night in a row, Jerry Adair had three singles and drove in three runs. His single with the bases loaded in the seventh put the game on ice. The A's got their run in the eighth, and it might have been more, except for the great one-hand grab Yaz made off Ken Harrelson. With Lonborg tiring, Williams brought in Sparky Lyle to get the last four outs.

Lonborg's army stint ends in Atlanta on Saturday morning.

THURSDAY, AUGUST 10

The team flew out of Kansas City for California. They begin a series with the Angels tomorrow night.

FRIDAY, AUGUST 11

The last time the Red Sox limped back from a bad West Coast trip, Dick Williams said something about the "extracurricular activities" and temptations in the Land of the Stars. Well whatever the reason, the California Horrors struck again. Tonight's game featured (if that's the right word to describe this kind of torment) only one run. Unfortunately for Boston, California scored it in the fifth.

Jimmie Hall led off against hard-luck Lee Stange. Hall went to third on Don Mincher's single, just past a diving Mike Andrews. Then Stange bore down to strike out Roger Repoz and get Woodie Held to foul out to Elston Howard. Just when it looked like

Stinger would escape, he threw a ball in the dirt with Tom Satriano up. The ball skipped by Howard, and Hall scored.

And that was it. Stange was brilliant the rest of the way. Jim McGlothlin was a shade better and gave up just three hits (two to Andrews). Not a single Red Sox runner got past first base.

Williams, peeved at George Scott for being a few pounds over his 215-pound weight limit, benched Scott and put Norm Siebern at first. Scott was grumbling, and there was quite a bit of second guessing from the media. Scott has hit .343 against the Angels this year, with four home runs and nine RBIs. On top of that, in his last three games against McGlothlin, he has hit three home runs.

"I was surprised to find Scott wasn't in the batting order. And happy, too," McGlothlin said. Scott did come up as a pinch hitter for Stange in the eighth, and he walked.

When asked about Scott's benching, Williams replied testily: "At what weight did Scott hit the home runs off him? A lot less than he does now."

Scott weighs 217. Williams wants him at 215. Until then Siebern's the first baseman. "This is the way I've operated all season, and I'm not going to change now just because we're in a race."

SATURDAY, AUGUST 12

Scott was still on the bench, but Joe Foy, who lost five pounds overnight in a steam bath, was put back in the lineup . . . to no avail. The slumbering Sox dropped into fourth place, two games out and just percentage points ahead of the fifth-place Angels. While Scott may be overfed, the offense was anemic again. They could scrape together just one run and wasted another fine pitching job. Final score, California 2, Boston 1.

It was the sixth loss in eight games on the western road swing. In those six defeats, the Red Sox have scored a total of five runs.

Don Mincher hit his eighteenth home run off Gary Bell to give California a 1–0 lead. The Sox got it back in the third on a base hit by Foy. In the sixth, the Angels scored the winning run on a Tom Satriano double and a single by Jim Fregosi. The Red Sox left runners on second and third in the third and left a runner on third in the seventh.

There was a minor incident in the third, when Mike Andrews fouled out against Jack Hamilton. Andrews argued with home plate umpire Ed Runge that the ball was wet. Hamilton is reputed to throw the spitter every now and then.

A Weighty Problem

The thing about Scotty's weight was this. Eddie Popowski was in charge of weighing George before each game. George kept coming in overweight, and Dick Williams stuck with Norm Siebern at first. Finally Eddie realized that the team needed George back in the lineup. When he reported to Williams that George was the correct weight, George was actually a couple pounds over; but they didn't tell the manager.

It was Pop's white lie that got George in there, and it may have meant the pennant. George went on to hit well immediately after returning to the lineup.

SUNDAY, AUGUST 13

The downbeat continued today as one-run madness has the team practically denying its collective sanity. The $3-2$ loss was bad enough, but there was more concern over Carl Yastrzemski, who banged his head into the left field wall in the first while going for a drive by Jose Cardenal. As Yaz crumpled to his knees, Cardenal circled the bases for an inside-the-park home run. Yaz was woozy and stayed down for a few minutes; then he said he was okay and remained in the game.

When Yaz came up for his last at bat in the eighth, there were two outs and runners on second and third. Bill Rigney brought in lefty Jim Weaver to face Yaz. Carl, looking bad, bounced feebly to second to end the inning. There seemed to be something wrong with him.

"I didn't see a pitch," Yaz said. "Everything was blurry. I figured it was water going into my eyes, and I kept stepping out and wiping them. But it didn't help . . . I couldn't focus. I think they were getting blurry because of the [first-inning] blow."

Buddy LeRoux said he didn't think it was serious. "He's tired. It wasn't blurring up to then. I think it might have been sweat in his eyes." To be safe LeRoux said Yaz's eyes would be examined when the team arrived in Boston tomorrow.

Jim Lonborg was ineffective and was gone after the fourth. The Red Sox made a go of it in the ninth. Rico Petrocelli hit a two-run home run to cut the gap to $3-2$. George Scott, batting for Mike Ryan, singled; but that's as far as it got, as George Thomas struck out to end the game and the terrible road trip.

The bad play on this trip has some people wondering if the Red Sox are about ready to fold. The pitching was generally fine, but the twelve regular batsmen were 49 for 245 for a .199 average. The losses were $2-0$, $2-1$, and $2-0$ in Minnesota; $5-3$ in Kansas City; and $1-0$, $2-1$, and $3-2$ here.

Williams said that following the off day Monday, everyone would be ordered to report to Fenway by 4 P.M. Tuesday, 3 1/2 hours before game time with Detroit. "Maybe they'll think a little baseball."

MONDAY, AUGUST 14

The team landed at Logan at 8:20 A.M. What a difference from the last homecoming. This time the Sox — losers of seven out of nine on the western trip — were greeted not by thousands of screaming fans, but by about fifty wives, children, and assorted friends and relatives.

TUESDAY, AUGUST 15

Dave Morehead held the Tigers scoreless in the top of the first; in the bottom half of the inning, leadoff man Reggie Smith blasted a home run. It was all Morehead needed in a six-hit, eight-strikeout, 4 – 0 victory. It was Dave's first complete major league game since September 16, 1965, the day he no-hit the Indians at Fenway. Tonight it looked as if two years of arm misery and frustration had never happened to Morehead. His fast ball was blazing, and his curve was in the Camilo Pascual category; it fell right off the edge of a flat world. When the game ended, the Fenway audience of 27,125 gave Morehead a standing ovation.

George "The Thin Man" Scott, off of his Henry VIII imitation, responded to his reinstatement to the lineup by cracking a first-inning home run of his own into the left field screen. Before the game, during batting practice, a few of the Tigers were riding George and Manager Williams on his weighty problems: "Nine teams have managers. The Red Sox have a dietician," someone cracked.

Morehead got insurance runs in the third (Joe Foy tripled, Yaz hit a sacrifice fly) and in the eighth (Yaz's twenty-eighth home run near the flagpole in center), but he didn't need them.

Dave Morehead chipped in five key wins down the stretch. (Photo courtesy Boston Red Sox)

"Dave's control [just one walk] was better than I've ever seen it," said Tiger star Al Kaline. "And he certainly had a good curve ball. Nothing to take away from the man off that performance tonight."

His only scare came in the fifth, when the Tigers loaded the bases with two out. Don Wert lined a ball to shallow right. Tony Conigliaro had a long run, ran out from under his cap, dove, one-handed the ball, and did a tumble as the crowd held its breath. They burst into cheers as Tony came up with the glove hand to signal the catch. Scott also made a couple of fine plays at first.

More details came out on George's "Battle of the Bulge." Scott said his troubles began on the team's day off in Anaheim on the recent road trip: "It was the day off there that killed me. Nothing to do. There was no colored people to visit in Anaheim like in the other cities. So I hung around the room all day, and I ate too much. I just look at food and I gain weight."

But he's below his 215-pound limit by a pound, a fact that prompted this line from the *Boston Globe's* Ray Fitzgerald: "The svelte Mr. Scott is a vision, a walking ad for rye crisp and zwieback toast."

The Red Sox also made another roster move by sending pitcher Hank Fischer to Toronto and catcher Russ Gibson to Pittsfield. Their spots on the roster were taken by Jose Tartabull, who was brought back from Pittsfield, and Jerry Stephenson, recalled from Toronto. Stephenson was 8 – 7 in International League play, but had three complete games, including two shutouts. With Gibson gone the Sox — incredibly — are down to two catchers. A few days ago, they had four.

Fischer just came off the disabled list, but Haywood Sullivan said Hank wasn't throwing hard and was still having arm problems.

WEDNESDAY, AUGUST 16

George "Twiggy" Scott caught two fat Denny McLain pitches, and the Boomer belted two long home runs to lead his mates to an 8 – 3 win over Detroit before another routine Fenway crowd: 32,051. One could sense the momentum — Old Mo — swinging back to the Red Sox with this resilient win.

Scott's first blast (a 420-foot job to left center) came in the first with Yaz aboard. Reggie Smith followed with a solo shot for a 3 – 0 lead, but the Tigers got them back with two in the second (Norm Cash's two-run homer) and one in the third. That brought on Darrell Brandon, and the righty responded with seven innings of shutout relief that practically had Dick Williams and Sal Maglie doing cartwheels in the dugout.

In the bottom of the third, the Sox took the lead for good as George Scott rifled a ball into the Tiger bullpen with Jose Tartabull aboard. Williams bounced up to the top step of the dugout and greeted Scott with a warm smile and a pat on the back. Tartabull was playing right for Tony Conigliaro, who had an army reserve meeting in Lynn. Jose made two super catches. In the eighth, he went to the bullpen wall and snared Jim Northrup's bid. In the ninth, he went to the same spot and took a home run away from Dick McAuliffe. He also stole third base after doubling in the fifth. He may never see Pittsfield again.

Williams was thrown out of the game (his third ejection of the year) in the seventh, when Scott was called out at first on the tail end of a double play. Williams stormed out of the dugout, jawed face-to-face with ump Frank Umont, pulled the chewing gum from his mouth, and threw it on the ground. That was enough for Umont, and he ran Williams. Williams stalked off to a rousing ovation from the fans.

People were joking when the team had four catchers. For the moment they now have one healthy backstop, as Elston Howard jammed his thumb in the third inning. Mike Ryan came in, and George Thomas will be used behind Ryan if Howard's injury lingers. Ryan hasn't been too thrilled about riding the bench in favor of Howard: "We were in second place when he [Williams] took me out. Then we went all the way to fifth. He can yank me. That's his privilege. But there's nothing that says I have to like it. This is the third or fourth time I've been taken out when I felt I'd done the job . . . so all this is discouraging."

THURSDAY, AUGUST 17

In a tight race, today's 7 – 4 loss to the Tigers in ten innings really hurt. The crowd of 28,653 put the club over the one million mark for the first time since 1960, Ted Williams's last year.

"Tony Goes Down" Friday, August 18, 1967

The last line of the unabridged box score from tonight's game is a line of agate type; its brevity reads almost like an epitaph chiseled in the well-polished but somber stone of a grave and it stands as harsh testimony to one of Boston's — one of sports' — all-time tragedies: HBP — Hamilton (Conigliaro), T — 2:16, A — 31,027.

ANGELS					RED SOX			
Name	ab	r	h	rbi	Name	ab	r	h	rbi
Cardenal, cf. .	4				Andrews, 2b. .	3			
Fregosi, ss. . .	4				Adair, 3b. . . .	3		1	
Hall, rf.	4	2	2	2	Yastrzemski, lf	3			
Mincher, 1b. .	4		1		Scott, 1b. . . .	4		1	
Reichardt, lf. .	3				Smith, cf. . . .	4			
Rodgers, c. . .	2				Conigliaro, rf. .	1		1	
Knoop, 2b. . .	3		1		Tartabull, rf. . .	1		1	
Werhas, 3b. .	2				Petrocelli, ss. .	3	2	1	1
Repoz, ph. . .	1				Howard, c. . . .	3			
Held, 3b. . . .					Bell, p.	3		2	1
Hamilton, p. . .	1								
Satriano, ph. .	1								
Kelso, p.									
Coates, p. . . .									
Morton, ph. . .	1								
Cimino, p. . . .									
TOTALS	30	2	4	2	TOTALS	28	3	6	2

Team	1	2	3	4	5	6	7	8	9	
Calif.	0	0	0	0	0	0	1	0	1	2
Boston	0	0	0	2	0	1	0	0	X	3

Name	IP	H	R	ER	BB	SO
Calif.						
Hamilton (l)	5	4	2	2	1	5
Kelso	⅔	1	1	1		2
Coates	1⅓	1				1
Cimino	1					2
Boston						
Bell (w)	9	4	2	2	1	5

It hangs there like a victim on the gallows tree, a hollow form without life. It summarizes the key play of this game the way wreckage strewn over an airstrip gives evidence of a crash or the way a lone and empty life raft bobs aimlessly in the ocean after a great ship has gone down. This little line of type bothers one like a death in the family; it is a pathetic but human sorrow that may lose its edge as time goes by, but that can never be forgotten. Its brand is permanent in the psyche. This, therefore, is a living sorrow, one that is outside of time and one that will always be with us.

We remember the night Tony Conigliaro was beaned and almost killed as a *true* memory. To have this kind of memory, so much must be forgotten. That's why such an event can live with us so strongly, so long. So many other facts about the 1967 season can fade away, but not this play.

Tony's injury is a story about the tenuous nature of our lives here on this Earth, about a heartache that will never go away. The sound of the ball hitting the left side of Tony's head rings in the dark corners of the mind like a sobbing, a crying that cries because there is nothing else that can be done. There are no words for this.

The game started out quietly enough. Gary Bell and Jack Hamilton matched each other for three scoreless innings. Bell retired the Angels in the top of the fourth, and then came the fateful Red Sox fourth.

George Scott led off with a single to center. Scott tried to hustle it into a double, but was thrown out. Then, like a bad omen, someone dropped a smoke bomb in left field. It billowed away in thick white clouds, and it took ten minutes for the air to clear. After the delay Reggie Smith flied to deep center for the second out. Up came Tony.

He assumed his usual stance in the right-handed batter's box, close to the plate. Hamilton looked into Bob Rodgers for the sign, went into his motion, and delivered a fast ball that moved in on Tony and toward his head. Tony instinctively threw up his hands in a gesture of self-protection. Judging by the loud cracking sound and the way the ball ricocheted, it looked at first like the helmet had absorbed the full impact of the pitch. It looked like the pitch knocked the helmet off Tony's head; but what actually happened was that the helmet flew off as Tony tried to jerk his head out of the way, and the ball struck him flush on top of the left cheekbone, just below the eye socket. Tony went down as if he were shot and for long moments remained completely motionless. The crowd gasped, and there was a rush, led by Dick Williams, from the Red Sox dugout. Tony was still motionless, and the worst fears crossed everyone's mind. Rico Petrocelli knelt over Tony and whispered in his ear that it would be okay. Finally Tony moved and seemed to regain semiconsciousness. The first thing he did was kick his feet in agony.

Bobby Doerr ran down from the first base coaching box: "He didn't move much. He just lay there."

When it was obvious that Tony wasn't going to get up, a stretcher was brought to home plate. Jim Lonborg, Joe Foy, and Mike Ryan carefully lifted Tony's limp body onto the stretcher; and it was carried off into the clubhouse by Lonborg, Ryan, Buddy LeRoux, and Angel trainer Fred Frederico. An ambulance was called. Dr. Thomas Tierney, team physician, was waiting and made a preliminary exam. By that time Tony was awake and talking though still in great pain.

"When I got to him," Tierney said, "he said 'It hurts like hell. I heard a hissing sound, and that was all.' "

Ryan said Tony's face was "swelled all around and a tough thing to look at."

His left eye was hideously swollen completely shut and an ugly reddish blue color. He was bleeding heavily from the nose. The ambulance rushed Tony to Sancta Maria Hospital in Cambridge, and he was examined by a neurosurgeon, Dr. Joseph Dorsey. X-rays showed a shattered cheekbone. Tony also suffered a scalp contusion. Dorsey said that if the ball had struck maybe an inch higher and to the right, the young outfielder might have died. The doctor said it was too soon to determine if Tony had sustained any permanent eye damage.

The Fenway crowd booed Hamilton, who had the reputation of throwing the spitter. He stood on the mound with his arms folded and looked in. "I've not hit anyone all year," Hamilton said later. "I certainly wasn't throwing at him. I was just trying to get the ball over. Tony stands right on top of the plate. He hangs over the plate as much as anyone in the league."

"The pitch was about eight inches inside," said Angel catcher Rodgers. "It took off when it got near Tony. It was a fast ball and it just sailed."

As play continued the Red Sox got two runs in the inning (ironically, the HBP had started a two-run rally) and went on to a 3 – 2 win. But the crowd was stunned, and the applause over what

Strange Irony

Not many people remember that before Tony went down with his horrible injury, Dick Williams had expressed concern about someone getting hit. This is how Hall of Famer Bobby Doerr noted the fact with this brief diary entry:

There was a real ironic, almost strange thing about the game tonight, especially in light of Tony's injury, which looks like it's serious. Jack Hamilton has been accused all during this season by a lot of people of throwing spitters. Well, in the first part of the game tonight, Dick Williams complained to the umpires of this. Dick also voiced a protest early on (maybe the second inning), that we all thought Hamilton was throwing spitters. The ball was acting strangely. Dick said he was afraid someone would get hurt. Unfortunately, he was right.

normally would have been a gratifying victory was perfunctory. When the game was over, the Sox, each player lost in his thoughts, filed slowly into the dressing room. Most just sat or stood silently as they looked off into space or down at the floor.

The phone rang in Williams's office. It was Bill Rigney calling to inquire about Tony. "Mr. Yawkey and I were talking before the game," Rigney told Williams, "and he said it would be a great race if nobody got hurt. Then this had to happen."

There was no retaliation against Hamilton, but there was a little something going on between the pitcher and Carl Yastrzemski. After the beaning Yaz made a gesture at Hamilton from the dugout, and he yelled some strong words to the mound. Hamilton looked in.

"All I know," Yaz said in the clubhouse, "is that the kid has a cracked head [because of Hamilton]."

Hamilton responded from the Angel clubhouse after the game: "He's got a nerve hollering [at me]. If he's such a great hitter, why doesn't he hit me? He's nothing-for-eight off me, and I'm a .500 pitcher."

When Yaz was advised of Hamilton's comments, he shot back with some angry, and unprintable, words.

And Tony himself? At first, of course, no press was allowed to see him, but he would say later: "I thought I was going to die. Death was constantly on my mind. The ball seemed to follow me in. I didn't freeze."

Another irony to the beaning was that Tony was hitting from the sixth spot in the order instead of his normal cleanup slot. He had been dropped because of a mild slump at the plate (one home run in three weeks). Williams thought that by dropping Tony down, some of the pressure to be productive would ease. His first time up against Hamilton in the game, Tony singled.

The first report from the hospital said Tony would "miss at least three weeks." But that was quickly revised, and doctors said that he'd most likely miss the rest of the season.

SATURDAY, AUGUST 19

Tony rested comfortably overnight at the hospital. This morning Tom Yawkey visited him. Jack Hamilton went to the hospital, too;

but he was denied admittance, as was the press. The team sent a fruit basket to help cheer Tony up; and cards, telegrams, and phone calls poured into Sancta Maria all day. Tony was reported wide awake, in good spirits, and was quoted as saying that he would watch today's nationally televised game on TV.

It was tough going out to play while knowing how seriously Tony had been injured, but — true to the spirit of this team — the Red Sox not only played, they played with heart and responded with a throbbing 12 – 11 win over the Angels. There were twenty-nine hits in the game (seventeen by Boston) and six home runs (four by the Angels) in the three-hour, thirty-five minute contest that saw twelve pitchers (six by each side).

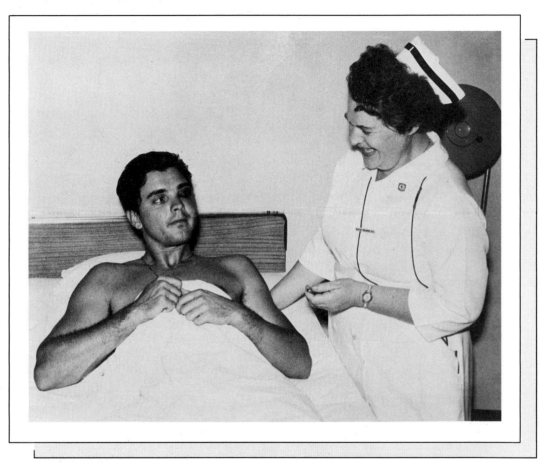

Tony Conigliaro endures the after-effects of his horrific beaning. (Photo courtesy Boston Red Sox)

Home runs by George Scott (his seventeenth; three hits on the day) and Carl Yastrzemski (his twenty-ninth; four hits on the day), plus Norm Siebern's bases-loaded pinch triple gave the Sox a seemingly safe 12 – 7 lead going into the ninth. Elston Howard and Reggie Smith chipped in with two hits. Darrell Brandon almost gave it all away, though, as he gave up four runs on home runs by Roger Repoz and Jimmie Hall and got only one out. Williams was angry over Brandon's performance, and he brought in Jerry Stephenson. Jerry got the second out, but then hit Rick Reichardt with a pitch. Moose Skowron followed with a single to right that sent Reichardt to third. Williams came out to the mound again. He was so desperate for the third out, he had Jim Lonborg warm up in the bullpen. But Dick played a hunch again and left Stephenson in the game. Bob Rodgers hit a chopper to Rico Petrocelli at short. It was a tough play and seemed off the bat like an infield hit, but Rico charged at full speed to get Rodgers by a half-step. It was a great play to end an exciting game.

Dan Osinski (3 – 1) got the win in relief over ex-Yankee Jim Coates (0 – 2).

ANGELS					RED SOX				
Name	ab	r	h	rbi		ab	r	h	rbi
Repoz, cf. . . .	3	2	1		Tartabull, rf. . .	3		1	
Fregosi, ss. . .	5	1	2	1	Wyatt, p.				
Hall, rf.	2	1	2	1	Howard, c. . . .	1			
Morton, rf.	2				Adair, 3b, 2b. .	4	2	2	2
Mincher, 1b. .	4	2	3	2	Yastrzemski, lf	2	1	1	3
Cardenal, pr. .					Scott, 1b. . . .	5		1	
Reichardt, lf. .	5		3	2	Smith, cf. . . .	5	1	1	1
Rodgers, c. . .	5	1	1		Andrews, 2b. .	4	1	2	
Knoop, 2b. . .	5	1	1		Petrocelli, ss. .	2			
Werhas, 3b. .	3				Landis, p. . . .				
Satriano, 3b. .	1				Foy, rf.	1	1	1	
Held, pr.					Ryan, c.	2	1		
McGlothlin, p.	2	1		1	Siebern, ph. .	1			
Hamilton, p. . .					Santiago, p. .				
Rojas, p.	1				Morehead, p. .				
Skowron, ph. .	1				Osinski, p. . .	1		1	
					Jones, 3b. . . .	2	2	2	2
					Thomas, rf. . .				
TOTALS	39	8	14	8	**TOTALS**	33	9	11	9

Team	1	2	3	4	5	6	7	8	9	
Calif.	0	6	0	2	0	0	0	0	0	8
Boston	0	0	0	1	3	4	0	1	X	9

Name	IP	H	R	ER	BB	SO
Calif.						
McGlothlin.	4⅔	6	4	4	2	4
Hamilton.	⅓	1	3	3	2	
Rojas (l).	3	4	2	2	2	3
Boston						
Morehead.	1⅔	5	6	6	2	2
Osinski.	2⅓	4	2	2	1	2
Landis.	2	1				2
Wyatt.	1	1				
Santiago (w).	2	3			1	2

"The Great Comeback" Sunday, August 20, 1967 Game 2

Some of the talk since two nights ago has it that Tony Conigliaro's injury (he's out for the year) was the Red Sox' death ticket, that a young team involved in a pennant race couldn't survive the loss of such a key player down the stretch. But this team apparently doesn't listen to such talk. Yesterday it was a wild 12 – 11 win. Today it was a 12 – 2, 9 – 8 sweep of the Angels that, owing mostly to the second game, defied description.

The sweep put the team just 1½ games out of first, as the Twins lost to the Yankees 7 – 2. The race looks like this:

Minnesota	67 – 52	.563	—
Chicago	66 – 52	.559	1/2
Boston	66 – 54	.550	1 1/2
Detroit	66 – 55	.545	2

The first game was a death march for the Angels. Presiding at the occasion was Lee Stange, who pitched a complete game and struck out ten. The Red Sox did it with the big inning as they got five in the first, one in the fifth, and six in the sixth.

Reggie Smith made history by becoming the first Boston player ever to hit home runs from both sides of the plate in the same game. He also became the first man *ever* to do it at Fenway. Yaz

added a starshot in the sixth as he hit one of the longest home runs of his career into the right field stands with a man on.

The most controversial play came oddly enough on the Angels' totally meaningless run in the eighth, which made it 12 – 2. It caused fury, not on the field, but later in the pressroom between games.

On the play Rick Reichardt hit a grounder to Mike Andrews at second; Mike booted it into left. Reichardt continued to second when the ball went to the outfield. Official scorer Cliff Keane of the *Boston Globe* ruled it a hit and an error, a hit because he said Reichardt would have beaten the throw to first and an error for allowing the extra base.

In the crowded pressroom after the game, Tom Yawkey confronted Keane about the call. An enraged Yawkey blasted Keane for scoring an error on the play and said it should have been ruled a double, but Keane stood his ground and the error held. The incident illustrates how tense things are in the Red Sox organization as the pressure mounts in the tight race.

In the second game, the unbelievable happened. The Angels seemed ready for revenge and stormed out to an 8 – 0 lead against Dave Morehead after 3 1/2 innings. Then it started to happen.

Reggie Smith makes Red Sox history on August 20 by homering from both sides of the plate. At right Reggie is greeted by George Scott (5), Elston Howard (18), and Carl Yastrzemski (8). Angel catcher Buck Rodgers looks on quietly. (Photos courtesy Boston Red Sox)

The Wave

When Yaz hit his home run in the second game to put the Red Sox back in the game, Nantasket Beach erupted. Nantasket is a beautiful, five-mile-long beach on the South Shore that, on Sundays in summer, is jammed with about one-hundred thousand people. Friends told me later that almost every party had a radio for the doubleheader. The broadcast could be heard running down five miles of coastline! When Yaz hit the home run, a roar went down the length of the beach. The sound wave was probably the biggest "wave" at the beach all year!

In the bottom of the fourth off All-Star Jim McGlothlin, Reggie Smith hit his third home run of the afternoon to make it 8 – 1. No one thought a thing about the run; but in the bottom of the fifth, Yaz hit his thirty-first with two on to make it 8 – 4. The crowd sensed the team might be onto something; and getting right back into the game, they reacted to each pitch. After Yaz's blast Rigney could be seen in the dugout pacing and fidgeting. He could see the foot descending on him, and the park was filled with Rigney's sense of inescapable doom. For Red Sox fans, the feeling was delightful.

The Sox were rolling now and were as unstoppable as a tidal wave. In the sixth, they tied it with four more. Some justice was served, for they did it in part against Jack Hamilton. The crowd was on Hamilton and so were the Red Sox. Foy led with a double. The rattled Hamilton then gave up two walks to load the bases. A resigned Rigney brought in Minnie Rojas, who hung a slider to Dalton Jones. Jones drove the ball off the center field wall to bring in two and up the score to 8 – 6. The crowd reacted like they were singing the "Hallelujah Chorus" on Christmas Day. There was more to come. Jose Tartabull hit a sacrifice fly to make it 8 – 7. Jerry "Do No Wrong" Adair then tied it with a single into left.

The game continued breathlessly into the eighth at 8 – 8. Jose Santiago held the Angels scoreless; and in the bottom of the inning, Adair came up. Jerry calmly administered the coup de grace by driving a ball from Rojas into the net in left. "I never thought it was going to make it," Adair said quietly. "I just let it fly out there, hoping it would hit the wall."

The crowd screamed ecstatically. Incredibly there was more excitement just ahead.

Rojas followed up on his gopher ball to Adair by plunking Yastrzemski in the elbow. With the Conigliaro beaning Friday night, this had the potential of a blowup. Buddy LeRoux and Williams ran out to see if Yaz was okay. He said he was and walked to first as he looked hard at Rojas, but Carl continued down the baseline and took first without a word. As Williams made his way back to the dugout, he looked down to first. When he got in the dugout, he yelled out something in the direction of first base. Williams wouldn't comment on what was said, but first base umpire Bill Valentine said this: "Williams was yelling at his player 'Cut somebody. Cut somebody open. When you go to second, go in spikes high, and you'd better cut somebody up.' I yelled at Williams to cut it out, and he came out of the dugout and ran to

Carl at first base. After he talked to Carl for a minute, he started back to the dugout. And then he spit on my shoes." Valentine then threw out the manager.

"I didn't spit on his shoes. I spit on the ground," Williams insisted.

Someone asked Yaz later if he thought Rojas was throwing at him: "No. I didn't think he was," Yaz answered. "Let me put it this way. Anybody who would fool around with a guy's career is crazy. They can be cut down at second base. Things like that."

Could there be an ounce of drama left in this delirious game? Yes — the Angel ninth.

With the 9 – 8 lead and Santiago on the mound, Don Mincher led off with a single and Reichardt doubled. The fans started squirming in their seats. Eddie Popowski, managing in place of the ejected Williams, brought the infield in. The move paid off when Bob Rodgers bounced to second, the runners holding. After Santiago fanned Bobby Knoop, the crowd felt better. But the Sox weren't out of it yet. Pop ordered an intentional walk to Tom Satriano to load the bases with Rojas due up. This forced Rigney to go to his bench, out of left-handed hitters. He had to bring up Moose Skowron against the right-handed Santiago. When Skowron was announced, Elston Howard went out to the mound. "Curve balls and keep them down," he told Santiago. Howard, after all, had played with Moose several years during the glory days of the Yankees. "He'll swing at the first pitch if it's even close," Howard said. He was right. Santiago came in with a low curve, and Skowron beat a ground ball to the shortstop hole. Adair went quickly to his right, back-handed the ball, and threw to Andrews at second for an extremely close force play, which ended the game.

They swept the Angels four straight and were six of seven on the important home stand. Sunday's game was one of the greatest comebacks in Red Sox history. The only game that old timers

Jose Santiago led the league in winning percentage with .750 on his 12–4 record. One of his wins was in the August 20 game against California, when the Sox erased an 8–0 deficit. (Photo courtesy Boston Red Sox)

could remember in which the team came from further back was on August 28, 1950, when they trailed Bob Lemon and the Cleveland Indians 10 – 0 and 11 – 1 and came back to win 15 – 14.

Another unusual aspect of the game was Joe Foy's playing an inning in right field. He looked kind of lost, but he handled his only chance without a problem. "I thought 'Uh oh, here I am out here and there goes the ball.' But after I caught it, I was all right. I was getting all kinds of instruction. Reggie moving me all over the place, and Andy [Andrews] telling me to back up, the wind was blowing out. I didn't know where I was at for a while."

Which is probably what Rigney and the Angels are thinking this very moment.

MONDAY, AUGUST 21

The Red Sox made it five in a row and seven of eight on the home stand against the Washington Senators tonight as they took a tight 6 – 5 decision. They continued their hero du jour mode; tonight it was Elston Howard's turn to shine, as the likable catcher singled home the winning run in the ninth before 26,018.

This was an up and down game. The Sox trailed 1 – 0, led 2 – 1, trailed 3 – 2, then led 5 – 3 until the Senators tied it in the eighth on Mike Epstein's two-run home run off John Wyatt. But in the ninth, Mr. Clutch, Jerry Adair, led off with a double. Yaz moved Adair to third with a ground out. George "Slim" Scott and Reggie Smith were purposely passed by Darold Knowles to get to Howard, who came in hitting at .194 and was 0 for 4 on the night. But the classy veteran had his moment as he singled to left center to score Adair. A contingent of players rushed the field to congratulate Howard, who was smiling and bouncing up and down like a rookie.

Carl Yastrzemski wore a helmet with an ear flap for the first time. The move comes after Tony Conigliaro's beaning and with pitchers working Yaz very tight.

In other news Kansas City A's owner Charlie Finley gave Ken Harrelson his unconditional release after the first baseman criticized Finley for causing disruption on the team. Harrelson said he received offers from six teams. He wouldn't identify them, but said that one of them was in the first division. There was talk about the Red Sox going after Harrelson, but the team — publicly, at least — remains cool to the idea: "We already have two good first basemen in George Scott and Norm Siebern," said publicist Bill Crowley. Rumors also abound that the Sox are seeking either Jim King of Cleveland or Jim Landis, who was just released by Detroit. They need extra help in the outfield with Conigliaro out. Incidentally, Tony officially went on the disabled list today.

TUESDAY, AUGUST 22

The fans are about ready to run the pennant up the flagpole, as the team continues to rock and roll its way nearer to first place. Tonight they swept the Senators and jumped to second place just one percentage point behind the White Sox. The Twins and Detroit are one game back.

In the opener comebacking Jerry Stephenson worked 7 2/3 strong innings and allowed just six hits while striking out five. The game was scoreless through six as Phil Ortega (winner of his last eight decisions) matched Stephenson pitch for pitch. But Dalton Jones lined a triple down the right field line with two on in the seventh, and the Red Sox led 2–0. In the eighth, the Senators got a run off the tiring Stephenson; but John Wyatt came on and got out of further trouble by fanning the dangerous Frank Howard to end the inning.

The top of the ninth started out disastrously for the Sox, but ended up miraculously. Wyatt loaded the bases on a single and two walks, and the end seemed near; but the next batter, Paul Casanova, hit a sharp grounder to Adair, who (what else?) was playing perfectly at second. Jerry fielded the ball cleanly and fired home to Elston Howard for the force at home. Howard then rifled the ball to George Scott at first for the double play. Bang, bang. The game ended with Wyatt blowing away Tim Cullen on strikes.

The thin jokes don't stop for Scott. In the fourth, he was called out for leaving third too soon on a tag up. Eddie Popowski argued vehemently and was thrown out. In the locker room after the game, Pop was still hot over the call: "Why," he asked rhetorically, "would anyone leave early on [Frank] Howard's [weak] arm?"

"Maybe Scotty thought he saw a banana split sitting on home plate," someone shot back, and everybody, including Scott, got a good laugh.

Name Game

There were two sets of two players who shared last names at different parts of 1967. Who were they?

Answer: Reggie Smith and infielder George Smith during the early part of spring training, and Bill Landis and Jim Landis following Tony Conigliaro's injury in August.

Between games a telegram arrived in the clubhouse. It read:

JUST LISTENED TO THE NINTH INNING OF YOUR FIRST GAME. CONGRATULATIONS ON A THRILLING WIN. BEST OF LUCK IN THE SECOND GAME AND FOR THE REST OF THE SEASON.

> YOUR FAN,
> TED KENNEDY
> U.S. SENATOR

The senator's good luck wish in the second game paid off, as Gary Bell, with help from Darrell Brandon, survived a shaky start to settle down to a 5 – 3 win. Bell gave up a pair of runs in the first inning, but didn't surrender the third until the seventh. In the sixth, Reggie Smith hit his sixth home run in his last ten games to make it a 2 – 1 game. The Sox tied it in the same inning on Adair's double (can he do anything wrong?) and Rico Petrocelli's single. In the seventh, trailing 3 – 2, Boston came up with a trio. Scott drilled a bases-loaded single to make it 4 – 3, and Yaz plated Smith for the fifth and final Boston run.

In the ninth inning and with the Sox in the field, a young man strolled from the stands and managed to shake hands with and hug six players before the blue coats could catch up with him. Who was this victim of terminal pennant fever? Duncan MacKenzie, twenty-five, of Dorchester. "I just lost control of my emotions. I love the Red Sox, and I'm proud of it." MacKenzie was hustled downtown on a charge of disturbing a public assembly, but he escaped a fine. Judge Elwood McKinney let him off with a lecture. The judge, you see, is also a big Sox fan.

Off the field they signed free agent outfielder Jim Landis. Jim will join the club tomorrow night. Williams said Landis would be the defensive member of the George Thomas–Jose Tartabull–Landis team that's trying to fill the shoes of Tony Conigliaro in right.

WEDNESDAY, AUGUST 23

The team was hoping to ride into a share of first place today; but in a classic case of counting chickens too soon, they overlooked their opposition, and the Senators took a 3 – 2 game before 33,680 at Fenway. The loss dropped Boston to a game out, as the White Sox beat the Yankees.

Country Clubbed

For many years before 1967, the Red Sox had the reputation of being a "country club"; but what really must be remembered about those seasons is the fact that the team wasn't very good. I think the constant losing in those years did a lot to develop that reputation.

When you're in a season where the team isn't going anywhere, I think players naturally dwell more on the things that are bothering them about their performance on the field and even on problems in their personal lives. They can seem to not care. You find a lot of nit-picking on such teams, players bickering about each other, that sort of thing.

But in '67, especially after the All-Star Game, everyone became so engrossed in the importance of each game that suddenly the games became fun. When a team is winning, that's when you hear things like "we are a team," "we are together," "we are family." You find players giving credit to each other. If a player has a bad day, but the team wins and moves closer to first place, the personal failure is easier to deal with.

Tony Conigliaro will be released from Sancta Maria Hospital tomorrow. His immediate plans include going on a vacation with his family.

THURSDAY, AUGUST 24

With Cardinal Cushing and 1,500 archdiocese nuns on hand, the Red Sox played like they had extra help from "up above" in the afternoon's heavenly 7 – 5 win over Washington. Boston, bless them, moved back to within a percentage point of first place, behind Chicago. Coincidentally the team embarks now to the Windy City for a crucial five-game set beginning tomorrow night.

Today the Sox did it with three long balls, all by newcomers: Jerry Adair, Jim Landis, and Elston Howard. Howard's three-run drive in the seventh (he also had a double) and Landis's solo shot in the eighth looked at the time like so much window dressing and

Also, as the season progressed, the team enjoyed what was for them unprecedented media attention, most of it favorable. What was to criticize, really, about a team like the Red Sox pulling off a miracle? We actually had to have a second bus to accommodate the overflow of press as the season went into August and September. Media types from all over the country were following the Red Sox — TV journalists, magazine writers, baseball writers from other cities, columnists.

In our own case, in the broadcasting booth, I arranged with our engineer, Al Walker, to cut away during our broadcasts to live broadcasts from other ball parks, for example, Ernie Harwell reporting from Detroit and Joe Garagiola reporting from New York.

Al set up the radio hookups to the other cities. In fact it was during one of these "check ins" to New York that Tom Yawkey called me from his private box at Fenway. His call was piped into the broadcasting booth. It was the only time that Mr. Yawkey ever called me while I was on the air. I was giving a report to Joe Garagiola in New York. I told him: "Joe, Elston Howard has just hit a home run in the screen for the Red Sox."

After the inning was over, there was a phone call in the booth. Al Walker answered it and told me, "It's Mr. Yawkey." I had no idea what he wanted. Mr. Yawkey got on and said: "Hey Kenny. Howard hit the ball *over* the screen." He wasn't being critical. He was just plain excited . . . so excited he had to share it with someone.

But getting back to the difference winning makes, it definitely affected the way we broadcast the games. One of our main sponsors in '67 was Narragansett Beer. Midway through the season, one of the company executives came up to me and told me he thought that my work on the air had picked up 100 percent over 1966.

On the surface of things, I was doing everything exactly the same in '66 that I was doing in '67. The only difference was that the club was playing so great and there were so many exciting things happening that I really got into it in a new way. The year before, we were out of it, nothing was at stake, there were a lot of one-sided games. But things were so exciting in '67, it made everyone just that much better.

---

gave the team a 7 – 2 lead. But they needed the runs as the pesky Nats roughed up Darrell Brandon in the ninth for three runs. It was a performance that didn't exactly set too well with Dick Williams, who was preparing a room in the doghouse for Brandon. He brought John Wyatt in with one out and the bases loaded. Wyatt got an out and needed only to get Ken McMullen to end the game. McMullen hit a fast ball to deep right. "When I hit it," McMullen said, "I thought it was good enough to go into the seats."

But some 1,500 prayers were offered up in the stands, and a gust of wind sprang up and caught the ball. Right fielder Landis did a tango under it: "I nearly lost it in the sun," Landis said. "The wind slowed it down and started to pull the ball away from me."

With all the runners circling the bases (three would have scored), Landis made a running, lunging, one-handed grab. The 31,283 fans (298,788 for the ten dates on the home stand) offered up a collective novena of joy because the Red Sox, on August 24, were in a virtual first place tie in the American League. Ex-mate Bill Monbouquette shut out Eddie Stanky's punchless White Sox 5 – 0.

The upcoming series in Chicago is the biggest for Boston since the last two games of the 1949 season in New York.

FRIDAY, AUGUST 25

A verbal battle preceded tonight's actual war. With all his braggadocio, Chicago manager Eddie Stanky sounded more like a man running scared: "Everybody's making a big to-do about how well Boston is doing . . . Boston . . . the City of Culture . . . that's a laugh! Well big deal."

The ever-quotable Stanky went on: "We don't belong in the same league with Boston, all those 'hairy chested' players and their 'new breed' manager . . . my boys are making a laughing stock of the American League. It embarrasses the other teams to pick up the paper and see the White Sox in first place. We'll probably wear out Lonborg with line drives . . . tonight, Lonborg probably won't last through four innings . . . The City of Culture is crying about Conigliaro's injury. Big deal. We've had injuries all season, but we aren't crying."

Carl Yastrzemski, who earlier this year got into a verbal joust with Stanky, wouldn't fall for the Brat's baiting: "I'm not going to let Stanky bother me," Yaz said.

There was also some other news before game time. The Red Sox announced they had acquired free agent Ken Harrelson. They reportedly paid Harrelson $75,000. He will report to the club Monday in New York. It was yet another of Haywood Sullivan's shrewd deals to strengthen the team.

Now to tonight's doubleheader. The "hairy chested" Bostonians slipped into first place by taking the opener 7 – 1 behind Lonborg, who won his seventeenth game and made Stanky eat his words by throwing a complete game. They relinquished the top spot in the nightcap by dropping a typically Chicagoan 2 – 1 win. The split left the teams tied for second, a half game behind Minnesota, who beat Cleveland today on a no-hitter by Dean Chance.

In game one the Red Sox gave Chicago a taste of its own medicine by punching out sixteen hits — fifteen of them singles. It was plenty for Lonborg, who had good stuff in going all the way for the first time since July 23. Jim allowed seven hits, walked no one, and struck out six. The game was over in the first, as the Sox scored three times after two were out on consecutive singles

The Brat

Eddie Stanky was certainly a controversial manager for Chicago. He did anything he could to get his players up. He'd also try to use every psychological edge he could think of. Sometimes it backfired on him, like when he called Yaz an All-Star from the neck down. Yaz went on from there to have some great games against the White Sox.

I saw Eddie play when he was with the Boston Braves. People used to say: "He can't hit, he can't run, he can't throw. All he can do is beat you." That's the kind of player he was. When he was a coach with the Indians in the early sixties, he never interfered with manager Mel McGaha. Eddie knew his place as a coach was in the background.

Off the field Eddie was and is a real gentleman.

by Yaz, Scott, Smith, Howard, and Petrocelli. They never looked back.

The second game was a tight one, with Lee Stange hooking up with rookie Cisco Carlos, who was making his major league debut. Chicago held a 1 – 0 lead until the eighth, when Boston tied it up when Smith singled to score Adair. But John Wyatt, who ironically had a blazing fast ball and great stuff, gave up a single to Ken Berry with two men on for the winning run. The hot-hitting Berry previously homered for his team's first run.

Petrocelli's base-running blunders killed the seventh. He was on second with one out. Dalton Jones looped a ball into short left, near the line. Eddie Popowski screamed from the third base coaching box for Rico to break and go home, but Petrocelli played it cautiously and got only to third. On the next play, Rico erred in the opposite way by running when he shouldn't have. Norm Siebern, batting for Stange, hit a check-swing roller in front of the plate. Rico hesitated from third, then unwisely decided to break for the plate, and was an easy out.

SATURDAY, AUGUST 26

For the first time in eighteen years, the Red Sox were in sole possession of first place this late in the year. Their 6 – 2 win over Chicago, coupled with Minnesota's 5 – 2 loss to Cleveland, put them on top. Just a game separates the first four teams:

Boston	72 – 56	.563	—
Minnesota	71 – 56	.559	1/2
Chicago	70 – 56	.556	1
Detroit	71 – 57	.555	1

The Sox chased Joel Horlen, Chicago's best pitcher, while Jerry Stephenson pitched five innings of no-hit ball before tiring in the sixth. Darrell Brandon came on and preserved the victory.

Boston took a lead with two in the third, one in the fourth, and two in the fifth. In the third, Jose Tartabull tripled and scored on Jerry Adair's single. Adair later scored on George "Twiggy" Scott's hit. Andrews's walk and Mike Ryan's triple made it 3 – 0 in the fourth, and they ran it to 5 – 0 the next inning on Reggie Smith's run-scoring single and Petrocelli's double. Their final run came in the seventh on Andrews's sacrifice fly.

The loss didn't quiet Stanky: "Except for the stupidity of the other manager, we would have lost three straight." The Brat claimed Williams managed too timidly in the second game on Friday night and cost his team a win. "I know why he did it. He was in first place for two hours, and he didn't know what to do. He wanted to play it safe. Well, we were in first place for two months. We didn't get there by playing safe."

Someone asked Stanky about his own questionable managing in today's game, when he sent Don Buford on an attempted steal of third with his team trailing 3 – 0 in the fourth (Buford was thrown out). Stanky stared icily at the questioner, then said: "There were 912 plays in that game, and you ask about one as if it meant the ball game."

He also got in the needle on Adair, who played for Stanky earlier in the year. Adair accused Stanky of ordering Tommy John to throw at him in the eighth inning, when John threw one behind Jerry. "John threw on orders from the dugout," Adair said.

When asked about it, Stanky took off his cap, placed it over his heart, and said in a tone of mock surprise: "Oh! Poor Jerry Adair, bless his heart. Is that what he said? How touching. Ask some of our pitchers how they liked him when he was here . . . but now you've ruined my evening. Tsk, tsk . . . poor Jerry Adair!"

In the Boston clubhouse, Dick Williams just smiled a Cheshire Cat smile when told of Stanky's comments. "Mr. Stanky is quite a manager," Williams said coyly. It was the cool and self-assured statement of a manager in first place.

"D.P. — Tartabull to Howard" Sunday, August 27, 1967 Game 1

This late in the season, with this close a pennant race, every day is life and death now. Each action and play — each is performed like a man defusing a bomb. For example, the first thing Carl Yastrzemski did when he got to the park was run up to the stands and check which way the wind was blowing. He studied the wind carefully for several minutes.

It was a friendly wind for Carl in the memorable first game of today's doubleheader. He ripped two long home runs in a pulsating 4 – 3 victory. But it was an outfield double play of a kind that no one could ever recall seeing before that ended the game and gave Boston what is now, and most likely will continue to be, its most memorable single play of the season. This play, in fact, has become one of the most memorable in Boston sports annals.

Yaz belted numbers thirty-three and thirty-four, and George Scott added a two-run single to build a 4 – 1 lead in the first game. But in the bottom of the seventh, the White Sox got a pair back, helped by Mike Andrews's error on what looked like a perfect double play ball. Things were still 4 – 3 when the White Sox came up for their last chance in the bottom of the ninth.

Ken Berry led off against Gary Bell with a double down the left field line. He was sacrificed to third by Ron Hansen, Scott to Andrews covering. With Duane Josephson announced as a pinch hitter and Bell tiring after 8 1/3 innings of baseball, Dick Williams went to relief ace John Wyatt.

On the first pitch to Josephson, Wyatt came in with a fast ball: "I threw as good a fast ball as I can," said Wyatt. "It was about knee high and on the outside of the plate. I think he was looking for some kind of breaking pitch. He was bending back from the plate and he just barely got the bat on it."

The swing sent a line drive to medium right field. Jose Tartabull ran in fast and one-handed the ball. Berry tagged up on Tartabull's weak throwing arm. So here was the race — Eddie Stanky's best runner against Dick Williams's weakest outfield arm. Berry broke, and Tartabull let go with everything he had. The ball came in surprisingly hard, but it had a bit too much arc and was much too high. There didn't seem to be any chance of

Jose Tartabull made the *throw. (Photo courtesy Boston Red Sox)*

getting the swift Berry.

Then Elston Howard made the play of the year. Howard jumped up for the ball, and Berry started his slide. Howard didn't have enough time to catch the ball two-handed, then come down with the tag. The amazing thing was that he somehow knew this with his back to the play. Maybe it was radar or instinct or luck, but Ellie made a play that no one — not even venerable Al Lopez, who was on hand — could remember seeing a catcher make. He came down and with his left foot (size 12B) caught Berry's left spike maybe one inch from the plate. He then deflected Berry's foot to the side of the plate. But that was just the first part of the problem of how to keep Berry from touching the plate; Howard still had to make the tag. When Berry realized he was blocked off the plate, he tried to reach it with his hand, but Howard's glove was there first. How? Ellie caught Tartabull's throw one-handed and in one motion swept down in a perfectly calculated descending arc to make the tag.

"When I had to jump for the ball," Howard explained, "I wasn't thinking of blocking the plate. I was just trying to get the ball down quick. But his foot came into the tip of my shoe, and it kept it from getting in, and that was it," the final out of the game. Umpire Marty Springstead was tight on the plate with a perfect view, and he didn't hesitate in making the out call on the extremely close play.

"It was a real gutsy call," Yaz said.

And what about the throw home? Here's what Tartabull said: "The line drive went deep into my web. I had trouble getting the ball out. I threw it all the way as hard as I could. I didn't worry about making a bad throw. I wanted to get it down, but she took off and . . . zip!" Jose then made the sign of a jet taking off. It was the only runner Tartabull threw out all year.

When Springstead made the out call, Stanky tore out of the dugout like a madman. He practically climbed into Springstead's shirt. But the second year ump stood his ground, and the play held. TV replays clearly showed that Springstead had made the right call. Stanky was frothing in the clubhouse as well. He pointed to a picture in today's paper that showed several Boston players holding up a big "No. 1" to signify first place: "We're in first place sixty-three blanking days, and you don't see one blanking picture like that," he growled. "They're up there overnight, and there's the picture."

RED SOX					WHITE SOX				
Name	ab	r	h	rbi		ab	r	h	rbi
Tartabull, rf. . .	5				Buford, 3b. . .	4	1	1	1
Adair, 3b. . . .	4	1	1		Causey, 3b. . .	4	1		
Yastrzemski, lf	3	2	2	2	Ward, lf.	3	2	1	
Scott, 1b. . . .	3	1	2		Agee, rf.				
Smith, cf. . . .	4				Boyer, 1b. . . .	4			
Howard, c. . . .	4	1			Martin, c. . . .	4	1	1	
Petrocelli, ss.	3				Colavito, rf. . .	4	1	1	
Andrews, 2b. .	4	1	2		Berry, cf.	4		1	
Bell, p.	4				Hansen, ss. . .	2			
Wyatt, p.					Alomar, ss. . .				
					Klages, p. . . .	1			
					Williams, ph. .	1			
					Locker, p. . . .				
					Burgess, ph. .	1			
					Wilhelm, p. . .				
					Josephson, ph	1			
TOTALS	34	4	7	4	**TOTALS**	33	3	7	2

Team	1	2	3	4	5	6	7	8	9	
Boston	0	0	2	0	1	0	1	0	0	4
Chicago	1	0	0	0	0	0	2	0	0	3

Name	IP	H	R	ER	BB	SO
Boston						
Bell (w).	8⅓	7	3	1	2	4
Wyatt.	⅔					
Chicago						
Klages (l).	5	6	3	3	2	2
Locker.	2	1	1	1		1
Wilhelm.	2					

Darrell Brandon, 1986. (Photo courtesy Dan Valenti)

But back to The Play.

"One other thing," Adair pointed out, "is that the grass is so high out there and the ground so soft that Berry couldn't get good footing to start rolling. The place is like a swamp so the ball won't get to the infielder and their little speed guys will beat out some hits. In this case it really backfired and Berry never really got rolling. That hurt them."

In a subplot to the game, a number of Boston batters were brushed back or knocked down. The most obvious one was in the fifth, after Yaz had hit the first of his two home runs. George Scott came up against White Sox starter Fred Klages, and Klages nailed Scotty on the arm. Just about everybody felt the pitch came on orders from Stanky. Scott was angry. "That bush so and

Retrospective: Darrell Brandon Looks Back

On Dick Williams:

"Dick Williams was a take-charge manager. The team at the time needed someone like that. He was exactly the right man for our situation. Dick made the difference between us being a .500 club that year and being a pennant winner. We had some real talent on that club, with Yaz, Tony C., George Scott, Jim Lonborg, Rico Petrocelli, and the like. I think Dick realized how good we could be before the players actually did. He knew it in spring training, that he had some good ball players.

"You hear a lot about his doghouse, and believe me, he had one. If you were going good, Dick was great to play for. But if you were not going well, he wouldn't speak to you for two or three weeks. That was hard to understand and accept. He'd totally ignore you. He'd walk right past you and not say anything. It worked for some players, and for some it didn't. But look at what we did. The record proves we won, so you'd have to say it worked.

"Usually on a team, you have two or three players who are always griping, and they can destroy the whole team, getting guys talking about each other. But there was never any of that I can remember in 1967. We were a *team*. Guys lived for one another and pulled for one another."

On the beaning of Tony Conigliaro:

"I was out in the bullpen. It was a scary feeling. I didn't realize he was hurt as bad as he was, though I knew it was serious. Unfortunately Jack Hamilton threw him a spitball that ran in on Tony. I played with Jack Hamilton later, and he admitted he threw a spitball that got away from him. Jack said he wasn't throwing at Tony, but a spitter is a dangerous pitch."

so. He's bush and will always be bush. I looked over at Stanky and he was yelling at his pitcher [when I came up] and was pointing to me . . . he's a bush leaguer."

"And George is right," said Golden Foot himself, Elston Howard. "I've never hated many people in this game, but I don't want any part of that runt, and you can quote me on that, too."

"I have an idea of what Stanky is up to," Williams chipped in. "He wants to hit our guys so we'll hit theirs to give him some kind of offense. That's the only way he'll get anybody on base, the way his men are swinging the bat."

After all this there was a second game to be played. Jose Santiago pitched 9 2/3 innings of shutout ball, but it wasn't enough as the Sox dropped a 1–0 heartbreaker in eleven. Chicago scored their run with a typical rally — four walks and a bunt. The granter of such largess was Darrell Brandon, whose wildness didn't improve his stock with Williams. The Red Sox could manage only four hits (two by George Thomas) off Gary Peters, who pitched all eleven innings.

There were a couple of injuries in the game. Santiago had to leave in the tenth after colliding with Mike Ryan and hurting his right shoulder while trying to field a bunt. Thomas hurt his hand sliding into a base and had to leave for x-rays. Both injuries were minor.

So despite two tough losses, the Red Sox did what they wanted to do in this series: win three. They go into Yankee Stadium now just one percentage point out of first.

MONDAY, AUGUST 28

It was Carl Yastrzemski night at Yankee Stadium, and more than 100 relatives and friends came in for the game from the east tip of Long Island. The fans presented Carl with a cream-colored Chrysler with Massachusetts plates that read "YAZ-8." Yaz gave most of his other gifts, which amounted to $10,000, to the Jimmy Fund.

Yaz was trying to hit one out, but he had to settle for three walks and a sacrifice fly as the Sox, behind Dave Morehead and Sparky Lyle, blanked the Yankees 3 – 0. The win keeps them .001 behind first-place Minnesota.

Elston Howard made his Yankee Stadium debut in road grays and drove in a run with a single. Reggie Smith kept up his power hitting with his thirteenth home run, twenty rows up into the right field bleachers.

Morehead (4 – 2) was strong through five; but in the sixth, he aggravated a blister on his pitching hand and had to leave. Williams brought in Lyle, who did the job the rest of the way.

Comings and goings. The team released Jim Landis today. His six-day stay with the team will be just a footnote to this season, but he did help out with his home run against the Senators and with his catch to end the game at Fenway on Nun's Day.

"I'm released and I get thirty days' severance pay from the Red Sox. That's all I know," Landis said. The move made room for Ken Harrelson, who reported to the ball club before the game and was promptly mobbed by the press. In the locker room after the game, Gary Bell yelled over to him: "You brought the good-looks rating of the clubhouse down, Hawk."

What made getting Hawk all the sweeter is that the Red Sox beat out Chicago for his services, and it wasn't money that made Harrelson decide for Boston. Hawk said the White Sox offered him $100,000, Boston, $80,000. But he came to New England for several reasons, he said, among them cozy Fenway, the fact that his wife is from Arlington, the team's youth, and the down-to-earth manner of Tom Yawkey.

Ken "the Hawk" Harrelson: free as a bird. (Photo courtesy Boston Red Sox)

TUESDAY, AUGUST 29

The rash of doubleheaders continued tonight against the Yankees. After the dust had settled on this long, long night of baseball, the Sox played twenty-nine innings, split two one run decisions, and found themselves in first place, one-half game ahead of the Twins.

In the opener Jim Lonborg won his eighteenth with a three-hit, eleven strikeout dandy. Jim dueled Mel Stottlemyre in the 2 – 1 game.

This was a tense 1 – 0 game through six. In the seventh, Reggie Smith used his speed to steal a run. He beat out an infield hit, stole second, and raced home on Lonborg's single. The Yankees got the run back in the bottom of the seventh, but that was it for the scoring as Lonborg walked off with a well-earned win. Jim didn't come close to walking a batter. "I had the best control of my life . . . I felt anytime Howard put up a target, I could hit it," he said.

As Lonborg was talking to reporters, George Scott chanted playfully in the background: "Here's the headlines back in Boston: 'LONBORG WINS OWN BALL GAME: GOOD HITTING, GOOD PITCHING, TAKES OWN CONTEST.' "

The second game took six hours and fifteen minutes to play and ended at 1:57 A.M. on Horace Clarke's single off Jose Santiago. The Red Sox looked like they had it won in the top of the eleventh, when they scored to take a 3 – 2 lead. But with two outs and two strikes on Steve Whitaker in the bottom of the inning, Sparky Lyle was squeezed. He came in with a nasty curve that looked like it was over the plate. Whitaker froze, took it, and looked back at home plate ump Ed Runge, who called it a ball. Lyle couldn't believe it; neither could the Boston bench. On the next pitch, Whitaker tied the game with a home run.

Police Are People, Too

Sox fan Tom Rodgers was running a bar in North Plymouth. On August 29 they listened to the entire twenty-inning second game against the Yankees in that bar. Rodgers was supposed to close at 2 A.M.; but the place was packed with fans listening to the game on radio, and they wouldn't let Tom shut down the bar. Finally the police came in to get everyone out, but they too wound up sitting there and listening to the rest of the game.

The Red Sox used twenty-one players, including eight pitchers. Yaz kept the game going in the fifteenth when he made a great sliding catch with a runner on second. The Sox loaded the bases in the top of the twentieth, but couldn't score.

Reggie Smith added three steals, giving him five in the doubleheader. Ken Harrelson made his Boston debut and hit a home run in four trips.

The team was dead tired after the game. "I feel like I might die now," said Rico Petrocelli as he sat numbly in front of his locker. "I might evaporate away." "I've never felt so tired in all my life," said Yaz.

Dick Williams was tired, too, but not too tired that he couldn't get mad at George Scott, who missed a hit-and-run signal in the fifteenth inning.

WEDNESDAY, AUGUST 30

Yaz was tired from last night. He showed up about an hour before game time and took a long treatment for his aching arms and legs from Buddy LeRoux in the trainer's room. He got to the bench, and Williams saw him.

"How do you feel?" the skipper asked.

"I can play a little defense and pinch-hit," Yaz replied.

"Well sit down and rest," the manager told him.

So with lefty Al Downing on the mound for New York, George Thomas took over in left. Once more the Red Sox and Yankees hooked up in a nail-biter. Through seven, Jerry Stephenson and Downing each gave up a run. By that time Yaz, pacing in the dugout, was eager to get in. When the Yankees came up in the eighth, he could take it no longer and told Williams he wanted in; and so he went out to play left.

In the ninth, he got on at bat; but, popping up, he looked terrible against Downing. The out extended the tired outfielder's hitless string to 0 for 18, one of the worst slumps of his career.

"I went out to the outfield after popping up," Carl said, "and I said [to myself] that no matter what, if I had another chance to hit, I would go for the long ball. I had the whole series. Why change now? It was the first series that I can remember when I thought of nothing but home runs. And finally I had another chance in the eleventh. I remembered that Downing had challenged me with a fast ball. I knew he would again. So there it was, and I whacked it out of the ball park."

The ball landed deep in the seats of right center. It was Yaz's thirty-fifth of the year and gave the Red Sox and John Wyatt a 2 – 1 win. It also left the team with a 6 – 3 road trip record. They will go home to Fenway in first place by 1 1/2 games.

Now Eddie "Brat" Stanky and cohorts come in to play on Boston's turf. Someone asked Williams if he would have his pitchers throw at White Sox hitters. Williams said no, he wouldn't. That later prompted a comment by Baltimore superscout Frank Lane: "Stanky was smart trying to agitate the Red Sox, but Williams was smarter not falling for it."

Which is about what Williams said: "He likes to agitate; but we didn't fall for it in Chicago, and we won't fall for it at Fenway."

THURSDAY, AUGUST 31

It was all in order, the perfect setup: Eddie Stanky was in town, the Red Sox were in first place, and 35,138 jammed the stands. Everything was in order . . . except the game and outcome, which went to the Pale Hose 4 – 2.

End-of-the-month Stats: 8/31/67

American League Standings
August 31, 1967

Team	W–L	PCT.	GB
BOSTON	76–59	.563	–
Minnesota	74–58	.561	½
Detroit	74–59	.556	1
Chicago	73–59	.553	1½
California	66–65	.504	8
Washington	64–70	.478	11½
Cleveland	63–71	.470	12½
Baltimore	59–71	.454	14½
New York	59–75	.440	16½
Kansas City	55–76	.420	19

Team Batting

Name	AB	R	H	HR	RBI	AVG.
Osinski	9		3		1	.333
Stephenson	9		3			.333
Yastrzemski	483	88	149	35	95	.308
Scott	467	64	142	17	68	.304
Conigliaro	349	59	101	20	67	.289
Adair	326	36	86	3	31	.264
Petrocelli	396	43	104	13	53	.263
Harrelson	266	34	70	10	42	.263
Smith	458	64	120	13	53	.262
Jones	110	13	28	2	15	.255
Andrews	421	67	105	7	33	.249
Foy	427	64	106	17	48	.248
Tartabull	206	22	47		8	.228
Thomas	78	9	17	1	6	.218
Ryan	204	19	43	2	23	.211
Brandon	42	3	8		1	.190
Howard	270	21	51	4	24	.189
Siebern	91	9	17		11	.187
Santiago	27	2	5	1	3	.185
Bell	61	5	8		2	.131
Lonborg	78	4	9		6	.115
Wyatt	11		1			.083
Stange	41	2	2		1	.049
Morehead	7					.000
B. Landis	2	1				.000

Team Pitching

Name	IP	H	BB	SO	W	L	ERA
Stephenson	23	14	8	14	2	0	1.57
Lyle	34	27	10	35	1	2	1.85
Osinski	57.2	54	13	36	3	1	2.37
Wyatt	79.2	57	33	62	8	6	2.39
Stange	150.2	133	25	83	8	8	2.64
Lonborg	218.1	178	64	194	18	6	3.26
Bell	191	162	59	122	10	11	3.30
Santiago	110.1	109	34	83	7	4	3.85
Landis	33.1	22	11	21	1	0	4.09
Brandon	147	137	59	88	5	11	4.16
Morehead	33.1	31	13	28	4	2	4.36

Leaders

Batting
(minimum of 300 at-bats)

Name and Team	At-Bats Avg.
F. Robinson, Balt.	.331
Yastrzemski, Bos.	.308
Scott, Bos.	.304
Carew, Minn.	.299
Kaline, Det.	.299
T. Horton, Cleve.	.297
Blair, Balt.	.292
W. Horton, Det.	.292
Fregosi, Calif.	.289
Conigliaro, Bos.	.287

Home Runs

Name and Team	#
Yastrzemski, Bos	35
Killebrew, Minn.	34
F. Howard, Wash.	31
F. Robinson, Balt.	26
Kaline, Det.	22

Runs Batted In

Name and Team	#
Yastrzemski, Bos.	95
Killebrew, Minn.	90
F. Robinson, Balt.	78
F. Howard, Wash.	75
Blefary, Balt.	70

Pitching
(minimum of 12 decisions)

Player and Team	Record	Pct.
Lonborg, Bos.	18-6	.750
Merritt, Minn.	10-4	.714
Horlen, Chi.	14-6	.700
McGlothlin, Cal.	11-5	.688
Peters, Chi.	15-7	.682

8 September and October

Lasting thirty pulsating days, September's song was the number one tune on New England's hit parade and a melody that had the entire region — and a good portion of the country — on pleasant edge. The Red Sox began the month in first place and, for the next four weeks, slipped in and out of the top spot like someone falling in and out of love. Incredibly they never trailed the leader by more than one game for the entire month (ten times they were a half game out, four times a game out). They were excitingly uneven. After winning on the first behind the bat of newcomer Ken Harrelson, the Sox lost three in a row, then won seven of the next eight, only to lose three in a row again. From September 18 to September 24, they came back (once more) to take six of eight.

Then came perhaps the lowest point of the year — two losses to Cleveland at home during the last week of the season. One loss was bad enough. By rights the second defeat (a 6 – 0 humiliation, with ace Jim Lonborg on the mound at that) should have killed them. But they wouldn't die, and miracles do happen. The other contenders were also losing. And the raw golden syrup of this fine season boiled itself down into the hard amber reality of the last two games against Minnesota. Trailing the tough Twins by one, Boston needed both games to take the flag. September's song ended on the thirtieth with a euphonious 6 – 4 win that put them into a flat tie and set up October's ravishing encore.

In the one-game season for everything, Lonborg, Yaz, and company met the challenge with a rousing 5 – 3 win. Later, when the Angels beat Detroit in the second game of the doubleheader in Motown, Boston had the pennant. The Impossible Dream came true.

All that followed, including the World Series against St. Louis, was a bonus, even a footnote. Yaz and Lonborg lived up to their star billing, as did Cardinal flamethrower Bob Gibson. The Sox took the heavily favored Cardinals to seven games to give us the end of a season that, for its innocence, can never happen again.

But once was enough . . . wasn't it?

FRIDAY, SEPTEMBER 1

The newest Red Sox player, Ken Harrelson, showed why he might have a home in Boston. Before a standing room crowd of 34,054, Hawk thrilled and drilled. His home run, triple, and double led the way as the Sox dumped the White Sox 10 – 2. The win kept Boston a half game ahead of the Twins, who beat Detroit 5 – 4. The Tigers fell to 2 out, while Chicago dropped to 2 1/2 off the pace.

Hawk, who's proving immensely popular with the Fenwayites, tripled in the first, homered in the fourth, and doubled in the seventh. He was hoping for another at bat and a chance for the cycle, but he didn't get it, as Hoyt Wilhelm set down the side in order in the eighth to leave Harrelson three batters shy. Ken had his strategy in order just in case he came up again. He was going to stop at first on any hit, no matter where it landed. "If I got up in the last inning," he said, "I was gonna stop at first no matter how far I hit the ball."

And he had permission to do it from Dick Williams, who indicated that he gave his okay given the one-sided score. But Hawk never got his chance at a 420-foot single.

His outburst at the plate, he said, was the result of an extra half hour of batting practice taken before the game from the offerings of Bobby Doerr and Dalton Jones. He also took fifteen minutes of extra practice handling fly balls in right. Ken's a natural first baseman, and it's obvious he's no Roberto Clemente in right, but he's gaining some confidence: "For the first time, I was hoping they'd hit the ball to me [in tonight's game]. The other day I was scared to death out there."

The crowd's growing affection for the Hawk is obvious. For example, after each hit today, the fans behind the right field bullpen gave him a standing ovation. "I've always had some fun with the people here," Hawk acknowledged.

His big day at the plate made a winner of Jose Santiago, who went all the way in upping his record to 8 – 4. Santiago and Harrelson aren't exactly strangers. They've been teammates on the same team in the minors and majors for five seasons.

Eddie Stanky kept a low profile all night. Maybe the Sox offensive explosion had something to do with it — they got four in the first and three in the second off the usually tough Gary Peters. After the Red Sox had made it 10 – 0 in the seventh, the fans really got on Stanky by chanting "Stanky is a bum."

"We got our brains beat out," The Brat said after the game. Referring to the fans, he had this to say: "It looked to me that in about the third or fourth inning, all those wonderful fans decided to go to the concession stands and make a night of it. And then the kooks took over."

SATURDAY, SEPTEMBER 2

After four nights in first place, the Red Sox dropped to the now disappointing climes of second place. Imagine, in spring training, being concerned about second place! After today's 4 – 1 loss to Chicago, the team is number two . . . maybe they will start trying harder.

The White Sox put this one away early by scoring three in the top of the first with two out off Jim Lonborg.

After the game the Red Sox announced that eighteen-year-old Ken Brett would be called up from Pittsfield and would join the club on Tuesday. Russ Gibson also will return from the same club. Gibson's return will give Dick Williams more flexibility in pinch-hitting Dalton Jones and Norm Siebern for Elston Howard and Mike Ryan, who are batting .188 and .210, respectively.

SUNDAY, SEPTEMBER 3

Once again the White Sox' fine pitching did the trick. Today it was lefty Tommy John's turn, and he shut out Boston's lumbermen 4 – 0. The loss, coupled with the Tigers' 5 – 0 win over the Twins, further tightened the pulsating American League pennant race.

The Twins are now in first, 1/2 game ahead of the Red Sox, followed by Chicago 1 game out and the Tigers at 1 1/2 games behind.

The team left immediately after the game for Washington . . . all except for Carl Yastrzemski, who's fighting a slump and stayed behind for extra batting practice at Fenway. He'll catch a later flight to D.C.

On the flight to Washington, Dick Williams was sitting in his seat and holding a piece of paper in his hand. He was laughing. He then shared a letter sent to him from Japan by Dr. Strangeglove himself, Dick Stuart, Williams's roommate when the two played for the Red Sox in '63 and '64. Stuart wrote, in part: "I see in the papers that come here once in a while to Japan that Yaz has a chance to lead the league in all three departments. I led the league once in all three, too, (a) most errors (b) most strikeouts and (c) best quotes in the press."

Stonefingers said he was hitting .290 for one of the Japanese teams and had twenty-eight home runs. He said nothing about his fielding.

MONDAY, SEPTEMBER 4

Lose one, win one. That was the story of today's Labor Day doubleheader in the nation's capital. In doing so the Sox kept pace with the Twins, who also split against the Indians.

After the Sox dropped their third straight game (and fourth in the last five) 5 – 2 against Camilo Pascual, Dick Williams — true to form — cleaned house and made a half dozen lineup changes. After posting the lineup card on the dugout wall before the second game, he announced in a loud voice: "Better check the lineup, men."

Players scrambled to see who was in and who was out. Changes included Jose Tartabull in right to replace Ken Harrelson, Jerry Adair going to third in place of Joe Foy, and Norm Siebern spelling the Boomer at first. The benched players said nothing; but when George Scott saw Siebern listed at first, he mumbled to himself, took a few chunks of ice from his soft drink cup, and whipped them the length of the dugout. He then lifted a bat bag, rattled it, and made a lot of noise. Williams ignored it.

In the past Scott has hit well after coming back from a chastisement at the hands of the manager. In the second game, Williams sent up Scott as a pinch hitter for Siebern in the ninth, and Scotty doubled. It was Scott's first extra-base hit in seventy-four at bats.

Since his last one in late August, he's had a Tartabullian string of twenty-one consecutive singles . . . not the kind of muscle you want out of the cleanup spot.

As they have so often this year, Williams's moves paid off, this time with a 6 – 4 victory. Jerry Stephenson hung in for five innings to get the win. Sparky Lyle (three innings, three strikeouts) and John Wyatt (a scoreless ninth) made the lead stand.

TUESDAY, SEPTEMBER 5

One for the money, two for the show. That was all Yaz needed to get ready and go, man, go. His two home runs — numbers thirty-seven and thirty-eight in the fourth and seventh — lifted the team to an easy 8 – 2 triumph over the Senators. The irony of Carl's performance was that he wasn't supposed to play. Dick Williams wanted to give him the night off so that, coupled with tomorrow's off day, Yaz could have two consecutive days of rest; but Yaz talked Williams out of it.

After Yaz won the Great Debate, Gary Bell went out and put an end to any discussion with Washington by shutting them out for eight innings before giving up two totally meaningless runs in the ninth. The win ran Bell's record to 11 – 11, but 10 – 6 since coming to Boston.

Gerry Moses was brought up from Pittsfield and was in uniform for tonight's game. The young catcher was originally supposed to join the team Thursday, but he got fidgety and was allowed to report immediately.

WEDNESDAY, SEPTEMBER 6

Team members gave Fenway a wide berth today, their first day off since August 14. It was a day pleasantly free of baseball and the pressures of the race.

Meanwhile, at Sancta Maria Hospital in Cambridge, Dr. I. Francis Gregory examined Tony Conigliaro's left eye and said somewhat ominously: "The hemorrhaging has cleared up, but we're concerned with the inner eye, now."

In the eye test, Tony's right eye registered an unusually good 20/10; but his left eye tested at 20/100.

Tony will be examined again tomorrow at the Massachusetts Eye and Ear Infirmary's Retina Clinic. After the results of that exam are in, doctors will decide on Tony's fate. There seem to be three possibilities: (1) he can come back later this year, (2) he needs further rest, or (3) he needs surgery.

"I was hoping I could start batting this weekend. Now I find out I have to go to another clinic," said a dejected Conigliaro. "My life has been spent in clinics since I started baseball. It's a hard game. Probably I should have played football."

In other off-the-field news, the office of baseball commissioner William D. Eckert gave the Red Sox permission to print World Series tickets . . . just in case. Prices fell out this way: box seats, $12; reserve grandstand, $8; standing room, $6; bleachers, $2.

THURSDAY, SEPTEMBER 7

It has finally sunk into everyone as a hard reality and not as some fanciful possibility: each game might literally mean the season. Everyone knows it, and everyone's wondering — in public or otherwise — how this young team will hold up under Pressure, capital P. Tonight, at any rate, they showed how as Jim Lonborg won his nineteenth, a dazzling three-hitter. The 3 – 1 triumph at Fenway versus the Yankees moved the Red Sox into second place .001 percentage points behind Minnesota, who topped Baltimore 4 – 2.

Lonborg fanned ten to run his league-leading total to 210. Jim is now 7 – 3 at home. How come he has just seven home wins versus twelve on the road? "That's a matter of coincidence. First off, I haven't pitched here that much. Besides, I don't know what park I'm pitching in. When I'm out there, it's like I'm in a closet, between me and the catcher." The team hopes he never comes out of that closet.

Rico Petrocelli backed up Lonborg by equaling the entire Yankee hit total with three (good for two RBIs). One of the hits was his fourteenth home run. Lonborg drove in a run with a ground rule double. Jim has been getting in a little extra batting practice, and he's been chipping in some hits. He's also working on bunting for base hits. The Yankee run came on Tom Tresh's home run in the seventh.

There was a funny play in the bottom of the sixth. George Scott opened with a single. Reggie Smith then drove a ball deep to right center. Scott, thinking it would fall in for a hit, barreled around all the way to third; but Yankee right fielder Steve Whitaker made the catch. Scott ran back to retag, but — inexplicably — stopped at second. He was easily doubled at first. When asked why he stopped at second, George explained that he had no chance of beating a throw to first, so he decided to stop at second and play possum so the Yankees might think he belonged there. That's what they mean by the old college try.

Tony Conigliaro had a further eye exam by a new doctor, Dr. Charles Regan of Wellesley. He reported that Tony's left eye was still swollen, which he termed "disturbing."

FRIDAY, SEPTEMBER 8

The Yankees came into tonight's game in ninth place, sixteen games below .500. On the mound they had old friend Bill Monbouquette, an early castoff from Detroit. It's the kind of game that pennant contenders simply shouldn't lose down the stretch, but it didn't work out that way. Monbouquette, who won ninety-one games in a Boston uniform after starring at Medford High School, tamed the Red Sox for 6 1/3 innings to post a 5 – 2 win. The loss dropped the Sox to third place, a half game behind Detroit and Minnesota, who are tied for first. The White Sox are in fourth, one game out.

SATURDAY, SEPTEMBER 9

Jerry Stephenson came up with a stomach problem at the last minute, and Dave Morehead became the emergency starter by default. In a big spot on little notice, Morehead did as so many of the unexpecteds have done this year: he came through. The Yankees put together two doubles in the first inning to take the lead; but between then and the eighth, Dave allowed just one hit. By that time the Red Sox had built up a 6 – 1 lead on thirteen hits, including Carl Yastrzemski's thirty-ninth home run and Rico Petrocelli's fifteenth. Andrews, Adair, Scott, and Smith chipped in with two hits each.

In the eighth, Morehead tired and loaded the bases with no outs. Dick Williams once more pushed the right button by bringing in Sparky Lyle, who fanned Jake Gibbs and got dangerous Tom Tresh to hit into a double play.

Stephenson and Elston Howard were both felled by the same stomach virus.

SUNDAY, SEPTEMBER 10

Dick Williams started his new job as manager of the Red Sox by brashly declaring his team would win more than it would lose. This promise brought some snickers, but no one's snickering now as today's 9−1 romp over the Yankees at Fenway assured the prophecy of its fulfillment. The victory was number eighty-two, so the club could lose every game from now to October 1 and end up 82−80.

The win, which pushed the Sox into second place, a half game behind the Twins, offered fans a nice blend of heavy hitting (nine runs, thirteen hits, a homer by Hawk Harrelson) and outstanding pitching (a complete four-hit, seven-strikeout game by Gary Bell). Bell ran his record to 12−11, 11−6 since coming to Boston. He showed his craftiness. His fast ball wasn't working, and he relied mostly on his curve and used the fast ball only as a setup pitch.

The game's big blow came in the bottom of the sixth. With the score 4−1, the Red Sox loaded the bases with light-hitting Mike Ryan due up. There were some cries from the grandstand managers for a pinch hitter, but Williams let Ryan hit for himself. Hit he did, smashing a bases-clearing triple into the left field corner.

MONDAY, SEPTEMBER 11

The team enjoyed another day off today. They resume the home stand Tuesday against Kansas City. No one was at the park . . . well almost no one. Against a green sea of thousands of empty seats, a solitary figure stood at home plate for the first time since August 18. Tony Conigliaro, needing to intuitively *know* if he could pick up a pitched ball well enough to hit, was taking batting practice. By workout's end Tony, walking slowly to the clubhouse, said to no one and to everyone: "Not good. Not good at all."

Tony began by taking twelve swings against his brother Billy, a Red Sox farmhand. He didn't hit any with authority. He then moved to the outfield to shag for his brother and catcher Don January, another Red Sox farmhand. He had enough of shagging. Tony ran in. "Now," he said to Billy, "get out there and throw hard."

This time Tony reached the wall with several balls. "It was better, but I know I'm not ready . . . I've never felt stronger. There's no pain. I've had no dizzy spells." He paused as if trying to find words for something too hard to say. "But the blur stays with me." Tony explained that he could see the ball, but he couldn't tell where it was, that is, how close it was to him.

TUESDAY, SEPTEMBER 12

It was a most satisfying night. Jim Lonborg got his twentieth win (the first Red Sox pitcher to do so since Bill Monbouquette in 1963). More importantly the 3−1 win over Kansas City put them in a flat-out tie for first place, thanks in part to Frank Bertaina and the humble Senators, who beat the Twins 5−4.

Lonborg and Catfish Hunter locked up in a tense duel. Reggie Smith gave Boston a 1−0 lead with a home run in the fifth. The A's tied it at 1−1 in the eighth on Bert Campaneris's home run, but the Red Sox came right back in the bottom of the eighth to score two runs. With one out Mike Ryan singled to center. Jose Tartabull ran for Ryan. That brought up Lonborg. The A's played for the bunt. Lonborg played along by shortening up on

Jim Lonborg won number twenty on September 12 to put the Sox back into a first-place tie. (Photo courtesy Boston Red Sox)

Retrospective: Rico Petrocelli Looks Back

On their brother's keeper:
"As a kid growing up, we didn't have many material things. I was the youngest of seven children, and all my brothers had to go out and work for the family. Because they did that, I was able to go out and play baseball and become a good athlete. It was all because of my brothers. They were working, bringing in the extra money we needed."

On high hopes for '67:
"During the second half of 1966, we played well. I think the Red Sox might have had the best record in the American League after the All-Star Game. So we were optimistic going into '67. Then Dick Williams came on the scene in spring training, with his aggressive attitude. Yaz had just come off a great conditioning program in Boston with Gene Berde at

The Colonial. So we felt encouraged. We were just hoping we would finish in the first division, then go from there."

On Eddie Popowski and Dick Williams:
"I played under Pop in the minors. He was a great teacher. He was a father figure to us, an older guy who had been around and taught us a lot about how to play the game. I thought Pop was the best instructor that I had ever seen in baseball. He quieted things down when Dick Williams got going. We'd go to him to get things out of our system.

"Dick Williams was very tough to play for. He was very good for our team at the time because we were young and needed direction. But in all honesty, it's no secret, he was arrogant at times. He wouldn't give in to us. If we made an excuse, he'd say, 'No

---

the bat; but at the last second, Jim drew the bat back, swung away, and lined Hunter's fast ball to the fence in right center. Jim legged it into a triple to make the score 2 – 1. Moments later he scored an insurance run on Mike Andrews's sacrifice fly.

The crowd of 27,976 loved the triple, but experienced an equal delight in watching Lonborg escape trouble four straight times. In the second and third, he got out of a first-and-third, one-out situation. In the fourth, Jim was Houdini himself, wriggling out of a bases-loaded, no-out quagmire. In the fifth, Lonborg slinked through a first-and-second, one-out noose.

WEDNESDAY, SEPTEMBER 13

Rico Petrocelli drove in three runs to pace a 4 – 2 win over the A's at Fenway. The park looked nearly empty: only 12,257 were on hand mostly because kids were now back in school. It was the lightest turnout since June 1. In the forty-four games since then, the gate has gone over 15,000 seven times, over 20,000 eight times, over 25,000 thirteen times, and over 30,000 sixteen times. Though the 12,257 is comparatively small, remember that a

way! Just get out there and play.' So you'd get angry at Dick and take it out on the other team."

On the motivator:
"Jim Lonborg lost a tough 2 – 1 game at California relatively early in the season. He lost it in the ninth inning. We were walking into the dugout after the loss, dejected, and Dick Williams was standing on the top step with his foot up and his hands folded. Boy, he was steaming! And as Jim and I got closer to Dick, right near him, I said, 'Jimmy, nice game. Tough luck.' Dick heard me and barked out, 'Tough luck, my ass!' Lonborg got angry and came back steaming at Williams. But his next few starts, and all the rest of the season, Jim came back aggressively on the mound. So I guess you'd have to say that Williams's approach worked."

On the last out:
"I remember the pitch. It was a great tailing fast ball by Jim Lonborg. It got right in the hands on Rich Rollins, and he hit it off the fists. It wasn't that high, but it seemed 1,000 feet high as I was waiting for it to come down. The fans were kind of quiet for a couple of seconds, waiting for it to come down. All of a sudden, it went into my glove. I squeezed it as tight as I could. Then there were cheers. My roomie, Dalton Jones, who was playing third, ran over to me; and we jumped on each other. Then Yaz joined us. We tried to get over to Jim Lonborg; but by that time, the fans were on the field. They had Jim on their shoulders and were taking him out to right field. It was scary."

---

year ago against Chicago, the Sox drew 1,010 at Fenway. Two years ago it was 1,247 against the Indians.

Today, with the score tied 1 – 1 in the eighth and Joe Foy on third with two outs, the A's intentionally walked Ken Harrelson to get to Rico. Rico foiled the strategy by doubling over Jim Gosger's head to score both runs.

Lee Stange gave up one unearned run in seven innings before leaving for a pinch hitter. John Wyatt pitched the eighth and ninth to pick up the win and up his mark to 8 – 6.

There was a bit of unwanted déjà vu for George Scott. For the second time in less than a month, Boomer was called out in the fourth for leaving third too soon on a fly ball. The entire Kansas City bench was screaming for an appeal. Home plate ump Bob Stewart ruled Scotty out. Of course George saw it differently.

THURSDAY, SEPTEMBER 14

The Sox had the day off, but there was more discouraging news for Tony Conigliaro. His injured eye was examined for ninety minutes, and the doctors made it official: Tony's through for the season.

The imbalance between the damaged left eye (20/100) and the healthy right eye (20/10) destroys his ability to adequately judge distance.

FRIDAY, SEPTEMBER 15

"We were due for something like that." Thus was the epitaph applied by Dick Williams to tonight's wretched effort against the Orioles at Fenway. The litany of seven walks, three wild pitches, a passed ball, and a wild throw from the outfield bore an uncanny resemblance to the writing on a tombstone, one marking this 6 – 2 loss.

Even the weather seemed to have gothic-horror undertones. A gloaming mist and fog crept in from center field like a nightstalker searching, on a lonely street, for his next victim. It would have been totally within the character of this evening if the Phantom of the Opera had replaced John Kiley on the organ.

The only bright spots were Reggie Smith's fifteenth home run in the fifth and Carl Yastrzemski's three hits, which lifted him, at .313, into a tie for first place in the batting race. Frank Robinson dropped two points tonight.

Starter Dave Morehead (2 2/3 innings, three runs, four walks) was wild high throughout his brief stint.

SATURDAY, SEPTEMBER 16

James Bond, look out. The Red Sox announced today that they have assigned a team of four scouts to trail the St. Louis Cardinals (in first place in the National League by thirteen games) for the last two weeks of the season. The team will be led by Eddie Kasko and Frank Malzone. What will they look for? "Everything," says Haywood Sullivan.

But the team has a more immediate task at hand, this little business of winning their own pennant. And for the second straight night against Baltimore, they seemed to lose sight of that fact. The 4 – 1 loss, coupled with Earl Wilson's twenty-first win of the season for Detroit against the Senators, put the Sox in second, one game out.

A Special Kind of Team

For what they did on the field, members of the '67 Red Sox proved they were part of a special team. But a little-publicized event demonstrated what kind of team this really was when it came time to voting on World Series shares in September. In an overwhelming vote, team members voted one full share to the Jimmy Fund, the club's official charity. The Jimmy Fund has for decades been one of the world's leading institutions for cancer research and for care of children with cancer.

SUNDAY, SEPTEMBER 17

With the season winding down, no one can afford to blow their chances; but once again it happened against the Orioles at Fenway. With a win the Red Sox could have regained first place. Washington cooled off the Tigers, and the White Sox beat the Twins . . . but all the Red Sox could do was lose again, 5 – 2. It could be worse, though. Despite scoring only five runs in three straight home losses to the Birds, they are still just one game out. The weekend record of the four American League contenders was a measly 5 – 7.

After the game an irritated Williams announced, in no uncertain terms, that he was angry with the play of the team and said there would be lineup changes for tomorrow night's big game against the Tigers in Detroit. "I'm putting Jose Tartabull in right field in place of Ken Harrelson. And I'm putting Russ Gibson behind the plate. Also Dalton Jones will be at third base. Jones has a good record hitting in the Detroit ball park. I've got to get him in."

The more Williams talked about the need to shake up the lineup, the more he lightened up and at one point cracked a joke: "Wouldn't it be something if I put Jose Tartabull up there in the cleanup spot? I just might."

The Tiger series is a GIANT one in so many ways. After the three losses against Baltimore, the team seems flat. Some are wondering if the team is starting to unravel in the pressure of the race. They need to turn it around, and there is little time left. As *Boston Globe* writer Ray Fitzgerald put it in a column: "The Red Sox need a spark. They need a happening."

As they go into Detroit, the race looks like this:

Detroit	85 – 65	.567	—
Chicago	85 – 66	.563	1/2
Boston	84 – 66	.560	1
Minnesota	84 – 66	.560	1

MONDAY, SEPTEMBER 18

Ray Fitzgerald called it. The Red Sox, on the verge of disaster, needed a "spark," a "happening." Tonight they got it as Dalton Jones had the game of his career in a wild, ten-inning, 6 – 5 win

Dalton Jones had the game of his life when the Red Sox needed it most: against the Tigers on September 18 in Detroit. (Photo courtesy Boston Red Sox)

over the Tigers. This was the kind of vintage comeback that for so long this season had become routine for the Sox. But tonight it was anything but routine . . . it was the event that Fitzgerald called for.

Boston came out determined with three in the first; but, because Jerry Stephenson couldn't get his curve over, the Tigers came back to tie it with three in the bottom of the fourth. After seven innings the score was still knotted at 4–4; then came the eighth, which by rights should have left the Red Sox completely demoralized and incapable of doing what they eventually did.

In the top of the inning, the Sox set themselves up nicely. Dalton Jones led off with his third single, and Rico Petrocelli sent him to third with a single to right. With nobody out and rookie Fred Lasher on the mound, things looked good. But a freak, unassisted double play quickly changed everything. With the infield in, Russ Gibson hit a one-hopper at Dick McAuliffe at second. McAuliffe looked Jones back to third, then saw Rico breaking toward second. When he saw McAuliffe in the base path, Rico put on the brakes and tried to scamper back to first; McAuliffe chased him, caught him, and tagged him out about five feet from the base. The scrappy Tiger second baseman simply continued running at full speed to first, where he beat Gibson to the bag for the double play. Jones held at third on the play ("I would have sent him, but it would have been a triple play" — Eddie Popowski). With two outs pinch hitter Norm Siebern walked to put runners at the corners. That brought up Jose Tartabull, who shocked everyone by hitting a ball to right that at first looked like it might go out; but Al Kaline stayed with it and made the catch right in front of the fence.

In the bottom of the inning, the Sox lost the lead as John Wyatt walked Kaline and surrendered a double to Jim Northrup to make it 5 – 4 Tigers. The Boston bench, looking out in glum silence, realized they were on a precipice, maybe on the verge of a fall that would begin the dismantling of a miracle season. The situation was desperate.

Inside Carl Yastrzemski something must have stirred. Who can say exactly what it was? But with one out and the bases empty in the Red Sox ninth, Yaz nailed a Lasher fast ball and sent it into the upper deck in right to tie the game. In a second the magic was back. The spark. The happening. The bench responded with enthusiastic fire. They knew, then and there, that they would not lose this game. Sure enough, in the top of the tenth, Jones launched his own upper-deck job, this one off Mike Marshall, to give his team a 6 – 5 win. It was Jones's eighteenth career home run for Boston and his sixth in Tiger Stadium.

"This had to be the best game of baseball I've ever played in the big leagues," said an ebullient Jones, who went 4 for 5 on the night. "This is my ball park . . . there's something about this place. I just feel better coming to the plate here than I do anywhere else."

Jones also made the final out of the game by spearing a Bill Freehan line drive that looked like it would be a double. Jones's heroics made a winner of Jose Santiago, who's now 8 – 4. "I wanted to give the ball to Jose Santiago," said Jones, "but Jose made me keep it." Until tonight Jones had been a forgotten man on the Red Sox bench. His last two starts came on Labor Day and on August 6.

Yaz was 3 for 4 with his homer and two RBIs; this ran his totals to .314, 40, 107, good for the Triple Crown lead. Another good performance almost lost in the drama was Stephenson's seven-inning stint. He struggled with his curve, but hung in with the fast ball.

Tuning In

As the Red Sox and Tigers squared off in this crucial series, a group of students were gathered around a radio at the University of North Carolina. One of them was Peter Gammons, who went on to become one of the country's finest sportswriters with *Sports Illustrated* and the *Boston Globe*.

Peter said they would pick up night games on WTIC in Hartford. There was one fellow from Detroit, Tom Haney, who was as much a Tiger fan as Peter was a Boston fan. He would go out to his car and listen to the Tigers on WJR from Detroit. During one game he actually ran his car battery dead from listening to the radio without the motor running. He then went into the dorm and called his father in Detroit. His dad put the phone receiver up to the radio, and the broadcast came through that way. There was no word on what the phone bill came to.

As much as this was a jubilant win for Boston, it was a depressing loss for Detroit. Their locker room after the game was as quiet as an empty library. "This game was a crusher," said Norm Cash, who homered twice in a losing effort.

Lasher, standing near his locker and almost in a daze, muttered about Yastrzemski's home run: "I'd like to have that pitch back. I'd love to have it back," he kept repeating. Finally he came out of his funk long enough to discuss the pitch: "It was right across the center [of the plate], belt high. Just a terrible pitch. I'm really disgusted with myself. Anybody could have hit that ball out. My grandmother could. Hell *I* could have. It was a lollipop." It was the first home run anyone hit off him in twenty-three innings with Detroit and seventy more at Montgomery and Toledo.

McAuliffe mumbled unintelligible monosyllables to questions.

The Boston victory created another three-way tie among Boston, Detroit, and Minnesota, with the White Sox 1 1/2 games out in fourth. Also of mild interest, the St. Louis Cardinals clinched the National League pennant tonight.

TUESDAY, SEPTEMBER 19

Just two nights ago, the Red Sox were a car with a dead battery and sitting alone in an empty parking lot in below-zero cold. Last night Carl Yastrzemski and Dalton Jones gave the team a jump start. But would the motor keep running? The answer came tonight: yes.

For the second straight night, the Tigers went into the ninth inning with the lead . . . and for the second straight night, they blew it.

Through eight, the Tigers led 2 – 1, although the Sox were lucky to be that close. They went ahead 1– 0 in the second on Russ Gibson's single. It was Gibby's first RBI since late July. Lee Stange was on the ropes all night, but the Tigers couldn't put him away. In the third, Detroit loaded the bases; but Stange got out of it by serving up a double play grounder. In the fourth, the Bengals, to no avail, put runners on the corners with no outs. In the sixth, they finally scored as Willie Horton's two-run home run made it 2 – 1. In the seventh, the Tigers had runners on first and second with no outs, but couldn't score. It was at this point that Dick Williams had seen enough. He brought in Sparky Lyle, and the rookie picked up where Stange left off . . . by getting out of the jam. In the eighth, the stuck record continued. Incredibly the Tigers loaded the bases with no outs against Jose Santiago, but failed to score a run. Norm Cash fouled out, and Bill Freehan hit into a double play.

As each chance went by the board, so grew a suspicion that the Red Sox would eventually make the Tigers pay for their lack of opportunism. Through eight, Mickey Lolich gave up the lone run and struck out thirteen. But in the ninth, Jerry Adair opened up with a base hit. Lolich then walked Yaz, and you could feel something building. A sense of doom hung over the Tiger bench. George Scott followed with a single up the middle to tie the score.

Tiger manager Mayo Smith, showing either signs of panic or a complete lack of faith in the bullpen (maybe both), brought in starter and twenty-one–game winner Earl Wilson for his first relief spot of the year. Reggie Smith moved the runners to second and third with a sacrifice, and Wilson intentionally walked Ken Harrelson. Dick Williams sent up lefty Norm Siebern to hit for Rico Petrocelli, and Wilson uncorked a wild pitch that allowed Yastrzemski to score the lead run. Siebern finally walked to load the bases again, and Scott scored on Gibson's sacrifice fly (for a change, George didn't leave too early).

Because of the pinch-hitting, the Sox opened the ninth with an infield of Scott at third, Mike Andrews at short, Dalton Jones at second, and Siebern at first. Trailing 4 – 2, the Tigers decided to agonize themselves and their fans just one more time for good measure. Yaz made a great sliding catch of Don Wert's sinking liner for the first out. Jose Santiago then got wild and walked Lenny Green and Dick McAuliffe. With Ray Oyler due up, Smith pinch-hit Eddie Mathews. Williams responded by playing a hunch and bringing in little-used left-hander Bill Landis. It was the youngster's first appearance since August 29 (he's pitched just twenty-nine innings all year). Williams imparted some last words of wisdom to Landis. What did he say? "I said to Landis, 'Do you know what that oblong thing is there?' He said, 'Yeah. It's the rubber.' I knew then he was all right," Williams said.

Actually Landis got advice even before leaving the bullpen. Before coming in Landis asked Gary Bell if low fast balls got Mathews out. "I told him 'yes,' " Bell said, "to make him feel good. But, heck, I didn't know what got him out."

Landis threw Mathews two sliders, one of which he fouled off, and two fast balls, both of which he missed.

With two outs Williams brought in Bell to face Al Kaline. Bell came in; and before he pitched, he looked around at the Red Sox infield: "When I went down for the resin bag and saw who was there at third [Scott] and short [Andrews] with Kaline up, I nearly choked," Bell said. On the first pitch, Kaline hit a screaming liner to center. Reggie Smith took it on the run, knee-high. The Boston bench exploded out of the dugout to mob Bell.

The 4 – 2 win gave the Red Sox a two-game sweep (Jose Santiago won both games) of the biggest series of the season and put them into a first-place tie.

Boston	86 – 66	.566	—
Minnesota	86 – 66	.566	—
Chicago	86 – 67	.562	1/2
Detroit	85 – 67	.559	1

The Red Sox dressing room was a combination madhouse, circus, and Three Stooges food fight. Andrews shouted, "Fabulous!" Yaz screamed, "Beautiful! Beautiful!" Tom Yawkey called the clubhouse to offer his congratulations. "After this, the World Series should be easy," Petrocelli yelled.

The Tiger clubhouse was predictably dead silent. A tomb. A funeral. You could hear the water running from the showers. You could hear Gates Brown crunching potato chips in the middle of the big room. That was it. Mathews sat with his shirt off in front of his locker and stared at the tattoos on his body as he shook his head.

WEDNESDAY, SEPTEMBER 20

It's becoming an addiction. In Cleveland tonight the Cardiac Kids pulled out another one in the ninth. With the score tied 4 – 4, Reggie Smith singled sharply to right to score Carl Yastrzemski for a 5 – 4 win before 6,003 . . . or over 70,000 empty seats.

Yes, once more, the ninth inning.

The Sox smashed three home runs off Sudden Sam McDowell, one each by Rico Petrocelli (his seventeenth), Yaz (his forty-first), and Mike Andrews (his eighth). But Jim Lonborg gave up three as well (Larry Brown, Max Alvis, and friend Tony Horton). The barrage left the score knotted, and . . . once more the ninth inning.

Taking a Stance

The following September 20 entry from Hall of Famer Bobby Doerr's diary contains what is perhaps the best, most detailed analysis of Carl Yastrzemski's swing as it was in 1967.

Yaz awaits the pitch in his familiar stance. (Photo courtesy Boston Red Sox)

Yaz hits best with his hands up [see Doerr's diary entry on May 14]. When he's hitting good, I can see his hands all the time. When he drops them, he dips under the higher strikes and fouls off his pitches. I believe a big reason for his big home run year has been the raising of his hands.

At times, Carl tries to pull the ball too much. When he's tired, he uses too much body, and overswings. I don't believe his hip action is at all a problem . . . his hips have been square all year. He also has his right shoulder pulled in pretty good, and this helps him pull the ball without too big of a swing.

Carl stands well back in the box, in fact, about as far as he can get. His left foot is pointing back a little; it is not straight with the white line. His stance is a little closed, with his left big toe about in line with his right arch. Yaz spreads his feet about 21 inches, but a shade back from straight up. He wraps the bat a little in back of his head, and chokes up about a half an inch.

He looks like he has more weight on his front foot when he's ready to hit. His hands are about twelve inches back from his ear, and are level to his left ear.

With two out and nobody on, Yaz singled to left center. George Scott walked. George Culver quickly got Smith down on the count, 0 and 2, and tried to blow the fast ball by him. But Smith was ready and lined it to right for the game winner. John Wyatt came on to protect the lead and the win. Again the ninth.

Yaz had four hits, giving him the league batting lead at .316 over Frank Robinson. Carl also leads in four other categories: home runs, 41; RBIs, 108; runs, 104; and hits, 173.

Luncheon Lines

At a luncheon on the twenty-first in Cleveland, Carl Yastrzemski spoke; and he mentioned how much Ted Williams helped him become a pull hitter. Yaz said that Ted worked with him all spring. Cleveland Indians' executive Al Rosen followed Yaz to the podium and had this line: "I think Ted Williams helped Yaz become a pull hitter by letting him see his checkbook."

Rosen predicted that Yaz would become the second $100,000 player in Red Sox history.

At the luncheon I asked Jim Lonborg about his comment that Yaz embarrasses him in left field when someone homers and Yaz doesn't even turn to look at the ball.

"He did it again last night on the homer to [Max] Alvis."

Jim then told a laughing Yaz: "You might at least look like you could catch the ball." Yaz replied: "I might have if they moved the stadium back a few hundred yards."

THURSDAY, SEPTEMBER 21

After playing such high-strung, adrenaline-laced baseball for the last three nights, a letdown was in order. The good thing — no, the lucky thing — about tonight's game against the Indians was that, despite the downtick, they still managed to win 6 – 5 in a nearly empty Municipal Stadium.

The Sox were once ahead 6 – 1. They had only seven hits (three by Mike Andrews), but used them to good effect. Sloppy play (Yaz misplayed a ball that was ruled a double and a through-the-wickets error by George Scott) made it close. Gary Bell got by (6 1/3 innings, four runs) for his thirteenth win against twelve losses. John Wyatt saved it with a scoreless ninth.

The win was the team's forty-first on the road this season. That means that for just the eighth time since Tom Yawkey's stewardship began in 1933, the club will be over .500 away from Fenway.

Back in Boston the crush for World Series tickets is on. A deluged ticket office is handling what requests it can. But for each 100 applications, there is only one ticket. All applicants are limited to a maximum of two tickets for each of two games: either Games One and Seven, or Games Two and Six.

They move on to Baltimore tomorrow night to play a twinight doubleheader.

FRIDAY, SEPTEMBER 22

After a 10 – 0 mauling from the Orioles in the first game tonight, Dick Williams pulled out all stops for the nightcap: he emptied out the doghouse. The woofers came out barking, with Ken Harrelson, Elston Howard, and Joe Foy back in there.

Game one was a disaster: Jim Hardin gave up just three hits and struck out ten in the shutout. Jerry Stephenson was bombed, as was his relief, including the recently recalled Billy Rohr, who was tagged for four runs in one inning. To rub some salt into this open wound, Dalton Jones threw in two errors.

In game two it looked like more of the same as the Sox dropped behind 2 – 0 through four; but the Red Sox came back with five in the top of the fourth, an inning that looked like Cartoon Carnival.

Yaz started it with a single. Scott walked. Reggie Smith then sent a fly to right. It looked like a routine out; but for some reason Curt Blefary didn't react to the ball, and it just dropped safely. Yaz scored, and runners were on first and second. Rico Petrocelli bunted the runners over.

Ken Harrelson reached on an error by shortstop Luis Aparicio to load the bases. Howard plated Smith with a sacrifice fly. A third run scored when Paul Blair's throw to the plate went to the backstop. Joe Foy cleaned up with a two-run double. With the Orioles throwing the ball around like the House of David (there was another error by Aparicio), the Baltimore fans started cheering for the Sox. Spurred on by the crowd, Boston added one in the fifth, two in the sixth, and two in the eighth. Foy and Harrelson had three hits, Scott and Smith two.

Jose Santiago gave the bullpen a much needed rest by pitching a complete game to run his record to 9 – 4.

SATURDAY, SEPTEMBER 23

Once again, this charmed team came back, climbing out of a 4 – 0 hole to take a 5 – 4 lead in the fifth on Carl Yastrzemski's forty-second home run; but the Orioles' other Robinson, Brooks, hit a two-run home run in the eighth to spark a 7 – 5 Bird win. The loss dropped the Sox to third place:

Minnesota	89 – 67	.571	—
Detroit	88 – 67	.568	1/2
Boston	89 – 68	.567	1/2
Chicago	88 – 68	.564	1

As the pressure builds up in the race, the Red Sox seem to be handling it well. Witness the following events, all of which have happened on this road trip:

• Rico Petrocelli and Mike Ryan reminding no one of the Everly Brothers as they try to harmonize on a song in back of the team bus.

• A pillow fight aboard the plane ride out of Detroit.

• A single by Frank Robinson skids off Petrocelli's glove. Foy yells over to Rico: "Yaz wants you to bear down on Robinson." The next batter, Brooks Robinson, hits a grounder at Rico, who starts a smart-looking double play. Rico shouts to Foy: "Which Robinson?" Foy trots off the field and into the dugout, where he collapses in laughter.

• Frank Robinson gets his two-thousandth career hit and asks for the base. Later in the 10 – 3 Sox victory, George Thomas is sent in to run and caddy for Yaz. Thomas asks the umpire for first base. "I told him it was the two-thousandth time I've been there."

SUNDAY, SEPTEMBER 24

This crucial road trip, the season's last, ended the right way as the Red Sox pounded the Orioles 11 – 7. The win left them 6 – 2 on the trip and feeling good in second place.

Minnesota	90 – 67	.573	—
Boston	90 – 68	.570	1/2
Chicago	89 – 68	.567	1
Detroit	88 – 68	.564	1 1/2

Boston built up a 7 – 0 lead. With Jim Lonborg on the mound and hunting for his twenty-first win, it looked safe. Dick Williams pulled Lonborg after six shutout innings so the tall right-hander could rest up for the final week.

Despite the victory Williams indicated sharp displeasure at "certain ballplayers." He didn't name names, but gave enough hints; it was clear he was referring to the bullpen performance of yesterday and today. "You find out about ballplayers in a series like this. I'm not naming men, but I said you learn things about people when things get tough," the manager said. Williams was also angry at the team's four errors.

Williams doesn't fool around. Yesterday Mike Andrews played poorly in the field. Today he was on the bench in favor of Jerry Adair. Mike Ryan, once the number-one catcher, didn't play at all on the entire road trip. He didn't try to hide his displeasure.

Adair, coming up with four hits, once again made Williams look like a genius. Dalton Jones did nothing to take away from that label — he had four hits and five RBIs after spelling Joe Foy at third. George Scott also banged out four hits, including his eighteenth home run. In all, the Sox had eighteen hits.

Bill Landis left today for a six-month army stint at Fort Polk, Louisiana. His absence will make Russ Gibson eligible for the World Series should Boston get in. Gibson's time spent in Pittsfield had put that matter in doubt.

The Red Sox finished 1967 with a road record of 43 – 38. This was the first time they were over .500 away from home since 1956.

As Lonborg rested in the clubhouse, he mentioned his performance versus Minnesota: he's 0 – 3 this year, 0 – 6 lifetime, a disquieting thought, considering that the final game may mean the pennant. "It's just one of those things," he shrugged.

MONDAY, SEPTEMBER 25

The team flew out of here for a day off today. There was a minor snag. Their chartered plane had a bad engine, and they had to switch to another ship at Friendship Airport in Baltimore.

Without playing today they actually gained some ground. The Angels defeated the Twins 9 – 2 to give Boston a share of first place.

The teams stack up like this:

Boston	90 – 68	.570	—
Minnesota	90 – 68	.570	—
Chicago	89 – 68	.567	1/2
Detroit	88 – 69	.561	1 1/2

The team got word that Darrell Brandon tore a muscle behind his right shoulder. He will be lost for the rest of the year. "I felt something rip apart in there [on Sunday] as soon as I let the pitch go. I was trying to reach back and put a little extra on the fast ball," Brandon related.

Yaz took an abbreviated batting drill at Fenway today and hit twenty pitches tossed in by Joe Foy. Carl has a three-point edge over Frank Robinson in the batting race. Carl leads in home runs and RBIs.

TUESDAY, SEPTEMBER 26

". . . and the games dwindle down to a very precious few."

A mysterious dark cloud, as alien as a hostile UFO, hovered over a hushed Fenway Park this afternoon. When it finally drifted away, the Red Sox could be seen in their clubhouse searching for an explanation. The Indians had just beaten them 6 – 3. The loss, coupled with Minnesota's 7 – 3 win over California and the Tigers' 1 – 0 win over New York (Chicago was rained out), left the race this way:

Minnesota	91 – 68	.572	—
Chicago	89 – 68	.567	1
Boston	90 – 69	.566	1
Detroit	89 – 69	.563	1 1/2

"This hurts a hell of a lot, but we played a bad game. It has to be our most damaging loss of the season," Dick Williams said as he sat in his office and puffed on a cigarette. He then listened to the clubhouse radio giving the results of the Twins' win. He showed no emotion. He sipped at his beer and continued to drag on his cigarette. Williams sat wearing just an undershirt and shower slippers. He sat staring into a crack in space, into a private world of what might have been, where what happened to his team today didn't happen at all. But it did.

The Red Sox showed the kind of self-destruction that at this point in such a close race is usually fatal:

- A simple pop fly falling safely between three fielders in shallow center
- Reggie Smith throwing a ball into the visiting dugout to give away a run
- A line drive off of Jerry Adair's glove
- An error by Rico Petrocelli
- A grounder, generously scored a single, under Dalton Jones's glove at third

The only bright spot for Boston was Carl Yastrzemski's three-run home run in the seventh. It made a 6 – 0 game 6 – 3 and stirred up the crowd a little. It also tied him with Ted Williams for the club's all-time home run mark for a left-handed batter at forty-three.

Before leaving the clubhouse, a glum Yastrzemski said: "Now we've got to win all three. We've got to win, win, win."

The crowd was thin, just 16,652. And it was a strangely quiet crowd from pregame to the final out. There was a weird, nervous kind of quiet in the park all day, a quiet that couldn't properly be explained.

Gary Bell (13 – 13) went just four innings to take the loss.

WEDNESDAY, SEPTEMBER 27

Today was a case of the nobodies going nowhere beating up on the somebodies trying to arrive. It was like that all across the American League. The Indians did their war dance again at Fenway by winning a love set 6 – 0. The Red Sox are still in this thing only because of the equally dismal showings of the other pretenders . . . er, contenders: the Angels beat the Twins 5 – 1, and — most shocking of all — the last-place A's beat Chicago twice 5 – 2 and 4 – 0. The White Sox got seven hits in the double-header. The Tigers didn't play.

Minnesota	91 – 69	.569	—
Detroit	89 – 69	.563	1
Boston	90 – 70	.563	1
Chicago	89 – 70	.561	1 1/2

Jim Lonborg, going with just two-days' rest, pitched a score-less first before collapsing in the four-run second. The Red Sox never got untracked. They loaded the bases twice without scor-ing, once with one out and the second time with no outs. That second occasion, in the sixth, was the backbreaker. Jerry Adair and Carl Yastrzemski started with singles. When Indian starter Sonny Siebert went to 2 and 0 on Reggie Smith, Manager Joe Adcock brought in Bob Allen from the bullpen. Allen complet-ed the walk. Adcock, managing as if *he* were playing for a pennant, pulled Allen in favor of Stan Williams. All Williams did was fan Dalton Jones, George Scott, and Rico Petrocelli on eleven pitches. The 18,415 in the stands let out a groan of disappointment and were silent the rest of the game.

They did get a chance to see young Ken Brett make his debut. The eighteen-year-old lefty pitched the eighth and ninth and gave up a run (Richie Scheinblum's single and Joe Azcue's triple in the eighth) and struck out two with his blazing fast ball.

Today's loss puts the odds against the Sox. Although not mathematically eliminated, they will need a near-miracle to clinch the pennant during the regular season. Today's results eliminated the possibility of a four-way tie, but a three-way tie could still happen.

"We just played poorly," said a calm Dick Williams after the game. Williams spoke deliberately, munching on potato chips and drinking beer. "It's as poor as we've played all year. . . . Our chances are not as good as they were yesterday. But I'll get a good night's sleep. The beer still tastes good," he said with a slight smile.

Williams said that no formal workout was scheduled for the off day tomorrow, though players could come to the park on their own. A practice session was scheduled on the second off day on Friday. He said he wasn't sure who would pitch the last two games against the Twins, though he said Lonborg would start one of them.

Indian manager Joe Adcock said he watched the Red Sox closely during the game and that he could see them reacting to the pressure, a polite way of saying they choked.

Tony Conigliaro was in uniform and on the bench for the game.

The Boston dressing room was what you would expect: glum and brooding. Yaz was gone in ten minutes. Lonborg left early after trashing his locker. Adair sat in front of his locker staring at nothing, a cigarette hanging from his lips, a beer bottle dangling from his hand. He took a drag off the butt, then flicked it to the floor and stamped it out. "A good year, and it turned into nothing in the last two days," Adair said.

THURSDAY, SEPTEMBER 28

It was a day to reflect, a time to gather one's hope and resolve and prepare for the last assault. For the Red Sox, the task was simple: they had to win their last two games against Minnesota. There were no other possibilities besides defeat if that didn't happen. The team got an enormous break when the White Sox dropped two to last-place Kansas City last night.

Dick Williams spent the day with his coaches and the front office, then announced that Jose Santiago would go Saturday with Jim Lonborg in the finale.

Several players—including Yaz, Rico Petrocelli, Lonborg, Santiago, and George Scott—worked out on their own today at Fenway. Yaz was in good spirits: "When I heard that Chicago had lost twice to Kansas City, I couldn't believe it. This whole thing is incredible. We've got to be the luckiest team in baseball, really. Maybe we are destined to win this thing like some people say," Yaz said.

The Twins worked out today in Minnesota and will fly into Boston later in the day.

The standings look like this:

Minnesota	91–69	.569	—
Detroit	89–69	.563	1
Boston	90–70	.563	1
Chicago	89–70	.561	1 1/2

FRIDAY, SEPTEMBER 29

Dick Williams revealed his lineup for Saturday, and there were some surprises. Ken Harrelson will bat cleanup and play right, Russ Gibson will replace Elston Howard behind the plate, Mike Andrews will start at second, and Jerry Adair will move over to third in place of the Joe Foy/Dalton Jones tandem. Here's the batting order:

Andrews, 2b
Adair, 3b
Yastrzemski, lf
Harrelson, rf
Scott, 1b
Petrocelli, ss
Smith, cf
Gibson, c
Santiago, p

The manager added that Gary Bell would be the first man out of the bullpen, but "everyone will be ready to go if needed." The lineup shows that Williams won't stop gambling now, one game away from elimination.

And then there were three. The Washington Senators defeated the punchless Chicago White Sox 1 – 0 to eliminate Chicago from the race.

After the morning workout at Fenway, the players went home to prepare. In slightly more than twenty-four hours, at 2:15 P.M., over 30,000 at Fenway and millions across the country will see what this team is really made of.

Let the games begin!

"One Down, One to Go"
Saturday, September 30, 1967

The two days off could have been two centuries, or two seconds. It didn't matter, because the team was in a real sense outside of time, on the verge of realizing (or losing) this impos-

MINNESOTA Name	ab	r	h	rbi	BOSTON	ab	r	h	rbi
Versalles, ss. .	5	1	1		Andrews, 2b. .	3	1	2	
Tovar, 3b.	5	1	1		Adair, 3b. . . .	4	1	1	1
Killebrew, 1b.	4	1	2	2	Yastrzemski, lf	4	1	3	4
Oliva, rf.	5		1	1	Harrelson, rf. .	3			
Allison, lf. . . .	2	1	1		Howard, c. . . .	1			
Carew, 2b. . . .	4				Scott, 1b. . . .	4	1	2	1
Uhlaender, cf.	4		2		Petrocelli, ss.	3			
Zimmerman, c	2				Smith, cf. . . .	4	1	1	
Reese, ph. . . .	1		1	1	Gibson, c. . . .	1			
Nixon, c.	1				Jones, ph. . . .	1	1	1	
Kaat, p.	1				Tartabull, rf. . .	2			
Perry, p.	1				Santiago, p. .	3			
Kastro, ph. . .					Bell, p.	1			
Kline, p.									
Rollins, ph. . .	1								
TOTALS	**36**	**4**	**9**	**4**	**TOTALS**	**34**	**6**	**10**	**6**

Team	1	2	3	4	5	6	7	8	9	
Minn.	1	0	0	0	0	1	0	0	2	4
Boston	0	0	0	0	2	1	3	0	X	6

Name	IP	H	R	ER	BB	SO
Minn.						
Kaat.	2⅓	3			1	4
Perry.	2⅔	4	2	2		4
Kline (l).	2⅓	3	3	2	1	1
Merritt.	⅔	1	1	1		
Boston						
Santiago (w).	7	7	2	2	4	7
Bell.	2	2	2	2		

sible dream. The task was clear: win the last two against the first-place Twins . . . against the team that has beaten you eleven out of sixteen times this season . . . win, after coming off two voodoo losses at home against Cleveland. Win, with the eyes of the achingly expectant home fans on you. Win, with the knowledge that all the cushion is gone from this dream. It's either fulfillment or banishment, joy or sorrow.

There is no time for thoughts now. Actions, not meditation, must be summoned; and they must be the unforced actions of players who will play with confidence. They must play with faith.

Faith. It poured out of the stands, out of 32,909 hearts and into the dugout on the first base side, where a group of men — young and young at heart — sat, stood, paced, hollered, and prayed in their red, white, and blue uniforms. The Red Sox walked off with a 6 – 4 win to force the final showdown tomorrow.

The strange quiet of the fans during the two Cleveland losses was gone and was replaced by electric enthusiasm: this crowd was ready. They were touched by this win and went collectively mad as George Scott and Carl Yastrzemski hit their nineteenth and forty-fourth home runs, respectively, in this *must* game. Jose Santiago came up big as he went seven strong innings to run his record to 12 – 4.

The victory was a microcosm of the entire season: the Red Sox fell behind, made some mistakes, came back to go ahead, got some lucky breaks, and made it stand.

Santiago drew the tough assignment of cooling off Jim Kaat, the Twins' hottest pitcher in September. In the dressing room before the game, Santiago went over to Yastrzemski and made him a pledge: "I promise you that Killebrew isn't going to hit any out of the park off me today, okay?" Yaz smiled. "Jose," the left fielder said, "you make sure none of his go out, and I'll make sure I hit one out for you." They shook hands on it.

Santiago admitted he was nervous when he walked to the mound in the top of the first: "Who would *not* feel nervous in a game like that?"

His early jitters showed. Zoilo Versalles led off with a single. After Cesar Tovar flied out, Harmon Killebrew walked. That brought up Tony Oliva, who promptly lined a single to right to score Versalles. Bob Allison followed with a single to load the bases. With only one out and a run already in, the crowd squirmed. Visions of all sorts of damnations and crawly things were going through the minds of the fans (except Vice-President Hubert H. Humphrey, of course, who was on hand to root for his home-state Twins), but Jose kept his cool: "I had good stuff, and I didn't worry." He settled down to get the dangerous Rod Carew on a liner to Jerry Adair and Ted Uhlaender on a ground out . . . on a 3 − 1 pitch.

No one could doubt Santiago's competitiveness after he got out of that, but there was more to come. For the next two innings, though, things were okay; Jose held the Twins scoreless. Kaat, meanwhile, was dominating Red Sox batters. He pitched shutout ball for the first 2 1/3 innings and struck out four, then something happened. His left elbow blew out like a set of cheap retreads. Kaat knew it was serious, and he motioned to the dugout. "It's the first time anything like that has ever happened to me," Kaat said.

Jim pulled a tendon and had to leave the game. He walked off the field dejectedly, his stiff elbow throbbing with pain. At that instant people had the feeling that maybe a larger power was in control of this thing. Cal Ermer brought in Jim Perry, who got the last two outs of the Red Sox' third with no incident; but the fans were glad to see Kaat out of there.

In the fourth, Santiago had another brush with disaster as he worked out of a jam not of his making. With one out Uhlaender lofted a fly to right. Ken Harrelson looked unsure of it, danced, got tangled up, and the ball bounced off his glove (and Reggie Smith's shoulder) for a triple. Jose reached back for something extra, found it, and struck out Jerry Zimmerman after falling behind 3 and 0. Santiago then got Perry on a deep fly ball to center.

Perry worked a scoreless fourth, Santiago an uneventful fifth. In the bottom of the fifth, the guiding force — one word for it is luck — that had been riding with the Sox all year made an appearance in the bright sunshine.

Smith started it with a hard double to left center. With Russ Gibson (.206) due up, Dick Williams went with Dalton Jones from the bench. Jones tapped a weak grounder to second. The ball was hit so softly that it seemed to wheeze its way out to Carew. The ball wouldn't have taxed the glove of Dick Stuart, so everyone was thinking of the bright side: at least it would move Smith to third. But at the last possible instant, as Carew reached down to make the play, the ball took a weird bounce. Practically defying the law of physics, the ball hopped up and hit Carew in

Yaz was tough in the clutch. (Photos courtesy Boston Red Sox)

the left shoulder to leave runners on first and third. It was now Perry's turn to bow his back as he struck out Santiago and Mike Andrews. That left it up to the quiet Oklahoman, Jerry Adair, who so many times came through this season. Jerry wasted no time and flicked the first pitch into right center for a hit to tie the score at 1–1.

Yaz was up (so was the crowd), and Perry worked him tough. Carl fought off an inside pitch and sent a bouncer to the right of Killebrew at first. Harmon made a stab at the ball, but it was just out of his reach. Carew, however, came over quickly and made a fine play. He stopped and set up to throw to first when he discovered — to his complete surprise — that the bag was uncovered. Perry, frozen on the mound, gave Yaz a base hit and an RBI as Jones scored.

More than any other play today, this one handed Boston the game and haunted the Twins and Ermer. "The pitcher has got to be there," Ermer said disgustedly. "It's automatic. You work on it all spring, drilling it into their heads. Yet this is the fourth time it's happened to us in the past month."

"I started over," Perry later explained, "but when the ball went past Harmon, I hesitated. Then I saw Carew get to the ball. I said to myself, 'Great play,' but what could I do then? Once you hesitate, you're dead."

Ermer said he didn't know how a manager could punish such a fatal mistake. He said a fine wouldn't be enough: "There's no use talking about how much [of a fine he'd impose]," he lamented like Job. "There's no way you can assess a punishment that would fit the crime."

The Twins, to their credit, came right back in the top of the sixth to tie the game 2 – 2. Santiago walked Allison and gave up singles to Uhlaender and pinch hitter Rich Reese. With a run in and the bases loaded, Jose needed the big pitch; and once more, he got it. He came in to Versalles with a wicked sidearm curve and got the shortstop to pop up. "I'd say that was my best pitch of the day," Santiago said later.

Ron Kline, historically very good against Boston, came on for the Twins in the bottom of the sixth. The first man he faced was George Scott. Scotty, given the green light to swing from the heels, went tater hunting and poked a shot five rows deep in the center field bleachers off Kline's first pitch. Scott trotted around the bases with his head down, his arms loosely pumping, as if attached by ball bearings. When he made it back to the dugout, the rousing greeting from the bench practically tore his shirt off.

With a 3 – 2 lead, Santiago pitched a scoreless seventh; then came the stretch inning, and utter pandemonium. Mr. Guiding Force took another bow.

With one out Andrews reached first when his check-swing roller died in front of Kline for a scratch hit. Adair followed with a comebacker to the box that looked like a certain inning-ending double play. Kline fielded it cleanly and threw to second in plenty of time. Just one thing went wrong. Versalles dropped the ball. The crowd cut loose as Yaz stepped in. Ermer went right away for lefty Jim Merritt. Yaz stepped in with his usual ritual: a tug on the belt, an adjustment of the helmet, the bat held high. Merritt worked Carl carefully and fell behind 3 and 1.

"When the count went to 3 and 1, I guessed he would throw me a high fast ball," Yaz explained. The guess was right on the money, and Yaz sent the ball into the Twins' bullpen for a three-run home run to give the Sox a 6 – 2 lead.

Carl Yastrzemski reaches the plate after his crucial home run in the seventh inning on September 30 against the Twins. Elston Howard (18), Jerry Adair (right), and Mike Andrews welcome Carl. (Photo courtesy Boston Red Sox)

"I knew it was gone as soon as I hit it," said Yaz. "I was out in front of the pitch good and knew it would be gone." So did the entire ball park. A mammoth, sustained cheer erupted and continued unabated for a couple of minutes. One of the few silent faces belonged to Vice-President Humphrey. The avid Twins fan had a look on his face similar to the one he wore on the day he lost the 1960 West Virginia primary to John F.

Kennedy, as someone cracked. To Humphrey's left, Ted Kennedy whooped it up.

In the eighth, Santiago walked leadoff man Bob Allison. Williams wasted no time in making a move. Santiago had thrown 120 pitches when Williams brought in Gary Bell. "I wanted to finish the game," Santiago said, "but I have to admit I was tired. [Trainer] Buddy LeRoux talked to me in the dugout and asked me if I was tired just before I went out to pitch the eighth. I told him I was, but not to tell Dick [Williams] because I wanted to try to finish."

Bell got out of the eighth with no further trouble and was okay until two were out in the ninth. Tovar doubled, and Killebrew cleared everything in left to make it 6 – 4 (it was Harmon's forty-fourth, tying him with Yaz); but it was too little too late for Minnesota. Oliva lined out to end the game. The loss was pinned on Kline; it was just his first loss in eight decisions.

Players streamed into the winning clubhouse and jumped up and down like kids. Santiago planted a kiss on Yaz and said: "You're too much, baby!"

Later, as he was soaking his right elbow in ice water, Santiago said: "I told them all the way down to San Juan, Puerto Rico, that I'd do it."

One of the first visitors to the clubhouse was Massachusetts governor John Volpe. "I don't know if I can make it for tomorrow's game," the governor told Williams. "I've lost my voice, you know."

Williams, getting into the spirit of the situation, pretended awe and made some remark about the wonder of being in the presence of a speechless politician.

One player was noticeable in his reticence . . . Jim Lonborg, who pitches the Game of the Century tomorrow. Jim sat on the table in the trainer's room and dangled his legs off the side of the table, swinging them back and forth. "This is the first *big* game of my life. I haven't seen a big one until tomorrow. Never," Jim said.

Lonborg (22 – 9) goes against Dean Chance (20 – 13). A full twenty percent of Chance's twenty victories have been against the Red Sox — he's 4 – 0 against them. Lonborg, meanwhile, is 0 – 3 against the Twins this year and 0 – 6 lifetime.

"They're just an unlucky team for me," Jim said tersely. Lonborg said he'd have a good dinner and try to get a good night's sleep. He said he'd try not to think about the game until game time: "I don't want to feel anything now. It can't help me now. I'll start thinking about it when I start warming up. That's what I've done all year. I don't want to stop now."

Most likely the winner of tomorrow's game will win the American League pennant. Today the Tigers split with the Angels; they took game one 5 − 0, but blew a 6 − 2 lead in the eighth in game two to lose 8 − 6. They need a sweep of the Angels in tomorrow's doubleheader to force a tie for first place and a playoff between the winner of the Boston-Minnesota game. The two straight doubleheaders were forced by rainouts. The Tigers have had a tendency to self-destruct while going into the late innings with leads.

But there's no thought of Detroit for the moment. The Red Sox have one more game to win.

Boston	91 − 70	.565	—
Minnesota	91 − 70	.565	—
Detroit	90 − 70	.563	1/2

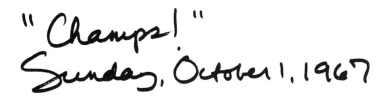

" Champs! "
Sunday, October 1, 1967

One game to decide the American League pennant. All along people had the feeling it would come to this.

Before the game Dick Williams gathered the team around him in the locker room. He looked at everyone without saying a word. The true commentary was unspoken. He then said: "I want to congratulate you men right now on a great season. I want to thank you for all you have given me. I know that you feel you can beat Minnesota today. So do I. Let's go get 'em."

The team filed out of the locker room, down the long runway that leads to the dugout. Jim Lonborg, the starting pitcher, did some stretching exercises. Lonborg didn't sleep in his apartment last night. He decided to change his routine in an effort to change his luck (0 – 6) against the Twins. "Ken Harrelson has a room at the Sheraton Boston, and I slept there. Maybe it sounds foolish, but I thought if I slept in a hotel, it might make me feel like I was pitching a road game," Jim explained. He said he fell asleep reading *The Fall of Japan* by William Craig. The way today's game turned out, it might have been titled *The Fall of Minnesota* by James Lonborg. "When I woke up this morning," Lonborg went on, "I just knew I was going to win. I was full of confidence. But early in the game, I thought it might be a long day when they got those unearned runs off me."

Those unearned runs caused much consternation for Boston fans. For a crowd that had been waiting twenty-one years for a pennant, each play was life and death, so much so that a Russian novelist and not a sportswriter would probably be better equipped to tell the story of today's game.

In the top of the first, the Red Sox started out like death. They were tight and looked ready to choke. The Twins' run in the first never should have scored. With one out Lonborg walked Harmon Killebrew on four pitches. Tony Oliva rifled a drive to left. Yaz made a wild dive, but the ball went over his head for a double. Killebrew went to third and couldn't believe it when coach Billy Martin waved him home. Yaz quickly ran the ball down and threw a perfect strike to George Scott in the cutoff position. Scotty had Killebrew dead at home. Any kind of a decent throw would have had the Twins' lumbering slugger by yards; but George rushed his throw, and it went high and to the left of Russ Gibson to make the score 1 – 0.

In the third, it happened again. With two outs Cesar Tovar drew a walk. Killebrew then singled to left center. Yaz, never giving thought to playing safe in a game of such importance, charged the ball to try and hold Tovar at second; but the ball got by Carl and rolled all the way to the wall to make it 2 – 0.

Meanwhile Dean Chance was shutting out the Red Sox. Through 5 1/2 innings, it was still 2 – 0; and some started to wonder about the likelihood of yet another comeback, about the jinx the Twins had over Lonborg, about the 6 – 11 record Boston had against Minnesota. "I figured Chance might pitch a shutout and beat me 2 – 0," Lonborg confessed, "but I kept throwing hard, hoping we could get some runs."

Dream on . . . dream on . . . and then came the bottom of the sixth, with Lonborg due to lead off. Any thoughts that Williams

MINNESOTA	ab	r	h	rbi	BOSTON	ab	r	h	rbi
Versalles, ss . .	3				Adair, 2b. . . .	4	1	2	
Reese, lf	1	1			Andrews, 2b. .				
Tovar, 3b	3	1			Jones, 3b. . . .	4	1	2	
Killebrew, 1b.	2	2	2		Yastrzemski, lf	4	1	4	2
Oliva, rf. . . .	3	0	2		Harrelson, rf. .	3			1
Allison, lf . . .	4	1	1		Tartabull, rf. . .	1	1		
Hernandez, ss					Scott, 1b. . . .	4			
Uhlaender, cf.	4	1			Petrocelli, ss .	3	1		
Carew, 2b . . .	4				Smith, cf. . . .	4			1
Zimmerman, c	2				Gibson, c. . . .	2			
Nixon, c. . . .	1				Siebern, ph. . .	1			
Rollins, ph . .	1				Howard, c. . . .	1		1	
Chance, p . . .	2				Lonborg, p. . .	4	1	2	
Worthington, p									
Kastro, ph . . .	1								
Roland, p. . . .									
Grant, p									
TOTALS	31	3	7	1	TOTALS	35	5	12	4

Team	1	2	3	4	5	6	7	8	9	
Minn.	1	0	1	0	0	0	0	1	0	3
Boston	0	0	0	0	5	0	0	0	X	5

Name	IP	H	R	ER	BB	SO
Minn.						
Chance (l)	5	8	5	5		2
Worthington	1				1	1
Roland	—	3				
Grant	2	1				1
Boston						
Lonborg (w)	9	7	3	1	4	5

Maybe the biggest hit of the year — Jim Lonborg races to first after laying down a perfect bunt to start the winning rally on the regular season's last day. Third baseman Cesar Tovar charges. Twins' catcher is Jerry Zimmerman. (Photo courtesy Boston Red Sox)

would send up a hitter for Lonborg disappeared when the tall pitcher trudged out of the dugout with a warm-up jacket covering his right shoulder and a bat in his hand. Jim ambled to the on-deck circle. "I didn't know what I was going to do," he said.

He shed his jacket like a prize fighter getting out of his robe before stepping to center ring for the moment of confrontation. As he walked to the plate, he looked around at the Twins' infield. He thought of something. "When I got to the plate, I saw that [third baseman] Tovar was back a little. My first time up, Chance threw me a fast ball right down the middle, and I slapped it for a single. From that I felt he wasn't going to waste any pitches on me."

The thought of a bunt flashed through Jim's mind. "A fast ball in the middle of the plate is the best pitch to bunt. I can run better than most guys on the team, and I knew I could get the hit if I got the ball on the ground."

Lonborg laid down a perfect bunt down third base. It was an audacious play. It was bold, daring, brilliant. Tovar was completely fooled. Chance had no play; so Tovar charged, picked the ball up, bobbled it, and took a bite out of it as Lonborg raced across first with his momentum carrying him halfway down the right field foul line. This was the switch that turned on the crowd. In an instant the 35,770 — including Hollywood stars Lee Remick and Cliff Robertson — were *into* this game. "Go! Go! Go!" they chanted.

Jerry Adair responded with a single up the middle. More hoopla. Williams put on the bunt with Dalton Jones up, but Jones fouled it off. Chance came in with a fast ball on the outside corner, and Jones smartly slapped it past Tovar for a base hit to set the stage for Yaz: bases loaded, nobody out.

Noise from a crowd can't have a life of its own; it can't independently decide to increase or diminish. But at this moment, it was as if this wall of noise were alive. It was as if there were no people . . . just an unvarying din that swept over everything.

Yaz stepped in. "I wasn't going to try for a home run," Carl explained later. "I just wanted to hit the ball hard somewhere and get some runs in. He gave me a pitch that I could have hit out of the park, but I hit it for a single."

The ball went into center field. Lonborg and Adair scored, and it was 2 – 2 with runners on first and third. Ken Harrelson was next up. "I never felt more calm or relaxed in my life," Hawk said. "I felt so good I thought I was going to hit a home run."

He worked the count to 3 and 2. Chance came in with a tough slider, down low. Harrelson did well to get some wood on it, and he sent a high bouncer to short. Zoilo Versalles fielded it and surprised everyone by throwing to the plate, where he really had no play. Jones was in easily to make it 3 – 2 and leave runners on second and first.

"I saw the man going home for the money," a downcast Versalles recalled, "and I always play for the money, so I threw home. It was the only play I had."

Actually it was the only play he didn't have, as Jones was in by five feet. Cal Ermer, pacing in the dugout, had seen enough. With George Scott up, Ermer went to the bullpen for Al

Worthington. Worthington furthered the unraveling of the heavily favored Twins by throwing two wild pitches, allowing Yaz to score and putting Harrelson on third.

"He was trying so hard to keep the ball down on me, trying to make me hit a grounder, that he bounced the pitch in front of the plate," Scott said.

Finally the Twins got the first out of the inning as Scott whiffed, but the magic began again. Rico Petrocelli drew a walk. Reggie Smith hit a grounder to Killebrew. Harmon didn't get the glove on it and misjudged the hop. The ball hit him in the left knee and rolled fifteen feet back toward home. Harrelson scored on the error to make it 5 – 2. Worthington got pinch hitter Norm Siebern and Lonborg to end the inning. As the Red Sox took the field for the top of the seventh, John Kiley played "The Night They Invented Champagne," and the crowd stood on its feet.

After a scoreless seventh, Lonborg had to work out of an eighth-inning scare. Rich Reese pinch-hit for Versalles and singled, then the Sox pulled two clutch defensive plays. The first was by Adair off of Tovar. The Twins' third baseman grounded to second. Adair charged the ball and fielded it in the base path. He coolly tagged Reese running by and threw to Scott for the double play. Adair paid the price for his great play: a deep spike wound, in his left leg, that required seven stitches to close. Jerry couldn't continue. As he limped off, the crowd gave him a standing ovation. Williams replaced him with Mike Andrews.

The significance of Adair's play quickly became evident. Killebrew and Oliva singled, and Bob Allison came up as the tying run. The tension in the stands was so intense that Carl Yastrzemski's wife, Carol, left her seat and moved under the stands out of sight. She clutched a pair of rosary beads and started praying.

And prayers are sometimes answered. Allison hit a liner that looked like a sure double into the corner in left; but Yaz, who seemed to be operating on radar, broke as the ball was hit, quickly dug it out, and made a beautiful throw into Andrews at second. Allison tried a hook slide; but when he reached for the bag, Mike slapped him with the tag. It was Yastrzemski's seventeenth assist of the year.

"I was out," Allison admitted. "Andrews just tagged me. I never did see what happened out there [in left]. I thought I had two; and I looked at Carl and I saw the throw coming, and I had to try and make it. But I didn't. It was just another great play by Yastrzemski."

Yaz had this to say: "I didn't care about Oliva [who held at third]. Let him score. I wanted to keep Allison from getting to second. He was the tying run. I cut the ball off before it got to the wall. It was a big play."

Williams had faith in Yaz: "When I saw Allison go, I said to myself, 'Yaz will throw one of his 800 strikes to second base.' "

Elston Howard said Allison's gamble didn't figure: "He had no reason to go. I was surprised. Really surprised."

Then came the Twins' ninth, the score still 5 – 3. Ted Uhlaender led off and grounded to Petrocelli, but the ball took a bad hop and hit Rico under the right eye. After an anxious minute, Rico got up and stayed in the game. Now it was déjà vu time. Rod Carew bounced to Andrews at second, and Mike gave it the "Jerry Adair Shuffle." He tagged Uhlaender in the base path and threw to Scott for the double play. Uhlaender tried to take Mike out. He rammed the infielder's left leg. The hurried throw was in the dirt, but Scott made a nice scoop to save it.

With catcher Russ Nixon scheduled, Ermer went against orthodoxy by pulling the left-handed-hitting Nixon in favor of righty Rich Rollins. Rich Rollins — the last man between the Red Sox and at least a tie for the pennant. Rollins lifted a soft, hump-backed pop-up to Petrocelli at short.

The arc circumscribed by the pop-up can be described in many ways. To a mathematician it is a series of axis points that can be expressed in numbers; to a physicist it is an event conforming to known and predictable laws of the universe. To a child it is the fanciful burst of freedom represented by things that rise: kites, balloons, planes. To the fans at Fenway Park, this arc represented the redemption of Boston baseball.

"The ball seemed like it was 1,000 feet high. I couldn't wait for it to come down," Petrocelli recalled. "I remember thinking Whatever will happen to me if I drop this ball? I would have had 36,000 people down my back. When I caught it, I started to run in toward the dugout. We were all ready to jump on Jim Lonborg, but the fans got to him before we could. My roomie, Dalton Jones, was at third base; Yaz was in left field. And we finally caught up with each other and, you know, everyone's jumping up and down, really happy about the way things turned out."

The Mighty Casey

My son Casey, who now works as a TV sportscaster in Cleveland, worked at Fenway in 1967 for the concession people. On the last day of the season, Casey went to Fenway. He wasn't scheduled to work that game, but figured he could get into the park with his concession pass to watch the game. He went into Boston with his friend Tom Keating, who also was a concession worker; but when they got to the park, they found they couldn't get in. There were no exceptions: if you weren't scheduled to work, you couldn't get into the game. So Casey and Tom went out behind the bleacher area behind the center field wall. They climbed on top of a ticket booth, jumped the fence that separates the grandstand and the bleachers, and watched the game from that area. At the end of the game, they jumped over the wall near the right field foul pole and ran into the infield to join the thousands of fans crushing in on Jim Lonborg.

There was no precedent, no way to prepare for what followed. After Rico squeezed the final out, Lonborg leapt up in the air. Andrews and Scott rushed over to Lonborg and lifted him up to their shoulders. Elston Howard came out to join in the celebration. The Red Sox' bench ran onto the field. Darrell Brandon almost collided with Rollins, who was running back to the Twins' dugout. Then came Dick Williams, a hatless Tony Conigliaro, and Joe Foy. Then the fans swarmed in. Jim was smiling and enjoying his ultimate joy. But as the crowd swelled, things threatened just for a moment to get out of hand. The throng surged and, like a tidal wave, swept Jim along far out to right field. The rest of the players made their way straight to the dugout out of a sense of self-preservation.

"Dear Lord," Lonborg thought, "how do I get out of here?" People clawed at him. They patted and pounded him. They hugged him and kissed him. They tore the buttons off his uniform shirt and tore his sweatshirt off completely. They took his cap and shoelaces. "It became a mania," Jim said. "I was scared to death."

Several policemen fought their way into the crowd, which had now drifted back toward the dugout, and ran interference for Jim as he made for the dugout and the runway leading to the Boston clubhouse.

"This made Roxbury look like a picnic," said patrolman John Ryan, a riot veteran. "Jim could have been hurt bad. We barely got him out of there."

Lonborg arrived in the clubhouse in rags. With Lonborg gone the crowd turned their attention elsewhere. Some made it out to left and dismantled the scoreboard. About twenty kids climbed the screen behind home, and several fell nearly forty feet below to the concrete walkways of the stands. People took chunks of grass and handfuls of dirt as souvenirs.

A man named Ray Copeland, from London, England, took a handful of dirt and put it into a small box. "Going to take this back to England," he said. "I've been working in Boston a year, became a Red Sox fan; and when I go back, some of the soil of Fenway goes with me."

In the locker room, players howled, cried, and laughed. There were actually two celebrations this day. The first one came right after the game, which had clinched at least a tie with Detroit. But the Sox had to wait for the outcome of the second game of the doubleheader between the Tigers and the Angels.

The Tigers had won the first game 6 – 4. If they also took game two, there would be a playoff between them and the Red Sox. If they lost the Sox had the pennant outright.

So the first celebration was the cut-rate celebration — thirty minutes of whooping it up with beer (not champagne) and shaving cream. Williams, covered in cream, looked like he had just emerged from the set of a Three Stooges comedy. He paused long enough to say that, should a playoff become necessary, Lee Stange would pitch. The manager found Stange, who

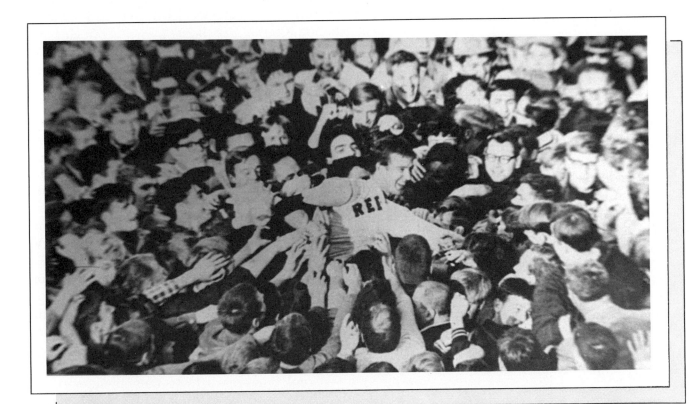

Jim Lonborg rides the crest of a human wave after the clincher. The crunch continued, and the moment turned scary for Jim. (Photo courtesy Boston Red Sox)

was sipping beer in front of his locker. "Take it easy with that stuff, Stinger. You're going tomorrow," he told Stange.

The most emotional moment of the first celebration came when Tom Yawkey entered the dressing room and gave Lonborg

Survivor

Before the game was over, I left the booth to go down into the locker room for a postgame TV show. Ned Martin was doing the radio call, and Mel Parnell was handling the television broadcast. When the game ended, I was in the locker room and saw the players rushing in. Some were crying; some were laughing. Everyone seemed to be shouting. Finally I saw Lonborg, lunging into the runway, jettisoned in by a sea of people and his police escort. His uniform was torn, and he looked completely disheveled. I went over and did an interview on the spot. Understandably Jim was breathless, but he did remarkably well in the interview, considering what he had just been through.

a bear hug. "Jim, you were terrific . . . you were terrif . . ." Yawkey cut the word short as tears appeared in his eyes.

"Mr. Yawkey," Jim offered, "I wish there was something I could say to you to show you how I feel. But I can't think of something appropriate. Isn't that silly?" Yawkey answered, "You did your talking on the field today."

The team then settled down to listen to Tiger broadcaster Ernie Harwell call the Tiger-Angel game. About eight players squeezed into the trainer's room where the radio was. They sent out half-inning updates. The Tigers went ahead 3–1 in the second, but then Don Mincher put the Angels ahead 4–3 with a home run in the third.

Scott came running out of the trainer's room. "Mincher hit one right in the kitchen, right in the kitchen, man. 4–3."

Yaz leapt up from his seat and yelled, "Go get 'em, Rig [Angel manager Bill Rigney]." He then yelled to a clubhouse boy, "Get the champagne, we're going to start to party now."

But no one was ready to do that. There was a long way to go in the game. To help pass the time and distract them from the tension, Joe Foy and some other players started taping up a couple of clubhouse boys like mummies. Yaz paced up and down the room. When a cheer would come out of the trainer's room, Yaz would yell impatiently, "What happened? What happened?"

People paced and prayed in the locker room. The game was piping out to the entire locker room on another radio. "I'm not going to send Rigney a telegram when this is over," said a confident Yaz. "I'm going to call him personally."

Later Yaz called out: "I want a beer. I need a beer. Would you please get me a beer, Fitzy?" Equipment manager Don Fitzpatrick brought Yaz a cold one.

At last the game reached the ninth inning with the Angels leading 8–5. Williams came down from Tom Yawkey's office upstairs to listen to the outcome with his troops. For his part Harwell was playing up the drama by giving a couple of long fly balls a big call in the eighth.

Yaz, Sparky Lyle, and Fitzpatrick sat in the middle of a host of media people. The Tiger ninth started out anxiously as Bill Freehan led with a double. Yaz hid his face in his hands and swore. "Bear down, Minnie," Yaz urged Angel pitcher Minnie Rojas, but Rojas walked Don Wert to put the tying run at the plate with no outs. Yaz ran his fingers through his hair and

looked up at the ceiling. Tiger manager Mayo Smith sent up Lenny Green to bat for Mickey Lolich. Rigney brought in lefty George Brunet.

"Let's send a wire to Brunet," said Yaz, "and promise him a year's supply of beer if he gets the side out."

After Rigney brought in Brunet, Smith sent up Jim Price to hit for Green. Price hit a pop-up behind the plate.

"There may be a play," Harwell called. "No, it's just on the screen." There was a loud groan. On the next pitch, Price flied to left to a great cheer in the Red Sox' clubhouse.

That brought Dick McAuliffe. Someone said softly and ominously: "This guy is tough. He can hit it out." But McAuliffe hit a ground ball to second baseman Bobby Knoop.

Harwell: "Knoop shovels to Fregosi for one. There's the throw to Mincher, and it's a double play!" It was only the second double play that McAuliffe hit into all year.

The Sox celebrate the pennant. Top left, Ken Coleman interviews Dick Williams. Bottom left, Lonborg and Yaz whoop it up. Top right, Yaz and Tom Yawkey share the moment. Bottom right, Rico Petrocelli sings in the shower. (Photos courtesy Boston Red Sox)

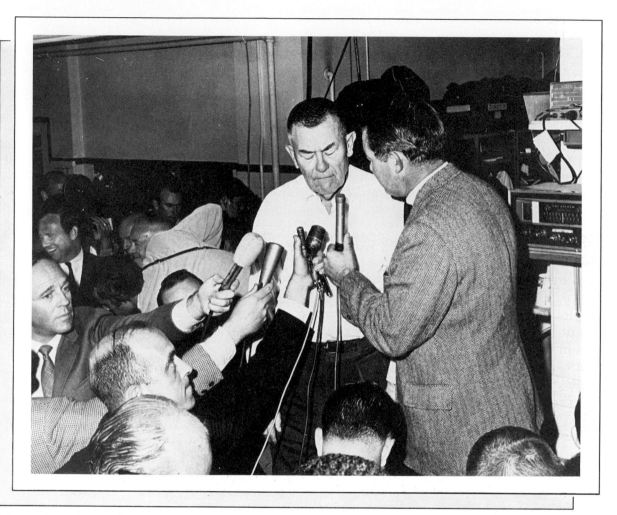

Ken Coleman interviews an emotional Tom Yawkey in the Red Sox' clubhouse after the clincher. (Photo courtesy Boston Red Sox)

Yaz shot out of his chair, and the walls came tumbling down. Dave Morehead and Jose Tartabull put Yaz on their shoulders. There was screaming, dancing, every joyous emotion imaginable. Mike Ryan looked around for someone to hug. He spotted batboy Keith Rosenfeld. "Nice going, Keith!"

Dick Williams hopped up and down and yelled, "It's over! It's over! It's unbelievable!"

Yaz, who today wrapped up the Triple Crown, had just completed one of the most incredible seasons any man has had in the history of the game. He went 7 for 8 in the last two games to finish at .326, 44 HRS, and 121 RBIs. Williams walked over to Yaz. "I've never seen a perfect player," the manager said, "but you were one for us. I never saw a player have a season like that." He then hugged and kissed Carl.

"Kiss him again," the photographers shouted. Williams obliged.

Yaz, wearing underwear and his baseball socks, walked around and shook hands with everybody. "I'm on a trip," he declared.

Tom Yawkey came down again and watched the celebration from inside of Williams's office. He was fighting back tears. Someone gave him a paper cup with champagne in it. "I haven't had one of these in four years," Yawkey said. He walked over to Williams. "I want to have a toast with you, Dick." "Fine," Williams said. He borrowed a glass of champagne from someone walking by. "Here's to you, sir, for giving me the opportunity," said Williams. "And here's to you, Dick, for making the best of it. This is the happiest moment of my life."

At one point in the festivities, Williams was so emotionally overcome that he went into the trainer's room to lie down for a couple of minutes. Coach Al Lakeman went in with him to calm him down. When he came out, Williams was okay and hugged each player. "Here are my kids," he said when he got to Reggie Smith and Mike Andrews. "I was a tough guy at Toronto and a tough guy up here . . . but [I was] a winning tough guy." He then hugged press steward Tommy McCarthy.

Joe Foy's cackle could be heard above the noise: "We win the pennant! We win the pennant! Aaaaaaaah!"

Coach Eddie Popowski was thrown, fully clothed, into the showers.

Williams later announced that Jose Santiago would start the first game of the World Series versus the Cardinals on Wednesday at Fenway. When Jose heard the news, he bolted out of the dressing room to the nearest public phone inside the park. Only trouble was, he forgot to get dressed. There he stood, calling Juana Díaz, Puerto Rico, in just his underpants and a sweatshirt. A group of young girls stood watching and giggling.

When Williams went up to Jerry Adair, he said: "You won it." Adair said nothing. He just smiled.

"Everybody else is dancing around like Indians, pouring champagne everyplace. Adair just sits there alone drinking his. Smart guy," Yawkey observed.

And so it went, this impossible dream. The Red Sox won the pennant.

Everybody Loves a Parade

Dick Bresciani, who is now public relations director of the Red Sox, was at the time working in the public relations department of the University of Massachusetts in Amherst. Dick said that when the final game was over, students filed out of their dorms for a spontaneous parade to downtown Amherst and back.

Final Stats:
10/1/67

American League: Final Stats

Batting

Name	G	AB	R	H	AVG.
Yastrzemski, Boston	161	579	112	189	.326
F. Robinson, Baltimore	129	479	83	149	.311
Kaline, Detroit	130	453	93	140	.309
Scott, Boston	159	565	74	171	.303
Blair, Baltimore	151	552	72	162	.293
Carew, Minnesota	136	514	66	150	.292
Oliva, Minnesota	146	557	76	168	.289
Fregosi, California	150	585	73	168	.287
Freehan, Detroit	154	515	66	146	.283
Clarke, New York	143	533	74	160	.282

Home Runs

Yastrzemski, Boston	44
Killebrew, Minnesota	44
F. Howard, Washington	36
F. Robinson, Baltimore	30
Mincher, California	25
Kaline, Detroit	25

Runs Batted In

Yastrzemski, Boston	121
Killebrew, Minnesota	113
F. Robinson, Baltimore	94
F. Howard, Washington	89
Oliva, Minnesota	83

Pitching
(winning %, based on ten or more decisions)

	Record	Pct.
Santiago, Boston	12-4	.750
Horlen, Chicago	19-7	.731
Hardin, Baltimore	8-3	.727
Wilhelm, Chicago	8-3	.727
Lonborg, Boston	22-9	.710

Team Batting

Name	AB	R	H	HR	RBI	AVG.
Osinski	9		3		1	.333
Yastrzemski	579	112	189	44	121	.326
Scott	565	74	171	19	82	.303
Jones	159	17	46	3	25	.289
Conigliaro	349	59	101	20	67	.287
Adair	415	47	111	3	35	.267
Andrews	494	79	131	8	40	.265
Petrocelli	491	53	127	17	66	.259
Harrelson	332	42	85	12	54	.256
Stephenson	16		4			.250
Lyle	8		2			.250
Foy	446	70	111	16	48	.249
Smith	536	73	131	14	56	.244
Tartabull	246	35	58		10	.236
Thomas	88	9	18	1	6	.205
Gibson	138	6	28	1	14	.203
Santiago	42	5	8	1	4	.190
Ryan	224	21	45	2	26	.201
Brandon	44	3	8		1	.182
Howard	315	22	56	4	26	.178
Siebern	102	10	18		11	.176
Bell	74	7	12		2	.162
Lonborg	97	7	14		8	.144
Morehead	12	1	1			.083
Stange	48	2	3		1	.063
Wyatt	11		1			.091
Landis	1	1				.000

Team Pitching

Name	IP	H	BB	SO	W	L	ERA
Lyle	43	33	14	42	1	2	2.30
Osinski	64	61	14	38	3	1	2.53
Wyatt	93	71	39	68	10	7	2.67
Stange	182	171	32	101	8	10	2.77
Lonborg	273	228	83	246	22	9	3.16
Bell	226	193	71	154	13	13	3.31
Santiago	145	138	46	109	12	4	3.60
Stephenson	40	32	16	24	3	1	3.83
Brandon	158	147	59	95	5	11	4.16
Morehead	48	48	22	40	5	4	4.31
Landis	26	24	11	23	1	0	5.19

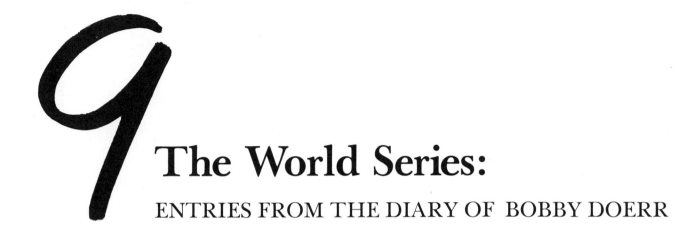

The World Series:

ENTRIES FROM THE DIARY OF BOBBY DOERR

With Boston's win and Detroit's loss on the last day, Fenway would see the October Classic for the first time since 1946. As it was twenty-one years earlier, the opposition would be the St. Louis Cardinals. And as it was twenty-one years earlier, the Cardinals would win in seven games.

One of the key participants of the '46 Series was Hall of Fame second baseman Bobby Doerr. In '67, of course, Bobby was the Red Sox' first base coach and batting instructor. During the season and the Series, Bobby kept a personal diary. His entries for the seven games of the World Series follow; they are published here for the first time ever.

World Series: Game One

WEDNESDAY, OCTOBER 4, AT BOSTON

The World Series atmosphere in Boston has been wonderful for me to experience. I cannot help but think back to 1946, when we also hooked up with St. Louis. The whole town is caught up in this in a way I wouldn't think possible. Yesterday, Dalton Jones, Rico Petrocelli, Dick Williams, Dick O'Connell, and I went to City Hall for ceremonies honoring the team. Mayor Collins

A Warning

Before the Series began, team wit George Thomas spoke at a celebration dinner held on Monday night. He warned Carl Yastrzemski: "Don't get overconfident because right now we both have the same average in the World Series — .000."

Thomas went on to say that what Yaz had done in the regular season wasn't so great: "He just had the kind of season I had in spring training." Thomas hit .400 in grapefruit league play.

presented us with inscribed silver cigarette boxes. The mayor predicted the Red Sox in five games.

Before the game, the clubhouse was generally relaxed. Some tension's inevitable, though. Dick called the team together and told us to just go out and do our best. He thanked everyone for their efforts to get us here. In the papers, Dick predicted that we'd win more than we lose in the Series, and said he looked for a lot of runs. I think the Series will be closer than a lot of people are saying. They have the Cards as 3 – 1 favorites, but we'll give them a battle. I think the pitching will be strong, with Jim Lonborg for us and Bob Gibson for them dominating.

We spent part of the morning going over scouting reports compiled by Frank Malzone, Eddie Kasko, and Don Lenhardt. Don scouts the St. Louis area for us.

In the game, it was bright sunshine. Gibson was overpowering. Jose Santiago did a good job for us. He held the Cardinals to just two runs in seven innings, and even hit a home run in the third to tie the game at 1 – 1. But Gibson showed why he's one of the best. Went all the way, fanned 10, including Rico three times. Rico and Ken Harrelson didn't look too good at the plate.

Yaz made a great throw to get Lou Brock at home, and also made a good catch against the wall off Curt Flood. George Scott had two hits.

World Series: Game Two

THURSDAY, OCTOBER 5, AT BOSTON

We evened the Series up today with a 5 – 0 win. Jim Lonborg was *great!* It had to be the best game he's ever pitched, anywhere. He had his sharp curve, good fastball, and great control (one walk). Jim had a no-hitter until two outs in the eighth, when Julian Javier doubled. Yaz had no chance to get the ball. After the hit, the crowd gave Jim one of the loudest ovations I think I've ever heard. We all felt the emotion on the bench. Jim came in the dugout after the inning was over, and couldn't say anything. He faced just 29 batters.

At the plate, Yaz did it again, with two home runs . . . a solo shot in the fourth and a three-run blast in the seventh that put the game out of reach, giving us the five-run lead. The second homer was off lefty Joe Hoerner. Before the game, Carl told me he'd be going for the fences. "If I hit one, it will shake things up," was the way he put it. He told me he thought he was too tentative yesterday against Gibson [0-for-4]. He said he needed the Big Swing.

There was great fielding also. Jerry Adair and Rico made terrific plays at third and short. Jerry's was a backhander off of Lou Brock; Rico went into the hole to throw out Curt Flood.

But the whole story was Lonborg. Elston Howard helped Jim out a lot, I think. Ellie said that he still had a "book" on the Cardinals around from that 1964 Series team.

After the game, everyone was after Jim for interviews. He told the writers that Javier's hit was a moment of "agony" in an otherwise great day. There were so many writers after Yaz, too, that he had to stand on a chair so they could all hear him. An hour after the game, Carl was still in uniform. He went onto the field to do interviews for the TV guys. Yaz has handled the press like a true pro.

Jim's performance got some of us talking about Don Larsen's perfect game in the '56 Series against Brooklyn. Sal Maglie, our pitching coach, pitched that day for the Dodgers. Sal pointed out that today's game was almost a repeat of the Larsen game. He said Mickey Mantle hit a home run off him in the fourth inning that day, and pointed out that Yaz also hit one in the fourth.

World Series: Game Three

SATURDAY, OCTOBER 7, AT ST. LOUIS

Gary Bell started for us today. Lou Brock led off the first with a triple. He scored quickly on Curt Flood's single. Seemed like after that, we lost some momentum. In the second, Mike Shannon hit a two-run homer off Bell on a high breaking pitch. Gary was just up with everything today, and lasted just two innings. Gary Waslewski came on next, and pitched three shutout innings. He didn't give up a thing, not even a hit.

We got a run back in the sixth to make it 3 – 1 as Dalton Jones singled to score Mike Andrews. But in the bottom of the sixth, Cards got it right back off Lee Stange. Brock beat out a bunt, and

October 5, 1967

ST. LOUIS	ab	r	h	rbi		BOSTON	ab	r	h	rbi
Name						Name				
Brock, lf	4					Tartabull, rf . .	4	1		
Flood, cf	3					Jones, 3b. . . .	5	1	2	
Maris, rf	3					Yastrzemski, lf	4	2	3	4
Cepeda, 1b . .	3					Scott, 1b	4	1	1	
McCarver, c. .	3					Smith, cf	3			
Shannon, 3b.	3					Adair, 2b. . . .	4		2	
Javier, 2b. . .	3	1				Petrocelli, ss.	2	1	1	
Maxvill, ss. . .	2					Howard, c. . . .	3			
Tolan, ph. . . .	1					Lonborg, p. . .	4			
Bressoud, ss.										
Hughes, p. . .	2									
Willis, p.										
Hoerner, p. . .										
Lamabe, p. . .										
Ricketts, ph. .	1									
TOTALS	28	1				TOTALS	33	5	9	5

Team	1	2	3	4	5	6	7	8	9
St. Louis.	0	0	0	0	0	0	0	0	0
Boston	0	0	1	0	1	0	3	0	X	5

Name	IP	H	R	ER	BB	SO
St. Louis						
Hughes (w)	5⅓	4	2	2	3	5
Willis.	⅔	1	2	2	2	1
Hoerner.	⅔	2	1	1		
Lamabe.	1⅓	2				2
Boston						
Lonborg (w)	9	1			1	4

October 7, 1967

BOSTON	ab	r	h	rbi		ST. LOUIS	ab	r	h	rbi
Name						Name				
Tartabull, rf. .	4					Brock, lf	4	2	2	
Jones, 3b. . . .	4	3	1			Flood, cf.	4		1	1
Yastrzemski, lf	3					Maris, rf	4	1	2	1
Scott, 1b. . . .	4					Cepeda, 1b. .	4		1	1
Smith, cf. . . .	4	1	2	1		McCarver, c. .	4	1	1	
Adair, 2b. . . .	4					Shannon, 3b.	3	1	2	2
Petrocelli, ss.	4					Javier, 2b. . . .	3	1		
Howard, c. . .	2		1			Maxvill, ss. . .	3			
Bell, p.						Briles, p.	3			
Thomas, ph. .	1									
Waslewski, p.										
Andrews, ph. .	1	1	1							
Stange, p. . . .										
Foy, ph.	1									
Osinski, p. . . .										
TOTALS	32	2	7			TOTALS	32	5	10	5

Team	1	2	3	4	5	6	7	8	9
Boston	0	0	0	0	0	1	1	0	0	2
St. Louis.	1	2	0	0	0	1	0	1	X	5

Name	IP	H	R	ER	BB	SO
Boston						
Bell (l).	2	5	3	3		1
Waslewski.	3					3
Stange.	2	3	1			
Osinski.	2	1	1	1		
St. Louis						
Briles (w).	9	7	2	2		3

Stange worried too much about his speed at first. Tried to pick him off, but threw the ball away, and Brock went to third. Roger Maris singled him home to make it 4 – 1.

Reggie Smith homered in the seventh to make it 4 – 2, but Osinski gave up a run in the eighth on Orlando Cepeda's double. Final score: 5 – 2, Cardinals.

Yaz was 0-for-3. He had some good pitches to hit, but was swinging too hard and missed everything. Jones had three hits and has looked good. He took extra B.P. before the game, and it paid off.

Nelson Briles was tough on us . . . nine innings, seven hits, no walks. But I believe we will get to him if we get another shot at him.

World Series: Game Four

SUNDAY, OCTOBER 8, AT ST. LOUIS

From the start, we just didn't have it today. Starter Jose Santiago couldn't get through the first inning, giving up six hits and four runs. He was pounded. Brock beat out an infield hit to lead it off. I thought Jones could have come in better on the ball, but he was too late with the play. With Brock's speed, you can't make any mistakes. That opened the gates for four runs. Then in the third, Jerry Stephenson came in and gave up two more. It was 6 – 0, and that's the way it stayed.

A bright spot was Dave Morehead, who pitched three innings of shutout long relief. And the kid Ken Brett came in for the eighth, and looked sharp, striking out one. He's fast, and has a great curve. Hard to believe he's still a teenager.

For them, it was Bob Gibson again. We couldn't touch him [four singles and a double in nine innings].

Now, we're down three games to one, and everyone realizes that we can't lose again. But we've come back all year, and I think we will again. One good thing is the mood in the clubhouse. No gloom and doom. There's still a lot of noise and talking it up. The writer Jimmy Cannon had a good line in the papers, something like, "Teams drown in silence when they give up."

We haven't lost spirit, and haven't given up.

October 8, 1967

BOSTON				ST. LOUIS			
Name	ab	r	h rbi		ab	r	h rbi
Tartabull, rf. . .	4	2		Brock, lf.	4	1	2
Jones, 3b. . . .	4			Flood, cf.	4	1	
Yastrzemski, lf	4	2		Maris, rf.	4	1	1 2
Scott, 1b. . . .	4	1		Cepeda, 1b. .	4	1	1 2
Smith, cf. . . .	3			McCarver, c. .	3	1	1 2
Adair, 2b. . . .	4			Shannon, 3b.	3	1	
Petrocelli, ss.	3			Javier, 2b. . . .	4		2 1
Howard, c. . . .	2			Maxvill, ss. . .	3		1 1
Morehead, p. .				B. Gibson, p. .	3		
Siebern, ph. .	1						
Brett, p.							
Santiago, p. . .							
Bell, p.							
Foy, ph.	1						
Stephenson, p							
Ryan, c.	2						
TOTALS	32	5		TOTALS	32	6	9 6

Team	1	2	3	4	5	6	7	8	9
Boston	0	0	0	0	0	0	0	0	0
St. Louis	4	0	2	0	0	0	0	X	6

Name	IP	H	R	ER	BB	SO
Boston						
Santiago (l).	⅔	6	4	4		
Bell.	1⅓					
Stephenson.	2	3	2	2	1	
Morehead.	3				1	2
Brett.	1				1	1
St. Louis						
B. Gibson (w).	9	5			1	6

World Series: Game Five

MONDAY, OCTOBER 9, AT ST. LOUIS

Once again, Dick Williams gathered the boys together before the game. He told them that we've been in tough spots before and got out of them, and that we'd do it this time too. He also said that no matter what happened from here on out, he was proud of all of them.

In the game, we got another brilliant game from Jim Lonborg. The best word I can use to describe Jim today was "determined." He was as determined and business-like as I've ever seen him. He went all the way, and gave up just three hits and a run. He didn't walk a batter and struck out four. Jim was getting his sharp curve over regularly, and used his fastball intelligently, in spots . . . did a great job at setting Cardinal hitters up.

Through eight, this was a 1 – 0 game as Steve Carlton and Ray Washburn gave up just the single run in the third . . . Foy singled, went to second on an error, and scored on Ken Harrelson's hit.

In the dugout and on the field, I could feel the tension mounting as we went into the ninth. Red Schoendienst [Cardinal manager] brought in Ron Willis to pitch the ninth. George Scott walked. Reggie Smith doubled him to third. They purposely passed Rico to get at Elston Howard. They brought in Jack Lamabe, and Ellie came through with a bloop hit down the line in right, in front of Maris. Two runs came in . . . one on the hit, the second on Maris' throwing error. Those two runs were big, because Maris hit a solo home run with two outs in the ninth, to make it 3 – 1. But Joe Foy robbed Orlando Cepeda for the last out . . . great play . . . Joe went to his knees to field the ball. Joe's been kind of a forgotten man for us, but he had a great game today . . . he made another great play off Dal Maxvill earlier in the game, backhand grab taking a double play.

Lonborg showed today that you can't beat that good pitching! Jim has now given up just four hits in his two games. Someone said that's a new Series record for fewest hits allowed in two consecutive Series games.

There was a lot of clubhouse talk about how the St. Louis papers have been calling us the "Dead Sox" when we were down three games to one. Dick taped the clipping on the dressing

He's My Brother

For the World Series games in St. Louis, the family of young Ken Brett made the journey from California to be on hand. Included, of course, was Ken's younger brother, George, who was destined to become a superstar in the seventies and eighties with the Kansas City Royals. George said that having his brother pitch in the World Series was a tremendous thrill for all the family, though they did have trepidations about Ken's going up against the mighty Cardinals on national TV. After all he was still a teenager.

George, who was fourteen at the time, also said that because he knew Red Sox catcher Jerry Moses, he was allowed to ride on the team bus from the hotel to the stadium for one of the games. He said that when they got to the park, he was later introduced on the field to Carl Yastrzemski. George said he was so thrilled, he was virtually speechless.

room wall. Everyone saw it. It really fired the boys up, especially Yaz, who led the charge out of the dugout in the first by yelling "Let's win this one!"

October 9, 1967

BOSTON					ST. LOUIS				
Name	ab	r	h	rbi	Name	ab	r	h	rbi
Foy, 3b.	5	1	1		Brock, lf.	4			
Andrews, 2b.	3	1			Flood, cf.	4			
Yastrzemski, lf	3	1			Maris, rf.	4	1	2	1
Harrelson, rf.	3	1	1		Cepeda, 1b.	4			
Tartabull, rf.					McCarver, c.	3			
Scott, 1b.	3	1			Shannon, 3b.	3			
Smith, cf.	4	1	1		Javier, 2b.	3			
Petrocelli, ss.	3				Maxvill, ss.	2		1	
Howard, c.	4	1	1		Ricketts, ph.	1			
Lonborg, p.	4				Willis, p.				
					Lamabe, p.				
					Carlton, p.	1			
					Tolan, ph.	1			
					Washburn, p.				
					Gagliano, ph.	1			
					Bressoud, ss.				
TOTALS	32	3	6	2	TOTALS	31	1	3	1

	1	2	3	4	5	6	7	8	9	
Boston	0	0	1	0	0	0	0	0	2	3
St. Louis	0	0	0	0	0	0	0	1		1

	IP	H	R	ER	BB	SO
Boston						
Lonborg (w)	9	3	1	1		4
St. Louis						
Carlton (l)	6	3	1	1	2	5
Washburn	2	1				2
Willis	1	2	1		2	
Lamabe	1	1				2

October 11, 1967

ST. LOUIS					BOSTON				
Name	ab	r	h	rbi	Name	ab	r	h	rbi
Brock, lf.	5	2	2	3	Foy, 3b.	4	1	1	1
Flood, cf.	5	1	1		Andrews, 2b.	5	1	2	1
Maris, rf.	4	2			Yastrzemski, lf	4	2	3	1
Cepeda, 1b.	5	1			Harrelson, rf.	3			
McCarver, c.	3				Tartabull, rf.				
Shannon, 3b.	4	1			Adair, ph.				1
Javier, 2b.	4	1	1		Bell, p.				
Maxvill, ss.	3				Scott, 1b.	4		1	
Hughes, p.	1				Smith, cf.	4	1	2	2
Willis, p.					Petrocelli, ss.	3	2	2	2
Spiezio, ph.	1				Howard, c.	4			
Briles, p.					Waslewski, p.	1			
Tolan, ph.	1				Wyatt, p.				
Lamabe, p.					Jones, ph.	1	1	1	
Hoerner, p.					Thomas, rf.	1			
Jaster, p.									
Washburn, p.									
Ricketts, ph.	1								
Woodeshick, p									
TOTALS	36	4	8	4	TOTALS	34	8	12	8

Team	1	2	3	4	5	6	7	8	9	
St. Louis	0	0	2	0	0	0	2	0	0	4
Boston	0	1	0	3	0	0	4	0	X	8

Name	IP	H	R	ER	BB	SO
St. Louis						
Hughes	3⅔	5	4	4		2
Willis	⅓					
Briles	2					1
Lamabe (l)	⅓	2	2	2		
Jaster	⅓	2				
Washburn	⅓					1
Woodeshick	1	1				
Boston						
Waslewski	5⅓	4	2	2	2	4
Wyatt (w)	1⅔	1	2	2		1
Bell	2	3				1

Gary Waslewski forever became a part of Red Sox lore when he was tapped by Dick Williams to start the must-win Game Six of the Series. (Photo courtesy Boston Red Sox)

World Series: Game Six

WEDNESDAY, OCTOBER 11, AT BOSTON

Dick Williams pulled the surprise of the Series today by starting rookie Gary Waslewski. But to those who've been around the

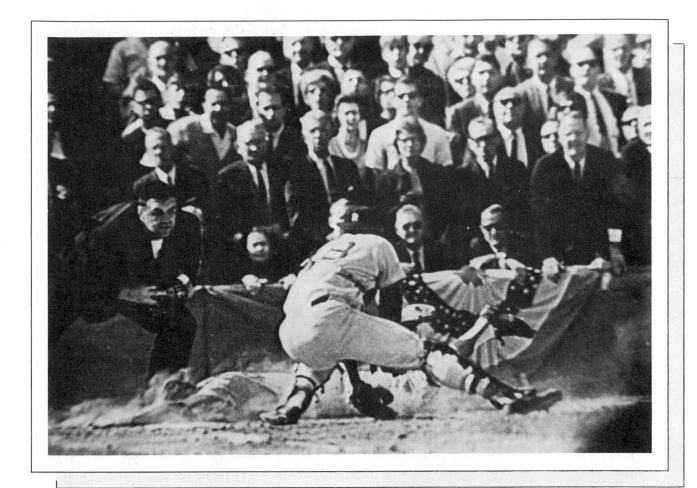

Cardinals' Lou Brock slides in head first just ahead of Carl Yastrzemski's throw in the third inning of Game Six. Elston Howard slaps the tag on too late. Sox won, however, 8–4. (Photo courtesy Boston Red Sox)

ballclub, it wasn't really a surprise. Gary's a real battler, much the way Jim Lonborg is. Plus, he looked good in game three with three shutout innings in relief. Dick's hunches have worked all year.

Gary did well... went five and a third innings [four hits] before tiring in the sixth. We had the long ball working... crowd loved it. Rico hit a solo shot in the second. In the fourth, we unloaded. Yaz, Reggie Smith, and Rico all hit home runs... set a record for home runs by a team in one inning.

The Cardinals tied it up 4–4 in the sixth on Lou Brock's two-run homer off John Wyatt, but in the bottom of the seventh, we came on again. The fans helped us out a lot. They were on their feet for the seventh-inning stretch, and they really started cheering and yelling. It gave the whole bench a lift.

We got four in the seventh. Jones singled and scored on Foy's double. Mike Andrews singled for run number two. Yaz singled. Adair hit a sacrifice fly to score Mike. Smith's bloop to center

Bob Gibson, about to rocket another pitch in the Series. (Photo courtesy Boston Red Sox)

scored Yaz. It was 8 – 4 (the final score), and the Fenway fans really went wild.

Gary Bell came on in the eighth, and had his troubles, loading up the bases. But Yaz made a great one-hand catch off of Tim McCarver. In the ninth, George Thomas took a home run away from Brock by taking the ball out of the Sox bullpen.

Scotty was swinging from the heels, and didn't do much.

So now the Series is tied at three games each. I remember being in this position in 1946 against the Cardinals. But what's different this time is that we weren't supposed to get this far. They said we couldn't win the pennant but did. When we were down to the Cards three games to one, a lot of people wrote us off. But we came back. Now, no matter what happens tomorrow, this team can be proud of itself. I know I'm so proud to be associated with these young men.

World Series: Game Seven

THURSDAY, OCTOBER 12, AT BOSTON

The World Title wasn't to be. Jim Lonborg came back after just two days' rest, and he didn't have it, although no one could have given it a better effort. Bob Gibson pitched on three days' rest, and I think that made the difference. Gibson was on top of his game again: outstanding fastball, good quick curve, fine control. We didn't get a hit off him until Scotty tripled in the fifth. I have to believe if Jim had three days' rest, we might have won it. He's been outstanding in his last three games, but today he just didn't "snap" the ball the way he was in his two previous starts in the Series.

We were all hoping we could win to bring the World Title to Mr. Yawkey. My thoughts were with Mr. Yawkey all day, thinking about how close we came in 1946, too.

The Cardinals got a pair in the second, two in the fifth, and three in the sixth. Brock, Maris, and Javier had two hits each. We got a run in the fifth when Scotty tripled and Javier threw the ball in the dugout. In the eighth, Rico doubled, went to third on a wild pitch (one of the few mistakes Gibson has made the entire

October 12, 1967

ST. LOUIS	ab	r	h	rbi	BOSTON	ab	r	h	rbi
Name									
Brock, lf....	4	1	2		Foy, 3b.....	3			
Flood, cf....	3	1	1		Morehead, p..				
Maris, rf....	3	2	1		Osinski, p....				
Cepeda, 1b..	5				Brett, p.....				
McCarver, c..	5	1	1		Andrews, 2b..	3			
Shannon, 3b.	4	1			Yastrzemski, lf	3	1		
Javier, 2b...	4	1	2	3	Scott, 1b....	4			
Maxvill, ss...	4	1	1		Harrelson, rf.	4	1	1	
B. Gibson, p..	4	1	1	1	Smith, cf....	3			
					Petrocelli, ss.	3	1	1	
					Howard, c....	2			
					Jones, 3b....				
					Lonborg, p...	1			
					Tartabull, ph..	1			
					Santiago, p..				
					Siebern, ph..	1		1	1
					R. Gibson, c..				
TOTALS	36	7	10	6	TOTALS	28	2	3	1

Team	1	2	3	4	5	6	7	8	9	
St. Louis........	0	0	2	0	2	3	0	0	0	7
Boston.........	0	0	0	1	0	0	1	0		2

Name	IP	H	R	ER	BB	SO
St. Louis						
Gibson (w).................	9	3	2	2	3	10
Boston						
Lonborg (l).................	6	10	7	6	1	3
Santiago..................	2					1
Morehead.................	1/3				3	1
Osinski...................	1/3					
Brett.....................	1/3					

Cards' Tim McCarver slides safely into second at Fenway. Rico Petrocelli's not doing a war dance; he's signaling for the cutoff man to "hold the throw." (Photo courtesy Boston Red Sox)

Series), and scored on a ground out to second. But by the time that run scored we were down 7 – 1. The run was the last run of the game, for a final of St. Louis 7 and Boston 2.

There were some tears in the clubhouse afterwards, but there was also a lot of pride and good feeling. This has been a truly amazing year. I'm sure that what happened this year will stay with us and the fans a long, long time.

World Series Batting Totals
(Players listed in order of appearance in Series games)

	G	AB	R	H	RBI	HR	AVG.
Adair.	5	16		2	1		.125
Jones.	6	18	2	7	1		.389
Yastrzemski.	7	25	4	10	5	3	.400
Harrelson.	4	13		1	1		.077
Wyatt.	2						–
Foy.	6	15	2	2	1		.133
Scott.	7	26	3	6			.231
Petrocelli.	7	20	3	4	3	2	.200
Morehead.	2						–
Brett.	2						–
Andrews.	5	13	2	4	1		.308
Smith.	7	24	3	6	3	2	.250
Gibson.	2	2					.000
Siebern.	3	3		1	1		.333
Tartabull.	7	13	1	2			.154
Santiago.	3	2	1	1	1	1	.500
Howard.	7	18		2	1		.111
Lonborg.	3	9					.000
Bell.	3						–
Thomas.	2	2					.000
Waslewski.	2	1					.000
Stange.	1						–
Osinski.	2						–
Stephenson.	1						–
Ryan.	1	2					.000
Totals.	**7**	**222**	**21**	**48**	**19**	**8**	**.216**

World Series Pitching Totals
(Players listed in order of appearance in Series games)

	G	CG	IP	H	R	ER	BB	SO	W	L	ERA
Santiago.	3		9.2	16	6	6	3	6		2	5.40
Wyatt.	2		3.2	1	2	2	3	1	1		6.00
Lonborg.	3	2	24	14	8	7	2	11	2	1	2.63
Bell.	3		5.1	8	3	3	1	1		1	5.40
Waslewski.	2		8.1	4	2	2	2	7			2.25
Stange.	1		2	3	1	0					0.00
Osinski.	2		1.1	2	1	1					9.00
Stephenson.	1		2	3	2	2	1				9.00
Morehead.	2		3.1	0	0	0	4	3			0.00
Brett.	2		1.1	0	0	0	1	1			0.00
Totals.	**7**	**2**	**61**	**51**	**25**	**23**	**17**	**30**	**3**	**4**	**3.39**

Composite Score by Innings:

	1	2	3	4	5	6	7	8	9	
St. Louis.	5	2	7	0	3	4	3	1	1	25
Boston.	0	1	2	4	1	2	8	1	2	21

World Series Stats

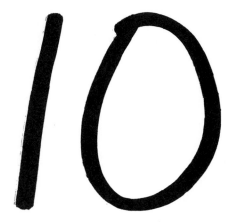

Echoes of a Dream

We heard a lot of claims made for 1967. In this book Don and I have made some of the strongest. But can it be any other way? A season such as 1967, while it is happening and especially after years of hindsight, pulls too strongly on our memories and our emotions. By its magic it elevates itself out of the ordinary, out of the simply unusual, and into a changeless and unaffected spot in our lives.

Is this making too much out of what happened over that summer more than two decades past? I don't think so. As head of the Red Sox' radio/TV broadcast team that year, I was one of just a handful of people who witnessed every game. I lived with that season as a major part of my life. I sat behind the microphone and described the action of a season that became a milestone in Boston sports history. I watched what by all logic should have been just another routine baseball year become history in the making.

Almost every time I get the chance to meet and talk with fans, the topic of The Impossible Dream comes up . . . someone will tell me where they were when they heard my call of Jose Tartabull's throw to the plate to get Ken Berry in Chicago; another will ask me how I remember a certain play. Whenever I discuss 1967 with people, it always sets up a mood, a tone, of happiness, of lightness, of joy — I can even call it freedom of spirit. Nineteen-sixty-seven was a year rooted on sacred ground, if you will. It was a year that defied cynical probing. Of course there were controversies, disputes, Dick Williams's doghouse. We have looked at these blemishes in this book. But the truth is that, as fans, we have allowed the dramatic push to the pennant to speak for itself and stand as the overriding commentary on that year. Almost instinctively we haven't tried to strap 1967 into the straitjacket that we sometimes buckle around many of the otherwise unqualified joys of our lives, because, in our lives, few joys are total. For example, the promotion and new job may mean more money, but also an overbearing responsibility. Baseball, though, is a game; and when a particular season passes, it becomes frozen in time. It will always be good for us.

This explains our approach in this book — to examine what happened and to relive the games for no other purpose than to remember, in detail, the truly special joy of that year. We were touched by an impossible dream that came true. A dream — always we must dream.

We dream because life is imperfect. There is always more to wish for, to reach for. There are always changes we'd like to make. For all of us — broadcasters, ballplayers, fans — life is a combination of joy and suffering, hope and dejection, fulfillment and failure.

And we dream because life is important. What we do, what we say, what we observe . . . it all matters as we go about living our lives. Because we occasionally know the partial tastes of momentary success, we have in our own minds the justification to dream. The greatest fool is one who ridicules a dream as foolish, because all accomplishments begin as dreams, and more often than I'm sure we realize, dreams do come true. If a desperate hope is achieved — just once — it gives validity to all hope. Maybe that's the true significance of what happened in Boston in 1967. The Impossible Dream was a shared dream for millions of people. What we all hoped for came true. How can we not think back and feel the idealism?

It's a fact that 1967 was a watershed year for the Boston franchise. It reestablished the Red Sox as winners and, for years to come, as legitimate contenders. It put millions and millions of fans into the stands. It changed the way the whole country thought about Boston baseball. They were a "topic" again, and they have remained to this day on the agenda of the nation's baseball fans. All this grew from 1967's seed. In a very real and literal way, the Cardiac Kids saved Boston baseball from slow death.

As we have seen, it wasn't so much the fact that they won, but *how* they won, beating 100 – 1 odds. It was a year of comebacks. It was game after game of never giving up and never giving in no matter how bleak the situation. It was a year of belief.

I'm convinced we all learned something from this. But what? We are, after all, talking about a game played by men for money, in other words, a business (though far less businesslike than today's game). However, that's no reason to ignore the emotional benefits of the game. Why should baseball be segregated from the rest of life as a valid life experience? Why should we prevent it from having its due importance? Why can't baseball be allowed the same capacity to elevate us into higher truths, about our human condition, that we freely and unthinkingly grant the more pretentious and manufactured dramas of movies, music, and MTV? The fact is this: a season like The Impossible Dream gives baseball this transcendent ability.

Baseball can be insignificant, irrelevant, and boring; but it also can be a cause for reflection, for meditation, for exhilaration. It can channel us into emotions that rejuvenate us and send us on our way into our daily lives uplifted. Baseball can be the catalyst for happiness and laughter. Out of millions of fans, sheer odds alone say that baseball must mean this to certain people. The lasting effect of 1967 proves this.

This book chronicles The Impossible Dream so that readers may remember and enjoy it more completely, at their own pace and leisure, and savor the nostalgic sense of happiness that a particular story or game may bring. "Savor" is a fitting word. It means the deliberate, unrushed enjoyment of some thing or experience. To savor is to appreciate in the fullest sense. You may say that's what this book aspires to be: an appreciation of 1967. Specific games and plays are, in fact, savored like fine wine from a bottle that never seems to run dry. We've looked at these plays, these games, in this book. On each rereading, these events can come alive and be fresh and new. You really hold in your hands a time machine.

Enough time has passed now for these special moments to have achieved an almost archetypal, mythical status in our minds. The mere mention of the two words *Tartabull's throw* conjures up an entire sequence in the mind's eye. This sequence is stored inside like a movie threaded in an endless loop on a projector. The words *Tartabull's throw* is the switch that turns the projector on. We've all experienced this type of thing with other events in our lives, moments whose timing and effects have lifted them out of the ordinary and the forgotten. Examples abound. Of course there are the personal milestones of life: births, graduations, weddings, and the like. Then there are communal milestones, those that derive an extra power from the fact that they were public events and so many people simultaneously participated in them. I think of such things as VJ Day's ending World War II, the moon landing on July 20, 1969, and even such tragedies as the assassination of President Kennedy in 1963 or the explosion of the space shuttle "Challenger" early in 1986.

To hundreds of thousands of fans, the Impossible Dream is such a mythical event. Those who lived through it share it in common; those who are too young to remember have their own joy: that of discovery, of reading about it and getting a small taste of the adventure.

In talking with people about 1967, I've often heard the word *miracle* come up. Miracle. An event for which there is no rational explanation. I must admit that at first I thought the term a little strong. Maybe this has to do with the fact that for so many years I've been part of baseball from the inside, where much of the glory disappears and what you see is the grind; but now I'm not so sure.

I'm not an expert on miracles; but I do think that if there are miracles, they are made for adults, not children. In childhood, miracles are *supposed* to happen. A child incorporates the miraculous into his or her life as an everyday reality. A miracle is no big deal. To a child a miracle is not miraculous. But with adults it's different. Part of the price we pay for losing our innocence is losing faith. So what do we do in the face of a miracle? We either accept this slap in the face of our cynicism as a cause to be more cynical, or we embrace it and find rejuvenation. And when a team like the '67 Red Sox wins the pennant, we find out where we stand.

Baseball has a special place in the hearts and minds of Americans. Sometimes, when I'm in a plane and I look down on the landscape below, I'm intrigued by the number of baseball diamonds I see: stadiums, little league diamonds, high school diamonds, sandlot diamonds. The ninety-foot base paths, the exact geometry, the green and brown colors stand out easily amid urban chaos and clutter. Baseball is literally part of our geographical landscape and equally a part of our psychic pastorals.

If baseball were not just a household word but also a household object, it would be a mirror for each action imparts an equal but reverse reaction. Each particular play can be broken down into a series of opposites: a run scored by one team is a run given up by the other; an RBI single raises both the batting average of the hitter and the ERA of the pitcher; a man reaches on an error by the shortstop — his batting average goes down on the 0 for 1 and the shortstop's fielding average drops as well.

Each at bat is also a batter faced, every double play turned is one hit into, a batter's home run is a pitcher's gopher ball, one team's home stand is part of another's road trip. It all depends on your point of view.

Each of these opposites, taken in totality and added together over a February-to-October time frame, equals a season. Each put out, stolen base, run, catch, error — all of it — is a piece to a large puzzle, which, when put together, forms a picture of ourselves at play.

Baseball is a perfectly devised game. All of its dimensions are just right. When considering the nature of this game, however, we must first remember one thing: baseball is play. To really be called baseball, the game must be fun. It must make us feel good whether we are playing it, watching it, or describing it. It must always be two teams of kids picking sides. Right field closed off. A jacket serving as third base. An old newspaper held down by a rock functioning nicely as the plate. Baseball must always be this. For if, between the lines, baseball cannot be innocent, it loses its character and becomes little more than a parody of itself.

In his mind a kid on the sandlot is a big leaguer. In the field he is Carl Yastrzemski in left throwing out a base runner. On the mound he is Jim Lonborg winning the pennant on the last game of the season. At the plate he is George Scott hitting a tater. And it should work the other way around. Every major leaguer must retain a little bit of that kid having fun, otherwise he becomes nothing more than a mercenary. In baseball a child is father to the man.

This is baseball: a simple game encased in carefree joy. When it masquerades as business, or when business masquerades as baseball, something's terribly wrong.

The game fits nicely with the pace of our lives. We may say that baseball coincides with life. Many things have changed since 1967: artificial grass, double knit uniforms, salaries; but baseball is still unlike life because there is no clock. In real life we live by the clock. We live by the artificial purpose and constant pressure it puts on our actions. In baseball purpose comes from the action itself, not from an underlying meaning placed on that action by a clock. In that sense maybe baseball represents or invokes a more distant past in each of us, an experience out of time that we as a race experienced in prehistory and as individuals in early childhood. In no other game is the cliché truer: it's not whether you win or lose, but how you play that counts. You can never run out of time in the bottom of the ninth. You may run out of determination, you may run out of will, you may simply run out of outs . . . but never time. Because of that deeds can be performed more deliberately, more strategically. Perfection is the goal because perfection is possible. Ask Don Larsen or even Billy Rohr.

The real miracle of 1967 is that it happened, not as the conscious effort applied to a preconceived plan, but in spite of just about everything. And because it happened, we have the memory, a point inside the heart where we can return time and again, a changeless region that, despite whatever snows and cold winds surround it, always remains temperate and calm.

This leaves us at the end of the story. But it's a temporary leaving, for so many will not forget. Which brings to mind a saying found on the Yad Vasham memorial in Jerusalem: "The mystery of redemption lies in remembrance."

So it is with the Impossible Dream.

Sox Survey

As part of the research for this book, players and coaches from 1967 were sent a survey. Here are a few selected responses.

What did it mean to your life to be associated with the 1967 Red Sox?

Ken Brett: "Being lucky enough to participate in a World Series at my age was unreal. To get a World Series ring at age twenty had quite an effect on my career and made me want to be in the majors all the more. Plus all the media, Yaz's great year, all the characters I met [Bell, Thomas, Gibson]. I only wish I was old enough to really appreciate what I was involved in at such a young age."

Mike Ryan: "1967 will always be a banner year for me due to three great events: (1) my brother Steven arrived home from Vietnam; (2) I was married; (3) I participated in my first World Series."

Billy Rohr: "The thrill of a lifetime and memories forever."

Bobby Doerr: "It meant a great thrill seeing players that I had worked with in the minors. It was wonderful to see them do so well in the majors and to be with them."

Dick Williams: "It started my major league managerial career after thirteen years in the majors as a player. If you win, you can stay on a few years."

Bill Landis: "It completed a dream I had from childhood to play in the majors and the World Series. It also meant the friendship of the players and the fans throughout New England."

Russ Gibson: "The biggest thrill of my life. Having always been a Red Sox fan from Fall River, it was something else. I'll never forget Mr. Yawkey, the finest man in baseball."

Jerry Stephenson: "Was happy for my dad because it meant at least one year I wouldn't have to listen to what's wrong with the Red Sox. My biggest thrill in a mediocre career."

Ken Harrelson: "Everything at the time."

Darrell Brandon: "A feeling of being part of turning baseball around in the New England area. There are no better fans anywhere, and they deserved that year as much as the players."

Galen Cisco: "The Red Sox were my team as a young boy. A dream come true — to be signed originally by the Red Sox. It meant a great deal to me as they were the team to offer me an opportunity."

Do you have a favorite "how tough was Dick Williams" story?

Jim Lonborg: "He called a curfew in Anaheim, California, the night after we were beaten in the bottom of the ninth 2–1. It wasn't unusual for Dick to call a curfew, but never did he do it when the next day was a day off. Needless to say he caught quite a few people out."

Bill Landis got some of the details wrong, but the truth still came through: "The first game I pitched as a member of the Red Sox was in relief at Yankee Stadium. There were 50,000 fans in the stands [actually it was 19,290 on Sunday, April 16]. I walked the first three batters [it was the first two]. After the third walk, Dick came to the mound and told me in his gentle way that if I didn't throw strikes, he was going to send me so far down in the minors that I wouldn't ever get out of his doghouse. He then left the mound. The next batter came up, and it didn't take me very long to walk him. Dick quickly returned to the mound, and without saying a word, he handed me a can of dog food. That was my first trip to his doghouse. The next time I pitched was twenty-eight days later."

Ken Brett: "This happened in 1968. I was playing for Louisville and came to Boston for an army reserve meeting. I went up and spent some time with Neil Mahoney, the minor league director; and by the time I got dressed and on the field, it was 5:10 P.M. The Red Sox players had to be on the field at 5 P.M. Let me reiterate I was playing for Louisville at the time. Dick walked over to me and said the next time I was late there wouldn't be a uniform for me. I was devastated."

Billy Rohr: "Sorry. I don't have any stories about Dick of which the word *favorite* would be an appropriate adjective."

Dick Williams: "Many! But all I know is I helped put money in a lot of people's pockets."

Russ Gibson: "First I must say he was then and still is the best manager in baseball. But in '67, after being bombed by Minnesota, he didn't talk to me the next day; and I thought for sure I wouldn't catch on Russ Gibson Day with 10,000 Fall River fans at Fenway. I am glad he let me catch, for his sake and mine."

Jerry Stephenson: "Never thought he was that tough. He just did not have an ingratiating personality."

Ken Harrelson: "Many, but he was the best manager I ever played for."

Darrell Brandon: "When Scotty [Boomer] would not be allowed to play when his weight went over Dick's limit, Scotty would be seen in the whirlpool early before the game to try to get his weight down to satisfy Dick. Boomer never realized the physical drain this was having on his strength."

The Day-by-Day Record: 1967

April

Opp.		Score RS–Opps	W/L	Pitcher of Record Red Sox	Opp.	Date	Club Rec.	Pos.	G.B.
Chi.	H	5- 4	W	Lonborg	Buzhardt	4/12	1- 0	1T	—
Chi.	H	5- 8	L	Fischer-R	Lamabe-R	4/13	1- 1	3T	1
N.Y.	A	3- 0	W	Rohr-C	Ford	4/14	2- 1	2T	1
N.Y.	A	0- 1	L	Bennett-C	Stottlemyre-C	4/15	2- 2	4T	1
N.Y.	A	6- 7 (18)	L	Stange-R	Downing-R	4/16	2- 3	8T	1½
Chi.	A	2- 5	L	Brandon	Howard-C	4/18	2- 4	9	2
N.Y.	H	6- 1	W	Rohr-C	Stottlemyre	4/21	3- 4	8T	2
N.Y.	H	5- 4	W	Santiago-R	Womack-R	4/22	4- 4	4T	1
N.Y.	H	5- 7	L	Santiago-R	Downing	4/23	4- 5	7T	1½
Wash.	A	7- 4	W	Wyatt-R	Lines-R	4/24	5- 5	6	1
Wash.	A	9- 3	W	Fischer-C	Richert	4/25	6- 5	4	½
K.C.	H	3- 0	W	Lonborg-C	Hunter	4/28	7- 5	2T	½
K.C.	H	11-10 (15)	W	McMahon-R	Aker-R	4/29	8- 5	1T	—
K.C.	H	0- 1	L	Brandon	Nash-C	4/30	8- 6	3	1

May

Opp.		Score RS–Opps	W/L	Pitcher of Record Red Sox	Opp.	Date	Club Rec.	Pos.	G.B.
Calif.	A	4- 0	W	Bennett-C	Rubio	5/1	9- 6	2T	½
Calif.	A	2- 3	L	Fischer	McGlothlin-C	5/2	9- 7	2T	1
Calif.	A	1- 2	L	Lonborg-C	Kelso-R	5/3	9- 8	3T	1
Minn.	A	2- 5	L	Rohr	Grant	5/5	9- 9	5	2
Minn.	A	2- 4	L	Brandon	Chance-C	5/6	9-10	6	3
Minn.	A	9- 6	W	Osinski-R	Perry-R	5/7	10-10	5	3
K.C.*	A	3- 4	L	McMahon-R	Krausse	5/9	10-11		
K.C.*	A	5- 2	W	Wyatt-R	Aker-R	5/9	11-11	5	3½
K.C.	A	4- 7	L	Stange-R	Lindblad-R	5/10	11-12	6	4½
Det.	H	4- 5	L	Brandon	Wilson	5/12	11-13	6T	5½
Det.	H	8-10	L	Wyatt-R	Korince-R	5/13	11-14	8T	6½
Det.*	H	8- 5	W	Lonborg	McLain	5/14	12-14		
Det.*	H	13- 9	W	Santiago	Lolich	5/14	13-14	3	6
Balt.	H	5- 8	L	Wyatt-R	Fisher-R	5/16	13-15	5T	6
Balt.	H	8-12	L	Cisco-R	Dillman-R	5/17	13-16	7T	7
Clev.	H	3- 2	W	Lonborg-C	Bell	5/19	14-16	4	7
Clev.	H	3- 5 (10)	L	McMahon-R	Bailey-R	5/20	14-17	7	7
Clev.*	H	4- 3	W	Wyatt-R	Siebert-C	5/21	15-17		
Clev.*	H	6- 2	W	Brandon-C	McDowell	5/21	16-17	4	5½
Det.	A	5- 2	W	Bennett	Lolich	5/23	17-17	4	5
Det.	A	1- 0	W	Lonborg-C	McLain	5/24	18-17	3	5
Det.	A	3- 9	L	Santiago	Wilson-C	5/25	18-18	3	5½
Balt.	A	3- 4	L	Rohr	Drabowsky-R	5/26	18-19	5	5½
Balt.	A	0-10	L	Brandon	Phoebus-C	5/27	18-20	6T	7
Balt.	A	4- 3	W	Lonborg	Barber	5/28	19-20	5T	6
Calif.*	H	5- 4	W	Osinski-R	Kelso-R	5/30	20-20		
Calif.*	H	6- 1	W	Bennett-C	Brunet	5/30	21-20	4	5½
Minn.	H	3- 2	W	Brandon	Perry	5/31	22-20	3	4½

June

Minn.	H	0- 4	L	Rohr	Chance-C	6/1	22-21	4	4½
Clev.	A	2- 1	W	Lonborg-C	Siebert	6/2	23-21	3	4½
Clev.	A	6- 2	W	Bennett	Bell	6/3	24-21	3	3½
Clev.	A	0- 3	L	Stange	Hargan-C	6/4	24-22	4	4
Chi.	A	3- 5	L	Brandon	Wilhelm-R	6/6	24-23	4	6
Chi.*	A	2- 5	L	Bennett-C	Horlen-C	6/8	24-24		
Chi.*	A	7- 3	A	Bell-C	Howard	6/8	25-24	4T	5½
Wash.	H	8- 7	W	Santiago-R	Humphreys-R	6/9	26-24	4	4½
Wash.	H	3- 7	L	Stange	Pascual	6/10	26-25	4	4½
Wash.*	H	4- 3	W	Santiago-R	Baldwin-R	6/11	27-25		
Wash.*	H	7- 8	L	Osinski-R	Cox-R	6/11	27-26	4	5
N.Y.	H	3- 1	W	Bell-C	Verbanic	6/12	28-26	4	4
N.Y.	H	3- 5	L	Lonborg	Talbot	6/13	28-27	4	5
Chi.*	H	7- 8	L	Bennett	Peters	6/14	28-28		
Chi.*	H	6- 1	W	Stange	Klages	6/14	29-28	3T	5
Chi.	H	2- 1 (11)	W	Wyatt-R	Buzhardt-R	6/15	30-28	3T	4
Wash.*	A	0- 1	L	Bell	Priddy	6/16	30-29		
Wash.*	A	3- 4	L	Wyatt-R	Cox-R	6/16	30-30	4	5
Wash.	A	5- 1	W	Lonborg-C	Moore	6/17	31-30	3	5
Wash.	A	2- 3 (10)	L	Santiago-R	Knowles-R	6/18	31-31	4	6½
N.Y.	A	7- 1	W	Bell-C	Stottlemyre	6/20	32-31	4T	5½
N.Y.	A	8- 1	W	Lonborg-C	Tillotson	6/21	33-31	3T	6
Clev.	H	8- 4	W	Stange-C	Siebert	6/23	34-31	3	5
Clev.	H	2- 3	L	Brandon	Hargan-C	6/24	34-32	3	6
Clev.	H	8- 3	W	Bell	Tiant	6/25	35-32	3	5
Minn.	A	1- 2	L	Lonborg	Kaat	6/26	35-33	3T	6
Minn.	A	3- 2	W	Waslewski	Chance-C	6/27	36-33	3	6
Minn.	A	2- 3	L	Stange	Boswell-C	6/28	36-34	3	7
K.C.	A	5- 3	W	Bell	Nash	6/30	37-34	3	5½

July

K.C.	A	10- 2	W	Lonborg	Dobson	7/1	38-34	3	5
K.C.	A	2- 1	W	Waslewski	Hunter	7/2	39-34	3	4½
Calif.	A	9- 3	W	Stange-C	Hamilton	7/3	40-34	2T	3½
Calif.	A	3- 4	L	Bell	Clark	7/4	40-35	4	4½
Calif.	A	3- 4	L	Santiago-R	Brunet-C	7/5	40-36	4	5½
Det.	A	4- 5 (15)	L	Wyatt-R	Marshall-R	7/7	40-37	4	6
Det.	A	0- 2	L	Stange	McLain-C	7/8	40-38	5	7
Det.*	A	4-10	L	Bell	Wilson	7/9	40-39		
Det.*	A	3- 0	W	Lonborg	Wickersham	7/9	41-39	5	6
Balt.*	H	4- 2	W	Stange	Phoebus	7/13	42-39		
Balt.*	H	0-10	L	Bell	McNally-C	7/13	42-40	5	6
Balt.	H	11- 5	W	Lonborg	Adamson	7/14	43-40	5	5½
Balt.	H	5- 1	W	Santiago-R	Richert	7/15	44-40	5	4½
Det.	H	9- 5	W	Brandon	Sparma	7/16	45-40	3T	4
Det.	H	7- 1	W	Stange-C	McLain	7/17	46-40	3	3½
Balt.	A	6- 2	W	Lonborg-C	McNally	7/18	47-40	3	2½
Balt.	A	6- 4	W	Santiago-R	Richert	7/19	48-40	3	1½
Clev.	A	6- 2	W	Brandon-C	Tiant	7/21	49-40	2	1½
Clev.	A	4- 0	W	Stange-C	Hargan	7/22	50-40	2	½
Clev.*	A	8- 5	W	Lonborg-C	O'Donoghue	7/23	51-40		
Clev.*	A	5- 1	W	Bell-C	Tiant	7/23	52-40	2	½
Calif.	H	4- 6	L	Waslewski	Newman-R	7/25	52-41	2	2
Calif.	H	9- 6	W	Landis-R	Rojas-R	7/26	53-41	2	1½
Calif.	H	6- 5 (10)	W	Lyle-R	Kelso-R	7/27	54-41	2	1
Minn.	H	2- 9	L	Lonborg	Chance-C	7/28	54-42	2	1
Minn.*	H	6- 3	W	Wyatt-R	Worthington-R	7/29	55-42		

(continued) 243

July

Opp.		Score RS–Opps	W/L	Pitcher of Record Red Sox	Opp.	Date	Club Rec.	Pos.	G.B.
Minn.*	H	3-10	L	Waslewski	Perry	7/29	55-43	2	1½
Minn.	H	5- 7	L	Brandon	Merritt	7/30	55-44	2	2
Minn.	H	4- 0	W	Stange-C	Boswell	7/31	56-44	2	2

August

Opp.		Score RS–Opps	W/L	Pitcher of Record Red Sox	Opp.	Date	Club Rec.	Pos.	G.B.
K.C.*	H	3- 4	L	Morehead	Dobson-C	8/1	56-45		
K.C.*	H	8- 3	W	Lonborg	Sanford	8/1	57-45	2	2½
K.C.	H	6- 8	L	Wyatt-R	Segui-R	8/2	57-46	2	2½
K.C.	H	5- 3	W	Morehead-R	Hunter	8/3	58-46	2	2
Minn.	A	0- 3	L	Brandon	Merritt-C	8/4	58-47	2	2½
Minn.	A	1- 2	L	Stange	Boswell-C	8/5	58-48	2	3
Minn.	A	0- 2	L	Lonborg-C	Chance-C	8/6	58-49	3	2½
K.C.*	A	3- 5	L	Morehead	Hunter	8/8	58-50		
K.C.*	A	7- 5	W	Wyatt-R	Stafford-R	8/8	59-50	3	2½
K.C.	A	5- 1	W	Lonborg	Nash	8/9	60-50	2	1½
Calif.	A	0- 1	L	Stange	McGlothlin-C	8/11	60-51	3	2
Calif.	A	1- 2	L	Bell	Hamilton	8/12	60-52	4	2
Calif.	A	2- 3	L	Lonborg	Clark	8/13	60-53	5	2½
Det.	H	4- 0	W	Morehead-C	Sparma	8/15	61-53	4	3
Det.	H	8- 3	W	Brandon-R	McLain	8/16	62-53	3	3
Det.	H	4- 7 (10)	L	Lyle-R	Gladding-R	8/17	62-54	4	3½
Calif.	H	3- 2	W	Bell-C	Hamilton	8/18	63-54	3	3
Calif.	H	12-11	W	Osinski-R	Coates-R	8/19	64-54	3	3
Calif.*	H	12- 2	W	Stange-C	Brunet	8/20	65-54		
Calif.*	H	9- 8	W	Santiago-R	Rojas-R	8/20	66-54	3	1½
Wash.	H	6- 5	W	Wyatt-R	Knowles-R	8/21	67-54	3	1
Wash.*	H	2- 1	W	Stephenson	Ortega	8/22	68-54		
Wash.*	H	5- 3	W	Bell	Cox-R	8/22	69-54	2	—
Wash.	H	2- 3	L	Lyle-R	Priddy-C	8/23	69-55	2	1
Wash.	H	7- 5	W	Morehead	Nold	8/24	70-55	1T	—
Chi.*	A	7- 1	W	Lonborg-C	Peters	8/25	71-55		
Chi.*	A	1- 2	L	Wyatt-R	Locker-R	8/25	71-56	2	½
Chi.	A	6- 2	W	Stephenson	Horlen	8/26	72-56	1	—
Chi.*	A	4- 3	W	Bell	Klages	8/27	73-56		
Chi.*	A	0- 1 (11)	L	Brandon-R	Peters-C	8/27	73-57	1T	—
N.Y.	A	3- 0	W	Morehead	Talbot-C	8/28	74-57	1T	—
N.Y.*	A	2- 1	W	Lonborg-C	Stottlemyre-C	8/29	75-57		
N.Y.*	A	3- 4 (20)	L	Brandon-R	Bouton-R	8/29	75-58	1	—
N.Y.	A	2- 1 (10)	W	Wyatt-R	Downing-C	8/30	76-58	1	—
Chi.	H	2- 4	L	Bell-C	McMahon-R	8/31	76-59	1	—

September

Chi.	H	10- 3	W	Santiago-C	Peters	9/1	77-59	1	—
Chi.	H	1- 4	L	Lonborg	Horlen-C	9/2	77-60	2	½
Chi.	H	0- 4	L	Stange	John-C	9/3	77-61	2	½
Wash.*	A	2- 5	L	Morehead	Pascual	9/4	77-62		
Wash.*	A	6- 4	W	Stephenson	Lines-R	9/4	78-62	2	½
Wash.	A	8- 2	W	Bell-C	Bertaina	9/5	79-62	2	½
N.Y.	H	3- 1	W	Lonborg-C	Stottlemyre	9/7	80-62	1T	—
N.Y.	H	2- 5	L	Stange	Monbouquette	9/8	80-63	3	½
N.Y.	H	7- 1	W	Morehead	Barber	9/9	81-63	3	½
N.Y.	H	9- 1	W	Bell-C	Downing	9/10	82-63	2	½
K.C.	H	3- 1	W	Lonborg-C	Hunter	9/12	83-63	1T	—
K.C.	H	4- 2	W	Wyatt-R	Aker-R	9/13	84-63	1T	—
Balt.	H	2- 6	L	Morehead	Phoebus	9/15	84-64	1T	—
Balt.	H	1- 4	L	Lonborg	Hardin-C	9/16	84-65	2	1
Balt.	H	2- 5	L	Bell	Brabender	9/17	84-66	3	1
Det.	A	6- 5 (10)	W	Santiago-R	Marshall-R	9/18	85-66	1T	—
Det.	A	4- 2	W	Santiago-R	Lolich	9/19	86-66	1T	—
Clev.	A	5- 4	W	Wyatt-R	Culver-R	9/20	87-66	1T	—
Clev.	A	6- 5	W	Bell	Hargan	9/21	88-66	1T	—
Balt.*	A	0-10	L	Stephenson	Hardin-C	9/22	88-67		
Balt.*	A	10- 3	W	Santiago-C	Richert	9/22	89-67	2	½
Balt.	A	5- 7	I	Wyatt-R	Miller-R	9/23	89-68	3	½
Balt.	A	11- 7	W	Lonborg	Phoebus	9/24	90-68	2	½
Clev.	H	3- 6	L	Bell	Tiant-C	9/26	90-69	3	1
Clev.	H	0- 6	L	Lonborg	Siebert	9/27	90-70	2	1
Minn.	H	6- 4	W	Santiago	Kline-R	9/30	91-70	1T	—

October

Minn.	H	6- 3	W	Lonborg-C	Chance	10/1	92-70	1	—

The '67 Roster: Yesterday and Today

Name	'67 Avg.	RBI	HR	What's He Doing Today?
Infielders				
Jerry Adair	.271	35	3	Working in Sand Springs, Oklahoma.
Mike Andrews	.263	40	8	Chairman of the Jimmy Fund in Boston. Also operates a baseball camp with Gerry Moses.
Joe Foy	.251	49	16	Working as a drug counselor in New York City, runs a bar in The Bronx.
Tony Horton	Traded in June			Banker in Santa Monica, California.
Dalton Jones	.289	25	3	Sells investment insurance in Baton Rouge, Louisiana.
Rico Petrocelli	.259	66	17	Owns commercial cleaning firm in Boston area. Also works as minor league coach for White Sox organization.
Ken Poulsen	Sent to minors			Residential construction, Simi Valley, California.
George Scott	.303	82	19	Does promotional work for a company that produces baseball card shows.
Norm Siebern	.205	7	0	Insurance business, Naples, Florida. Also scouts for Kansas City Royals.
George Smith	Injured, spring training: DNP			Living in St. Petersburg, Florida.
Outfielders				
Tony Conigliaro	.281	67	20	Lives at home with parents in Nahant, Massachusetts, where he is recovering from a heart attack.
Don Demeter	Traded in June			Minister; also owns team in the American Association, Oklahoma City, Oklahoma.
Ken Harrelson	.246	61	15	Former executive vice-president, Chicago White Sox; lives in Lisle, Illinois.
Jim Landis	Signed and released in August			Sign-manufacturing business, Napa, California.
Reggie Smith	.244	56	14	Retired as active player in Japan League, 1984.

Name	'67 Avg.	RBI	HR	What's He Doing Today?
Outfielders				
Jose Tartabull	.223	10	0	Manages the Sarasota club in the Florida State League.
George Thomas	.213	6	1	Lives in Minneapolis, where he's involved in fund-raising. Before that, baseball coach at University of Minnesota.
Carl Yastrzemski	.326	121	44	Promo work for Kahn's Meats. Also, part-time hitting coach in spring with Red Sox, and TV work for Boston station.
Catchers				
Russ Gibson	.203	15	1	Lives in Swansea, Massachusetts. Works for Massachusetts State Lottery.
Elston Howard	.178	28	4	Deceased.
Gerry Moses	Called up in September but did not play			Runs baseball camp with Mike Andrews.
Mike Ryan	.199	27	2	First base coach, Philadelphia Phillies; lives in New Hampshire.
Bob Tillman	Sold in August			Executive with food brokerage company in Gallatin, Tennessee.

Pitchers	ERA	W–L	What's He Doing Today?
Gary Bell	3.31	13–13	Works with the San Antonio minor league baseball club.
Dennis Bennett	Traded in June		Owns restaurant on West Coast.
Darrell Brandon	4.16	5–11	Life insurance sales, Aetna Company in Hanover, Massachusetts. Also owns and operates baseball instructional school.
Ken Brett	4.50	0–0	Salesperson, Sorg Printing Company; member, Miller Lite All Stars; part owner with family, Spokane Indians; owner, sports restaurant, Hermosa Beach, California.
Galen Cisco	Released		Coach, San Diego Padres; lives in St. Mary's, Ohio.
Hank Fischer	Released		Restaurant business, West Palm Beach, Florida.
Bill Landis	5.19	1–0	Sergeant with King's County Sheriff's Department. Lives in Hanford, California.
Jim Lonborg	3.16	22–9	Practicing dentistry in Hanover, Massachusetts. Lives in Scituate, Massachusetts.

(continued)

Name	'67 ERA	W–L	What's He Doing Today?
Pitchers			
Sparky Lyle	2.30	1–2	Works for casino in Atlantic City, New Jersey.
Don McMahon	Traded in June		Scout for Los Angeles Dodgers.
Dave Morehead	4.31	5–4	Executive for sporting goods company; lives in Tustin, California.
Dan Osinski	2.53	3–1	Steel fabrication salesman, Oak Forest, Illinois.
Billy Rohr	Sent to minors		Practicing personal injury and product liability law in Orange County, California.
Jose Santiago	3.60	12–4	Baseball broadcaster, Puerto Rico.
Lee Stange	2.77	8–10	Minor league pitching coach for Red Sox.
Jerry Stephenson	3.83	3–1	Scout, Los Angeles Dodgers.
John Wyatt	2.67	10–7	Real estate business, Kansas City, Missouri.

Coaches	**What's He Doing Now?**
Bobby Doerr	Retired and doing lots of fishing and hunting in Junction City, Oregon.
Al Lakeman	Deceased.
Sal Maglie	Retired near Niagara Falls, New York.
Eddie Popowski	Minor league coach with Red Sox.
Dick Williams	Resigned as manager of San Diego Padres in early 1986. Named manager of Seattle Mariners in May 1986.

Awards Won in 1967

Carl Yastrzemski
Most Valuable Player, American League
Most Valuable Player, Boston Chapter, Baseball Writers of America
Triple Crown Award, National Brewery, Baltimore
Triple Crown title, American League
Van Heusen Award, for outstanding achievement
S. Rae Hickock Belt, Professional Athlete of the Year
Babe Ruth Crown, for Outstanding Athlete of the Year
Ty Cobb Award, Atlanta Chapter of the Baseball Writers
M.V.P. Award, Washington Chapter of the Baseball Writers
Top awards from the Minnesota and New York chapters of the
    Baseball Writers of America
Sporting News, Player of the Year
Associated Press, Male Athlete of the Year
UPI, Major League All-Star Team
Silver Bat for A.L. batting crown
Gold Glove Award, Rawlings Sporting Goods Company
Sport Magazine, Man of the Year
Sports Illustrated, Sportsman of the Year
UPI, Comeback Player of the Year
Academy of Sports, Man of the Year

Jim Lonborg
Cy Young Award, American League
Sporting News, Pitcher of the Year
Dickie Kerr Award, Houston Chapter, Baseball Writers of America
Most Valuable Pitcher, Boston Baseball Writers
UPI, Major League All-Star Team

Dick Williams
Associated Press, Manager of the Year
UPI, Manager of the Year
Manager of the Year, Boston Baseball Writers
Sporting News, Manager of the Year
Top award from the Washington chapter of the Baseball Writers

George Scott
Gold Glove Award, Rawlings Sporting Goods Company

Dick O'Connell
Sporting News, Major League Executive of the Year
UPI, Major League Executive of the Year
Executive of the Year, Boston chapter of the Baseball Writers

Index

loss, 95; used in relief, 123; wins Boston debut, 86-87; wins second straight for Boston, 90; wins 10th game for Boston

Bennett, Dennis, 18, 21, 25, 28, 31, 73; drops 1–0 decision, 47; has words with Dick Williams, 37; raises record to 3–1, 79; shuts out California, 60; traded to Mets, 104–106; in trouble with Dick Williams, 11–12; wins fourth game, 83

Berde, Gene, 27, 34

Berry, Ken, 86, 93, 166; thrown out by Jose Tartabull, 168–170

Bertaina, Frank, 185

Blair, Paul, 69, 122, 123, 197

Blefary, Curt, 197

Boggs, Wade, 28

Bosox Club, the, 83

Boston baseball writers, 60, 114–115

Boston Braves, 2

Boston Celtics, 48

Boston, Globe, The, 150, 189, 191

Boston Red Sox: and attendance, 4, 104, 186; awards won in 1967, 249; beat Minnesota in last two games of season, 203–221; and brawl at Yankee Stadium, 98–101; and celebration after season finale, 216–221; and comeback wins, 70–71, 91–95, 131–135, 156–160, 190–194; co-set American League record for extra base hits, 69; as "country club," 8, 10, 163; day-by-day record, 242–245; drop to .500 on 6/18, 6½ games out, 97; early pitching problems, 70; extend winning streak to 10 games, 127–130; and fans, 1, 6, 7, 149; 41st road win clinches winning road record, 196; and grapefruit league opener, 18; and lack of offense, 144, 148; listed as 100-to-1 underdogs, 37; lose 20-inning game in New York, 173–174; lose two key games to Cleveland at Fenway, 199–202; make six errors in game, 77; move into third-place tie, 124; 1967 payroll, 55; 1967 as watershed year, 7–9, 235–236; and pennant fever, 127–128, 130–131; play first major league game in history of the Virgin Islands, 35; slumping, 64–67, 118; sweep California in doubleheader, 78, 156–160; sweep Cleveland, 71; take over first place, 166; take over sole possession of second place, 126; and team identity, 98–99; team members surveyed,

240–241; team sets World Series record for home runs in an inning, 229; tops one million in attendance, 151; and trouble winning in Minnesota, 61; turn triple play, 122–123; and uniforms, 78–79; and waiver wire, 27–28; where players are today, 246–248; and World Series, 223–233; and years of decline, 4–7

Boston University, 3

Boswell, Dave, 107, 144

Boswell, Thomas, 15

Bowens, Sam, 77

Brandon, Darrell, 24, 31, 37; injury ends his season, 199; looks back on 1967, 171; pitches complete game win to put Boston in second place, 126; strong relief outing, 150; wins first game of season, 71–72

Brandt, Jackie, 5

Bresciani, Dick, 221

Brett, George, 227

Brett, Ken: and brother George, 227; called up from Pittsfield, 179; makes major league debut, 201; pitches in World Series, 226

Brinkman, Ed, 96, 97

Broadcasting: radio versus television, 46–48

Brock, Lou, 120, 224, 229, 231

Brown, Gates, 194

Brown, Larry, 194

Brown, Mace, 20

Brown, Paul, 39

Brunet, George, 79, 117, 131, 219

Buford, Don, 93, 167

Burgess, Smokey, 95

Buzhardt, John, 93–94

California Angels, 60–61, 78–80, 116–117, 131–134, 146–148, 151–160

Cambridge, Mass., 40, 153, 181

Camp Drum, N.Y., 65, 93

Campaneris, Bert, 185

Cannon, Jimmy, 226

Cardenal, Jose, 148

Carew, Rod, 136, 143, 204, 205, 206, 207

Carlos, Cisco, 166

Carlton, Steve, 227

Casanova, Paul, 96, 161

final game, 216–218; and pennant clincher versus Minnesota, 209–211, 215–216, 218; pitches one-hitter in Game Two of World Series, 224–225; on season's final game, 104–105; shuts out Kansas City, 54; shuts outs Detroit, 73–74; as stopper, 70, 118–119; success in spring outing, 26; three-hits Cleveland, 83; three-hits New York for 19th win, 182; three-hits St. Louis in Game Five of World Series, 227; and Tony Conigliaro beaning, 153; trashes locker, 202; triple helps him win 20th game, 185–186; wild pitch loses game in Anaheim, 61; wins 18th game, 173; wins 15th game, 140; wins season opener, 41; wins 17th game, 165; wins 10th game, 113; wins 13th game, 125; wins 20th game, 185; and working out of jams, 186; works out with Atlanta Braves, 137
Lopez, Al, 169
Los Angeles Angels, 6
Los Angeles Dodgers, 30
Lyle, Sparky, 132, 134, 140; makes major league debut, 116
Lynn, Mass., 150

McAuliffe, Dick, 143, 151, 191–193; grounds into double play to give Boston the pennant, 219
McCarthy, Tommy, 221
McCarver, Tim, 231, 232
McDowell, Sam, 194
McFarlane, Orlando, 79
McGaha, Mel, 165
McGlothlin, Jim, 60, 132, 133, 147, 158
MacKenzie, Duncan, 162
McKinney, Judge Elwood, 162
McLain, Denny, 25, 73, 118, 125
McMahon, Don, 30, 52, 57, 86; traded to Cleveland, 84
McMullen, Ken, 95, 96, 164
McNertney, Jerry, 86
Maglie, Sal, 11, 16, 132, 150, 225
Magrini, Pete, 13, 18, 25, 26
Malzone, Frank, 6, 188, 224
Mantilla, Felix, 40
Mantle, Mickey, 6, 69, 225
Marcott, Dan, 39
Marichal, Juan, 120
Maris, Roger, 6, 227, 231

Martin, Billy, 211
Martin, Ned, 4, 46, 88–89, 218
Marshall, Mike, 118, 191
Massachusetts Eye and Ear Infirmary, 181
Massachusetts Turnpike, 122
Mathews, Eddie, 193, 194
Maxvill, Dal, 227
Maye, Lee, 25, 129
Mazeroski, Bill, 120
Medford High School, 183
Mele, Sam, 87
Memorial Stadium, Baltimore, 125
Memorial Stadium, Kansas City, 116
Merritt, Jim, 143, 207
Miller, Stu, 69
Mincher, Don, 117, 131, 134, 146, 147, 159, 218
Minnesota Twins, 6, 31, 61–62, 80–83, 106–107, 135–137, 143–144, 202–221
Moby Dick, 94
Monbouquette, Bill, 6, 165, 183, 185
Monday, Rick, 55, 113, 115
Montgomery, Ala., 192
Montpelier, Vt., 2
Moore, Barry, 97
Morehead, Dave, 13, 24, 26; and clutch performance in emergency start, 183; makes first appearance, 140; and 1965 no-hitter, 148; picks up first win, 141; pitches three shut-out innings of relief in Game Four of World Series, 226; recalled from Toronto, 136; shuts out Detroit, 148
Morton, Bubba, 134
Moses, Gerry, 26, 181, 227
Most, Johnny, 48
Municipal Stadium, Cleveland, 196

Nantasket Beach, 158
Napp, Larry, 95
Nash, Jim, 109
Nelson, Lindsey, 3
Nen, Dick, 96
New York Mets, 20, 23, 37
New York Yankees, 4, 23, 28, 37, 42–48, 51–53, 90, 98–101, 172–175, 182–184
Nixon, Russ, 215
Nolan, Gary, 25

Rosenfeld, Keith, 220
Rudi, Joe, 20
Runge, Ed, 147, 173
Rutland Royals, 2
Ryan, John, 216
Ryan, Mike, 68, 137; drives in two runs, 113; grumbles over lack of playing time, 151, 198; hits pinch-hit home run, 140; suicide squeeze beats Minnesota, 80; and Tony Conigliaro beaning, 153; triples with bases loaded, 184

Sadowski, Bob, 11–12, 26
St. Claire, Ebba, 2
St. Louis Cardinals, 4, 34, 188, 192, 223–232
San Juan, Puerto Rico, 209
Sancta Maria Hospital, 15, 153, 155, 163, 181
Sands, Charlie, 101
Santiago, Jose, 7, 28, 33, 87; beats Minnesota to force first-place tie 9/30, 204–205, 207, 209; named to open World Series, 221; perfect in relief, 84; pitchers nine and two-thirds innings of shutout ball in losing effort, 171–172; raises record to 8–4, 179; and trade rumors, 27; wins two games in two nights in big Detroit series, 191–194; and World Series, Game One, 224
Satriano, Tom, 147, 159
Saturday Evening Post, The, 104
Saverine, Bob, 87, 97
Schall, Paul, 134
Scheinblum, Richie, 201
Schilling, Chuck, 6, 40
Schoendienst, Red, 227
Schwall, Don, 6
Score, Herb, 3
Scott, George: awards won in 1967, 249; benched, 49, 76, 180; blasts Eddie Stanky, 170, 171; chided by Dick Williams, 22; and defensive brilliance, 67, 68, 74, 94; on Williams, 74, 76; and disagreements with Williams, 23, 26, 27, 49, 180; and Eastern League Triple Crown, 50; has four-hit game, 198; hits back-to-back home runs with Tony Conigliaro, 132; hits crucial home run versus Minnesota 9/30, 204, 207; hits 12th home run, 132; hits two home runs in game, 150; home run caps big rally, 71; injured running into outfield wall at Winter Haven, 30–31; leaves game with back spasms, 117; makes two errors in game, 107; praised by Williams, 72–73; put in outfield, 15; razzed by opponents, 149; and trade rumors, 27; and triple play, 123; and weight problems, 50, 74, 76, 147–148, 150; on winning the pennant, 76; wins first base job over Tony Horton, 33
Scottsdale, Ariz., 105
Serling, Rod, 95, 96
Sheraton Hotel, 211
Siebern, Norm, 40, 131, 135, 147, 214; hits three-run pinch triple, 155; and key ninth-inning single, 145; makes Boston debut, 126; obtained from San Francisco, 125
Siebert, Sonny, 201
Skowron, Bill, 134, 155, 159
Slaughter, Enos, 4
Smith, Charlie, 43, 48, 100
Smith, George, 32, 40; dealt to San Francisco, 125; injures knee in spring training, 14–15
Smith, Mayo, 118, 193, 219
Smith, Reggie: becomes first player in Boston history to hit home runs from both sides of plate in same game, 156–157; has three hits in game, 77; hits big triple in 10th versus California, 134; hits home run in Game Six of World Series, 229; hits home run in Game Three of World Series, 226; hits sixth home run in 10 games, 162; as second baseman, 31, 37, 40; and speed, 173, 174; and Yankee Stadium brawl, 100–101
Snow, Rob, 21; traded to Chicago, 84
Snyder, Russ, 122, 123
Soar, Hank, 41
South Yarmouth, Mass., 119
Sparma, Joe, 118
Speaker, Tris, 19
Sporting News, The, 114
Sports Illustrated, 105, 191
Spring training, 21, 26, 32, 33, 38; rituals of, 15–20; at Winter Haven, Fla., 10–40
Springstead, Marty, 169
Stafford, Bill, 145
Stange, Lee, 31, 35, 47; beats California, 116; hard-luck loss, 146–147; pitches complete game win, 102, 125; shuts out Cleveland, 126; shuts out

Minnesota, 137; and trade rumors, 77; wins complete game with 10 strikeouts, 156; wins first game, 90

Stanky, Eddie, 175, 179; and Carl Yastrzemski, 28, 90, 91; criticizes Boston, 165–167, 169; criticizes Jerry Adair, 167; ejected from game, 95

Statistics, end-of-month: 58, 81, 111, 138, 176, 222

Stephenson, Jerry, 20, 22, 28, 145, 174; called-up from Toronto, 150; sent to minors, 38; strong game, 161

Stewart, Bob, 86, 187

Stottlemyre, Mel, 35, 46, 47, 51, 173

Stroud, Ed, 95, 96

Stuart, Dick, 6, 60, 105, 205; and letter to Dick Williams, 180

Sullivan, Haywood, 38, 137, 150, 188; deals Bob Tillman to New York, 145; and Elston Howard trade, 142–143; and Jerry Adair trade, 84; and Ken Harrelson deal, 165; and trade possibilities, 65, 77

Swaton, Vicki, 107–108

Tartabull, Jose, 14, 21, 30, 32, 37, 41; and character, 62; and great defensive play, 150–151, 167–170; has three hits in game, 62; hit beats Kansas City in 15th inning, 56; recalled from Pittsfield, 150; sent down to Pittsfield, 142; throws-out Ken Berry at home, 167–170; 234, 236

Thomas, George, 14, 25, 27, 34, 50, 52; as backup catcher, 151; has two hits in game, 172; hits first and only home run of year, 117; injures hand, 62; pitches batting practice to Tony Conigliaro, 88; plays left for resting Carl Yastrzemski, 174; reinstated, 83; robs Lou Brock of home run in Game Six of World Series, 231; starts in place of benched Yastrzemski, 62; takes over at first for injured George Scott, 117; as team comedian, 132, 197, 198, 224

Tiant, Luis, 129

Tierney, Dr. Thomas, 153

Tiger Stadium, 118, 192

Tillman, Bob, 25, 27, 98, 99, 100; beans Wyatt with throw, 66; has three hits in game, belts first home run, 103; reinserted in starting lineup, 98; replaces Russ Gibson in lineup, 62; sold to New York, 145

Toledo, Ohio, 192

Toronto, Canada, 11, 14, 105, 136, 140, 145, 150

Torrance, Jerry, 105

Torre, Joe, 120

Tovar, Cesar, 135, 136, 204, 209, 211, 212, 213

Tresh, Tom, 41, 47

Triple play: turned by Boston, 122–123

Uhlaender, Ted, 135, 204, 207, 215

Umont, Frank, 151

University of Massachusetts, 221

University of North Carolina, 191

Updike, John, 5

Valenti, Dan, 17, 75, 102, 170

Valentine, Bill, 158, 159

Valentine, Fred, 96

Verbanic, Joe, 90

Versalles, Zoilo, 62, 144, 204, 207, 213, 214

Vietnam War, 8

Vineyard, Dave, 33

Virgin Islands, 35, 37

VJ Day, 237

Volpe, Gov. John, 41, 209

Wagner, Leon, 85, 103

Wahoo Club, 83

Walker, Al, 89, 164

Wallace, Don, 79

Ward, Pete, 95

Warren, Chief Justice Earl, 97

Washburn, Ray, 227

Washington Senators, 38, 53–54, 87–89, 95–97, 160–165, 180–181

Waslewski, Gary, 24, 32; beats Minnesota, 106; cut in spring training, 38; makes major league debut, 89; pitches nine shutout innings, 94; pitches three-hitter, 115; pitches three shutout innings in Game Three of World Series, 225; sent down to Toronto, 136; surprise starter in Game Six of World Series, 228–229; and Yankee Stadium brawl, 101

Weaver, Jim, 148

Weis, Al, 94

Wellesley, Mass., 183

Werhas, Johnny, 132

of World Series, 229; hits 17th home run, 98; hits two home runs in doubleheader, 67–68; hits two home runs in game, 80, 87, 224–225; hits 20th home run, 122; hits 25th home run, 132; hits 27th home run, 137; honored at Yankee Stadium, 172; and improvement as player, 6–7; as interviewee, 125; on last two games of season, 32; in locker room after final, 218–220; as locker room cheerleader, 129, 134, 194; looks back on 1967, 27–33; misses game because of flu, 106; moved to center field, 145; and next-to-last game of season versus Minnesota, 204, 206–208; ninth-inning home run ties vital game versus Detroit, 191–192; and off-season training program, 34; on the pennant race, 80; and pressure of pennant race, 64; runs into wall and is shaken up, 148; on relationship with Dick Williams, 31; and rookie year, 6, 29–30; strains back, 38–39; and tape-measure home run, 156–157; on team attitude, 31; and Tony Conigliaro beaning, 30, 154; tooth pulled, 24; and trade rumors, 13; and Triple Crown, 220; 21st home run sets career high, 124; two home runs defeat Minnesota, 80; two-run home run defeats Cleveland, 83; wears helmet with ear flap following Conigliaro beaning, 160; wins game in New York with pinch-hit home run in 11th, 174–175

TOPPS 406 — MICHAEL JAY ANDREWS

HT: 6'3" WT: 195 BATS: R
THROWS: R BORN: 7/9/43
HOME: PEABODY, MASS.

An All-American Junior College end before signing with the Red Sox, Mike was originally a shortstop. Switched to 2nd base in 1966 when he led IL in Runs. Hit .308 in 1967 World Series, had fine year in 1969.

MIKE WAS VOTED RED SOX "MAN OF THE YEAR" IN 1968.

MAJOR AND MINOR LEAGUE BATTING RECORD

YEAR	TEAM	LEA.	G	AB	R	H	2B	3B	HR	RBI	AVG.
1962	Olean	N.Y.-P.	114	398	89	119	24	2	12	62	.299
1963	Winston-Salem	Carol.	39	149	21	38	11	0	3	18	.255
1963	Waterloo	Midwest	75	251	40	81	16	2	4	41	.323
1964	Reading	East.	139	491	73	145	21	7	4	54	.295
1965	Toronto	Int.	127	426	41	105	13	3	4	34	.246
1966	Toronto	Int.	144	439	97	128	23	4	14	46	.267
1967	Boston	A.L.	5	18	1	3	0	0	0	0	.167
1967	Boston	A.L.	142	494	79	130	20	0	8	40	.263
1968	Boston	A.L.	147	536	77	145	22	1	6	45	.271
1969	Boston	A.L.	121	464	79	136	26	2	15	59	.293
Major League Totals		4 Yrs.	415	1512	236	414	68	3	30	144	.274

TOPPS 297 — RUSS GIBSON

CATCHER BOSTON RED SOX

Ht: 6'1" Wt: 195 Bats: Right Throws: Right
Born: May 6, 1939 Home: Seattle, Wash.

This strong armed receiver led three minor leagues in double plays. In his first A.L. start, Russ caught 8⅔ innings of hitless ball against the New York Yankees. Two days later, he played an 18 inning ballgame.

MAJOR & MINOR LEAGUE BATTING RECORD

YEAR	TEAM	AB	H	2B	3B	HR	RBI	AVG.
1957	Corning	9	4	0	0	0	1	.444
1957	Lafayette	138	43	10	1	2	26	.312
1958	Waterloo	358	91	14	1	4	59	.254
1959	Raleigh	239	64	10	2	1	33	.268
1960	Raleigh	287	86	12	7	7	50	.300
1961	Win.-Salem	360	99	18	7	11	71	.275
1962	York	384	100	24	6	7	59	.260
1963	Seattle	221	54	8	3	7	33	.244
1964	Seattle	467	129	20	1	17	69	.276
1965	Toronto	376	81	13	3	10	52	.215
1966	Toronto	339	99	13	2	9	50	.292
1967	Boston	138	28	7	0	1	15	.203
1967	Pittsfield	59	13	1	0	0	5	.220
Maj. Totals 1 Yr.		138	28	7	0	1	15	.203

Q.—WHO HIT .400 FOR THE SOX IN THE 1967 WORLD SERIES?

A—CARL YASTRZEMSKI.

TOPPS 123 — JOSE SANTIAGO

PITCHER BOSTON RED SOX

Ht: 6'2" Wt: 188 Throws: Right Bats: Right
Born: Aug. 15, 1940 Home: Juana Diaz, P. R.

Jose was the Sox's hottest pitcher during the closing weeks of the 1967 A.L. pennant race and Mgr. Williams chose the righthander as his pitcher for the opening game of the World Series. 8 of Jose's 12 victories were in relief.

MAJOR & MINOR LEAGUE PITCHING RECORD

YEAR	TEAM	W	L	PCT.	SO	BB	ERA
1959	Olean	6	3	.667	34	44	3.44
1959	Grand Isl.	3	6	.333	64	45	3.91
1960	Albq'que	15	6	.714	217	96	3.30
1961	Shreveport	0	0	.000	1	4	27.00
1961	Visalia	13	13	.500	218	130	4.26
1962	Alb'q'que	16	9	.640	188	93	3.88
1963	Portland	12	15	.444	153	82	3.66
1963	Dallas	0	0	1.000	6	2	9.00
1964	Kan. City	1	0	1.000	2	0	0.00
1964	Kan. City	0	6	.000	64	35	4.71
1965	Vancouver	6	3	.667	135	42	2.19
1966	Boston	12	13	.480	119	58	3.66
1967	Boston	12	4	.750	109	47	3.60
Maj. Totals 5 Yrs.		25	23	.521	306	146	4.01

Q.—WHO LED BOSTON IN STOLEN BASES IN '67?

A—REGGIE SMITH—17.

TOPPS 212 — DAVE MOREHEAD

PITCHER BOSTON RED SOX

Ht: 6'1" Wt: 200 Throws: Right Bats: Right
Born: Sept. 5, 1943 Home: San Diego, Cal.

Twice a ten game winner for the Red Sox, Dave is trying to shake the arm trouble which has curtailed his activity during the past two campaigns. The righthander's big moment in the majors was a 2-0 no-hit win against the Cleveland Indians in late '65. Dave graduated from the same San Diego high school that Ted Williams attended.

MAJOR & MINOR LEAGUE PITCHING RECORD

YEAR	TEAM	W	L	PCT.	SO	BB	ERA
1961	Johnstown	4	8	.333	66	27	4.80
1962	Seattle	10	9	.526	159	90	3.72
1963	Boston	10	13	.435	136	99	3.81
1964	Boston	8	15	.348	139	112	4.96
1965	Boston	10	18	.357	163	113	4.06
1966	Boston	1	2	.333	20	7	5.46
1967	Toronto	11	5	.688	109	68	3.10
1967	Boston	5	4	.556	40	22	4.31
Maj. Totals 5 Yrs.		34	52	.395	498	353	4.32

Q.—WHO SLUGGED THREE WORLD SERIES HOMERS IN 1967?

A—CARL YASTRZEMSKI.

TOPPS 116 — ALBERT WALTER LYLE

HT: 6'1" WT: 190 THROWS: L
BATS: L BORN: 7/22/44
HOME: REYNOLDSVILLE, PA.

The Bosox bullpen ace had an excellent year in 1969. Tops on the club in ERA he saved 17 games and was 4th in the AL Fireman Derby, and averaged almost one K per inning. Originally signed by Baltimore.

SPARKY ONCE STRUCK OUT 5 MEN IN A 17 INNING GAME.

MAJOR AND MINOR LEAGUE PITCHING RECORD

YEAR	TEAM	LEA.	G	IP	W	L	PCT	SO	BB	ERA
1964	Bluefield	Appal.	7	33	3	2	.600	44	25	4.36
1964	Fox Cities	Midwest.	6	35	3	1	.750	51	18	2.31
1965	Winston-Salem	Carol.	37	87	5	5	.500	79	55	4.24
1966	Pittsfield	East.	40	74	4	2	.667	54	43	3.65
1967	Toronto	Int.	16	21	2	2	.500	17	11	1.71
1967	Boston	A.L.	27	43	1	2	.333	42	14	2.30
1968	Boston	A.L.	49	66	6	1	.857	52	14	2.73
1969	Boston	A.L.	71	103	8	3	.727	93	48	2.45
Major League Totals		3 Yrs.	147	212	15	6	.714	187	76	2.50

TOPPS 481 — JOHN WYATT

PITCHER BOSTON RED SOX

Ht: 6'0" Wt: 205 Throws: Right Bats: Right
Born: April 19, 1935 Home: Kansas City, Mo.

John won game #6 of the 1967 World Series.

MAJOR LEAGUE PITCHING RECORD

YEAR	TEAM	W	L	PCT.	SO	BB	ERA
1961	Kansas City	0	0	.000	6	4	2.57
1962	Kansas City	10	7	.588	106	80	4.46
1963	Kansas City	6	4	.600	81	43	3.13
1964	Kansas City	9	8	.529	74	52	3.59
1965	Kansas City	2	6	.250	70	53	3.24
1966	K.C.-Boston	3	7	.300	88	43	3.69
1967	Boston	10	7	.588	68	39	2.61
Maj. Totals 7 Yrs.		40	39	.506	493	314	3.51

Q.—HOW MANY SHUT-OUTS DID THE RED SOX STAFF COMPILE IN 1967?

A—NINE.

TOPPS 12 — STRIKEOUT LEADERS

AMERICAN LEAGUE

Player	SO		Player	SO
Lonborg, Bos.	246		Dobson, K.C.	110
McDowell, Clev.	236		John, Chi.	110
Chance, Minn.	220		Santiago, Bos.	109
Tiant, Clev.	219		Pascual, Wash.	106
Peters, Chi.	215		Horlen, Chi.	104
Kaat, Minn.	211		Peterson, N.Y.	102
Boswell, Minn.	204		Stange, Bos.	101
Hunter, K.C.	196		Drabowsky, Balt.	97
Nash, K.C.	186		Brandon, Bos.	96
Wilson, Det.	184		Krausse, K.C.	96
Phoebus, Balt.	180		Perry, Wash.	94
Lolich, Det.	174		Watt, Balt.	93
Downing, N.Y.	169		Kelso, Cal.	91
Brunet, Cal.	165		Bertaina, Balt.-Wash.	87
McLain, Det.	161		Knowles, Wash.	85
Merritt, Minn.	161		McMahon, Bos.-Chi.	84
Bell, Clev.-Bos.	154		Lindblad, K.C.	83
Sparma, Det.	153		Rojas, Cal.	83
Stottlemyre, N.Y.	151		Clark, Cal.	81
Hargan, Clev.	141		O'Donoghue, Clev.	81
McGlothlin, Cal.	137		Cimino, Cal.	80
Siebert, Clev.	136		Locker, Chi.	80
Richert, Wash.-Balt.	131		Worthington, Minn.	80
Ortega, Wash.	122		Coleman, Wash.	77
Barber, Balt.-N.Y.	117		Wilhelm, Chi.	77

TOPPS 87 — DICK WILLIAMS

(Boston Red Sox — Manager)

The Cinderella story of the baseball world in 1967 starred Dick Williams as Prince Charming. The Boston Red Sox who had struggled to a ninth place finish in 1966 surprised the skeptics with their pennant victory on the final day of the '67 campaign. Mgr. Dick Williams was rewarded with a three year contract from Boston's owner, Tom Yawkey. A three year contract to manage a ballclub is practically unheard of today! Not content to rest on the laurels of the past, Mgr. Williams has plans to improve the 1968 club. He feels the addition of another starting pitcher, a lefthanded hitting catcher and some additional bench strength would prepare the Red Sox for their 1968 bid to recapture the American League pennant flag. With performers such as Carl Yastrzemski, Jim Lonborg, George Scott and several others, Mgr. Williams will have some of the game's finest talent at his fingertips.

TOPPS 156 — 1967 WORLD SERIES — GAME #6

Boston tied the World Series at three games apiece as surprise starter, Gary Waslewski held on long enough while the Red Sox bats went to work. Home runs by Carl Yastrzemski, Reggie Smith and two by Rico Petrocelli crushed the Cards.

GAME #6 — AT BOSTON

ST. LOUIS	AB	R	H	O	A	E
Brock, LF	5	2	2	3	0	0
Flood, CF	5	0	1	2	0	0
Maris, RF	4	0	2	0	0	0
Cepeda, 1B	4	0	1	10	0	0
McCarver, C	3	0	0	2	0	0
Shannon, 3B	4	0	0	0	1	0
Javier, 2B	4	1	1	3	3	0
Maxvill, SS	3	0	0	1	1	0
Hughes, P	0	0	0	0	1	0
Willis, P	0	0	0	0	0	0
Spiezio	1	0	0	0	0	0
Briles, P	0	0	0	0	0	0
Tolan	1	0	0	0	0	0
Lamabe, P	0	0	0	0	0	0
Hoerner, P	0	0	0	0	0	0
Jaster, P	0	0	0	0	0	0
Washburn, P	0	0	0	0	0	0
Ricketts	1	0	0	0	0	0
Woodeshick, P	0	0	0	0	0	0
TOTALS	36	4	8	24	12	0

BOSTON	AB	R	H	O	A	E
Foy, 3B	4	1	1	3	3	0
Andrews, 2B	5	1	2	2	2	0
Yastrzemski, LF	4	2	3	2	0	0
Harrelson, RF	4	0	0	0	0	0
Tartabull, RF	0	0	0	0	0	0
Adair	0	0	0	0	0	0
Bell, P	0	0	0	0	0	0
Scott, 1B	4	1	1	10	1	0
Smith, CF	4	1	2	4	0	0
Petrocelli, SS	3	2	2	1	3	0
Howard, C	4	0	0	4	0	0
Waslewski, P	2	0	0	0	1	0
Wyatt, P	1	0	0	1	0	0
Jones	0	0	0	0	0	0
Thomas, RF	1	0	1	0	0	1
TOTALS	34	8	12	27	10	1

ST. LOUIS ... 0 0 2 0 0 0 2 0 0 — 4
BOSTON ...... 0 1 0 3 0 0 4 0 X — 8

©T.C.G. PRINTED IN U.S.A.